THE

HOLLOW

BOOK ONE IN THE
ORDER OF THE VEIL SERIES

LESLIE LENZ

The Hollow
Copyright © 2026 by Leslie Lenz

For information visit:
www.authorleslielenz.com

Book Cover Designed by: Chitin Scarab Ink
Map Design: Andrėja Dikšaitytė
Dinkus Designs: Morgan Teal
Line Editor: Paige Lawson

ISBN: 979-8-9949219-0-6   (Paperback)   979-8-9949219-1-3 (Hardcover) 979-8-9949219-2-0 (E-book)

SIGN UP FOR MY NEWSLETTER!

Be the first to learn about Leslie Lenz's new releases and receive exclusive content.

www.AuthorLeslieLenz.com

To every person who felt they were too late to start doing something they loved. It is never too late. Write your story.

BIRCHGROVE
RIVEN HOLLOW
STAR HOLLOW
ROOTS HOLLOW
RAVEN HOLLOW
DER OVE
BUNKER
MOON HOLLOW
MASK HOLLOW
ASHMERE HOLLOW
OAKGROVE
MAPLEGROVE

THE

BOOK ONE IN THE
ORDER OF THE VEIL SERIES

LESLIE LENZ

Chapter 1

The morning sun spilled golden light over Eldergrove, but Leah barely noticed the tremor in her hand or the strange heaviness in the air as she habitually wiped down the counter of the Bluebird Café. But the familiar hum of regulars and their endless stream of orders no longer grounded her. Something was off. Even as she tried to pretend the restless ache in her chest was just exhaustion.

Outside, children darted beneath the skeletal oaks, laughing and chasing one another before school. Leah's eyes followed them, distant. Memories of younger days drifted in unbidden— hours spent exploring forgotten corners of town, her grandmother's stories letting her imagination run wild like the wind. Those carefree afternoons felt impossibly far away now, buried beneath the quiet ache of the ordinary life she led.

Back then, the world had seemed larger, softer, and filled with possibility. She had always dreamed of adventure and wondered who she would become. But growing up with only her grandmother had made her childhood unlike that of the other kids at school. Whispers and rumors followed her everywhere. Most of the children were cruel and quick to judge her and her grandmother, whom they found odd and eccentric.

It was true that Selene Gardner was certainly odd. She grew herbs in chaotic garden beds and sang strange songs to the stars.

But to Leah, Selene was simply home and the only family she had ever known.

Selene taught her to recognize the healing in nature, to notice how a plant leaned toward the sun or how the air shifted before a storm. But with all her curious teachings, she also had a way of keeping the world small. For as long as Leah could remember, Selene had gently discouraged her from wandering too far beyond town, as if safety could only be found within its borders.

Still, there had always been something mysterious threaded through Selene's bedtime stories and daily conversations. She spoke in riddles that didn't always make sense to Leah growing up and told tales too vivid to be pure imagination.

Leah sensed early on that there were things left unsaid, but she learned not to press. She had known since she was old enough to understand that her parents had died shortly after she was born. Selene never shared much more than that, and Leah never asked. Part of her had always wondered what truly happened, but she kept that curiosity tucked away. Whatever the truth was, it seemed easier to leave it in the past.

Selene had given her a life full of care and meaning, and for a long time, that had been enough. But those memories felt like they belonged to another lifetime now. The scent of coffee grounds had replaced herbal teas, and the hum of locals filled the space where Selene's stories used to live.

Just before the lull between the morning rush and the afternoon pastries, Leah was wiping down the front counter when she overheard two young women seated near the window. Their voices were lowered, but not enough.

"That's the one up on the hill, right?" one asked, stirring her coffee. "The one practically pressed into the forest? We passed it as soon as we drove into town."

"Oh yeah," the other said, brightening. "People at the inn were talking about it. Apparently, some witch lives there. Super reclusive and strange. They said she doesn't have any friends and lives cooped up in that place."

Leah's hand stilled mid-wipe. Her jaw tightened until she felt pressure bloom in her temples.

She was still new to adulthood, only recently out of high school, and these women, who looked to be in their mid-twenties, reminded her far too much of the girls who had made her last years at school unbearable. They had the same glossy, effortless confidence. Somehow, these strangers carried the same amused cruelty and easy superiority as the girls in her school.

"They said she's weird," the first woman added, smirking. "One of the shopkeepers said she talks to the stars. Honestly? I believe it. That place looks creepy."

"Totally creepy," her friend laughed. "Kind of want to go up there later to see if the rumors are true."

"Well, careful," the first teased, nudging her. "You might get hexed. Or sacrificed."

Their laughter clawed at Leah. Her fingers curled tighter around the rag, white-knuckled. They didn't know Selene. They didn't know anything. And yet, they spoke with the same smug certainty of people who treated someone else's life like entertainment.

She had hoped graduation would let her escape the rumors and start fresh. Guess that had been a dream. As long as she stayed here, they would follow her.

Just as she braced herself to snap, a gentle voice pulled her back from the edge.

"Hey, you okay?"

Thomas, the café's newest hire, appeared beside her with a quiet stack of clean mugs. He'd moved to town recently, just in time to fill the hole Edgar had left when he quit. Edgar had been irritable and snarky, making Leah's mornings unnecessarily tense. Thomas, by contrast, was a breath of fresh air.

She blinked up at him. His dark curls were half-tamed beneath a backward cap, his green eyes already scanning her expression.

"Yeah," she said quickly. "Just tired."

He followed her gaze to the women by the window and raised a brow as he lifted a mug. "People say stupid things when they don't know better. That doesn't make them true."

Leah exhaled slowly, the tension in her shoulders easing just a little. There was something about the way he said it that made her feel as if he already knew exactly what those words meant to her.

"She isn't crazy," she said softly, not looking at him. "She just... sees the world differently."

Thomas nodded, setting the mugs down gently. "Sounds like someone I'd love to meet."

Leah gave a faint smile that didn't quite reach her eyes. "You would like her."

"Well," he said, offering a crooked grin, "if I can't meet her, I guess I'll settle for liking her granddaughter instead."

Warmth crept into Leah's cheeks, sudden and unexpected. She wasn't sure why, but the easy confidence in his voice caught her off guard. She opened her mouth to reply, only for the bell above the café door to chime.

"Morning, Sunshine!!"

Sage breezed in, her usual bright smile lighting up the room. Within seconds, Leah was enveloped in what could only be described as a full-force bear hug. A customer nearby flinched, nearly spilling his latte.

"Sage..." Leah wheezed, trying to pry her arms free. "I can't breathe."

Sage loosened her grip just enough for Leah to inhale, then pulled back. Her eyes darted between Leah and Thomas in a quick, instinctive scan. It lasted no more than a second, but something in her posture shifted as a mischievous grin spread across her face.

"Well, Leah," she said, wiggling her eyebrows, "and who do we have here?"

Still rubbing her shoulder, Leah froze, then groaned. Oh no.

"Sage," she said firmly, pointing at her, "this is Thomas. He started two days ago. Be nice."

Sage narrowed her eyes, pretending to scrutinize him like a bouncer at a club. "Hmm. Suspiciously cute for a new hire. And conveniently standing next to you during peak drama hour..."

Thomas raised both hands. "Innocent bystander, I swear."

Leah rolled her eyes, warmth creeping into her cheeks again. She wasn't used to being caught off guard like this, and it made her feel oddly self-conscious. "Sage, stop."

"Fine," Sage laughed. "I'll behave. For now."

She turned back to Leah, pulling her into a gentler, one-armed hug. "I missed you. You still hoarding lemon bars in the back, or did you finally learn to share?"

Thomas chuckled and slipped away toward the back counter, giving Leah a subtle nod of support before disappearing.

Leah laughed softly. "Maybe a little hoarding. You know me too well."

"Some things never change," Sage said.

Leah smiled. "Apparently not."

She took in Sage's familiar wild curls and unmistakable hazel eyes. Sage hadn't changed at all since she moved away. There was still that magnetic energy that drew people in like firelight on a cold night.

Unlike Leah, Sage had always been certain of her future. Animals were her whole heart, and she'd known since childhood that she would become a vet. True to form, she'd landed one of five coveted spots in the Bravo Veterinary Apprenticeship Program which was a grueling full-time rotation that took her to a town called Oakgrove. She'd spent the last few weeks working long days at a clinic and volunteering at a local shelter in the evenings. But that was Sage: relentless, vibrant, and utterly incapable of doing anything halfway.

Leah smiled, grateful for the steady friendship. Sage was her anchor and reminder that not all of life's mysteries had to be so heavy. Her warm smile and confidence were a comforting contrast to the quiet hum of the café. Sage had been part of Leah's world since they were seven years old— two scrawny girls meeting beneath the twisted branches of the old elm tree by the schoolyard.

Other friendships had come and gone, light as leaves on the wind, but Sage had been the one who stayed. She had listened when Leah had no words, understood the restless spirit behind Leah's quiet nature, and grounded her when the world felt too big—or too small. Their conversations drifted seamlessly from silly jokes to the kind of deep talks that left Leah feeling a little lighter and a little less alone, reminding her she didn't have to carry everything by herself.

"So," Sage said, leaning on the counter with a playful grin, "how's life treating you? Same old, same old?"

Leah smiled, the corners of her mouth tugging up more easily than they had in days. "Busy as ever. The café keeps me on my toes."

Sage nodded. "And your new coworker? Thomas, right?"

Leah laughed softly. "He's easy to be around. Feels like he's been here longer than a few days."

"Ohhh," Sage said. "Comfortable already."

"Don't start," Leah said. "He just fits."

Sage smirked. "I'll keep my eye on him."

Leah laughed. "You're ridiculous."

"Obviously," Sage said with a mock bow. "That's why you keep me around."

A comfortable silence settled between them as the mid-morning rush ebbed, leaving only the soft clinks of cups and the low murmured conversations.

Leah glanced around, then back at Sage. "So, how's the apprenticeship going? You still survive those marathon shifts?"

Sage threw her head back dramatically. "Barely. Last week I was on my feet for twelve hours straight, and then I volunteered at the shelter after. I swear, I'm one coffee away from becoming a permanent resident there."

Leah smiled, admiring her friend's relentless energy. "You're like a machine. I don't know how you do it."

Sage shrugged with a wink. "It's all about caffeine...and probably some stubbornness."

Leah pressed her fingers to her temple, wincing. "Speaking of caffeine...I think I've had a little too much today. Headache's been nagging at me all morning."

Sage's eyes softened immediately. "Hm. Maybe you should take it easy. You know, actually rest instead of working until you drop."

Leah shook her head, forcing a small smile. "I'll be fine. Just one of those days."

Sage didn't look convinced but didn't press, which Leah was thankful for. Instead, she grabbed Leah's hand, giving it a squeeze. "Promise me you'll take care of yourself?"

Leah nodded, her chest feeling lighter. "Promise."

Sage grinned. "Good. Because I'm holding you to that. Besides, I came down here to celebrate you. I cannot have you stuck in bed all weekend with a headache! It's bad enough already you didn't take tomorrow off."

Leah's smile faltered for just a moment. Her birthday. She'd almost managed to forget it was tomorrow. Another year older, another reminder that nothing in her life felt like it was moving forward. It would just be another day of pretending everything was fine. But she didn't want Sage to see any of that written on her face.

"Yeah," Leah said lightly, forcing a grin. "I know."

They shared a quiet laugh before the bell above the door chimed again, signaling another wave of customers. Leah exhaled slowly, feeling a little more grounded. She was thankful Sage had decided to visit this weekend, but she couldn't help the weird sense of dread that lingered.

Once the early afternoon rush was over, Leah made her way to the corner booth where Sage was curled up, deeply absorbed in what looked to be an essay on her laptop about...cats? The glow of the screen lit her face as she leaned forward, completely immersed. Only a few hours into her short trip, and she was already working. Sage really was too loyal.

Leah smiled softly and sat down next to Sage. "Hey, thought you might want a refill," she said, setting down a fresh cup of coffee beside Sage's laptop.

Sage looked up, a grateful grin spreading across her face. "You're a lifesaver. This day needs all the caffeine it can get." She nudged her laptop a few inches to the side, the screen tilting just enough that the reflection of the window replaced whatever she'd been working on.

Leah let out a short laugh. "I'm heading home a little earlier today. Hopefully rest helps this headache," she said, pressing her fingers lightly to her temple.

Sage's brows furrowed as she studied Leah's face. "Are you sure you're okay? You look pale."

"I'm fine," Leah said quickly, brushing her temple again. "It's just a headache. Not actively dying yet."

"You're never one to complain. Hang on." Sage dug into her oversized canvas bag and pulled out a thin, woven bracelet. It was soft blue, with silver threads knotted into a pattern that shimmered around a cool metal center. "Here," she said, reaching across the table and gently looping it around Leah's wrist. "I found this at a market last week. The woman who made it said it's supposed to help with stress and emotional regulation. Figured you could use a little of both."

Leah chuckled, touched. "You know you didn't have to bring me anything."

"I know," Sage said, tying it off with a practiced tug. "But I wanted to. Besides, it's supposed to be waterproof, flameproof, life-proof, the whole shebang. And maybe it'll remind you to take care of yourself when I'm not around to nag you."

Leah looked down at the bracelet. It was simple, a little imperfect, and somehow completely comforting.

"Thanks," she said softly.

"Of course," Sage replied with a shrug, brushing it off like it wasn't a big deal. But her eyes lingered on Leah a moment longer than necessary. "I'll pass by Selene's tomorrow when I'm free." She winked before signaling to Thomas. "I think he'll need some company to end his shift today."

Before she grabbed her coat, Leah glanced toward Thomas at the counter. He was wiping down tables, looking calm and focused. She gave him a small nod and a quick smile, silently checking if he needed anything before she left early. Then she turned back to Sage, who was already teasing Thomas with a playful grin. Leah raised an eyebrow and shook her head slightly, mouthing, *Behave.* Sage just winked in response.

Shortly after, Leah made her way up the winding path to her house. The garden rose up around her, wild and tangled, spilling past the stone borders in deliberate abandon. Flowers bloomed where they pleased, softening the chaos with color and various floral scents. She pushed open the creaking gate and followed the trail to the front door. The women's voices from the café echoed in her mind, along with the comments they'd made about the house. A knot tightened in her stomach. Of course they'd talked about the house. Anyone driving in from that side of town would pass the edge of the property. She glanced toward the trees lining the road, suddenly aware of how secluded it must look to strangers. The thought stung more than she wanted to admit.

She exhaled, rubbing her thumb along the cold doorknob before pushing it open. Inside, warmth wrapped around her, settling into the ache at her temples.

Selene sat in her favorite armchair by the fire with a light blue cloth spread across her lap. She was stitching that same symbol, two gold concentric circles joined by a line across their center that Leah had grown up seeing all her life. Her grandmother never explained it, and Leah had long since learned that pressing her when she slipped into one of her quiet, private rhythms was pointless. It wasn't fear that kept her from asking, just respect for the small, repeated quirks that made Selene...Selene.

Leah sank onto the couch beside her, letting the quiet of the room seep into her bones. The familiar smell of herbs pressed against the ache in her temples, easing it little by little.

"I am exhausted..." Leah said softly, her voice barely above the crackle of the fire.

Selene looked up, her faded gray eyes gentle beneath softly lined lids. Her silver-white hair fell around her shoulders. Even seated, her tall, lean frame carried a quiet, steady presence. "You've been working too hard again." She reached over and tucked a stray strand of hair behind Leah's ear.

Leah gave a small smile. "I've had to cover a lot of shifts after Edgar quit, but I'm training someone who seems promising and hopefully won't quit after two weeks." She chuckled dryly.

"The world outside these walls can take more than it gives," Selene said gently. "That is why we must learn to rest when we can."

Leah hesitated. The words had been pressing against her all day, caught beneath her headache and that strange sense of dread. "Gran...do you ever feel like there's more out there?"

For a moment, Selene's smile faltered. A shadow passed through her expression, gone almost as quickly as it came. "I have lived long enough to know there is always more, Leah. But not everything is meant to be sought before its time."

The fire popped, sending a tiny spark into the air. Silence pressed in again, broken only when Selene's gaze drifted to Leah's wrist. She reached out, brushing her thumb near the edge of the bracelet.

"That's new," she said, her voice calm but thoughtful. "From Sage?"

Leah glanced down at it. "Yeah. She said it should help ground me or something. She passed by the café. She came to visit for the weekend."

A faint smile touched Selene's lips. "She's always known how to choose her timing." She paused, her thumb still hovering over the bracelet. "I'm glad you have her."

Leah looked over, surprised by the weight in her grandmother's tone, but Selene had already returned her gaze to the cloth on her lap.

"You're becoming someone I'm so proud of, you know that?" Selene said softly, her voice catching slightly. "You have this light in you, Leah. Strength that runs so deep."

Leah swallowed the lump in her throat. "I wish I felt it."

Selene looked at her then and reached out to squeeze her hand. "Strength is not always loud," she said softly. "Sometimes it waits in silence, until the moment you need it most."

Leah let herself linger in the quiet as the words settled slowly. The silence felt unusually tender, given how rarely Selene spoke so openly. After another long moment together, Leah's stomach gave a small, traitorous rumble. Selene chuckled.

"Well," she said, brushing a hand over Leah's hair with a tenderness that tightened her throat, "I suppose that's enough heart-to-heart for one day. Let's eat something."

Leah laughed, grateful for the way Selene always knew when to let the silence stretch and when to break it. They moved to the kitchen, where Selene warmed a pot of lentil stew while Leah sliced bread and grabbed two bowls. The kitchen was small but cozy, its wooden beams overhead catching the soft glow of the late afternoon sun filtering through the windows. A small round table occupied the center of the room surrounded by four chairs, though only two showed signs of regular use. The scent of herbs lingered in the air, fresh and earthy, drifting from the windowsill where freshly plucked sprigs from the back garden lay drying.

They didn't say much as they ate, but it was never uncomfortable. Their silence was full of meaning, the kind of quiet that said everything words didn't need to. After scraping the last of the stew from the bowl, Leah leaned back in her chair with a long exhale.

"I think I'm going to shower," she said, rubbing her temples. "Maybe hot water might help."

Selene smiled gently and began to gather the dishes. "Go on. I'll take care of this."

Leah squeezed Selene's shoulder in thanks before standing and stepping into the narrow hallway that led to her room. Along the walls, faded photographs of a younger Leah and pressed flowers were tucked into frames. She passed the other two bedrooms, Selene's room and her study, both modest and filled with familiar things. Her thoughts drifted briefly to the attic above, a space heavy with dust and things Selene rarely spoke about before getting to her room at the end of the hallway.

The shower was quick but much needed. The warmth eased the ache from her limbs, and for a few blissful minutes, the sense of dread she'd felt all day faded away with the steam. She dressed in soft cotton clothes and wrapped her damp hair in a towel, planning to say goodnight before heading to bed. But when she returned to the kitchen, the lights were dim and the space was empty.

Frowning, Leah stepped outside, the cool night air brushing against her warm skin. She found Selene in the garden beneath a sky of silver stars. Selene was kneeling on the soil, her fingers tracing quiet symbols into the earth before her gaze turned skyward, searching the constellations like they might answer a question only she could ask.

Leah lingered at the edge of the porch, silent. The stillness of the scene made her hesitate, as if she were intruding on something private. The candlelight from the kitchen window barely reached this far, casting Selene in soft shadow. She watched as Selene paused, her fingers resting lightly on the soil, her gaze still lifted, lips moving soundlessly as if speaking to the stars. Only then did Leah take a quiet, reverent step forward.

"Gran?"

Selene turned slowly, but her gaze was still skyward as if finishing the conversation, before finally looking at Leah. When her eyes settled on her, they softened. "I'm sorry, Leah," she said gently. "I didn't mean to pull you out here in the cold."

Leah stepped into the garden, the damp grass cool beneath her feet. "I was coming to say goodnight...I didn't know where you'd gone."

Selene gave a quiet hum before rising slowly and brushing her hands clean on her skirt. "Sometimes I come out here when I'm feeling restless. The stars have a way of making the world feel small enough to hold."

Leah followed her gaze. "What were you thinking about?"

A moment passed before Selene answered. "You, mostly." She smiled again, more wistful this time. "You, and how quickly time passes. One moment you're crawling into my lap with your blanket, and the next...you're eighteen and grown."

Leah wrinkled her nose. "Well...not yet technically. In a few hours."

Selene's smile deepened, though it didn't quite reach her eyes. "Ah, yes. Still seventeen...clinging to childhood by a thread."

"You make it sound so tragic," Leah teased, nudging her gently. "It's just a birthday."

Selene looked at her then, and something in her expression changed. "Maybe. Or maybe it's the beginning of everything."

Leah blinked. "What?"

But Selene only reached out, letting her hand rest on Leah's head. When she spoke again, her voice was soft and careful.

"Do you remember our promise?"

Leah blinked, caught off guard by the shift. "Our promise...from when I was little?"

Selene nodded slowly and turned to look out again. "If I'm ever not here...you must trust the signs, however they reveal themselves."

A hush settled over the garden, colder than the night air. The words weren't new, but their delivery today carried something heavier, and it made Leah feel uncomfortable.

Selene's gaze was distant now, fixed somewhere beyond the sky. "Not all whispers need words, Leah. Some are waiting quietly and patiently for the right moment to awaken."

Leah felt her chest tighten as that sense of dread returned full force. She stepped closer, searching her grandmother's face for meaning. "Gran...why are you saying this now?"

Selene turned fully to her, placing a gentle hand over Leah's. Her touch was warm, but her eyes looked sad.

"Because sometimes," she said, "the wind carries whispers we don't want to hear, and we don't always get to choose when it's time."

Leah's brows furrowed. "But...is something wrong?" she asked cautiously.

Selene's smile returned, but it trembled slightly at the edges. "Not more than usual," she said gently. "And nothing you need to worry about tonight."

"Come now," she added, threading her arm through Leah's as they walked back inside. "The wind's turning cold."

Selene lit a single candle in Leah's room and sat beside her on the edge of the bed. It wasn't customary for Selene to make a big deal of birthdays, but she had a quiet tradition: the night before, she would hum a familiar tune and sing the lullaby that had cradled Leah to sleep since childhood. Tonight, however, the song carried new weight, sounding less like a simple melody and more like a quiet prayer.

Selene leaned down, caressing Leah's cheek softly, and sang in a low voice threaded with aching tenderness:

When darkness finds you where you least expect,

And the road ahead leaves your heart unchecked,

Keep the quiet light within your soul,

It will lead you onward and make you whole.

Leah's eyes drifted shut, lulled by the warmth in her grandmother's voice. But even as sleep claimed her, she felt the gentle squeeze of Selene's hand and the way it lingered a moment longer than usual, as if trying to hold on. Instinctively, Leah squeezed back, fingers brushing weathered skin as she clung to Selene's hand and to the warmth of the moment. She pressed into it, willing away the strange ache in her chest and refusing to believe this could be anything but another quiet night.

Chapter 2

The morning was unusual, wrapped in a thick, ghostly fog that blurred the edges of the streets and softened the shapes of the weathered buildings. The air was heavy and still, carrying a damp chill that seeped into bones. No birds sang in the skeletal oaks, no leaves stirred, and even the faint murmur of distant voices seemed swallowed by the gray haze.

Inside her modest bedroom at the edge of town, a loud **BEEP BEEP BEEP** shattered the silence. Leah yelped and thumped against the floor, tangled in sheets and hair.

"Ugh—third alarm?!" she groaned, blinking against the morning sun. "I must have slept right through them!"

For a moment, she just lay there with the sheets twisted around her legs and the weight of the day pressing down before it had even started. Today was her birthday—eighteen—but the thought barely registered. Every birthday seemed to blur into the last, another mark on the calendar without much to show for it. Even graduating high school hadn't changed the rhythm of her days. Same town. Same job. Same...everything.

She tried to summon a flicker of excitement, but all she felt was late. Late to grow up, late to leave, late to start anything at all. Did eighteen even mean anything if she was still caught in the same loop?

Her pulse quickened as she pushed herself out of bed. There was no time for a shower, and breakfast would have to wait. Leah pulled on yesterday's jeans, grabbed a cardigan that smelled faintly of lavender, and hurried down the hall toward the front door where her boots waited.

"Gran, I'm late! I'll grab something at the café!" she called, but no answer came.

The house was oddly quiet, the kind of quiet that made her skin prickle. She slowed, lingering in the hallway, and glanced toward the back window, frowning at the empty garden bed. No sun hat bobbed among the leaves like it usually did at this time. Maybe she had already gone into town, Leah thought, pausing halfway out the door. She was probably picking up that fancy tea she liked that got delivered every Saturday.

The doorbell above the café chimed loudly as she burst in, nearly slipping on the polished floorboards.

"Thomas! I am so sorry I'm late—!" Panic and apology tangled in her voice as she skidded to a stop.

Thomas stood behind the counter, wearing that too-calm smirk of his as he handed a steaming coffee across the bar. Sitting on the stool, holding the cup with both hands and blinking at her with mock innocence, was Sage.

"Well, look who finally decided to show up. I was starting to think you'd skip your own birthday and play hooky."

Leah blinked. "Wait, what are you doing up this early?"

"Well," Sage said, nodding toward Thomas, who was wiping down the espresso machine, "had to make sure the birthday people got all the celebrations they'd need for a weekend."

Leah turned to Thomas, surprised. "Wait, your birthday's today too?"

"Tomorrow," he said with a polite smile. "Seems like the universe lined us up back-to-back."

Leah laughed softly. "Whoa, that's so cool! Happy early birthday, then. I guess we'll both be eating cake all weekend."

Sage pulled a small bunch of balloons out from behind the counter with a flourish. "Exactly. Double the parties, double the trouble."

"You didn't," Leah said, grinning despite herself.

"Oh, but I did." Sage reached into her tote bag and pulled out a flat, wrapped gift, setting it on the counter with a thud. "Don't get misty-eyed on me. It's not sentimental...much."

Leah peeled back the paper and stared. Inside was a small, hand-bound photo journal with thick pages. The cover was plain but all too familiar. It was the same sketchbook they used to pass back and forth in middle school, the one they filled with doodles, notes, and weird little memories.

"You kept this?" Leah whispered, tracing her fingers over the frayed edges.

"Of course I did," Sage said, suddenly quieter. "It's our disaster scrapbook. I added some new pages, too, but don't worry. None of your exes made the cut. I do have standards, after all."

Leah laughed, blinking fast to fight back the sting in her eyes. "This is...perfect." She hugged the scrapbook to her chest.

"Yeah, yeah. I know." Sage nudged her shoulder. "Now go make some coffee before Thomas starts thinking I came here for him."

Leah shot a glance at Thomas, who raised a brow, then back at Sage, grinning.

"Also..." Sage slid her phone across the counter. On it was a blurry selfie of her and Thomas from the night before. He was grinning, and she was mid-laugh, a candlelit table behind them.

"You did not!" Leah gasped, half-whispering, half-laughing.

"Oh, but I did," Sage said smugly. "Dinner. Drinks. A walk under the lanterns by the river. He's actually pretty charming when he's not elbow-deep in a coffee grinder."

Thomas chuckled under his breath but didn't look up.

"You little liar," Leah said, nudging Sage's arm. "I thought you hated café boys."

"I do. Except for the ones with forearms like his." Sage wiggled her eyebrows and glanced at Thomas, a flicker of something unreadable passing through her eyes. "Also, he knows how to make the perfect dirty chai."

Thomas cleared his throat. "Thank you. I aim to please."

Sage smiled slyly before turning back to Leah. "I'll swing by Selene's later today since I'm already heading back tomorrow. I miss her!" She glanced at her watch, then added, "But I've got some things to take care of first."

With that, she slung her bag over her shoulder, hugged Leah briefly, and headed toward the door.

"See you later, birthday girl! Try not to sleep through your alarms next time!"

Leah rolled her eyes with a grin. "No promises."

The door swung closed behind Sage, and Leah let out a quiet sigh. The odd sensation from that morning still hovered at the edge of her thoughts, but she brushed it off as nothing more than the chaos of the day.

Thomas leaned on the counter, a crooked grin tugging at his lips. "Well, you two have a lot of energy in the morning."

Leah shot him a look of amusement. "We?" she asked, grinning.

Thomas froze for a moment, then grinned sheepishly.

Leah smirked. "So...dinner and lanterns by the river, huh? That was fast."

He shrugged, playful. "I make friends quickly."

Leah laughed, shaking her head. "Friends? That photo makes it look like you two were planning a heist or something."

"Just a highly coordinated dessert heist, at her request, of course," he said, raising an imaginary glass.

Leah rolled her eyes, smiling. "You're too much."

"Only when someone's watching," he replied, smiling as the café filled with its morning rhythm.

She let out a quiet chuckle at Thomas's grin, grateful for this lighthearted moment amid the chaos of her morning. The café was filling fast now with sleepy locals dragging in for their caffeine and the usual hum of conversation and clinking mugs. Leah slipped into the flow, pouring lattes, wiping tables, and laughing at Thomas's jokes between orders.

Somehow, it felt easier being around him. Maybe it was because they were both August babies, and maybe that little coincidence was enough to make the day feel a bit steadier and warmer, even when everything else felt off.

For a few hours, everything felt almost normal. The café was the kind of busy that made the hours pass quickly and kept the mind from wandering. As the last customer made their way out the door, Thomas sighed, a hand rubbing the back of his head.

"Long day."

"I didn't think it was too bad. Being busy always helps," Leah said as she closed the register and grabbed her cardigan from the employee room, happy she had the next day off.

"So, what's the plan for your birthday tomorrow? Big party? Skydiving? Or maybe another highly coordinated dessert heist?" Leah asked, slipping on her cardigan with a mischievous grin.

Thomas snorted. "Tempting...but I'm trying to pace myself. Can't keep up that kind of criminal energy."

Leah chuckled. "Okay, then at least cake. You do like cake, right?"

"I never really celebrated birthdays," he said, shrugging as though it were nothing. "It's usually just another day."

Her expression softened. She understood more than he realized. She hadn't really celebrated birthdays either, not in any big way. Most years had passed quietly, marked only by a card from Selene or a small treat at the café. It wasn't sad to her anymore, just the norm.

She nodded slowly. "That's...kind of depressing," she said softly, though a small smile tugged at her lips. "I get it, though. I've never been much for big birthday things either."

He smirked, grabbing his bag from beneath the counter. "Given the fact you chose to work on your birthday, I can see that."

Leah laughed. "Look who's talking! Don't you work tomorrow? You're at least getting one cupcake with a candle. No arguments."

Thomas gave a mock sigh, brushing a hand briefly over his temple as they stepped toward the exit. "A cupcake, huh? Dangerous. I might get used to this whole 'being celebrated' thing."

"Good," she said, shooting him a grin. "Then I'll consider it my civic duty to corrupt you with sugar on your workday."

Thomas chuckled. "Well, we still need to see if I survive this cupcake of yours."

Leah shook her head, amused, but as she stepped outside into the crisp air, the laughter faded faster than expected. The strange stillness settled over the street again, pressing quietly at the edges of her awareness.

"See you later, Leah."

"Goodnight! See you tomorrow," she called back, distracted by the odd tension she felt.

There was no rustle of leaves or chatter from the locals, just the sound of her own boots crunching against the gravel path. The lights inside other stores were beginning to dim, marking the end of another workday. Faded signs swung lazily on creaking hinges and the streetlamps flickered, casting long shadows across the pavement. With each step, the path back home seemed to stretch endlessly and the silence around her grew denser, broken only by the occasional shop door locking up for the night.

By the time she reached the crooked gate of her home, her steps had slowed. The garden remained untouched, not a single tool out of place. She looked around as she turned the key to open the door, then paused with her hand on the doorknob, a knot tightening in her stomach.

"Gran?" she called, stepping inside the house. "I'm home!"

Silence answered.

She wandered through the living room, noting every detail. Everything was exactly as they'd left it the night before. The tea they had brewed still sat cold on the stove. The half-finished knitting project remained draped over Selene's chair, needles paused mid-stitch as if Selene had only stepped away for a moment.

"Gran?" Leah's voice wavered, louder this time. She checked her bedroom, the study, the back garden, and even the small reading nook where Selene sometimes dozed off. She could feel it now. It wasn't just silence, it was absence. A subtle void, like the warmth had been drained from the walls. A flicker of unease tightened her chest. Selene was never this quiet.

Maybe she had gone out again and had gotten distracted by a conversation with the owner of the butterfly nursery, as she often did. But Selene had a habit of making sure she was home by the time Leah finished her shift. Something just wasn't right.

Leah stood frozen in the kitchen, tension rising in her chest. *Where is she?* The stress built into a pressure that crept up behind her eyes. Leah leaned against the kitchen table, trying to focus on anything other than the dread curling in her stomach and the headache beginning to form once more.

Her eyes scanned the kitchen and settled on Selene's mug. *Is that a new cup of tea? Is the tea still warm?* Leah stepped hesitantly toward it, and the instant her fingers touched the handle, something shifted.

For the briefest second, she saw her grandmother's hands locking a small chest in the attic. She felt as though she were standing right behind her, watching every careful motion. The image vanished as quickly as it appeared, leaving Leah blinking at the mug in her hands while her heart raced in sudden, frantic circles.

The mug was cold...almost as cold as the air outside. Leah set it back down, unease and confusion tightening her expression. Acting on instinct, she made her way to the hallway, drawn toward the attic door above. She reached for the rope and pulled, the hatch creaking loudly as it groaned against years of disuse. The sound was startlingly sharp in the hush of the house, but Leah didn't notice.

Fogged, disoriented, and with every nerve on edge, she drew a slow breath and began to climb the stairs. Each step seemed pulled by the memory of a vision that wasn't hers—a silent secret waiting just beyond the attic door.

Hours earlier, at dawn on that very morning, long before Leah's footsteps ever touched the garden path, another story had already come to its end.

The candle on Selene's desk had long since burned low, but she hadn't moved. Her hands trembled as they hovered over the book she had sworn to protect. A soft incantation slipped from her lips, sealing it with a protective spell. Around her neck hung a pendant of deep green stone set in tarnished silver.

Selene rose slowly, joints aching beneath the weight of years and knowledge she had carried alone. She climbed the attic stairs and faced the old chest, a pang of fear and sadness settling in her chest at the thought of the life Leah would soon inherit. Carefully, she placed the book inside, knowing it would call to Leah once she was gone.

With a weight heavier than her heart could bear, she left the attic and moved silently through the house, her slippers barely audible against the old wooden floorboards. She paused in Leah's doorway, watching her sleep soundly with the sheets tangled around her legs and one hand curled loosely beneath her chin.

Her throat tightened. Eighteen. It was always meant to play out this way. When the Seer's blood awakens on her eighteenth birthday, the one who sheltered her must pay the price. That was the pact. The cost of shielding a bloodline the world believed long extinct.

Selene stepped closer, brushing hair from Leah's face. "You were always made for more, Leah. Today you awaken," she whispered, her voice barely audible. "Forgive me for leaving you this way."

She would not run. Her death would be her final act of protection— a cloak, a severing, and a sacrifice— that would keep Leah hidden just long enough. Selene stepped back as Leah murmured something in her sleep and rolled over, unaware. Tears welled in Selene's eyes, but she didn't let them fall.

Moving through the house, she murmured soft incantations, weaving old magic tightly around the cottage. The enchantments were precise and powerful, shielding Leah from harm and concealing the house itself from detection by anyone on the other side of the Veil for a precious few days. It didn't matter if The Order sensed something had changed. By the time they traced it, Leah would already be beyond reach.

With one final breath, Selene stepped into the chill of the autumn morning, protective magic wrapping around the cottage like an invisible veil.

The wind howled through the trees in the Hollow, rattling branches and stirring dry leaves across the desolate hills.

Beneath the shadow of an ancient stone tower, Selene stood alone, her cloak tugged tight around her shoulders. This place had once been a refuge. A gathering point. Now it was only a graveyard of what used to be.

She had stood here many times in her youth, when laughter filled the hills. But that was before the town burned. Before the tower fell silent. Before everything changed.

She had known this day would come the moment she took Leah in. That was when she made the sacred pact that bound their fates forever. A promise etched in magic and sealed with sacrifice. As soon as the child turned eighteen, Selene's own life must end. Only then would the dormant power within Leah awaken, ready to face the darkness gathering beyond their fragile sanctuary.

A cold prickle ran down her spine. The unmistakable signal she had dreaded for years. The Order had found them at last. She had sensed The Order's agents as she exited Eldergrove. They, having stalked her every step for years, had finally infiltrated the town—posing as tourists and mapping residents for any trace of magic. The quiet hours were over. There was no running or hiding anymore. All that remained was the sacrifice she had prepared for years.

In her trembling hands, she held the delicate pendant she had crafted for Leah long ago, a simple stone cradled a memory that could only be unlocked through this final act. Through it, she would pass on the answers Leah needed, answers she could not give her tonight.

Selene closed her eyes and let the weight of everything press down on her. Years of fear, hope, whispered promises, and stolen smiles had all led to this. The ache beneath her ribs was heavier than any spell, a reminder that magic was never free of sacrifice.

Her thoughts drifted to Leah, the child she had raised, protected, and loved like her own. Selene's voice broke the silence, trembling at first, then growing stronger as she began to chant. Each syllable wove into a spell, sending ripples through hidden currents of magic and calling allies long scattered across the Hollows.

Each note was both a shield and a summon. Her eyes glowed bright green as the pendant pulsed against her chest, drinking in her voice. As the chant neared the end, her breath grew shallow, her body weakening, but her spirit clung fiercely to the pendant and to the child who would carry everything forward.

With a final, shuddering note, the chant wove itself into the morning mist— a blessing, a burden, and a beacon all at once. Selene opened her eyes one final time to the rising sun, letting its warmth brush her face as she whispered the words she had carried for years.

"You were always made for more, Leah. I love you."

A tear traced down her cheek before her knees gave way, and she collapsed among the ruins. Her body stilled, but her sacrifice and her love lingered in every pulse of magic she left behind.

The wind outside had quieted. But in the attic of Leah's home, beneath layers of dust, something had begun to stir, a newly awakened thread of power.

The narrow staircase creaked under Leah's weight as she climbed, dust thick in the air when she entered the room. The dim light seeped through a grimy window, illuminating boxes, old furniture, and yellowed photographs stacked haphazardly around her. Leah took a slow step forward, letting her hand brush the faded wallpaper as the scent of aged wood lingered in the air.

She hadn't been up here in years. The last time she had climbed these steps, she'd been no more than eight, trailing after Selene while new bedroom furniture was hauled in downstairs. She remembered wobbling up the ladder, wide-eyed at the treasure trove of forgotten things. But Selene had gently steered her back toward the hatch almost immediately, her tone warm but firm, saying there were things up here "best left to rest."

Then she saw it.

A small brown chest tucked beneath a pile of old quilts and curtains. It looked mundane, but she was almost certain it was the same one she'd seen in that strange vision. Leah stopped, staring at it, willing herself to break the trance she felt floating in. This was ridiculous. What was she even doing up here? The stillness was unsettling, and yet something inside her stirred, insisting the chest held something important.

Her fingers trembled as she brushed the dust away. The lock was old, but it clicked open easily. Nestled inside on a bed of velvet lay a thick, leather-bound book. Faded gold filigree traced the cover, but the title had worn away, leaving only a few illegible marks.

Leah's heart raced as she lifted it. It felt warm in her hands, as if the velvet had kept it that way. She slowly turned the fragile, yellowed pages, only to discover they were all blank.

That didn't seem right.

She flipped through them again, and this time fleeting traces of shimmering ink appeared across a page. She squinted, ignoring the pressure building behind her eyes, leaning closer to inspect it. Before she could think further, the book seemed to come alive, flipping itself to a page near the center. A shimmer rippled across it in waves. Compelled, Leah traced her finger along the flickering spots.

Cold seeped into her bones the instant she touched the page. The room shifted and the air thickened with a strange energy that froze her in place. The pressure behind her eyes was pulsing now, and she was sure she had to be hallucinating from a terrible migraine.

Then, just before she decided it was probably best to go back downstairs, images began surging into her mind. She did not recognize them as memories, at least not her own. These visions and flashes seemed off and distant, almost as if they were visions of the future, sharp and vivid, unfolding faster than she could process. She saw faces—some familiar, some unknown—places she had never been to, and snippets of events flashing too fast to comprehend.

The shimmer on the page flared bright, flooding Leah's vision in white. She squeezed her eyes shut, but the images came anyway, snapping in and out of focus—A stone archway, a man wearing an emerald cloak, a room lit by candlelight, and a sinister smile.

Then, in the midst of it all, a voice whispered her name.

"Leah."

Her name pulled her upright, just enough to catch a breath, before it was knocked right back out of her. When she opened her eyes, she was no longer in the attic.

Mist curled around her ankles and before her, a dead, ruined town stretched silently in every direction where Selene's boxes should have been. What had once been homes and shops were now little more than broken shells. Walls were split open, roofs had collapsed inward, and doorways gaped. Stone and timber lay scattered across the ground, swallowed by ash and creeping moss.

Leah staggered back, grabbing for something that wasn't there. "What—" Her heartbeat thundered in her ears. "Hello?" she called, her voice trembling.

From the haze, a figure emerged. A man, not much older than she was, stood watching her. His hood shadowed his face, his cloak shifting in the fog. Leah took a step forward, only for the world to spin again.

The ruins dissolved, and a man's voice spoke softly.

"The time has come. Your power is unlocked. Hold the book close. Its power will guide you."

The vision cracked like glass and Leah collapsed to her knees, the book slipping from her hands as nausea rolled through her. Her breath came shallow and ragged, spots flickering at the edges of her vision.

When she lifted her head, the attic felt different. The walls felt closer, the shadows deeper. Dust clung to her skin as her eyes locked on the leather-bound book at her feet. Its edges fluttered slightly, disturbed by no breeze.

Your power is unlocked.

The words echoed in her head. Leah squeezed her eyes shut, shaking her head as nausea twisted again.

"Power? I don't have power," she whispered. "I make lattes. I schedule supply orders."

A brittle laugh escaped her, then died. This wasn't a dream. It wasn't even a nightmare. She had seen unfamiliar places and people and heard a voice that sounded so familiar. This was definitely a hallucination. It had to be. She picked up the book with unsteady hands and hugged it to her chest, trying to steady the rush of emotions crashing over her all over again.

Once the pressure behind her eyes eased and her breath evened out, she simply stared at the book. She couldn't think of anything that she had eaten or drank prior to getting home that could have been tampered with to create such intense hallucinations.

"What are you?" she asked the book, half-expecting it to answer.

The attic creaked, making Leah spin, expecting the hooded man or another vision, but the room was empty. She let out a small, incredulous laugh, shaking her head.

What is going on?

Flipping the book open again, she paused at a page where the shimmers spiraled inward. The pull was irresistible.

"Okay," she muttered.

Her finger traced the page again, and the room responded instantly. Cold rushed in, the page growing brighter and brighter until she stood at the edge of a cliff.

Wind tore at her from every direction, whipping her hair and tugging at her clothes as if trying to hurl her into the sea below. Waves smashed against the rocks with a thunderous force that vibrated through her bones.

Her heart thrashed. This couldn't be real. This wasn't real. But every sensation was too sharp and too loud.

And she wasn't alone.

The realization crawled up her spine. A presence stood behind her, close enough that the air shifted the moment she felt it. Fear coiled tight in her chest, stealing her breath.

Turn around.

With a deep breath, she turned, but the world twisted again.

She blinked, and a library replaced the cliff. Hundreds of books lined the walls, the air scented with parchment and soil. A lantern swayed gently overhead, and at the center of the room stood a figure cloaked in deep blue.

Nico.

The name, whispered in her grandmother's voice, landed like thunder in her bones.

Before she could think, another vision surged forward. Chaos this time. Faces she didn't recognize, some kind, some terrifying. And at the center of it all, a man with a crooked smile and dark, unreadable eyes.

When he locked eyes with her, Leah gasped and stumbled back, the air punched from her lungs.

The attic tilted and shadows crowded in. Her breath came in short bursts as the familiar panic clawed its way up her throat. She grabbed the nearest box and forced herself to focus, counting floorboards, steadying her exhales, and blinking away the cold sweat that had gathered at her brows.

Instinctively, her fingers slid to the bracelet around her wrist. She clutched it until her pulse began to slow beneath her touch.

When the world finally steadied, she glanced down at the book. It lay on the floor like any ordinary object, and yet a knot tightened in her chest. She had lived in this house her entire life. She knew every drawer, every crooked step, every hiding place. But this...she had never seen this. Not once.

Is this why Gran didn't want me up here?

The thought lodged like a splinter just as a soft knock echoed from downstairs, followed by a familiar voice.

"Leah?"

It was Sage.

Leah blinked, disoriented. The attic suddenly felt suffocating, dust swirling like ghosts in the half-light.

"Yeah," she called hoarsely, her voice catching. "Coming."

Chapter 3

Leah left the book behind and made her way down the creaking stairs. The scent of something sweet reached her before she even saw Sage, a familiar presence she hadn't realized she needed until now.

"Coming here was so weird. Everything looked so eerie outside," Sage said, making her way toward Leah. "Maybe it's going to storm or something." A moment later, she appeared by the attic stairs holding two takeaway coffees and balancing a small bakery box in one arm.

Her usual grin lit up her face. "Happy birthday again, birthday girl," she said, holding up the box. "It's not much, but it's your favorite. Chocolate raspberry mini cake from Larry's."

Leah barely managed a nod. The smile faded from Sage's face the second she caught sight of Leah's expression.

"You okay?" Sage asked, passing her one of the drinks. "You look like you've seen a ghost or something."

Leah took the cup without thinking, her fingers curling around it more for something to hold than for warmth.

"I...I don't know," she murmured.

Sage's eyes narrowed as she stepped closer, the box still in her hand. Leah could see her playful energy draining away.

"Where's Selene?" Sage asked gently, without looking away.

Leah froze. She'd been so caught up in everything that had happened since she got home that she'd forgotten the one thing that made all of this so terrifying. Selene.

"I..." she started, but the rest lodged in her throat. Panic, anguish, and fear surged all at once, and before she could stop herself, the tears came.

The coffee slipped from her hand and hit the rug with a soft thud, causing a tiny splash to spill and mark the fibers, before she crumpled to the floor. Grief tore through her in waves she couldn't contain. A keening cry broke from her lips as Sage rushed forward, catching her in a hug, the coffee cups forgotten on the floor. The truth was unbearable. Selene was gone, and Leah could feel it in her bones.

Sage sat with her on the floor for a long moment with one hand firmly on Leah's shoulder, saying nothing. This silence was different. It was comforting, not hollow. When Leah's sobs finally eased, she wiped her face on her sleeve, aware of how red and swollen her eyes felt.

"I don't know what happened," Leah croaked. "She's just...gone."

Sage glanced around the house, her voice low and tight. "No sign of a struggle? No call? Nothing?"

Leah shook her head. "No note. No message. But something happened...I can feel it." She paused, eyes haunted. "And that's not even the strangest part."

Sage's brows lifted, patient but concerned.

"There's something I need to show you," Leah said quietly, pushing herself to her feet. "It's in the attic."

Sage opened her mouth as if to protest, then closed it again. Her face paled slightly, but she nodded and stood, brushing her hands on her jeans. "Lead the way."

The attic hadn't changed, not that Leah expected it to. Dust hung in the air as if suspended in time, and shadows curled in the corners like they were watching.

Sage hesitated at the threshold. "Okay, wow. Creepy."

Leah didn't answer. She crossed to where the book sat, still open to the spiraling shimmers. Her fingers hovered over the page, hesitant to touch it again.

"I found this," she said quietly. "Or...it found me."

Sage stepped closer with her arms crossed tightly. "It's just a book."

"It's not." Leah turned, holding it up carefully. "Sage, I heard someone. A man's voice. He knew my name and said this book would guide me."

Sage's brows pulled together as she stepped closer to get a better look. "You heard...a voice. Up here. In the attic."

Leah nodded, though the motion felt heavy. "And when I touched it, I saw things. Places I've never been. People I've never met. They were almost like memories, but not mine. They felt..." She swallowed hard. "They felt like they belonged to me somehow."

Sage stared at the book like it might bite her. "Leah, that sounds like...I don't know. Are you sure it wasn't a panic attack? A trauma thing? Maybe your brain's just trying to—"

"It wasn't a dream," Leah cut in, her voice sharp despite her trembling hands. "I know what I saw. I know what I felt."

Sage fell silent, studying her. Leah saw the subtle calculation behind her eyes, her best friend trying to make sense of something that didn't make sense. Then Sage stepped beside her and folded her arms.

"Well," she muttered, "if the haunted book tells you to start sacrificing goats, I'm staging an intervention."

A shaky laugh escaped Leah, half relief, half disbelief. "You know, this bracelet of yours really does work. And wouldn't I know it, as soon as you crossed my mind, you showed up."

Sage gave a small smile. "I'm glad it helped, Leah, but this," she gestured around the attic, "this is strange. Even for Selene. It's not like her to just vanish, especially without leaving some kind of clue."

"I know." Leah wrapped her arms around herself as the chill of the attic crept under her skin. "That's exactly why I think something horrible happened to her. And the visions...they feel connected somehow."

Sage eyed the book warily. "Can I see it?"

Leah hesitated, unease flickering through her, then handed it over. Sage's expression tightened as she took the book, as if expecting it to disintegrate in her hands. When nothing happened, she exhaled and flipped through a few pages.

"It's blank?"

"Yeah. It was locked up, though, which doesn't make much sense. Why lock something that has nothing written in it?" Leah said softly. "Then I started seeing something shining on the pages. When I touched it, that's when everything happened."

Sage searched Leah's face, then looked back at the empty pages. She waited for something to appear, but the book stayed blank. Frustration flickered across her expression before she shrugged. "Maybe it only works for you."

Leah frowned. "I don't get it. Maybe if I tried again—"

"No." Sage's voice came out sharper than expected, making Leah flinch. Sage quickly softened her tone, running a hand through her hair. "Not yet. I don't think you've recovered from whatever you saw the first time."

Leah looked down at her faintly trembling hands. "I just...I don't understand," she whispered. "Why would she hide something like this from me? And why am I finding it now?" Her throat tightened. "It's like she knew she wasn't coming back."

The weight of that thought hung between them. Sage shifted, crossing her arms. "Selene always had reasons," she said carefully. "Even when we couldn't see them."

Leah took the book back and hugged it to her chest. "Do you think she wanted me to find it because she's...gone?"

Sage rested a hand briefly on Leah's shoulder before pulling it back. "I think she wanted to make sure you'd be ready, no matter what happened. And maybe this is part of that."

Leah traced the book's worn cover with her thumb. "It doesn't feel like I'm ready. It feels like everything is falling apart."

Sage smiled, though Leah caught the strain behind it. "Then I'll help you hold it together. That's what best friends are for, right?"

Leah nodded, grateful for the one steady thing she still had. She set the book gently on the old chest near the window. Its pages no longer moved.

Sage rubbed her arms. "This room gives me chills. What was Selene even doing up here?"

"I don't know," Leah murmured, scanning the rafters. "She never let me up here. Said it was full of things not meant for kids." She paused. "I thought she meant boxes and old furniture."

Her words trailed off, leaving a heavy pause.

"Maybe I'm losing it," Leah said finally. "People don't just see things. Not unless something's wrong with them."

Sage's head snapped toward her. "No," she said firmly. "Nothing is wrong with you."

Leah blinked at the intensity, but Sage quickly forced a lighter tone. "Classic grandma move though," she added, attempting a laugh. "Hiding spooky heirlooms in the attic like it's a family tradition."

They sat in silence for a moment before Leah spoke again. "I don't know what any of this means."

Sage leaned back on her hands, posture stiff. "Then let's start here. One mystery at a time." Her eyes flicked to the book, lingering, before she plastered on exaggerated cheer. "But first..."

She sprung to her feet, striking a dramatic pose. "We must fuel ourselves. Snacks. Possibly cake and coffee."

Leah cracked a small smile as Sage headed down the attic stairs. She sat on the floor with the book closed in front of her, fingers hovering over the cover. Why did it feel like it was calling to her? The pressure behind her eyes crept back.

Without warning, the book snapped open and its pages began flipping rapidly before stopping on one that glowed faintly. A low hum filled the air.

Leah's eyes darted between the book and the stairwell. "Okay," she whispered. "What are you trying to show me?"

The hum grew louder. Without thinking, Leah touched the page, and the sensation was like falling into the book itself.

The attic dissolved.

A stone tower rose against a gray sky. At the center of the field stood her grandmother, arms outstretched. Leah couldn't move or speak. She was trapped, a spectator in the vision.

Selene lowered her arms and turned slightly, as if sensing Leah's presence without seeing her.

"Leah," Selene whispered. "My final breath lies where the river bends to ash. There, the earth will give you what I could not."

Leah's chest tightened so sharply she felt she might suffocate. She tried to call out, but no sound came. Her voice was stolen by the vision. Then the scene blurred and tore away, flinging her back into the attic.

She gasped, clutching the book. Sweat beaded on her forehead and her limbs shook violently.

Where does the river bend to ash?

The words burned in her mind as footsteps creaked on the attic stairs.

"Leah?" Sage's voice was careful.

She appeared in the doorway with the cake box and the newly-warmed coffees. Her eyes flicked to the book, then to Leah's pale face.

"Oh god. You're pale," Sage said, hurrying over. "What happened? Are you okay?"

"I'm fine," Leah whispered, though her voice betrayed her. "Sort of."

Sage crouched beside her, pushing the cake box towards her. "Eat something. Drink."

Leah reached for the cup but didn't drink right away. Her hands were still shaking too much. Sage covered her wrist gently, steadying it until Leah's hands stopped shaking.

"Hey, look at me. Whatever that creepy book showed you, it's over now."

Leah swallowed hard, forcing her eyes away from the book's cover. "It was Selene." Her voice was raspy with emotion. "I...I saw her."

Sage froze. For a fraction of a second, Leah saw her composure crack. Her mouth opened slightly, then closed again.

Leah could see the sharp intake of breath and the way Sage's eyes lingered on her face, but she couldn't read the expression fully.

"You saw Selene?" she asked carefully.

Leah nodded. "She spoke to me. She told me where to find her."

Sage knelt in front of her, taking both Leah's hands. "You've got this, Leah. We'll figure this out." Sage said, urging her to focus.

Leah blinked rapidly and let herself take in Sage's presence. When her breathing steadied, Sage eased back slightly, eyes fixed on her with furrowed brows. "Did Selene ever talk to you about any of this? The book? Visions? Any weird magical crap?"

Magic. The word felt odd when said aloud like that, but also uncomfortably fitting. Either that, or this was the start of a full mental breakdown. Leah shook her head. "No. Never. I had never even seen this book until today." She looked down, her voice growing smaller. "I feel like I'm in a nightmare."

Sage exhaled hard and glanced toward the floor, silent for a moment. Leah watched her, unsure what to make of her reaction.

"Okay." Sage finally said. "So, we have a magic book now."

Leah gave a small, humorless laugh. "Apparently."

"It's like she was preparing you for something but never got the chance to explain it?"

"Or maybe she thought she was protecting me. Maybe knowing would've been worse."

Sage chewed thoughtfully on a bite of cake. "But she was always so protective. Why wouldn't she want you to know more about this book?"

Leah hugged her knees to her chest. "What if I wasn't supposed to find it? What if something bad happens every time I open it?"

Sage followed her gaze to the book. "Do you think...it's alive?"

"I don't know," Leah said quietly. "But it's definitely not just a book."

Silence settled thickly around them.

"Should I go to the police?" Leah asked after a moment. "What if they could help me find Selene?"

"Leah," Sage said gently, "the police are going to have more questions than answers if you tell them about a blank book with shimmering ink and visions."

Leah nodded, staring at the book. Whatever this was, it wasn't something she could make public.

"Let's call it," Sage said with a groan, rising to her feet. "We've been in this attic all night. You're trembling. I feel like I've aged five years. We need real sleep."

Leah didn't protest. "Yeah. Okay."

Sage grabbed the empty cups and cake box, then looked back at her. "You coming?"

"In a minute," Leah said but made no attempt to leave.

Sage frowned but set everything down again and sat on a nearby stack of dusty boxes. Leah stayed where she was with her arms wrapped around her knees with the book by her side. Night crept in making the shadows thicken, even as moonlight sliced across the floor. At some point, Sage fell asleep under an old quilt, but Leah remained awake.

This had to be a nightmare.

How could her grandmother disappear and leave her with nothing but questions? She replayed their conversation from the night before, the weight in Selene's words. Even then, Selene hadn't explained anything.

Leah didn't sleep at all as she tried to make sense of the visions, the grief, and the impossible truths.

Morning light crept into the attic, casting soft golden slants across the worn floorboards. Leah stirred in the old window seat, the book resting heavily on her lap. Her eyes were shadowed with exhaustion; she had not really slept. The night had passed in broken fragments of questions, tears, and silence.

Across the room, Sage lay curled in the corner, wrapped in a faded quilt Selene had knitted years ago. Leah watched her for a moment, a soft smile tugging at her lips. Anyone else would have bolted the second she started rambling about visions and voices. Honestly, Leah would've expected them to. It was ridiculous that she'd even let the thought cross her mind when it came to Sage. Sage, who had always shown up. Who never hesitated, never doubted her, even when Leah doubted herself. The steady rise and fall of Sage's breathing eased something in Leah's chest. Loyal to a fault. Of course she stayed.

A sharp alarm cut through the quiet. Sage groaned, fumbling for her phone with one hand while the other clutched the blanket tighter around her shoulders.

"Ugh, my head," she mumbled. Then her eyes snapped open as her gaze met Leah's, and everything that had happened the night before came rushing back.

"Morning," Leah said softly, her voice hoarse. "It's time, isn't it?"

Sage glanced at her phone. The screen confirmed what Leah knew she'd completely forgotten: her train back to the city was in less than two hours. Her weekend in Eldergrove had vanished in a blur of grief.

Her face fell. "I...I didn't even realize—"

"I figured," Leah said gently, managing a small, tired smile. "We definitely let the time pass us by. I know you were supposed to leave earlier this morning, but it looked like you could use a little more sleep."

Sage looked up sharply. "How are you so calm about this?"

"I'm not," Leah admitted. "But I've had all night to think. You worked so hard for that apprenticeship. I'm not letting you blow it for me."

Sage ran a hand through her tangled hair, frustration simmering beneath the sadness. "You collapsed, Leah. You were shaking. You barely slept, and now you want me to just...walk away?"

Leah looked down at the book resting beside her like a quiet sentinel. "This is mine to carry, Sage. I don't know how I know that, but I do. Gran left it to me for a reason, even if she didn't explain it."

Sage shook her head, rising to her feet. "I can always try to figure things out and stay a little longer."

Leah stood too, slower, her movements heavy with fatigue. "No matter how much I want you to stay, I think the best thing is for me to figure this out. This feels really big, but I can't explain why. I just know I need to put the puzzle together."

Sage nodded. "Yeah."

"And..." Leah stepped closer. "You stayed. You stayed when I needed you the most. That means more to me than you know."

The attic held stillness like breath caught in the lungs. Dust swirled gently in the golden light creeping in through the window, the day waking around them while something deeper cracked underneath.

Sage nodded slowly. "How will I know you're okay? You don't have a cell phone..."

"I'll figure out a way," Leah said. "I promise."

"And if I don't hear from you," Sage warned, half-smiling through the ache, "I'm coming back with cops. Or a psychic. Maybe both."

Leah laughed, fragile but real. "Deal."

Then Sage pulled her into one of her bear hugs, except this one felt different. Leah could feel the fear in her grip, and the unconditional love and understanding that let her give Leah the space she needed.

"Don't do anything reckless," Sage whispered.

"No promises," Leah murmured against her shoulder.

Sage pulled back just enough to look her in the eyes. "Then promise me you'll reach out when you know a little bit more. I'll be back here as soon as I can."

"Once I have a better idea of what all this means, I'll do my best to reach out. Promise," Leah said.

They descended the attic stairs in silence, the floorboards groaning gently beneath them. The house felt heavier now as they walked toward the front door where they lingered, neither of them reaching for the knob right away. Sage hugged her again, burying her face in Leah's shoulder. When they finally let go, a quiet sense of trust and grief clung heavy in the air.

The door clicked shut behind Sage, leaving Leah standing there for a moment with her hand still resting on the knob, as if letting go too quickly would unravel her. The house settled back into a deeper silence.

Leah moved to the front window, brushing aside the old lace curtain. Outside, Sage crossed the overgrown path to her rental car at the edge of the gravel drive. Her steps were slow and reluctant. She opened the car door, paused, and looked back.

Leah raised a hand in farewell, and Sage lifted hers in return, just for a second. Then she got in, started the engine, and drove off. The sound of tires crunching over gravel echoed through the trees until it faded into nothing.

Leah stayed at the window long after the car disappeared. The wind stirred the trees beyond the yard, and the sky had begun to cloud over with soft shades of gray. Everything felt suspended. When she finally stepped away, the quiet pressed in all around her once more.

She turned slowly, her eyes drifting over the worn floorboards and the shelves lined with Selene's strange old books. The absence of her best friend was a tangible thing, heavier than she'd expected.

For a while, Leah remained in the kitchen with her fingers wrapped tightly around a mug, though the liquid inside had long since gone cold. She couldn't shake the chill that had settled into her bones.

The book now sat on the table between her hands. After what felt like forever, lost in thought, a flicker of movement caught her eye. Tucked beneath the edge of the book was a slip of parchment, aged, yellowed, and curled at the corners. Leah hadn't noticed it before.

Her pulse quickened as she unfolded it, recognizing her grandmother's looping handwriting immediately.

Leah,
If you're reading this, then I'm no longer with you.
I can't begin to express how much it breaks my heart to leave you like this. More than anything, I wish I could have stayed to see your face, to hold you close and explain all of this in person.

But time has run out, and there are truths you need to know—truths I could no longer keep from you.

The book found you, which means the time has come. I know you don't understand what that means yet, but trust that it was always meant to be yours. You carry something inside you, Leah—something rare and powerful—even if it hasn't awakened yet.

You are not safe in Eldergrove anymore. The protective spells I placed around you are fading fast, and there are those who would do anything to find you. You need to leave, quickly and quietly, before 48 hours pass from the moment the book found you. After that, all my enchantments will fail completely.

Take the book with you and guard it closely. It's more than just an heirloom. It holds pieces of a much larger truth—about who you are, and what you're meant to become. I know that sounds frightening, but I also know you. You have always been brave, even when you didn't feel it.

There is someone beyond the Veil who can help you. His name is Nico. I trust that he will protect you now. My enchantments have hidden you from even him, but once you step through the Veil, he'll be able to find you. Let him.

I know this must feel impossible. You're grieving, confused, and probably angry. And still, I need you to trust me one last time. Follow the call of the book. Let it guide you. You'll understand in time.

No matter where I am now, know that I am still with you in the quiet moments and in the warmth of sunlight through the trees.

Be strong, Leah. Shine as you always have.

With all my love,

Grandma Selene

Leah stared at the paper, her throat thick with grief and disbelief.

If you're reading this then I am no longer with you.

The words landed like stones in her chest. A cold rush of dread swept through her. She read the letter again, slower this time, trying to anchor herself in her grandmother's voice, but the more she read, the less any of it made sense. Her eyes caught on certain words and refused to move on.

Spells? The Veil? No. No, that was...this had to be something else. Some elaborate metaphor Selene had woven because she always spoke like her thoughts were a puzzle. Magic wasn't real. Spells weren't real. People didn't leave instructions about disappearing protection charms like it was a recipe to reheat lentil soup.

Her pulse thudded in her ears. Was this really what Selene had meant to leave her with? She pressed the letter to her chest, the paper crinkling under her fingers. Selene had known she'd be gone. Known Leah would be alone, and still she'd trusted her to understand and survive whatever this was.

A laugh bubbled up her throat, bitter and shaky. Magic and Veils, she thought bitterly. It's insane. But even as she told herself that, some quiet, unreasonable part of her believed it. A part that clearly wasn't logical. She looked up at the attic where shadows still lingered at the edges of the stairs. Part of her longed to wait, to catch her breath, and to make sense of any of this...but the clock was ticking.

Forty-eight hours.

That meant the spells would be completely broken by tomorrow evening. She stood slowly, looking around the house. Her hand curled around her wrist, fingers brushing the simple bracelet Sage had given her. The moment she touched it, a strange calm washed over her, the bracelet reminding her of Sage's steady voice, just enough to help her take a grounding breath.

The house, once warm and full of Selene's presence, felt hollow. Leah turned toward the door with the book and letter clutched tightly in her arms. She didn't know who Nico was, and she didn't know how to find that mystery Veil, but she knew one thing with aching certainty.

She couldn't stay.

Chapter 4

Leah stared at the door, unable to take her hand off the handle. She debated whether she should leave in a rush or take these last few hours to breathe. The house felt eerily still, and it seemed smarter to pause and think through a plan, to linger one final night before stepping into the unknown. And so, she stayed.

The afternoon passed as she gathered supplies and packed a small bag of clothes and other essentials before stopping to eat something. After finishing the last of the lentil soup, Leah curled up in Selene's favorite chair, tucking her knees beneath her and wrapping herself in the half-finished quilt that still held a strand of her grandmother's silver hair. All of it felt like something pulled straight from a nightmare, but the book resting on her lap told a different story. She traced its worn edges absently, as if trying to memorize it by touch. Her eyes drifted to the window, where the trees swayed gently, unbothered by the storm of change inside her.

It should have been a happy birthday. She blinked slowly, hollow with the thought. Cake. Wishes. Laughter. That was what birthdays were supposed to be. But hers had unraveled like a pulled thread, vision after vision, truth after truth, until the fabric of her life had come undone. She'd never liked birthdays much, and this one had only sealed the reason why.

With a sudden rush of exhaustion, Leah let herself drift off to sleep, attempting to make up for the loss of it the night before, and perhaps make up for any lack of rest that she would face moving forward.

The morning fog clung low to the earth, curling around Leah's ankles as she stepped beyond the threshold of the house. She paused on the porch, locking the door behind her for what felt like the last time. The key felt strange in her hand, small and useless, almost symbolic now. She wasn't due to work today, so there was no need for calls or farewell messages. She didn't want to explain. How could she, when she didn't even have the words herself?

Still, as she stared at the locked door, a pang of guilt tugged at her chest. Thomas. She'd promised him a cupcake for his birthday, and she'd completely forgotten in the chaos that ensued after coming home from work on her birthday. And Nora, the café owner, deserved better than an abrupt disappearance.

Leah hesitated at the bottom of the steps, cool air brushing her cheeks. Her boots crunched lightly on the gravel as she turned toward town. It was early enough that Eldergrove's streets were still quiet, and the fog was still softening edges and muting sound. The bell above the café door chimed as she pushed it open. The smell of roasted beans and cinnamon wrapped around her, and for a moment, she realized how much she would miss this place.

Behind the counter, Nora looked up from a stack of paperwork, surprised. "Leah? Aren't you off today?"

"I am," Leah said, adjusting her bag as she stepped forward. "I just...I was hoping to see you. I needed to say something."

Nora tilted her head, setting her pen down. "Is everything okay?"

Leah gave a tight smile. "Not really. I have to go away for a while. I don't know for how long."

Concern crept into Nora's expression. "Is it family? You don't have to explain if it's personal, but—"

"It's...complicated," Leah said quickly. "And I know this isn't the best way to do it. I should've called. I should've given more notice." Her words tumbled out faster than she could shape them. "Things just happened fast, and I needed time to think. I didn't want to disappear without saying something."

Nora nodded slowly, kindness softening her features. "I understand. Life has a way of pulling us off track sometimes. You've always been dependable, Leah. If you need to go, go. I'll figure things out."

Relief and guilt collided in Leah's chest. "Thank you. I know this probably means there won't be a job waiting when I get back."

"We'll cross that bridge when we get there," Nora said gently. "Just take care of yourself."

Leah nodded, throat tight. "Thanks. And...tell Thomas I'm sorry I didn't get to say goodbye."

Nora blinked. "Oh, he's not here. He called out last minute this morning. Said something about family, I think."

Leah frowned slightly. The words felt off, but she pushed the thought aside. "Right. Okay." Maybe he'd ended up celebrating his birthday with them after all.

With one last look at the café, the chipped mugs, the crooked sign, the stool that always wobbled, Leah turned and walked out, the bell chiming one final time behind her.

By the time she reached the edge of Eldergrove, the fog had begun to lift, the trees ahead still wrapped in early morning light. The path into the woods shimmered faintly beneath the sun. Leah reached into her bag, fingers brushing the book as if it might vanish. Whatever was happening, it was happening because of this book. She had to protect it.

There was no map. Just the letter, the name Nico, and the strange certainty that she would know the way when the time came. Now, that certainty flickered as she reached the forest's edge. The trees rose tall and quiet, trunks damp with dew.

Suddenly, something moved just beyond the mist, a shimmer or shape gone as quickly as it appeared. Leah held her breath, waiting for something to happen or for someone to appear, but silence answered. Then a breeze stirred, raising goosebumps along her skin. She cursed under her breath for not bringing a heavier coat. Still, she couldn't shake the feeling that it wasn't the wind unsettling her. It was the way the forest seemed to watch her, urging her forward.

As she followed the marked path, her footing shifted, and without realizing it, she stepped off the road and onto a narrow trail she'd never noticed before. It wasn't marked, but it felt right.

The forest and the scent of trees stirred old memories. They surfaced uninvited: afternoons spent wandering through these woods as a child, slipping out of school to escape relentless bullying. Back then, the trees had been a refuge, a place where she could breathe freely and speak aloud without fear. Selene had never allowed her to roam alone, so those moments had been rare, but the memories still carried that old thrill for the unknown.

She walked for what felt like hours, waiting for something to guide her. But the farther she went, the more time seemed to smear at the edges. The forest thickened, and with it came a strange awareness, as if someone were trailing her just out of sight. The book gave a single pulse against her ribs.

Then she noticed it: the low trill of birdsong cutting through the silence. A distant branch snapped, and she noticed that the shadows of the trees slanted differently than they should. The path ahead twisted and vanished into a curtain of silver mist that shimmered where sunlight should have been.

She stopped at a fork marked by a cluster of stones. One trail curved toward a thicket of brambles and the other dipped downward into a pit framed by weeping willows. She hesitated and stopped to listen, but once again, the quiet felt wrong. Her pulse quickened. If she'd ever wondered whether she could survive in the wild, this answered it. She would probably die within a day.

Another branch snapped to her left, and she followed the sound like a moth to a flame.

As she stepped between the willows, the pressure she'd felt behind her eyes returned full force. Leah pressed both hands to her temples and squeezed her eyes shut. It wasn't painful, but it was strong enough to drive her inward.

When she opened her eyes, the forest fractured. Light scattered like shards of glass, sound thinning to a whisper. And then she wasn't in the forest anymore.

She stood in the kitchen of her home. The familiar scent of warm cinnamon and dried orange peels filled the air. The kettle hissed softly. Selene stood at the stove, humming a low, haunting melody. Her silver hair was twisted into its usual loose bun, tendrils curling at her neck. A worn mug steamed in her hand.

Leah's throat tightened. The sight stole the breath from her lungs.

"Grandma?" Her voice cracked with everything she'd lost.

Selene turned, eyes kind, her smile exactly as Leah remembered from childhood nights spent hiding from nightmares. Leah ached to step forward, but her legs wouldn't move.

"You're almost there, darling," Selene said gently. "Just a little further."

"I'm not ready," Leah whispered. "You said you'd always be here. You promised."

Selene was already fading, and the kitchen was warping like wet paper, making the light fracture again. Leah reached out, her fingers grasping at air, but only smoke slipped through her hand.

"Don't leave..."

Warmth lingered in Selene's eyes as she vanished, the comfort and loss almost too much to bear.

"You have more strength than you know, Leah."

Tears welled, blurring Leah's vision. Then the scene shattered.

She collapsed to her knees among the willows, her breath coming in jagged gasps. The ache in her chest was raw and unbearable. She pressed a hand over her heart as if she could hold it together.

Pushing herself up, Leah wiped her eyes and kept walking.

The trees thinned, opening into a clearing ringed with weathered stones. At its center stood a tall, silver-barked tree crowned with pale leaves that rustled without wind. As she stepped forward, the air shifted again. The quiet wasn't empty; it was aware. A low hum vibrated through the soil and into her bones.

On the far side of the clearing stood a stone archway woven with ivy. Leah squinted, feeling a flicker of recognition. She had been here before, as a child. Back then, she had simply run through the archway carefree, imagining the world beyond as a place where the darkness of school and taunts couldn't touch her. Now, though, it felt different—almost as if something on the other side didn't match the world around it.

Leah approached the archway cautiously, half-expecting it to shift or dissolve before her eyes, or for another vision to show. Her pulse quickened as she stepped closer, every instinct screaming that something might be waiting on the other side. She held her breath, closed her eyes and stepped through it, bracing for a sudden jolt. When she opened her eyes, the clearing greeted her unchanged. Her chest tightened with a mixture of relief and irritation. She turned around to face the archway, almost angry at it for deceiving her. "Hello!?" she yelled, frustration cracking her voice.

With an exasperated sigh, she slumped her shoulders and tilted her face to the sky in defeat. Maybe she really was losing her mind. She leaned back against the stones, scanning the clearing for anything she might have missed, anything that could explain the strange pulse of anticipation she still felt. Maybe she should have taken the other path.

Leah began to retrace her steps mentally, but something caught her eye before she started walking back. A carving etched into the stone of the archway. Her stomach tightened at the sight. Symbols. Spirals, moons, and what looked like half-closed eyes. She recognized the symbols from her grandmother's embroidered blankets, ones she had long thought were just fanciful designs, a product of her grandmother's fascination with symmetrical shapes. They were there, carved into the stone.

Instinctively, Leah pressed her palm against one of the symbols, and like a switch, the world beyond the archway changed. She could no longer see straight through it; mist now obscured what appeared to be an entirely different forest. Leah glanced back one last time before taking a hesitant step forward, facing the archway. As she stepped through, the air thickened around her, turning almost liquid and muffling sound. For a moment, she could barely breathe, as if diving deep underwater. The book pulsed against her ribs, anchoring her amid the blur.

Then the Veil released her, and the forest beyond was completely unfamiliar. This wasn't Eldergrove or anywhere she'd ever been. Whatever this place was, it lived on the other side of something that felt different. Light filtered through impossibly tall trees, their leaves shimmering with hues no season could explain: violet, gold, and the palest green, like frost.

Leah took one step forward. The second came slower, and by the third, the trees had shifted again. For the first time since she'd started this journey, fear took hold. She turned around and realized the path was gone, and the archway had been swallowed by mist.

"Nico?" she called. Her voice was loud, but it didn't echo as it should.

The mist began to move. It slid toward her, wrapping around her legs, her waist, her throat, until the forest dissolved into white.

Familiar shapes formed within it: a narrow hallway lined with crooked picture frames, the soft creak of old floorboards, her grandmother's laugh drifting from somewhere close. Then, Selene's attic flickered into focus, just as it had looked the night Leah found the book. But something was wrong. The light pulsed unnaturally and the shadows seemed to be twitching impatiently. The air smelled wrong, and the groaning of the floor only heightened the sense that something was deeply off. This felt different from the other visions she'd seen so far.

The floor groaned behind her, and Leah whirled toward the sound, panic tightening her chest. Selene stood inches away, her face pale, her eyes vacant. When she opened her mouth, darkness spilled out like smoke.

"You're too late."

Leah's breath hitched.

"This isn't real," she whispered.

Selene flickered, her form stuttering in jagged bursts like a broken reflection on water, then vanished. The attic buckled and warped, walls bending under heatless pressure. Leah staggered back as the space twisted again, reshaping into something new and painfully familiar.

Desks. Chalkboards. The peeling yellow walls of her childhood classroom.

She was small again, seven, maybe eight. Her legs dangled from the plastic chair, too short to reach the floor. Her fists clenched in her lap as children laughed behind her, their whispers sharp and cruel.

"She doesn't have real parents."

"Her grandma's a witch."

"She lives in that creepy house by the woods."

The words cut into her like knives. Her child-self clenched her fists harder, jaw trembling as she fought back tears, her bottom lip quivering anyway. The laughter sharpened. Someone yanked her hair and hissed, "Freak," as a paper ball struck her cheek. Pain and shame burned through her, leaving her shaking.

Her vision blurred with tears, and the classroom melted away. Wind roared, deafening, and somewhere in the storm a man shouted something she couldn't understand, followed by a woman's urgent cry.

"Leah, run!"

Her heart pounded. She spun, but the trees were wrong. Shadows poured from the gaps between them, slithering closer. Then another voice cut through the chaos, but this time, it was calm and merciless. It wasn't that of a child's, nor that of anyone she could recognize. A stranger's voice struck deep inside her.

"They bear the blood of The Unheard. Kill them."

The words weren't shouted, but they burned through her like acid. She tried to scream, but no sound came. The shadows lunged, swallowing her child-self whole. She collapsed onto the forest floor, gasping, the book pressed to her chest like a lifeline as terror closed in.

"Stop," she whispered, barely audible. "Please. This isn't real."

But it was.

The pain. The shame. The loneliness. The gnawing certainty that she would always be different. Always haunted. Always alone. It crushed her with the weight of truth.

The wind rose. The world cracked. And then—silence.

The mist unraveled like thread pulled from a seam, and the forest snapped back into place. Leah stood in the clearing, breath ragged, eyes wet, knees trembling. She looked down. The book had opened in her hands, and on the page was her grandmother's handwriting.

Pain is a door. Step through it and trust in yourself.

Leah swallowed hard. The first test, she realized, hadn't been about magic at all. It had been about surviving truth. These weren't just visions. Some were memories clawing their way back.

She took a moment to steady herself, then stepped forward, once, then again. The path unfurled beneath her feet, guided by instinct and a quiet, stubborn resolve not to let the past dictate her future.

The air shifted again. Warmer, but charged enough to raise the hairs along her arms. She felt it before she understood it: pressure, a prickle at the back of her neck, the unmistakable sense that she was no longer alone.

She turned.

He leaned casually against the twisted trunk of a white-barked tree, arms folded as if he'd been waiting all along. His sharp jaw and dark cloak faded beside the intensity of his eyes. Blue. Fixed on her with unnerving stillness.

"You made it," he said calmly, as if she were late to a meeting.

Leah stared at him, her mind scrambling. Another vision? A real person? A stranger...or not?

She blinked. "You're...Nico." The name scraped out of her. At this point, a full mental breakdown still felt like the simplest explanation.

He inclined his head, a ghost of a smile touching his lips. "In the flesh."

Her fingers tightened around the book. Run, collapse, demand answers—she couldn't decide. How long had he been there?

"How did you know I'd be here?" she asked.

"Let's just say I had a feeling." His voice was steady, his gaze unwavering.

"So it's true," she said slowly. "This is all real."

She stepped closer despite herself, every muscle tense, balance unsteady. Nico moved as if to meet her, but she lifted a hand, stopping him. Dizziness still clung to her, shock and disbelief tangling together. She couldn't fall apart again. Not now.

"How did you know I'd be here *now*?" she asked, her voice wavering.

Nico straightened. "I didn't need to know. I just waited."

"Why?"

"I'm your mentor of sorts," he said simply.

Her laugh cracked the air. "Mentor? I don't even know who you are."

"I recall you calling my name a moment ago," he said mildly.

Heat rushed to her cheeks as she realized she had. Annoyed, she glared at him. "I don't trust you."

"I wouldn't expect you to."

The honesty disarmed her, if only briefly. He stood there like he hadn't just watched her unravel, like it had all been routine. Had he seen everything? Anger and humiliation burned behind her eyes.

"I saw things," she said. "Visions. Shadows. I saw my grandmother..." Her voice broke. "They weren't real, but they felt real."

"They were tests," Nico said. "The Veil doesn't let anyone through without cost. It reflects the truth you bury."

"So that was the Veil?" Leah asked, incredulously. The Veil had been such an intangible thing before. A meaningless word written in a letter. Leah took a deep breath in, letting it all sink in. Slowly, things were starting to come together.

Leah looked up, eyeing Nico suspiciously. "So what now?"

"Now," he said, stepping closer, "you learn how to use what's inside you. Before The Order finds you. Before it's too late."

The Order?

He extended his hand as she stared at it. Everything about him whispered danger. He was unreadable which put her on edge. She had met guys like him before and she had stayed far away from them then. But something in her stirred at his presence which thoroughly confused her. Her hand hovered near his and then, barely touching, she let her fingers graze his palm.

The connection sparked, sending a rush of energy flaring between them, sudden and wild. Leah sucked in a breath as the pull beneath her ribs was sharp enough to make her dizzy. Across from her, Nico stilled, and for a moment, she was certain that he felt it too. His composure slipped enough to tell her he was just as shaken.

"What was that?" she whispered.

He didn't answer. His gaze held hers with unsettling intensity.

"It's not safe out here," he said quietly. "I'll answer your questions somewhere safer."

Leah didn't know who The Order was, but Nico was the first person who had any answers at all. So she followed.

They moved through the forest with Nico leading them without hesitation, and Leah followed with cautious steps and mounting questions. The forest around them was strange and dim, filtered with a kind of dream light. She couldn't tell if it was dawn, dusk, or something entirely in between, but the air smelled of damp bark and distant rain.

She had not noticed it before, but shadows seemed to follow him. Even in the dappled light, shadows clung to him like they were extensions of him. They didn't move like shadows should and that realization sent a shiver down her spine. How had she missed it earlier? Now that she saw it, she couldn't unsee it.

They stopped in a wide circle of stone and moss, where runes were etched into the earth in looping, ancient-looking patterns. Nico finally turned to face her, and for the first time since they met, she saw him fully.

He was tall and lean, built with quiet strength. A thin leather band circled his wrist, and he had a kind of tension in the way he stood, ready to react if needed. His dark hair fell just past his jaw, slightly messy but not unkempt. His features were sharp—high cheekbones, a strong jaw, and a firm set to his mouth that seemed to rarely soften. But just as before, it was his eyes that caused her to stare. Deep blue, and watchful. They were focused and unreadable. She hated that. She hated being unable to read someone.

He wore a dark blue cloak over fitted black clothing, practical and worn. Someone used to hiding in plain sight.

"This place is protected," he said. "We're outside The Order's reach for now."

Leah wasn't paying attention. She was still watching him, trying to make sense of him. "What are you?"

Nico's brow lifted slightly. "Not the question I was expecting."

"Well, you pretty much stepped out of a vision. You're surrounded by shadows. You knew my name...and you apparently knew my grandmother." Her grip tightened around the book in her bag. "You talk about whatever that nightmare was back there as if it's just something you happen to see every day, but I didn't even know any of this...stuff was real until two days ago." She lifted the book like a shield. "So, you'll have to forgive me if I'm struggling to make sense of all of this."

He nodded slowly. "Fair enough."

Leah's gaze drifted nervously to the shadows at his feet. At first, she thought they were just forest shadows, but then they moved again. They stretched, curling like smoke against the ground.

Her breath caught. "What...what is that?"

Nico's eyes followed her gaze, calm and measured. "Watch."

He lifted a hand slightly, and the shadows responded instantly, rising, twisting, and forming thin, arching streams that wove through the air. Leah froze, every muscle locking. The shadows seemed alive, sniffing at the air and brushing against her boots before retreating again.

Her voice trembled. "Are they...alive?"

"They're reacting," Nico said plainly. "To you. To the magic you carry. They sensed it the moment you called for me."

The shadows swirled closer as if circling her, then flickered in midair before retreating. Leah's pulse raced, but her eyes stayed glued to them. "I didn't call for anyone. I was just—" She stopped, remembering the moment she'd very clearly called his name like an idiot.

"Why do you call them 'they,' as if they're separate from you?" she asked, hoping to steer the conversation.

Nico hesitated before answering. "They are part of me, but also more than me. They remember things I cannot, perceive what I cannot, move where I cannot. They respond to intent, to presence, and to danger."

Leah's eyes widened. "So they're part of your magic? This is your magic?"

"They are my magic," he said. With a flick of his wrist, the shadows folded inward and retreated fully to him.

Leah exhaled shakily, her gaze lingering on the space where the shadows had been, still seeing the echo of their movement in the air.

"I...I've never seen anything like that," she admitted.

"Few have. It's not a common form of magic."

Leah let out a short, humorless laugh. "No magic is common for me. Honestly, I keep thinking I'm losing my mind."

"You're not," Nico said, stepping closer. "You weren't raised in a world that prepares you for this. That's all."

A flicker of relief warmed her chest, but it was quickly overtaken by frustration. Her gaze narrowed. "I feel like you know more about me than you're admitting."

Nico met her eyes, calm and unflinching. "I do."

Leah froze. The words landed heavier than she expected, and a shiver ran down her spine. She suddenly felt exposed and she didn't like being caught off guard.

"I also know that you have a lot to learn," he continued, "and that we don't have much time before The Order notices you're here."

"You keep talking about The Order. Who are they?"

"They're the ones who enforce control over magic," he said carefully. "They decide who can wield it and who cannot."

Leah's hands trembled slightly around the book.

Nico stepped closer, the shadows at his feet brushing faintly against the mossy stones. "And they're the ones Selene was protecting you from."

For a long moment, Leah couldn't speak. Her chest rose and fell unevenly, her mind racing through everything she'd heard, everything she'd seen, and everything she was about to face. Her fingers found the bracelet Sage had given her, the cool metal biting into her skin. *Breathe.*

The realization settled in with a cold weight. The life she had known, everything she believed to be true, had been a lie. Her grandmother's careful rules and the fear that had always lingered in her eyes hadn't been caution. They had been protection.

A chill ran down her spine as she finally accepted it. This wasn't a dream. The danger Selene and Nico had warned her about was real, and it was closer than she'd ever imagined.

The Order was out there.

And she was no longer invisible.

Chapter 5

Leah drew a slow, steady breath. "Where...where are we exactly?" she asked, her voice a mix of curiosity and caution.

"We're on the outskirts of Roots Hollow," Nico replied.

His calm, matter-of-fact tone made something inside her bristle. How could he sound so unfazed when her entire life had just capsized? And now this name, dropped casually, as if it were common knowledge.

"I have no idea what that is," she said flatly. "I've never heard of that name in my life."

Nico sighed, lowering himself onto a mossy stone and gesturing for her to do the same. Leah hesitated before sitting across from him. In her experience, people only asked you to sit when something bad followed. Bad news. Hard truths. The kind of conversations that left you gutted. After the emotional whiplash she'd just endured, she wasn't sure she could take another hit. But if she was ever going to understand what was happening to her, this might be her only chance.

"Some areas of the world are non-magical," he began. "Places like Eldergrove are called quiet towns and are normal by design. They're said to be protected, though I suspect they're more closely monitored."

Leah frowned, trying to ignore the edge of annoyance in his voice. "Protected from what?"

"From us. From anything touched by magic." He glanced at her. "A long time ago, a group of people defected from The Order when the current leader rose to power. They called themselves The Drift. They weren't interested in The Order, its vision, or its control. But walking away came at a cost. They relinquished their powers, stripping themselves of everything that once made them magical. The Order then created the Veil, separating the magical world from the non-magical one, and banished the members of The Drift."

Leah's stomach twisted. Her whole life, she'd thought of Eldergrove as just an ordinary town. Hearing how it came to be sounded less like a home and more like a cage.

"So...Eldergrove isn't the only town?"

"Far from it. The non-magical world is set up similarly to ours. There are four main areas to the North, South, East, and West. Eldergrove is West, which coincides with this area, Roots Hollow."

She tried to absorb it, but the words tangled in her mind. It sounded like the bedtime stories Selene used to tell her, except Nico's tone left no room for disbelief.

He paused, letting the explanation settle. "When the current leader of The Order rose to power, everything changed. Freedom ended, and the four magical Pillars, Elemental, Seer, Blood, and Spellweaver, could no longer coexist. Each Pillar was forced into its own Hollow, and the Hollows have reflected those divisions ever since."

He turned fully toward her, and the intensity of his stare made her pulse stumble. His expression remained unreadable, but his voice sharpened. "That's how The Order of the Veil began. They claimed they were preserving balance and purity. In truth, it was about control."

"So they started separating everyone?" Leah asked.

"They created their version of order," Nico's tone darkened. "Hunting down anyone who wouldn't bow to them. Especially the Seers."

"Seers?" she echoed, the word sending a chill through her chest.

"People born with the ability to see things others can't. Glimpses of what was and what could be. Some saw buried truths. Others saw entire futures. They didn't need spells or rituals. It was in their blood."

Leah realized she was staring, but she couldn't stop. Her thoughts raced as she focused on steadying her breath. Glimpses of what could be. Images from Selene's attic flashed through her mind, memories and visions colliding. Was that what she was?

His jaw tensed. "They were dangerous to The Order. Too unpredictable. Too honest. They couldn't be bought or broken. Worse, some of them saw The Order's collapse. So when control failed—"

"They erased them," Leah finished.

Nico nodded once. "And your bloodline…" His eyes narrowed slightly and Leah saw hesitation again before he spoke. "You were never supposed to exist."

She felt like the air had been pulled from her lungs, and she couldn't help but start putting some pieces together. "The visions I saw in the attic…" she murmured, more to herself than to him.

"You're a Seer, Leah. But you're not just a normal Seer, you come from the bloodline they feared most."

The word cracked through her even though she half expected it to be true. Her knees felt weak and she had to bite the inside of her cheek to stop from trembling. She stared at him, blinking like she might wake up from a dream if she focused hard enough.

"A Seer?" she repeated numbly. "So …you're saying I'm basically some kind of magical psychic." She chuckled. "Next thing you'll tell me is that you're a hundred- and five-year-old vampire."

Nico blinked. "I'm twenty-five."

She blinked back, cheeks warming. "Oh." She cleared her throat. "Right. Just checking."

The corner of his mouth twitched, but his voice remained firm. "You're part of one of the oldest and most powerful Seer bloodlines. They were called The Unheard."

The word rang through her, cold and sharp. '*They bear the blood of The Unheard. Kill them.*' The memory of the voice in the Veil slammed into her and for a moment, she thought she might throw up.

Nico noticed the tension but continued. "The Order believed that bloodline was wiped out eighteen years ago. They erased every trace. What they didn't know was that your mother had already given birth. That you were alive."

"No," Leah said, shaking her head. "That's not possible. I never had visions. I wasn't different."

"You weren't," Nico said evenly. "Because you couldn't be. Selene suppressed your power. It was part of a pact she made with your parents. As long as she lived, the suppression held. The moment she died, it broke."

Leah stared at him as if the ground might split open. Tears stung her eyes, not just from grief, but from anger. "She kept so much from me that I don't even know what to think anymore."

"She kept you alive."

Silence pulsed between them before he added, "There's more."

"Of course there is," Leah muttered.

"The Order has been searching for a relic tied to the Seers. The Echodex. Ancient. Powerful. It's said to contain everything they once knew. Visions. Warnings. The legacy of the bloodlines."

Her hand dropped to the book.

"That," Nico said, nodding to it, "is the most dangerous thing in the world to them. They've burned libraries trying to find it. Killed for it. And for decades, they found nothing."

He met her eyes, something raw breaking through his calm. "And now, somehow, you have it."

Leah tightened her grip on the book. "So now what?"

Nico chuckled softly. "Now I keep you alive."

She studied him, searching for any hint of deceit. Her grandmother had mentioned that Nico would be the one to help her, a mentor, but could she really trust him? Leah rubbed at her temples briefly. "And how do I know this isn't some elaborate setup? That you're not here to deliver me to The Order instead?"

Leah noticed the immediate change in his expression and a small tendril of shadow slinking along the ground before dissolving into the moss.

"Because," he said, voice low and edged, "if I was going to betray you, Leah… I would have done it already."

Silence hung, heavy as the fog around them. She wasn't sure she believed him, but what were her options, really? Selene had asked her to trust her one last time and even despite the anger burning in her chest, Leah wanted to believe there was a reason for everything she'd done.

Finally, Nico stepped into the center of the circle. "This is a safe place to train."

"Train?" Her voice cracked, disbelief and exasperation mingling. Was he serious right now?

Nico's eyebrows lifted, as if it were the most obvious next step in the world. Had he already forgotten how clueless she had been her whole life about any of this? Leah's jaw dropped as she stared at him, trying to reconcile the calm authority in front of her with the chaos in her head.

"So just to recap," she said, ticking off fingers. "The Order wiped out my entire bloodline, I was hidden by a secret pact, my powers were suppressed until my eighteenth birthday, and now I'm the accidental keeper of the world's most dangerous relic— one that people have been slaughtered over for decades." She let her hand drop. "And you just want to, *train*?" she finished, incredulous.

Nico exhaled softly, a sound that might have been a laugh or a sigh, she couldn't tell. "Well yes, you'll need to know what you can do if you want to defend yourself."

Leah let out a short, humorless laugh. "Ha! Sure thing…Right after I finish crying, throwing up, and hiring a therapist." She rolled her eyes as frustration took over.

He tilted his head, faint amusement tracing his features. "The Order won't wait."

"No, of course not," she muttered, flinging her arms as if arguing with the sky. "Why would genocidal cult assassins wait until after I emotionally recover from the worst week of my life?"

Nico said nothing. His arms remained crossed, and he was still infuriatingly composed.

She pinched the bridge of her nose. "Fine. But before I pass out or break something, can we talk about you for a second?"

He blinked. "Me?"

"Yes. You. The walking shadow man." She gestured behind her. "Those shadows. Is that your only power?"

"It is," he said after a moment. "Shadowbinding."

"Sounds dramatic," Leah muttered.

"It is."

There it was, that calmness in his face, as if none of this was completely ludicrous. She raised an eyebrow in frustration. "Fine. Show me again how you can use them."

"Careful," he said. "You'll regret asking."

He raised one hand. The shadows lashed out, striking the ground on either side of her with a crack that echoed through the clearing. Dust and leaves spiraled upward in their wake. They didn't touch her, but they came close. Close enough to raise the hairs on her arms. Close enough for her to feel the cold seeping off them, colder than the night air.

Nico's eyes darkened, his irises swallowing the lighter tones, black bleeding into blue. The shadows circled him like a storm. When they finally retreated, they curled back into his outline like smoke. Nico lowered his hand. The unnatural darkness faded with them, but tension lingered in the air.

"Well," Leah said, her voice scratchy but steady, "you definitely win Most Dramatic Use of Powers."

She saw his mouth give a tiny, involuntary twitch.

"Wasn't trying to win anything."

"Could've fooled me," she crossed her arms and pretended her heart wasn't trying to sprint out of the forest.

He glanced down, brushing invisible dust off his coat. "I told you it was dangerous."

"You also said you live with them, which sounds an awful lot like being haunted."

A smirk appeared on cue, a trained reflex that made her jaw clench.

"Well, look at that," he said dryly. "Five minutes into meeting me and you've already earned your merit badge in psychoanalysis."

Leah gave him a flat look. "Is that a thing? Do I get a sash?"

"If you're lucky. But I'd hold off on the embroidery, we haven't even gotten to your trust issues yet."

A thin, humorless snort slipped past her lips. "Oh, you're hilarious."

"I try."

He turned as if to pace again, and she caught the quick wall snapping back into place, his guard going back up. He was definitely a strange one, she thought, but there was something about him that kept her curious, and she hated how pulled she felt toward him.

"Come on," he said, deliberately moving away from the tension. "If I start your training now, you'll pass out, and then I'll have to drag your unconscious body through the woods."

Leah gave an exaggerated gasp, the delirium of the past few hours still clinging to her. "You mean we're not doing life-threatening magical tests on zero sleep and no food? Wow. You are getting soft."

He didn't turn around, but his voice carried back, dry as sand. "Don't tempt me."

She jogged to catch up, boots squelching slightly on the damp ground. *Focus, Leah. Just focus.*

"So...where exactly are we going? Or are you one of those charming wilderness types who plans to sleep in a tree and call it character building?"

Nico cast her a sideways glance. "Would it kill you to trust me for more than three minutes at a time?"

"Would it kill you to answer a question directly?" She shot back.

"That depends. Are you always this exhausting, or is it just a post near-death thing?"

Leah couldn't help the smirk that crept onto her face. "Only when I'm hungry."

He sighed, but for a second she thought she saw something softer in him. "There's a shelter not far. It's old, but it's hidden and protected."

"And food?" she asked cautiously, still bracing herself for some survivalist horror.

"There might be something edible if the squirrels haven't eaten it all."

Leah rolled her eyes. "Fantastic. I've always wanted to share dinner with forest rodents."

"You'll fit right in then." He glanced at her again, and this time there was a small smile on his face. "Come on, Firecracker."

Leah followed closely behind him until they reached the place he called the shelter, which wasn't much to look at. Just a shallow cave half swallowed by moss and gnarled roots, hidden behind a thick veil of tangled brush. If you didn't know it was there, you'd walk right past it.

Nico reached through the brush with practiced ease, pushing aside a few branches until the opening revealed itself. He paused at the entrance and rested his hands on the branches. "After you," he said, gesturing inside.

Leah blinked, taken aback by the unexpected chivalry. There hadn't been many boys she'd known growing up who were courteous like this. She ducked under a low-hanging root and stepped inside with a small thrill of amusement.

The air was cooler, tinged with earth and the faint scent of old firewood. The walls glistened with a faint mineral sheen, and the floor looked recently swept, judging by the faint tracks of Nico's boots near the entrance. In the corner, a small fire ring waited, blackened with ash.

She crossed her arms, eyeing the space. "So this is your idea of five-star accommodations?"

He arched a brow, unimpressed. "Would you prefer I conjure a castle?"

"Only if it comes with a spa and room service," she shot back, smirking. "I just hope this roof doesn't come with bats."

Nico stepped in behind her, close enough that she could feel the warmth radiating off him. He knelt near the entrance and scanned the tree line, as if expecting danger to crawl out of the shadows. "Be grateful the bats are the worst thing you'd find in here," he said flatly.

Leah scoffed. "Is this where you live or something?"

"No," Nico said with a tang of annoyance in his voice. "We're a little ways away from where I stay, so we will travel there slowly while you start your training. In the meantime, we'll stay in the safe shelters I'm familiar with."

Leah caught the way his eyes flicked toward the trees, sharp and searching. He muttered something under his breath and traced a symbol into the dirt with two fingers. The air pulsed faintly around them, a quiet shimmer, like heat off pavement. Then he stood and moved to the other side, repeating the motion.

Leah watched him, awe rising in her chest. All her life she'd thought magic belonged in fairy tales, and now she was watching it happen inches away. It felt surreal, and undeniably cool.

"And that is...?" she asked, brow furrowed.

"Spells," he said shortly, brushing his hands on his coat. "To keep us from being tracked and to make sure nothing unpleasant wanders in, besides bats, of course."

She narrowed her eyes but chose to ignore the last part. *Jerk.* Still, it didn't bother her as much this time. She tilted her head, studying the space between them.

"Wait. Weren't you saying earlier that your only power was the shadows? Since when can you cast spells?"

He didn't look at her. "Only when I care what happens to the person inside."

Her breath caught, and she looked away, tucking her arms tighter around herself. Heat crept into her cheeks, but she pushed it aside. He was just being careful, that was all. They had just met, after all.

"So," she said lightly, forcing the mood back to casual, "do these spells also make dinner appear? Or should I start chewing on tree bark?"

Nico rolled his eyes, but he didn't look annoyed, which made her smile. "Tree bark won't kill you, but I'd prefer you didn't test that theory. There's dried fruit and bread in my bag. It's not gourmet, but it'll do."

"Comforting."

He tossed her a small satchel. She caught it awkwardly, nearly dropping it.

"You could've just handed it to me," she muttered, sinking onto a smooth patch of stone. Rude.

"You'll live."

She tore off a piece of bread and chewed it like it had personally offended her. It was dry and crumbly, but her stomach didn't care. She swallowed hard, trying not to look as exhausted as she felt.

Nico sank onto the opposite wall of the shelter, stretching his legs out in front of him with a long, tired exhale. "You should sleep," he said. "We'll start training in the morning."

"Oh good," she said with mock enthusiasm. "A full night of rock pillows."

He gave her a sidelong glance, almost amused. "You really do have something to say about everything."

"I cope through sarcasm."

"I noticed."

His head tipped back against the cave wall as he closed his eyes. Even though he seemed calm and collected, Leah could see the tension still coiled in his jaw. He didn't speak again.

She told herself to stop staring and caring about the brooding stranger who'd just told her that her entire life had been a lie. She watched him a moment longer before lying down and turning to face the cave's ceiling. Her eyes scanned the space to make sure there really were no bats. She'd never seen one up close or anything, but she wasn't trying to either. They just creeped her out.

The flicker of magic still lingered at the edge of the cave's mouth, like threads of moonlight in the dark. Leah shook her head slowly. Magic. Who would've thought it was actually real.

Sleep came slowly.

When she stirred again, the cave was dimly lit by the first pale shafts of dawn slicing through the narrow entrance. The air was cold as she blinked against the blur of shadows and stone, letting her eyes adjust. Her body was stiff and sore from the hard ground and her neck ached and her shoulders protested, but she didn't move right away.

Nico sat at the cave's entrance, his back partially to her, one knee bent, the other stretched out. His head was bowed slightly, morning light catching in his dark hair and casting a faint shimmer across his shoulders. He was silent, still and guarded, like a statue.

Despite the ache in her limbs, Leah found herself frozen, watching him. There was something magnetic about him, something that tugged at her curiosity even as it unsettled her. After everything—the journey, the magic, the Veil—he looked like someone who belonged in the quiet. She realized he most likely hadn't slept at all. He'd stayed facing the entrance the entire night.

She finally pushed herself up onto one elbow. "You know, I get that you're the strong, silent type," she said, her voice husky from sleep, "but watching over me all night without blinking once is giving me very strong vampire guardian energy."

Nico didn't turn.

"Are you trying to freak me out?" she added, stretching. "Because...it's working."

A pause. Then his voice came quiet, edged with faint, maddening amusement. "You snore."

Leah's mouth dropped open. "Excuse me?"

That earned her a glance over his shoulder, just a glance, but she caught the smirk playing on his lips.

"You're lying," she said, narrowing her eyes.

"I never lie," he replied smoothly, turning his gaze back toward the forest. "I withhold."

Leah sat up fully, brushing her hair back with an indignant flick. "You know, it's wild. I didn't realize brooding and sarcasm were such a potent combo until now."

"You've clearly been sheltered."

She gave him a long look, unsure if he was teasing her or simply incapable of normal human interaction. "And you clearly need sleep."

He didn't respond. Instead, he stood and moved farther toward the cave's entrance, reaching for something in the air. A shimmer stirred, barely visible where his fingers moved. It was subtle, but as Leah squinted, she caught the faint ripple of a spell.

"You set more of those up last night?" she asked, pushing herself to her feet.

"I always do."

There was something heavy in the way he said it. Automatic. Like it wasn't precaution anymore, just reflex. Leah studied him quietly, the morning light tracing the sharp line of his jaw.

"You know, most people don't cast a web of defensive spells over someone they just met."

"Most people don't have assassins and trackers after them by nightfall."

The dryness in his tone wasn't sarcastic, just blunt. The words settled heavily, reminding her what her reality looked like now. Memories of the previous day rushed back, and with them, the realization of what was supposed to happen next.

Training.

A knot of apprehension tightened in her stomach. She drew her knees up, resting her chin on them. How was she supposed to train?

"I get why you're here," she said. "Why I need to learn my magic. But how am I supposed to train for something I barely understand?"

That made him turn to face her fully. His gaze wasn't cold, but it pinned her in place.

"You understand more than you think," he said. "You've held the book. You've experienced the visions."

She hesitated, searching for the right words. "But it's like trying to walk in a dream. I catch glimpses. Flashes. I don't know what's real and what's not."

He stood slowly, brushing dirt from his palms. "Then I'll teach you how to tell the difference."

He turned toward the exit, pausing only briefly while glancing over his shoulder. "Come." he said. "Before the sun burns off whatever peace this place still has."

Chapter 6

The forest outside the cave was soaked in dew, mist rising from the ground. A hush lingered between the trees as distant birdsong filtered through the canopy. Nico stood just beyond the entrance with his back to her, arms crossed. They had only just started the day, but his shadows already clung to his every movement.

Leah stepped out, book in hand. "So, how exactly will I train?"

"We figure out what your base power is."

"Base power?" she echoed, frowning. "I thought you said I was a Seer."

"I did." He crouched, sweeping damp leaves aside with one hand, then began plucking through the underbrush. "But I have a theory I want to test."

"A theory?" Leah sighed. "Great."

He laid out what he'd gathered: a large droplet of water resting on a fallen leaf, a green leaf still slick with dew, a branch, and a fist-sized rock.

She arched a brow. "You just carry teaching props around with you?"

"Improvisation," he said smoothly, without looking up.

She huffed, lowering herself to sit cross-legged across from him. "Alright, Professor. What do I do? Stare at them until they burst into flame?"

"If you set anything on fire," he said, a corner of his mouth tugging upward, "lesson complete, I suppose. But let's start with water."

Leah stared at him. "Water?" Was he serious right now? Clearly, he'd already forgotten she'd been thrown into this loony world less than twenty-four hours ago. "Start with water...as in drink water? What are you even talking about?"

Nico drew a slow breath, the kind that suggested he was reconsidering every decision that had led him here. The faintest crease formed between his brows, which made Leah bite back a laugh. She knew she was testing his patience far too early in the morning, but honestly, it made this more fun.

"I need to see if you have any elemental magic," he finally said.

Leah blinked. "Elemental as in...fire, water, earth?" Her voice came out half incredulous, half amused. He could not be serious. Yes, she was suddenly in a crazy magic world. Yes, she was standing across from a broody shadow man. But her? Actual magic? That was still a stretch.

He nodded once. "I need you to aim your palm at the leaf and focus on the water droplet."

Leah scoffed softly but lifted her hand. Sure. She'd just move water with her mind. Totally normal day. She stared intently at the droplet, aware of Nico watching her from the corner of her eye. She shifted under his gaze, squinting in concentration and pictured the droplet lifting and gliding toward her, but nothing happened. The droplet didn't even tremble.

"Don't force it," he said quietly. "If your magic resonates, the element will answer."

Resonates? What did that even mean? She glanced at him, but he offered nothing more. So she turned to the leaf, assuming it represented wind. She pictured it lifting and floating. Again, nothing. She sighed and tipped her head back in frustration.

"How do I know if I'm even doing this right? It feels ridiculous to just stare."

"You'll know," he said simply.

His calm grated on her nerves. She couldn't help the heat that crept into her face as irritation and embarrassment tangled together. Fine. If he wanted effort, he'd get it.

She turned to the branch next. Fire. Of course it had to be fire, the one element most likely to blow her up. She pictured flames licking along the wood. Nothing happened.

Then the rock. Earth. She tried to picture it lifting, then sinking, then the ground swallowing it whole. Still nothing. She leaned closer with her palm hovering over the stone before grabbing it, her jaw tightening as frustration coiled in her chest.

"I can't do this! Why can't I do this?" she snapped, gripping and lifting the rock hard enough that it bit into her skin.

When she slammed it down, a sharp sting bloomed across her palm. She hissed as blood welled instantly, followed by intense heat. A pulse throbbed through her hand and echoed throughout her body, racing through her veins. It burned.

Her eyes flew to Nico. "I—I didn't do anything," she said, voice trembling, even as the warmth in her chest and the blood on her palm told a different story.

Nico's gaze didn't waver. His eyes flickered black for a moment before returning to blue. "You did," he said quietly. "Your blood responded. That wasn't Seer magic."

Her pulse spiked. Her blood?

Nico's eyes lingered on hers, the intensity making her cheeks flush despite the heat in her veins.

"Your eyes told me everything I needed to know. Now take a breath and come toward me."

Leah looked down at her palm. The cut hadn't clotted. Instead, the blood pooled and hovered above her skin. Fire rushed through her veins, sharpening her awareness. She sensed Nico moving closer, but it he was slow and deliberate. The blood rippled, stretching into the rough shape of a blade.

"Leah." His voice was low. He crouched beside her, stopping just short of touching her. Something in his expression held him back. "Look at me," he said.

Her head lifted instinctively. When their eyes met, the burning flared again. He reached out, tilting her chin just enough to hold her gaze.

"Breathe," he murmured. "Focus on me."

She swallowed, heat rushing up her neck at his touch. "Calm...right," she managed, forcing a shaky exhale. Her eyes stayed locked on his before the world started dimming until there was only him and the strange pull of magic in her blood.

The blood blade wavered, then collapsed, dropping back onto her skin where it settled, motionless.

"It's gone." She brushed her finger across the shallow cut, relief washing through her as the blood finally behaved like blood. Her voice shook. "What...was that?"

"Blood magic," Nico said.

Nausea rolled through her. "Blood magic? That's a thing? I thought it was just elemental magic...stuff you can see."

He shifted closer again, lifting her chin briefly to study her eyes before releasing her. The tension in his shoulders eased, just slightly.

Leah looked away, cheeks warm. "What's with all the intense staring?"

He ignored the comment. "Magic has a tell. Our eyes glow depending on the magic we use."

Her memory snapped into place. "So they actually change? I wasn't imagining it when your eyes went black?"

"You weren't," he said. "Each Pillar shows itself differently. Black for shadowbinding. Gray for air. And so on. Your eyes glowed red just now."

Leah stared at the dried blood on her hand. "Red...so how many magical Pillars are there?"

Nico studied her, weighing his words. She hated that pause. It made her feel like he was holding things back.

"You have elemental magic: earth, water, fire, air. Then Spellweavers, Seers, and Blood mages. But..." He stopped.

"But?" She pressed.

"But Seers and Blood mages are rare."

"Why?"

"Because they were hunted by The Order," he said. "Just like your bloodline."

A sudden chill spread through her chest. "Why does that feel...dangerous?"

"Because it is." His tone left no room for comfort. "You're what they call a Hybrid."

"Hybrid," she repeated. The word felt unreal.

"I've never met one," he added, "outside of my father."

Unease settled in her stomach. He hadn't expected this; she could feel it. The air around them had cooled now, shadows stretching across the clearing as birds stirred overhead.

"You said Seers are rare too," she said softly. "But that's what I am, isn't it?"

"That much is certain," Nico replied. "But Selene was always vague. I don't think she knew what to expect when your powers awakened. A suppression like yours...I'd never seen one before."

"Suppression," Leah repeated. "You mean she hid it?"

"She hid you," he said. "The suppression came from the pact with your parents."

Her throat tightened. Right. The pact. The one meant to keep her magic dormant until Selene's death.

"I've had visions," Leah said. "Flashes. Like dreams that aren't dreams. Sometimes voices or places I've never been to. They come too fast. I don't know what to do with them."

Nico tilted his head. "And those visions, were they triggered by something specific?"

"Yes," she said quickly. "That day, it was my birthday, but the day itself felt strange. It wasn't until I got back home that I felt this really weird pull toward the attic. That's where I found the book." Leah shifted her weight, grounding herself as she replayed the memory. "The trigger was the book. I held it and wanted to read it, but..."

Nico waited in silence, watching as she grabbed the book and flipped through it absentmindedly.

"It's just...empty," she said, showing him the faded parchment. "Then I saw something shining on some of the pages, like invisible ink or something, and as soon as I touched them..." She exhaled slowly, remembering the rush of color and sound. "That's when it happened."

She closed the book with a soft thud and looked up at him. "Is that how this works?"

"No." Nico held out his hand for the book.

Leah hesitated, the instinct to keep it close battling her curiosity. Finally, she placed it in his palm. She watched closely, half expecting something to happen, but nothing did. Nico flipped through the pages, frowning slightly, and she realized just how alien the book was, even to him.

"Nico?" Her voice pulled him back.

He exhaled, closed the book, and handed it to her. "Seer magic can be triggered by connection. An artifact, a place, or a person. What you see depends on what you interact with. Some Seers glimpse the past, present, or future of the trigger. But there are limits."

Leah leaned forward, her eyes bright despite the heaviness in her chest. "Limits?"

"Yes." His tone was deliberate. "I don't know all of them myself. You're the first Seer I've ever met. But I do know this power is dangerous. If you don't learn to control it, it will control you."

She stayed quiet, watching the tight line of his jaw.

"Seers walk the thread of time," he continued. "Most people are bound to the present. You aren't. You glimpse fragments of the past, present, and future, but not always in that order."

"So...every vision matters?"

"Not always. That's the danger. A vision can be truth, or it can be noise. The gift isn't seeing, it's knowing what to trust and what to ignore."

"That sounds impossible," she whispered.

"It might feel that way at first. You need to learn how to anchor yourself to separate yourself from what you see."

Her hand drifted unconsciously to the bracelet on her wrist as she drew her knees closer.

"And if I can't?"

His jaw tightened. "Then the visions own you. They take pieces of you each time. Your sense of time. Your sense of self. Eventually...you won't know which world you belong to."

Fear curled in Leah's stomach. It was terrifying, too much to process, and yet a strange thrill sparked beneath it.

Her heart hammered in a way it hadn't in years. Life had been predictable, safe, with days blurring into one another. But now, she stood on the edge of something that mattered. Something dangerous.

Even as her mind screamed that none of this made sense, that she had to still be dreaming, another part of her leaned in. Curious. Hungry. Could she survive this? Could she step beyond the life she'd been living and into something extraordinary?

"How exactly do I learn to anchor myself?"

"You start by listening differently," Nico said. "Not with your eyes or ears, but with your instincts. A vision presses against your mind like a hand on glass. You can't shove it away or throw yourself through it. You touch it lightly. Test it. If it feels jagged or chaotic, you leave it. If it feels steady, you let it in."

Leah blinked, heart racing with terror and awe. "You make it sound so simple."

"Maybe it is." He stood and offered his hand.

She hesitated, then placed her hand in his and pushed herself unsteadily to her feet. Nico turned her hand gently, his thumb brushing against her skin as he inspected the wound. The bleeding had stopped, but the cut still glimmered.

The contact was careful and kind, and she became acutely aware of how long he held her hand, how warm his fingers felt against her cooling skin. Instinct told her to pull back, but she didn't. After a moment, he let her hand fall.

"Alright," he said. "Let's try."

Her head snapped up. "Wha—now? What if—"

"If you wait," he cut in, "the fear will only grow."

Her breath stuttered, but she nodded. Nico led her deeper into the forest until they reached a scarred stretch of land where the ground was blackened and the trees were split and charred as if lightning had struck.

Nico crouched, brushing aside brittle fragments until he lifted a jagged piece of scorched wood.

"Here," he said, handing it to her. "Focus on this. Feel your body as it is now. Notice the birds, the air, the earth beneath your feet. *That* is your anchor. Remember it."

Leah's heart pounded as she stared at this piece of wood. Just as with the tests for elemental magic, she wasn't sure what she was supposed to think about to activate a vision. Until now, the visions had come from the book, or from crossing the Veil from Eldergrove. Leah's eyes shifted to the area directly in front of her, then back at the piece of wood as the familiar pressure she'd felt behind her eyes began to stir again. This was not the time for a headache.

At first, nothing came. But then, a ripple appeared around her, distorting the forest like water disturbed by stone. She tightened her grip on the wood and willed herself on, reminding herself that she could do this. Her pulse throbbed loudly in her ears and for the first time, she felt a strange surge of exhilaration through the fear. This...this was real. And she was doing it.

The ripples slowed and the forest shifted into night while smoke curled through the vision, thick and suffocating. Leah's pulse hammered in her veins as flames licked at her senses. Panic clawed at her chest, threatening to overwhelm her. She gasped and shook her head, trying to force herself forward, desperate to hold onto control in this nightmare she had brought into her mind.

"Leah." Nico's voice cut through, but it was mixed in the chaos of the scene before her. "Anchor. Where are you?"

Her lips trembled as she willed herself to recall her surroundings before this vision came. "In the forest. The sun is out. You are with me."

"Don't lose it." His voice was closer now, guiding her. "Breathe in. Out. Let the vision pass through you, not into you."

Her fingers clung to the wood like a lifeline. Slowly, she let the fire and smoke dissolve, curling away from her mind until it vanished. She gasped and opened her eyes. Sweat dampened her brow, and she could feel her pulse thundering in her ears.

Nico was watching her closely. "What did you see?"

Leah pressed a shaky hand to her chest, trying to slow her pulse. "Smoke...fire. I felt like I was going to burn along with it."

"You didn't burn," Nico said, and for the briefest instant, his eyes softened. "You anchored. You took control. There was a fire here a few weeks ago." he said at last, turning back toward the cave. "Luckily it died out before it spread too far."

Leah, still reeling from the fear that the vision brought her, instinctively reached out to Nico as he started to walk away, unaware that her eyes were still glowing. Her hand closed around his wrist, brushing against the bracelet there and a sudden tremor surged through her before another ripple began, making her breath hitch.

The forest was gone. She stood in a sunlit clearing with the most gentle and warm breeze she had felt in a long time. Leah looked up and noticed a boy practicing martial arts in the open field. The boy's movements were precise and disciplined. He couldn't have been more than eight years old. Leah squinted, trying to get a better view of the boy. There was something familiar in the way he stood, and in the way the air around him moved. The way the shadows clung to his body.

Before she could grasp it, another voice rang out behind her. She spun, her heart lurching as another child barreled toward her too fast. Leah panicked, realizing that there wasn't enough time to move before the boy would collide with her. She closed her eyes instinctively, bracing for the impact, but the boy passed through her like mist, laughing and smiling.

"I finished it!!" he called out excitedly to the boy practicing in the clearing. The dark-haired boy stopped mid form and looked over, a big smile crossing his face. Leah's heart fluttered, the joy between them was magnetic, pulling her closer. She wanted to stay and see more.

"Stop."

The command cut through the vision like a blade. Leah jerked as the clearing shuddered and the world around her began to shift. Now, screams could be heard in the background, tearing away the sunlight and the calm as darkness pressed in. Her lungs seized. She pressed her hands over her ears as panic threatened to swallow her.

"Leah! Anchor yourself. Come back." Nico's voice was a lifeline, taut with urgency.

She clung to it and reminded herself of where she was. Not a clearing, a forest.

"Leah!" Nico yelled again.

Slowly, the screams ebbed, the darkness dissolved, and she opened her eyes. She was in the forest once again, clutching Nico's wrist.

His expression froze her. Shadows clung to him, his eyes nearly black. For a moment, she saw the raw edge of his fury, but it was restrained and controlled. The realization that she had crossed a boundary hit her like ice.

Leah jerked her hand away. "I—I'm sorry Nico...I didn't know..."

He inhaled sharply, jaw tight, his lips pressing into a thin line. The air between them felt heavy. His hand was now clenched around his own wrist, but a slight tremor betrayed the struggle beneath his calm exterior. Leah wasn't too sure what to do or where to go from here. She clearly crossed a line she didn't even know existed.

Suddenly, she started feeling lightheaded and her vision started to blur. Nico noticed the change in her balance— the tilt of her shoulders, the way her knees wobbled. Before she could steady herself, her vision went black and she collapsed.

Chapter 7

The experience was unlike any he'd ever had before. She had slipped past his defenses, invading his head, and he'd had absolutely no control over it. Nico's mind wasn't a place meant for company—he'd built walls there long ago, the kind even sleep rarely breached. Yet in a single moment, Leah had seen what no one else ever had. It left him raw in a way that unsettled him more than he cared to admit. Vulnerability was a feeling he'd buried years ago, and he had no intention of unearthing it again, especially not by accident.

He shifted her limp body carefully over his shoulder. The rhythmic motion of his steps helped steady his own pulse as he made his way back toward the cave. The forest was beginning to dim into twilight but his mind, however, remained rattled by the experience.

Selene had always been cautious when it came to Leah. She'd spoken of the girl like she was both a blessing and a storm waiting to break. There was never any extra information given beyond what he absolutely had to know. Nico thought back to the day Selene had led him to the quiet room in the bunker, which held nothing but a single woven basket at its center. He'd looked back at Selene, confused, and then heard the smallest grunt from within the basket.

"One day," she'd said softly, her hand resting on his shoulder, "you will help guide her."

The baby had been so helpless then. He hadn't realized what kind of force she would grow into. A stubborn and reckless woman, he thought, the corner of his mouth twitching. A firecracker.

The wind had cooled by the time he reached the cave. He lowered Leah gently onto the ground and folded his coat beneath her head like a pillow, but his movements remained mechanical, his thoughts elsewhere. He brushed his fingers along the cave's entrance, where faint threads shimmered beneath his touch. The enchantments still held, but he could feel their strain, a subtle hum in the air that hadn't been there before.

He exhaled through his nose. The surge of power Leah had released when she entered the Hollow hadn't gone unnoticed, he was certain of it. Just as he'd felt the pull the moment she slipped into the Veil, others would have too. It was only a matter of time before someone came looking. His bunker was the next logical step, fortified and hidden underground, but bringing her there now, before they understood the full extent of her power, might expose more than it protected.

Nico's gaze flicked to his bag. He knelt and rummaged through it, pulling out something he hadn't used in years, a ring fitted to his pinky. He hadn't needed to communicate with anyone in a long time, but the revelations of the day meant certain people needed to be warned. He rolled the ring between his fingers, lost in thought. For a moment, he was no longer in the cave.

He stood instead in Mask Hollow with his mother, heart pounding as she led him through the Hollow marked by Elementalists. The streets buzzed with noise and laughter from its residents as they got closer to the town's marketplace. This day was special because it marked his fifth birthday and the day that he would finally get a familiar.

Nico wondered for as long as he could remember what kind of familiar he would get. He knew early on that every Pillar had a known familiar type. His mother had a Bengal cat she named Mila, and his father had a tiger named Arman. Nico had seen them often growing up, and wondered what kind of cat species he would get.

"Ilya! There you are!" a woman called as she flipped a sign on her shop door from closed to open.

"I made it," his mother replied with a big smile, ushering Nico inside.

The moment he entered, he was immediately distracted by the items in the store. A long table stretched in front of the small counter toward the back of the room covered with rings of every kind. Gold and silver bands gleamed under warm light. Some plain, others embedded with stones that caught the eye in subtle flashes of color. Nico stepped closer as his mother continued a conversation with the woman he had overheard was named Raya.

The table was divided neatly into three sections. The middle section held a small selection of simple rings. The section to the right appeared to have stones and crystals already embedded into them, and the space to the left had another set of simple ones but with a sign listing stones that could be embedded and personalized.

To the left of the store, there were displays of various candles and to the right of the store was a display of various jewelry. His mother had told him this shop was run by a fire mage, which made more sense now that he looked at the item descriptions. Ever burning candles, Volcanic Salts and Crystals, and a variety of stones to personalize any piece of jewelry.

"So this is the birthday boy?" Raya asked, interrupting his exploration. "I remember the first time I got a familiar. You must be nervous."

Nico approached her calmly and confidently. His father had taught him never to let others see his emotions, and so he would not show how truly excited and nervous he was.

"I'm fine," Nico said evenly. "I just want to be able to communicate for missions."

Raya looked taken aback and glanced at Ilya who simply smiled and shook her head, though Nico noticed the sadness in her eyes and the smile that didn't quite reach her eyes. "You must forgive him," she said gently. "I fear he's spending too much time training with his father lately."

Ilya stepped behind Nico and guided him toward the table full of rings. "Pick one Nico. Whichever one calls to you."

Raya moved behind the counter, watching closely.

"What's the difference?" Nico asked.

"Style, mostly," Raya replied. "These rings all act as conduits to a familiar, but they all require a link to activate."

"So, the stones don't change anything?"

"No," Ilya said, stepping closer. "Only preference."

Nico stared at a gold ring and took it, anticipation and impatience twisting in his stomach. "This one."

Raya took the ring and shared a look with Ilya, who gave a small nod.

"Okay then," Raya started, placing the ring on a metal plate on the counter and signaling for Nico to approach. She took his hand. "Which finger?"

Nico stared. Did it matter? "The pinky," he said. "So it doesn't get in the way of my training."

Raya nodded. She held his hand above the plate and traced a symbol in the air with her free hand. Four tiny fireballs appeared and began to circle in place, catching Nico's attention briefly before a sharp sting snapped his attention downward. A thin cut had opened on his pinky finger and blood dripped onto the plate and ring.

When Nico looked back at the fireballs, they were gone. A distraction, he concluded.

Raya closed her eyes and began to murmur an incantation. The blood on the plate began to glow bright red, then ignited before being absorbed entirely by the ring. Once the blood had disappeared from the metal plate, she opened her eyes again and smiled at Nico, taking the ring and handing it to him.

"Here we go," she said. "Put the ring on and place it on your forehead."

Nico did as he was told and placed the warm ring on his forehead. Within seconds, he felt the air around him stir. When he opened his eyes, shadows and curling smoke coalesced before him, forming the shape of a black wolf. Ilya's eyes widened, and Raya gasped, placing a hand over her mouth.

Nico didn't understand the reaction, but he realized he was smiling. A true smile. This was better than he ever imagined.

"Hi, Dimitri." he whispered, reaching out.

Leah's sharp intake of breath snapped him back to the present, making him alert and aware of their surroundings once more.

Slipping the ring onto his finger, he pressed it to his forehead and closed his eyes. Shadows and smoke merged, forming Dimitri's familiar shape. The wolf stepped closer to Nico, whining softly with emotion.

Nico smiled. "Hey bud. It's been a while."

Dimitri nudged into him, pressing his head against Nico's shoulder before noticing Leah behind him. The wolf stiffened, staring.

"She's a friend," Nico murmured, redirecting him gently. "It's ok. I'm sorry, we don't have much time."

Dimitri sat in understanding before Nico rested his forehead against his, communicating the message he needed to send. The wolf's gaze shifted toward the cave entrance, then dissolved into smoke.

Once it vanished, Nico crouched near Leah again, indecision weighing heavily on his shoulders. For now, all he could do was wait.

Leah stirred, mumbling something unintelligible before suddenly sitting up, confusion written across her face. Her gaze landed on Nico, just inches away.

"It's okay," he said quickly, raising both hands in a calming gesture. "We're back in the cave."

She blinked, her breathing uneven at first, then slowly settled as her eyes focused on him. The panic ebbed from her expression. He could see her studying him. He knew the way he'd looked at her back there must have shaken her, but the past she'd touched wasn't something he could ever share willingly. It wasn't her fault she'd stumbled into it, but that didn't make it any easier to bear.

Nico exhaled, trying to shake the lingering ache from his chest. He hated moments like this, the stillness after chaos, when emotion crept back in. Vulnerability always followed, and that was something he'd spent years locking away. He didn't know how to comfort people. Not really. Years alone had made him efficient, not gentle. Still, Leah looked disoriented, guilt already pooling behind her eyes, and something in him tightened, the same instinct that had driven him to pull her from the clearing before anyone else could find them.

"Nico," she said quietly, eyes on the floor. "I'm sorry. I had no idea that was going to happen."

He sighed, dragging a hand through his hair, a familiar motion meant to calm himself. "I know," he said softly. "And I'm sorry for how I reacted. It's just..." He paused, the words catching. "It wasn't something I wanted to remember."

He saw her hesitation before she spoke again with uncertainty written across her face. There were probably a hundred questions behind those eyes, and he dreaded every single one of them.

"Could you...did you feel me? When I was looking in?"

His jaw tightened. "Yes." The word came out rougher than he intended. "It felt like being frozen in place, watching someone pry open a locked memory and not being able to stop it." He looked away, firelight fracturing across his face. "Don't apologize. You didn't know."

Leah nodded, guilt still clinging to her expression. "So does that mean anything I touch can show me a vision?" Her voice wavered.

Nico studied her, seeing the same fear he'd once carried when he'd lost control of his own power. His gaze dropped briefly to his wrist, where her touch had lingered, before he took a deep breath.

"No. Visions only happen when the magic is active. Back in the forest, your eyes were still glowing. You hadn't fully detached from the first vision when you touched me."

Her brows knit. "How am I supposed to detach?"

"It takes time, Leah. The line between vision and reality doesn't sharpen overnight. But it will."

She nodded shakily, exhaustion weighing her down as the adrenaline finally faded. Nico reached for a canteen and handed it to her. Their fingers brushed briefly, sending an uneasy spark through his chest.

"Thanks," she murmured, taking a sip.

He nodded. "Rest. Uncontrolled magic takes a toll on the body."

He'd meant it as an order, but it came out softer than expected. Leah drew her knees up and stared into the fire, quiet. The cave filled with the soft crackle of flames, and Nico felt the weight of her thoughts pressing between them. He'd avoided this kind of closeness for so long he'd forgotten how disarming it could be.

He shifted restlessly. He didn't know what to do with her sorrow, or with the urge it stirred in him to reach out. Comfort wasn't something he knew how to give. He'd built his life on silence and control—two things that didn't coexist with compassion. Still, the words escaped him.

"You did well today."

Leah blinked, surprised. "You think so?"

He nodded once. "You anchored. Most don't, not on their first attempt."

A small smile tugged at her lips. "I thought I was going to burn."

"You didn't." He met her gaze. "You faced it."

Her smile softened. "It's strange," she said after a moment. "This still feels like a dream. A terrifying one sometimes, but..." She hesitated, eyes flicking toward the fire. "I don't feel empty anymore. Ever since that night, those visions...I've felt..."

He watched her with growing interest, the firelight catching in her gray-blue eyes and along the dark waves of her hair. Freckles dusted her nose and cheeks, making every emotion impossible to hide.

"Complete," she finished quietly. "It sounds silly."

He said nothing, letting the word settle. There was a steadiness to her now, even beneath the fear. Selene had been right. Leah carried something that would draw the world's attention. What frightened him was how much it already drew his.

"Get some sleep," he said.

She nodded and curled against the cave wall. Within minutes, her breathing evened out.

Nico leaned back against the stone and let the quiet return. The fire dimmed to embers, warmth barely reaching him. He'd lived years without another presence breaking the silence and told himself he preferred it that way. But now, listening to her breathing, unease stirred again. Not fear of danger, which he knew was inevitable, but fear of what her presence was beginning to undo in him.

He dragged his hand down his face, exhaling slowly. Vulnerability was a luxury he couldn't afford. Not now. Not ever.

Still, he traced a faint sigil into the dirt beside the fire. The wards shimmered briefly, confirming his suspicion. The magic around them was weakening.

It was only a matter of time before the forest stirred again. They would have to move soon, but for now, he'd keep watch.

Chapter 8

By the time Leah stirred, the fire had burned to ash and the light filtered faintly through the cave's entrance. Nico was already awake, of course. He sat near the entrance, still scanning the tree line. She was finally picking up that this wasn't only for vigilance, but more of a habit. She shifted her position, making him turn slightly at the sound of her movement.

"Morning," he said simply. His tone was neutral, but the faint roughness in it told her he hadn't slept much…again.

"Morning," she echoed, rubbing the sleep from her eyes. She lifted herself into a sitting position, feeling every muscle in her body ache. She secretly hoped their time in this cave would be over soon and that they could go somewhere with something softer than stone. Her body hurt every time she woke up on the ground.

"So, what's on the schedule for today?" she asked lightly.

Nico stood and retrieved the Echodex from beside the fire pit. "I think we need to figure out more about your Seer magic so that what happened yesterday doesn't happen again," he said, handing her the Echodex.

Of course. More training.

Leah tucked her hair behind her ear as he passed her the book. She had been so consumed by the aftermath of her magic that she'd almost forgotten the book existed. Her eyes lingered on the cover as the memories of how this book had apparently caused innumerable deaths and unimaginable suffering began to surface. She sighed. No matter how she looked at it, it was hard to understand how a book could create such chaos. Yet, if The Order sought it for their twisted plans, she wouldn't let them succeed. And if she hoped to stand a chance against them, she had to understand it far better than she did now.

"Call on your Seer magic," Nico said, pulling her from her thoughts. "You need to recognize when it's active and have control over it. Otherwise, the visions will overwhelm you."

Control. It always came back to that. Leah looked down at the book, remembering the intensity of the visions she'd first experienced in the attic—the ripples, and the way the world had folded in on itself. She took the book and closed her eyes, drawing in a deep breath before opening them again.

"Nothing," Nico said after a moment. "Try again. Close your eyes and focus. Magic has a pulse. You'll know it when you feel it."

Leah obeyed, closing her eyes once more. For a moment, there was nothing but her shaky breathing until finally, pressure loomed behind her eyelids—a sensation that climbed up her spine and spread to her face. Her brow furrowed as she realized that this whole time, the feeling behind her eyes might not have been a headache at all. There was only one way to test that theory. She opened her eyes and looked directly at Nico.

"Is it working?" she asked, hoping her theory was right.

"Yes," he replied simply, giving a small nod.

"Wow." Her voice trembled, disbelief woven into the word.

Nico nodded again. "Now see what you can do with the book."

Leah frowned, her heart thudding as she struggled to keep the pressure behind her eyes steady. She pressed her fingertips lightly to the Echodex, waiting for the rush, the pull—but nothing came. Just cool leather beneath her fingers.

Her lips parted in frustration. "It's not working."

Nico leaned back, watching her with that unreadable calm that drove her mad. "It won't always. The Echodex is peculiar...or so I read."

"Peculiar how?"

"You'll have to learn that," he said simply. But his eyes betrayed a fleeting shift, as though he knew more than he was willing to share.

Leah slumped back in frustration, her pulse still thrumming from the magic inside her. A faint glow prickled at the edges of her vision. "So it's not just me failing..."

"Not failing," Nico corrected. "Relics choose what they reveal. You might not be ready yet. Try something else."

Her gaze darted around the cave. Their belongings lay scattered in the dim light, including their bags. She emptied the bag, placing her change of clothes to the side before sitting back down with the bag in hand. The leather strap was worn and the stitching slightly frayed, but the moment her hand closed around it, the pressure in her eyes intensified and the cave blurred away.

She was smaller, sitting cross-legged on the rug in Selene's office. Selene's voice floated to her.

"For any of your future journeys," she said, placing the small bag in Leah's lap. "I saw you eyeing it the other day. Take care of it."

The vision rippled away, leaving Leah blinking back tears. When her sight cleared, Nico was watching her closely.

"What did you see?"

"Selene," Leah whispered. "The day she gave this to me." She pressed the bag to her chest, clinging to the fading warmth of the memory. "It felt so real. Like she was right here."

Nico's expression softened for a brief moment before he masked it again.

"That's what can happen with ordinary objects. They show you fragments. Impressions tied to them. Sometimes trivial, sometimes useful, but I don't think you can decide which you'll see."

Leah traced the bag's worn edges with her thumb. "So...it's just whatever the object wants?"

"Not necessarily," he said, his gaze flicking to the Echodex. "Some things are just objects. Others—like the book—are far more than simple artifacts."

Leah looked back at it, frustration flaring again. "Then why won't it work?"

"Because you're asking for doors it doesn't want to open. At least, not yet," Nico said quietly.

The words made her frown. The Echodex seemed almost alive, hoarding its secrets until it deemed her worthy. She hated that thought, hated the helplessness wrapped up in it.

"What about people?" she asked suddenly, meeting his eyes. "If I touch someone, will I see everything? Their memories, like I did with you?"

Nico's expression sharpened, and his shoulders visibly tensed.

"Not everything," he said. "Only what they allow."

She blinked. "Allow?"

"Most people guard themselves. They can either show you glimpses or lock you out entirely." He shifted before continuing. "When you saw that vision yesterday, you touched my bracelet. The item itself has meaning, and the vision came from the time it was tied to me." Nico moved to sit in front of her. "But if you were to touch me while I was aware—" He gestured toward her hand.

Leah straightened, unsure if she was ready. The memory of his expression in the forest still haunted her—the cold fury and the betrayal in his voice. She hadn't meant to invade something private, yet here he was, offering her the chance to try again—to do it right.

She hesitated. "Are you sure?"

"I wouldn't ask if I wasn't ready."

That was a lie, she thought. Or maybe half of one. She could still see the tension in his jaw and the stiffness in his shoulders. He was bracing himself, but he wasn't pulling away. Part of her wanted to refuse, but another part—the one craving meaning— refused to retreat. This was real. Terrifying at times, yes. But real. And if she wanted to stand up to The Order, she had to face her fears.

She had to stop running.

Her hand trembled as she raised it, hesitating only a second before pressing her palm to his chest. Instantly, magic flared beneath her skin, the pressure behind her eyes swelling as the cave dissolved into darkness.

She looked around, confused. She couldn't see anything. She stood in a vast void where shadows stretched endlessly in every direction, like the ones that clung to Nico's feet.

Her heart pounded. She tried to focus, to find a thread or a spark of memory, but there was nothing. No images, no voices, not even the faintest impression of Nico's thoughts. Only emptiness pressing in from all sides.

It felt suffocating, like being submerged beneath deep water. A chill swept over her. Was this what his magic felt like? The shadows she'd seen rise from his hands? She shivered. If this emptiness lived inside him, she understood why he carried it so carefully.

She pulled back slightly, panic flickering. "I...I can't see anything."

Nico's voice cut through the darkness, calm but firm. "Good. That's exactly what you should be seeing."

Her confusion deepened. "What do you mean?"

"You felt the pulse," he said. "That means your power is working. But not everything will open to you. People guard themselves instinctively. They choose what to reveal—especially if they sense you coming."

Leah removed her hand from his chest, blinking rapidly as the darkness faded and the cave returned. The pressure behind her eyes dimmed until her vision cleared, and she released a shaky breath.

"So with objects, I see fragments...but with people, I can only see what they allow?"

"Exactly." Nico leaned back on his hands, watching her closely. "Fragments, echoes, traces. Your power shows you pieces, not necessarily the whole. The Echodex might withhold what you want most because you wouldn't be able to handle it. That's why control matters. You need to feel the moment it activates and learn when to step back."

Leah leaned against the cave wall. The sensation of the void lingered at the edge of her senses. There had been something strangely comforting about it. Maybe because it had been his.

She sighed. "It's a lot to take in."

"It is," Nico said quietly. "And it'll get more complicated. But you'll learn—with practice and patience."

She nodded, determination flickering through the fear. The void hadn't been nothing—it was a boundary—and boundaries were something she had to learn to respect before she could push past them.

Nico stood, brushing dirt from his pants. "Try another object," he said. "Anything around here. Sense the pulse first and let the vision come—or not. Don't chase it. I'm going to see if I can find us something to eat. I won't be long."

Leah watched him head toward the cave entrance, pulling his cloak back on. Once he was gone, a strange mix of relief and anticipation filled her chest. She had the space to herself now, and for the first time, she could test her abilities without the fear of crossing boundaries again. The familiar pressure behind her eyes returned and her heart began to beat faster. She realized she was excited to be alone with her magic.

She turned back to the scattered objects: her bag, stone, and ash from the fire pit. Tentatively, she reached for the charred wood. A flicker of warmth ran along her fingertips, followed by a brief vision of Nico gathering firewood, his breath misting in the cold. The image dissolved almost instantly, leaving her blinking.

"Okay," she whispered. "That's something."

Next, she picked up a smooth stone. Nothing. She tried again, her pulse quickening as she called on her magic, but the stone remained inert. Frustration prickled, but she remembered Nico's words: Don't chase it.

She moved carefully from object to object, hovering her hands before committing to touch. Some offered tiny glimpses— a memory of Selene humming while sewing a patch onto her bag, a shimmer of sunlight caught on a polished rock. Others yielded nothing at all. Slowly, she noticed the pattern. Not every object held a vision, and those that did, revealed only what they were ready to give.

Time passed without her noticing. Her eyes glowed faintly with each pulse of magic, and though she couldn't control what she saw, she began to recognize the feeling that preceded a vision—the subtle shift in air pressure, the hum beneath her skin. When she finally lowered her hands, her body sagged with fatigue. The cave felt strangely peaceful now, wrapped in silence.

She was exhausted, more aware than ever of her limits. But the possibilities, if she could master them, were intoxicating. A current of exhilaration pulsed through her weariness, and deep inside, a spark of determination ignited.

She would learn control. She would uncover the Echodex's secrets. And one day, she would see exactly what she was meant to see.

Leah sat curled near the mouth of the cave with her arms wrapped around her knees. At some point after testing her magic, she'd finally changed into her only other set of clothes since Nico was away. They were a little warmer than the thin shirt she had on before, but it still did not help with the chilling air outside. The forest had sunk into a hush, broken only by the occasional rustle of leaves or the distant hoot of an owl. The fire had long since gone out, and with it, the warmth. The cold crept in, slow and patient, biting through her clothes until her fingers ached. She'd tried to light another fire but found herself fumbling with the stones and brittle stick, searching for a spark that never came. Fire magic would have been useful right about now, but summoning a flame felt as impossible as calling magic on command, so she waited for Nico to return.

When she heard the soft tread of footsteps through the underbrush, relief rippled through her. Moments later, Nico appeared at the cave's entrance, shadows sliding off his shoulders like a second cloak. Even in the dim light, he carried that same quiet gravity, always keeping himself just out of reach. Yet instead of fear, Leah felt a strange pull. The longer she stayed with him, the more she noticed what lay beneath the mask: the faint ease in his posture whenever she was near, and the way his gaze softened when it lingered on her just a little too long.

He set down a small bundle wrapped in leaves, crouching beside her. "You didn't light a fire."

Leah shook her head, embarrassed. "I don't know how."

Without a word, he arranged a circle of stones and placed dry kindling at the center. Sparks leapt from flint to steel, and soon, flames crackled to life, washing the cave walls in amber light. Leah let out a quiet sigh as warmth spread across her chilled skin, easing the ache in her fingers.

Nico fed the flames before unwrapping the bundle. Inside were roots, berries, and a few wild mushrooms. "It's not much, but it should hold us until tomorrow."

He skewered a root on the tip of his dagger, holding it over the fire until the skin blackened. When he broke it in half and handed her a piece, their fingers brushed, and a spark of warmth jumped up her arm.

"Thank you," she murmured.

He only nodded. They ate in silence, and to her surprise, it wasn't uncomfortable. It reminded her of dinners with Selene.

"You've done this before," Leah said. "The fire, the foraging...surviving like this."

"More times than I can count."

His tone was flat, but not unkind. She hesitated, wanting to press further—to ask what those times had been like, what had driven him to this kind of life—but she held back, sensing he wasn't ready. Instead, the words slipped out before she could stop them.

"I don't think I'd last a day without you." Heat rushed to her face. "Because of the fire," she blurted, stumbling. "It's too cold without it."

Nico paused mid-bite, his eyes lifting to hers. Then, without comment, he reached for the small pile of berries and offered them to her. Leah took them, and when she did, her fingers brushed his again. She quickly took a handful of berries and shoved them in her mouth to distract herself from the moment. The tart sweetness grounded her, though her pulse still fluttered.

As firelight painted shifting gold across the cave walls, Leah found herself studying him again. The sharp lines of his face, and the quiet steadiness of his movements. He was still a mystery—guarded and distant—but there was something in his silence that no longer unsettled her. Instead, it felt safe.

Nico leaned forward, feeding another branch to the fire. When he looked back at her, his expression softened almost imperceptibly.

"I'll keep watch tonight," he said quietly.

Leah wanted to argue, to insist she wasn't as tired as she felt, but her body betrayed her. The weight of the day pressed heavily on her shoulders, dragging her eyelids down. She nodded and curled closer to the fire.

The exhaustion from the visions was different—deeper, seeping into her mind as much as her muscles. It felt like sinking into something dense and dark, with her thoughts fraying at the edges. Every use of her power left her emptier, as if the magic took something she couldn't see. She wondered if that was what Nico meant when he said visions could take pieces of you. Within minutes, her breathing slowed, warmth seeping into her skin as sleep claimed her.

But sleep was not empty.

A shadowed void stretched before her, thicker than the cave's darkness. Indistinct whispers echoed in the distance—chains rattling, a faint echo of her name. She turned toward the sound, though her body didn't move. From the dark, hands reached for her throat before cloaked figures emerged, their faces covered and their voices merging into a single chilling word that shook the ground beneath her feet.

Found.

Leah jolted awake with a strangled gasp, her pulse racing as the dim glow of dying embers flickered against the cave walls. Nearby, Nico sat watchful and still, his shadows dormant, but his posture tense with constant vigilance. At the sound of her breath, his gaze lifted immediately, and within moments, he was at her side.

"What is it?" His voice was low, braced.

Leah pressed a trembling hand to her chest. "The Order," she whispered. "I think they know I'm here."

Nico's head snapped toward the entrance of the cave and his entire body stilled.

"What?" she whispered again, dread curling in her gut.

He didn't answer. His eyes stayed locked on the darkness beyond the cave, as if tracking movement only he could sense. The silence stretched thin until Leah could hear her own heartbeat. Then she felt it—a faint hum threading through the air.

"They found us," he murmured, already moving.

Nico caught her wrist and pulled her toward the entrance. Leah stumbled after him, clutching her bag with the Echodex to her chest as cold air rushed over her skin and they burst into the trees.

The forest erupted the moment her boots hit the moss— branches shifting too close, then the sharp twang of a bowstring.

Before the sound fully registered, Nico shoved her behind a thick root. She slammed into the ground as an arrow hissed through the space where her head had been. Her ears rang and her throat burned with a scream she didn't release.

From the tree line, shadows surged forward—three figures cloaked beneath gray-black armor moving as one. Moonlight grazed the half-closed eye pin at their collars, turning the mark of The Order into a cold, watchful glare.

"Stay low," Nico growled, his voice colder than she'd ever heard it. Commanding.

He was already in motion, rising fluidly to meet the attacks. His shadows shot out like living whipcords, intercepting the first agent who lunged toward Leah. The figure collided with the dark tendrils and was yanked backward, crashing into a tree with a grunt of pain and an impact that echoed through the clearing.

Leah pressed the Echodex tighter to her, white-knuckled. Hours of testing her magic hadn't prepared her for this—this chaos, this danger. Her Seer power wasn't something she could aim or summon like a weapon. It came and went, still wild and unpredictable.

She was useless.

Terrified.

Magic thickened around them, pulsing with every flare of Nico's power beyond the tree line. His movements were sharp, decisive, and deadly—each one a reminder of how much he risked by staying near her. A surge of helplessness pressed against her ribs until it ached. She tried to step forward, to help him, to be more than fear, but her limbs wouldn't budge. All she could do was cling to the book like it was the only thing keeping her from shattering.

A blur of motion caught her eye as another agent emerged from the left. Leah opened her mouth to warn Nico, but he was already there, shadows whipping from his fingertips like live wire. They hissed through the air and wrapped around the man's throat, lifting him off the ground. Leah gasped. This wasn't the quiet, watchful Nico she had come to know. This was someone else. The tendrils of darkness pulsed with fury, constricting until bone snapped beneath them.

"Nico—" she whispered.

He didn't hear her. His face was carved in fury, his eyes pitch black, and his body coiled with the stillness of a predator ready to strike. The final agent hesitated when Nico turned.

"You," the man breathed, disbelief in his eyes. "You're supposed to be dead."

Recognition flickered in his features, but it didn't stop him. With a roar, he lunged past Nico toward Leah with his blade drawn. Leah barely had time to react before rough hands grabbed her arm, yanking her forward. She gasped, the sound caught somewhere between a cry and a breath with each inhale stabbing her lungs with pain. Her vision blurred at the edges, and heat seared through her side where the blade had buried itself deep. She wanted to scream, to wail, to make the world stop—but her throat refused, leaving only a ragged, choked gasp. Every nerve in her body burned, and the pain pressed down on her chest.

"Leah!" Nico's voice snapped through the chaos, low and wrathful. "Get away from her!"

The shadows snapped like a whip. They tore the man backward, wrenching him off his feet and slamming him hard into the ground. His weapon flew from his grasp, clattering against the moss as he thrashed, clawing for air, but Nico didn't stop.

"You should have stayed dead," the man spat between ragged breaths. "You were never one of us."

Nico's voice dropped to a whisper that felt colder than steel. "I never was."

The darkness surged. It struck all at once, coiling around the man's limbs, his chest, his throat. His final scream was cut short, swallowed whole as the shadows crushed the life from him. Then nothing. The forest stilled.

Leah gasped, each breath shallow and jagged. Pain flared along her side, and warm, sticky blood seeped heavily through her fingers. She lifted her gaze, and Nico was already there, kneeling beside her. Shadows twitched faintly beneath his skin, restless, as if alive and echoing the fury coiling in his chest.

"You're bleeding," he said. His tone was sharp, and Leah couldn't tell if that was panic in his voice.

"I'm okay," Leah whispered, though the words trembled. Her vision wavered at the edges as darkness creeped in. She wasn't okay.

Nico pressed his hand against her side and Leah gasped as sharp pain flared like fire beneath his touch. Blood soaked through his fingers, and she saw his jaw go rigid and a flash of controlled panic cross his face. Then his eyes darted toward the trees again. She heard it too—a subtle, deliberate rustle in the shadows that didn't belong. Her stomach clenched. Another presence shifted in the shadows, then fled. A fourth agent retreating into the cover of the forest.

"Damn it." Nico muttered. The word vibrated with anger.

She could feel it in the air, a tension that made the shadows around him squirm and stir. He wanted to go after them, she could see the restraint in his posture and the conflict in his eyes, but his hand didn't leave her wound. Her blood was still warm against his skin as he exhaled through clenched teeth.

"We need to move."

Leah tried to stand, but her legs gave way, folding beneath her. Before she could fall, Nico caught her, his arms held her with a strength that made the spinning world feel momentarily still. In a fluid motion, he lifted her, his shadows swirling around them like a protective veil.

"Put me down—" she tried to argue, though the words barely formed

"Later," he snapped. "Bleed out if you want, but not here."

Nico quickly retrieved the bag with the Echodex as his shadows rose and followed, sliding over the ground as he carried her through the trees. They moved like a living barrier and through the haze of pain and exhaustion, Leah couldn't tell if the shadows were meant to keep the world out—or to keep Nico from breaking apart inside them.

Chapter 9

They threaded quickly through the trees until the path narrowed, forcing them between jagged ridges. Ahead, a seemingly random pile of large stones jutted from the earth, nothing more than a natural feature at first glance. Nico slowed, muttering a phrase in a language Leah didn't recognize. Then, with a low groan, the stones shifted, sliding smoothly apart. The earth beneath them split as roots twisted aside, revealing a stairway spiraling down into darkness.

"This place," she whispered, her breath ghosting against his collar. "It was always here?"

He didn't answer, just descended, carrying her as if she weighed nothing.

"Where does it lead?" she tried again, her voice thin.

His reply came quiet and sharp. "To a place The Order can't follow."

The passage twisted for what felt like hours, though it couldn't have been more than minutes. Moss glimmered faintly along the walls, and torches flared to life as they passed. Leah's head spun. Maybe it was the blood loss, or maybe it was the strange, hidden space unfolding before her.

At last, the passage widened, opening into a cavernous chamber—stone-walled and domed like the inside of a hollowed seedpod. The air was warmer here, touched with the scent of old paper and mineral earth. One entire wall was consumed by bookshelves, crammed edge to edge with loose scrolls and ink-smudged journals.

A fireplace carved directly into the stone sat beneath a mantle cluttered with mismatched trinkets. Across from it, a battered but cozy armchair sagged invitingly, its worn cushions soft despite their age. It reminded Leah of Selene instantly. Nearby, a small round table sat with four chairs clustered around it. Lanterns hung at even intervals along the curved walls, casting the space in a warm glow.

In one corner, a curtained alcove suggested a bathroom, the fabric swaying slightly as if stirred by an unseen draft. On the opposite side, a single closed door likely led to a bedroom, she guessed. Between them, a narrow stone counter served as a makeshift kitchen, complete with a kettle and a few cracked mugs hanging from hooks. It wasn't luxurious, but it was lived-in and strangely homey. For a moment, Leah couldn't shake the feeling that she had seen this place before.

She tilted her head weakly, managing a ghost of a smile. "So...this is your evil lair?"

Nico stopped mid-step and looked down at her. "It's not evil."

"Sure. Right. Just happens to be underground, filled with a hundred books and suspicious lighting." Her lips curved faintly despite the pain. "What do you even call this place?"

"It doesn't have a name."

"It does now," she murmured. "Welcome to the Book Bunker of Brooding. Population: one extremely intense shadow man."

His jaw twitched, and she caught the hint of amusement he tried to hide as he looked away. It shouldn't have mattered, but it did. She was starting to realize she liked pulling reactions from him—those fleeting moments when the mask cracked and something real slipped through. No matter how distant he pretended to be, she knew there was more beneath the armor.

"I'm not brooding," he muttered.

"You glared at a wound. That's peak brooding."

He didn't reply. Instead, he shifted her carefully, lowering her onto a padded bench tucked beneath the wall of books. The sudden stillness made her dizzy.

"You're hurt." He crouched in front of her with one knee pressed to the stone floor, and eyes fixed on her side. "Let me see it." It wasn't a request.

Leah hesitated. He was too close. Lantern light traced the line of his jaw, catching the dark strands of hair that fell forward as he studied her. She swallowed, forcing a casual tone. "It's fine."

His eyes lifted briefly, a warning in their darkness. "It's not."

Her pulse tripped. "Right. Fine. Fix me, then."

Nico shrugged off his cloak and pulled a satchel from a nearby shelf. Inside were herbs, bandages, and small glass vials of amber liquid, all neatly arranged—prepared for emergencies, as if he'd been expecting this.

"How do you have all this down here?" she asked.

"I live here."

She frowned. "You live in a cave under a forest?"

"It's safer underground," he said calmly, ignoring her incredulity.

He knelt closer, and before she could protest, his fingers brushed her side, lifting the hem of her shirt just enough to expose the wound. Leah froze and the air thickened; her skin prickled beneath his touch. He focused only on the injury, but it didn't matter—her breath caught anyway.

"You're lucky," he said. "It doesn't look like the blade hit anything vital, but it went in deep."

"I thought I would heal, like my hand did the first time I used my blood magic." Leah admitted.

Nico dipped a cloth into water, then into one of the vials.

"Blood magic is not widely understood," he said before pressing the cloth on the wound. The liquid stung when he pressed it to her skin and Leah hissed, but the pain faded quickly as the bleeding slowed.

She clenched her jaw. "That's supposed to help?"

"It is helping."

She studied him—the faint furrow in his brow, the way his jaw tensed whenever she flinched. He was being careful, almost gentle. It didn't match the man who had summoned shadows to kill moments earlier.

"Where did you learn to do this?" she asked.

He paused, fingers still against her skin. "I was trained."

"By whom?"

Nico looked up then, his eyes still dark from the fight—fury simmered beneath his restraint.

"By the same people who just tried to kill us."

Leah's stomach dropped. "The Order?"

He nodded once and returned to his task. His hands moved with precision, but tension lingered beneath every motion. When he wrapped the bandage around her waist, his knuckles brushed her ribs and the metal ring on his pinky grazed her skin. She hadn't noticed the ring before. The contact was brief, but heat skittered through her.

He tied the bandage with a firm tug and leaned back to assess his work. His face was unreadable, but she sensed the storm beneath it. Her thoughts flickered to the last man and the recognition in his eyes, before the shadows claimed him.

"That man," she paused. "He knew you, didn't he?"

Nico's hands stilled. "They thought I was dead. I let them believe it."

Dead. The word pressed uncomfortably against her chest. She traced the calm control in his movements, the shadows clinging to him, and realized part of her didn't want the full truth.

"Why would they think you were dead?" she asked. "What happened?"

"It doesn't matter," he said quickly.

"Doesn't matter?" Confusion sharpened into something tighter. "They recognized you, Nico. They knew you."

He exhaled slowly. "And now they'll know you too."

The distance slid back into place. Shadows stirred faintly behind him, restless. Whatever history lay there, he wasn't ready to share it. Leah saw it in the way his gaze slipped away.

Her frustration melted into guilt, and she began twisting the hem of her shirt, trying to distract herself from the tight, rising ache in her chest. "I'm sorry."

"For what?" Nico frowned.

"If it wasn't for me, you wouldn't have had to kill someone you knew."

A shadow crossed his eyes. "He hurt you. That man meant nothing to me."

She blinked. "You killed him because he hurt me?"

Nico didn't answer right away. He sat back on his heels, rolling the bloodied cloth between his hands. When he looked up, the dangerous edge in his voice had returned.

"I killed him because he would've kept coming. They all would. The Order doesn't bargain; they silence." He paused. "They just didn't expect me to be there."

Leah stilled.

"They thought you were alone," he continued. "The ones who found us were scouts—trackers. They weren't prepared for a fight, and they certainly weren't prepared for me. If they had known..." His shadows tightened, darkening the space around him. "They would have sent someone far stronger."

He crossed to the mantle and struck flint. The fire caught, casting low light across the chamber.

"Because of your blood, because the book is with you, they won't stop," he said. "They fear what they can't control. The moment you opened that book and your powers returned, you became unpredictable. An anomaly. And to them, anomalies must be eradicated."

Leah watched firelight move across his face, noticing the exhaustion he couldn't hide. He was still standing between her and danger, still choosing to protect her. Silence stretched, filled only by the crackle of flames. She pressed a hand to her bandage, dizzy.

"So do I hide in this...Brooding Bunker until they find me again?" she whispered.

"No." Nico's voice was steel. "You've made progress, but you still have much to learn—and you need to heal before we push further." He studied her, then stepped closer.

Leah's pulse jumped as he lifted her again. She leaned into him without meaning to, drawn to his warmth. His arms held her steady, and for the first time since the fight, there was no panic—only the solid rhythm of his heartbeat beneath her cheek.

He opened the door she'd assumed led to a bedroom. Inside, a low bed sat beneath sagging shelves, and a rough-woven blanket was folded at its edge. Her chest jumped. *Are we going to share a bed?!* Panic rushed through her and she forced herself to slow her racing heartbeat before Nico could hear it. She drew in a deep breath. *No, Nico would never.*

As if on cue, Nico laid her down gently, adjusted the pillow at her neck, and placed the book within easy reach. Then he stepped back.

"I'll keep watch," he said. "Sleep as much as you need. I'll see you in the morning." He didn't wait for her reply, he just turned and padded silently back to the main chamber.

Leah sank into the bedding with a soft sigh, grateful to finally be lying on something that wasn't cold rock. The ache in her body eased, replaced by a heavy kind of exhaustion.

She closed her eyes and couldn't help the faint, self-conscious thought that had flickered through her mind. *I'm so ridiculous, why would I think that?* Relief washed over her that Nico hadn't noticed her brief panic, and she pressed her face into the pillow, letting the exhaustion pull her under. Her thoughts scattered, twisted like roots in the earth. Somewhere near the edge of sleep, she heard Nico's voice again from the other room.

"I'll be back soon," he said. "Just need to reinforce the spells."

She didn't answer, only nodded drowsily, already half beneath the tide of exhaustion. The lantern's glow was low and golden, flickering against the walls. She drifted into a dream where a forest appeared around her in hues of burnt gold. Trees rose like silhouettes of ash, their branches long and spindled, their shadows stretching across uneven earth—until she saw her.

Selene stood at the base of a great silver tree, her gray hair rippling in wind that never touched Leah.

"Gran?" Leah's voice caught. "Is this...are you really here?"

Selene looked at her then. "You are not safe anymore," she said. "They know who you're with now."

Leah stepped forward. "Nico—"

But Selene's expression darkened.

"There is danger in his shadow," she said. "And power. He walks a line even he doesn't fully see. But he is bound to you now. Whether that saves you or destroys you remains unwritten."

The wind surged, making leaves spiral and the ground tremble. Suddenly, Selene's face was closer, her hand reaching for Leah's.

"You must learn to see," she whispered. "Not just with your eyes, but with your blood. Look deeper, Leah."

Leah's eyes snapped open, unsure how much time had passed. The bunker was quiet, and the book rested beside her, closed as it always was when it wasn't ready. Out of the corner of her eye, shimmers began to outline the cover. She hadn't seen the book react like that in a while, and fear tightened her chest. She wanted to ignore it, to close her eyes and pretend she hadn't seen anything—but the Echodex never called in vain.

Her fingers hovered above the cover. The shimmer pulsed once, and she felt the familiar tug beneath her ribs, the same pull that always came before the world fell away. When she touched it, that's exactly what happened.

A flash tore the world apart as the vision slammed into her.

She stood at the edge of a battlefield. Shadows surged and collided with bursts of white light. Faces blurred and bodies warped like ripples in water. She thought she saw Nico, but the image twisted away before she could be sure. They weren't alone. Other figures appeared—indistinct, braced as if waiting for what was coming.

A beam of yellow light burned in the distance, growing brighter. Knives shimmered like mirages, making her heart race. She spun, searching for meaning, but when her gaze snapped back to the light, a blade sliced through it with lethal precision, aimed straight for her head.

The blurred figures surged toward her, as if to stop it, but her feet were rooted to the ground. Fear clawed at her chest as the blade closed in, making Leah draw a breath and shut her eyes, bracing for impact.

Instead, the steel pierced the air around her and the vision shattered.

She fell back into herself, before the chamber's golden light replaced the battlefield.

Leah blinked against the firelight, sweat beading along her neck. The book lay open beside her, its pages glowing faintly before fading back to stillness. The images burned behind her eyes—Selene's warning, the silver tree, the yellow light, the shadows. She pressed a shaking hand to her chest, trying to calm her racing heart.

The half-closed door creaked open, and Leah jolted upright, her hand snapping away from the book as if it had burned her. Pain flared along her side, and she hissed, clutching the wound and cursing herself for moving too fast. Why did she always react before thinking? She was almost certain she'd reopened it. She struggled to sit upright on the narrow bed, watching firelight flicker through the doorway.

"Leah?" Nico's voice came softly before he stepped into view, brushing droplets of water from his shoulders. His coat was damp, and his black hair caught the firelight. The moment his eyes fell on her, they narrowed in concern, making her chest tighten again.

"You had a vision again." His tone was more a statement than a question, and Leah felt the heat rise to her cheeks.

She had wanted to hide it, to stop worrying him, but she never was good at hiding her emotions. Before she could reply, he was at her side, one hand holding her steady as the other hovered over the wound on her right side.

"Show me," he said.

The heat from his body pressed against her as he crouched, and for a moment, Leah felt a helpless warmth— one that came from the pull of his concern, the closeness she couldn't escape, and the way he moved instinctively to protect her. Her stomach fluttered despite herself.

"I—It just hurt when I moved," she admitted, her voice small. Her hand hovered near the bandage, afraid to touch it, aware of how exposed she felt under his gaze.

"Okay, let me check it properly," he said, adjusting his stance to bring her more securely into his view. The shadows at his back stirred faintly, echoing his vigilance, and Leah realized how utterly alone she would be without him and how much she relied on his strength even as her pulse throbbed from the pain. She hated it. She hated how little control she had in all this.

"You're tense," Nico murmured, his voice threading through the quiet room.

She hated it. The way it was so easy for him to read her. The way it was hard for her to read him.

"I—" she started, then stopped.

How could she explain that it wasn't just pain? That it was him—how close he was, how intently he looked at her. The thought of moving her body made her flinch even harder.

Her fingers twitched, hovering near his hand at her side, as if she could somehow lend him a fraction of the comfort he always seemed to give her. Part of her ached to brush the dark strands of hair out of his face, to rest her hand lightly on the warmth of his skin, and to anchor him like he had anchored her. She imagined, fleetingly, pressing her palm to his, letting him feel the weight of her concern, of her gratitude, and of the unspoken pull between them.

Her heart thundered at the thought, and warmth rushed to her cheeks. What was she thinking? She couldn't—shouldn't. And yet, before she could pull back completely, her hand moved of its own accord, sliding just enough to rest briefly atop his—a fleeting brush meant only to thank him. The contact was almost imperceptible, but it sent a jolt through her, and a spark that reminded her of the first time their hands had touched in the clearing.

She froze, panic clawing at her chest. Her mind screamed to pull away, but when she glanced up expecting him to recoil or step back, she found him still there, unmoving. His dark eyes met hers, steady and unflinching. Her pulse roared in her ears and she realized that she felt exposed in a way that had nothing to do with her wound now.

After what felt like hours staring into each other's eyes, she withdrew her trembling hand. She knew, even as her chest tightened, that something was growing between them.

Nico's lips parted slightly as if to speak, but no words came out. Instead, he finished adjusting the bandage with the same careful precision and got up as if he needed a bit of room to breathe the tension away.

Leah wrapped the blanket tighter around herself and let her gaze drift to the shadows dancing along the far wall, willing her pulse to slow down. Perhaps if she changed the topic...

"It started to shine again," she started. "It wanted to be seen, I guess."

Nico's shoulders relaxed slightly, and he moved to seat himself at the foot of the bed, leaning back just enough to create distance without breaking the shared space.

"The book doesn't want things. It responds."

"To what?"

"To you." He met her gaze. "What did it show you?"

She hesitated. The truth felt too sharp and too dangerous to disclose right now. "Selene," she said instead. "She warned me about you."

"Of course she did."

"That's it?" Leah blinked. "No denial?"

"You wouldn't believe me."

She felt the cracks then—his wall threatening to snap shut again. This time, she let it be. She just wanted him to stay.

"The magic in the book is so strange," she murmured, half expecting him to leave. But he didn't and relief bloomed in her chest.

Nico shifted beside her, folding his long legs beneath him. His voice was quieter when he spoke again, but it still held the same control it always carried.

"Magic has rules," he said. "Old ones. Etched into the fabric of the world."

Leah tilted her head toward him, curiosity stirring despite her exhaustion. "Start with the first."

A faint, wry smile flickered across his mouth. "Alright, apprentice. Lesson one." He lifted a gloved finger. "Magic always comes at a cost."

Leah frowned. "You mean like... energy?"

"I mean like blood. Or memory. Or time." he said, briefly meeting her gaze. "Nothing is free. The more powerful the magic, the greater the price. You don't get to choose the toll—only whether you're willing to pay it."

Chills crept down her spine as she thought about the visions that tore through her and left her fatigued and unable to stand.

"Lesson two," he continued. "Magic obeys intent. Thought shapes reality. But thought without discipline…" his gaze held hers. "That's how wildfires start."

Leah exhaled slowly. "Then why does the Echodex show me things I don't think about?"

"The Echodex is not bound by the same rule," he said after a pause. "The book is older than intent. Older than most things we understand."

He hesitated, the faintest crease forming between his brows. "When I was a child, I studied what little was known of it. Even then, no one could explain how it worked. Some believed it fed on echoes, memories or moments—the residue of what was. Others thought it held the world's unfinished stories." His tone shifted, quieter now. "Whatever truth it holds, it's not meant to be controlled."

There was something in the way he said it, like he was remembering something painful. A past she didn't yet know how to ask about.

"And me?" she asked softly. "Should I be afraid of it too?"

He looked at her for a long moment. "Lesson three," he said finally, leaning in just enough that she could feel the warmth radiating from him, the brush of his sleeve near her arm. "Magic remembers," he said. "Every spell, every lie, every wound. The land holds it. The shadows hold it. And so do we."

The fire popped, shattering the moment. Nico blinked as if waking from a trance and stood abruptly, the space between them cooling. "You should rest," he said, his voice controlled again. "Sorry to have woken you. I'll see you in a few hours."

Leah nodded, though she didn't move. She watched him step toward the doorway with his shadow stretching long across the floor. When he disappeared into the dim corridor beyond, the silence felt heavier. The fire still burned, but the air seemed colder without him. She lay back slowly, staring at the Echodex where it rested beside her. Its cover was dull again, but she could still feel it pulsing faintly—just like her.

Chapter 10

Nico closed Leah's door with a quiet click. For a long moment, he stood there, listening for any movement—or the faint rhythm of her breathing through the door. The silence that followed wasn't peace, it was weight. He let out a breath and turned toward the fireplace, its flicker painting the walls in trembling light.

He should have left then. Should have gone outside, run the perimeter wards, done anything but linger in the glow of what had just passed. But he didn't move. He stood there with his pulse still unsteady from the way she'd looked at him.

He'd told himself for months before she crossed that Veil that she was only a duty. A charge entrusted to him by Selene herself. That was the only reason she mattered. But something about that truth had begun to blur, and he could no longer tell whether the pull he felt was born of obligation or something else entirely. He ran a hand through his hair, trying to chase the thought away. It didn't work.

He made his way outside into the chill of the night. The forest around the bunker was quiet, but not still. The spells he'd cast along the perimeter shimmered faintly—lines of protective light weaving through the mist. He reached out and touched one, feeling its pulse answer the magic beneath his skin. The shadows around him stirred faintly, restless as they always were whenever he allowed himself to feel too much, but he pushed them back.

Control. That was the rule. Always control.

He'd been mastering that discipline since he could walk—his father had seen to it. A memory slipped through before he could stop it: the black marble floors of Raven Hollow's training chamber, the echo of boots, the sharp scent of metal. His father's voice, low and exacting. "Again, Nico. Again." The weight of command had been all he'd known. His mother's voice had been softer, but even she'd been bound by duty, her weaving of spells more graceful but no less precise.

Now, years later, he could still feel the same tension that had ruled every part of his childhood—the balance between obedience and rebellion, between shadow and light. The same balance that threatened to slip every time Leah looked at him like she wanted to understand him.

He'd stopped believing in innocence very young, after accompanying his father on missions and seeing what those missions truly were. Nico never let his mind wander too far back though, because when it did, the images came uninvited. He closed his eyes, the memories burning like salt. He'd long since buried those years, smothered them under discipline and distance. But lately, since Leah had arrived, the walls he'd built had begun to crack in small, traitorous ways.

He sank near the entrance to the bunker with his elbows braced on his knees. His hand still tingled faintly from where it had brushed hers earlier. He flexed it as if that might erase the memory. It didn't. He told himself it was the magic, not her. The residue of the Echodex. The way it warped the air between them. That was easier to believe than admitting what truly unsettled him.

The book had always been a myth within The Order. He remembered finding mention of it once in the archives, buried between ledgers of bloodlines and lost relics. A Seer's codex that remembered time itself. The few scholars who spoke of it called it a 'mirror of eternity'—a book that saw rather than recorded. He'd dismissed it then, like everyone else. Even the Seers of Raven Hollow had laughed at the notion that something so ancient could still exist, having not seen it for themselves. And yet here it was, in Leah's hands, answering her as if it had been waiting all along.

That realization unsettled him more than he wanted to admit. He rubbed a hand over his face and leaned back against the rock by the entrance with his eyes half-closed. The silence welcomed a feeling he hadn't known in a long time.

Guilt.

It coiled low in his chest. The image of Leah stumbling with blood blooming at her side, replayed again and again. He had frozen for only a moment—but it had been enough. Recognition of The Order's insignia and the face from a past he'd buried, had rooted him in place. And because of that hesitation, she'd been hurt.

His fists clenched until the leather of his gloves creaked, making the shadows around him stir, feeding on the storm inside him. He forced them still with a sharp breath. He could never let that happen again. Not to her.

Concern overtook the guilt. Had he cleaned the wound well enough? Had he missed corruption on the blade? She'd still been pale when he left her, still weak. The wound had taken more from her than she'd ever admit. She always tried to look composed, but her face betrayed her every time—every flicker of doubt, every attempt at bravery.

A faint chuckle escaped him. "Firecracker," he murmured.

She reminded him of Selene in her stubbornness and defiance, but Leah was different. Her defiance wasn't forged by power or certainty; it came from instinct—from the reckless need to protect even while bleeding. It made her unpredictable, and that unsettled him. She was the type to burn herself alive before showing weakness.

He exhaled and pushed the thought away. She'd need days before she could stand without wincing, longer before she could channel magic properly. He had decided that she would do light training only such as grounding exercises and focus work. Nothing beyond that. He'd considered blood magic, but like Seer magic, it was unstable, and with a wound like that—without knowing how blood magic truly worked—the risk was too high.

He told himself again that it wasn't emotion, it was precaution. Attachment was a weakness, and weakness got people killed. He had seen it. Caused it.

Still, even as he tried to steady himself, he could still feel her gaze burning into him. He stood abruptly, as if the act of moving could smother the feeling before it took root and made his way back down to the bunker, willing the memory of her out of his head.

He would have to keep his distance. But deep down, he already knew that distance was a lie. Because every time he closed his eyes, he could still feel the warmth of her hand brushing his. And for a man who had lived half his life in shadow, that warmth was the most dangerous thing of all.

Two weeks had passed since the attack, and each day felt like a careful negotiation between pain, recovery, and the discipline he demanded. Leah sat on the low bench in the bunker with her shoulders drawn back, the faint pink scar along her side no longer raw but still tender beneath his hands. He'd insisted on dressing it himself until she could do it properly, and the shift— from her initial hesitation to the way she no longer flinched at his touch—unsettled him more than he cared to admit.

Her skin was warm where his fingers brushed the healing cut, and the closeness of their bodies made him acutely aware of every breath she took. He forced himself to focus, securing the cloth with care, noting the slight catch in her breath whenever he adjusted the edges.

It wasn't difficult for him to see what was happening beneath her composure. Her flinches weren't pain anymore; they were awareness. He noted every tightening muscle and every shift of her body against his hands.

A small, almost predatory thrill ran through him. He liked the way she reacted, liked how her subtle movements betrayed her focus, her tension, her awareness of him. It made him want to linger, to trace the lines of her body, and to see how far he could push the teasing spark between them. The thought made his pulse quicken, sharpening the otherwise clinical motions of tending to her wound

Her eyes followed him constantly. Every time she adjusted her body and her waist pressed closer to him, he felt the urge to pause, to lean in, to feel more. But he restrained himself. It was healing. Precaution. Nothing else.

"You're doing well," he murmured, though his voice was loud in the quiet of the bunker. He rose to stand, bandages in hand, and then he noticed a tiny, pale leaf caught in her hair, tangled near her temple. He stopped, bending just enough so he was level with her eyes.

For a moment, he just looked at the leaf and the movement of her hair brushing against his gloved fingers before he reached out to remove it.

Their faces were suddenly close enough that he could feel the warmth of her breath and the faint scent of her skin. Her eyes widened, flicking to his with a mix of curiosity and restraint that made his chest tighten. She didn't pull away; her fingers hovered just above his hand, twitching as if unsure whether to move. That hesitation and silent permission was dangerous.

He cleared his throat, forcing himself to stand up again and to focus, though every instinct screamed against it.

"You'll be able to do this on your own soon," he said, his voice suddenly tight again.

Her eyes followed his hand when he offered it and for a moment, he almost saw disappointment in her eyes. She hesitated before taking it, but when she did, her palm was warm against his. He guided her carefully to her feet, supporting her as she tested her weight. The tension between them didn't fade. If anything, it settled deeper, day after day.

Nico tried to stay busy—drawing baths, preparing salves and keeping whatever she might need within reach. But all the while, he felt her eyes on him, tracking his movement. There was an ease there now, a willingness that hadn't existed two weeks ago that both thrilled and terrified him. She trusted him. Trusted him to touch her, to guide her, to manage the vulnerability she had been forced into. He could feel the weight of it and the danger inherent in that trust.

The days blurred into a rhythm of quiet movements and careful silences. Leah was healing too slowly for her liking, but too quickly for his peace of mind. Every morning, he found her trying to do something she wasn't supposed to: bending to reach the kettle, leaning too far when she thought he wasn't looking.

"Sit," he would mutter, and she'd shoot him that stubborn look that always made his jaw tighten.

"I'm not helpless," she'd insist.

"No," he'd reply, steady as a blade. "But you're not invincible either."

She would roll her eyes and sit anyway, pretending she was doing it by choice. He hated how much he admired her stubborn defiance and refusal to let weakness settle. Every day that passed, she would seem better. She'd learned to breathe through the pain and even managed to change her own bandages, though he still insisted on inspecting them.

"Still looks clean," he murmured one evening, kneeling beside her as she sat by the fire. "You're healing faster than expected."

"Maybe I'm just stubborn."

"You think stubbornness can stitch flesh?"

"It's worked so far."

Her laugh slipped into him like sunlight through a crack and disarmed him in a way that no magic ever had. He smiled before catching himself and as he reached for the edge of the bandage, she stilled. His fingers brushed her skin but she didn't pull away. When he looked up, he saw awareness in her eyes. Mutual and dangerous.

"Keep breathing," he said softly.

"I am," she whispered.

He forced himself to finish quickly. "That's it," he said, sitting back, needing the distance like air. But distance, as he had concluded early on, was nothing more than a lie.

Even during meals, the awareness persisted. The small brush of her hand when she passed him a cup. The soft sound she made when she laughed at something he said. Every little moment became a fracture in his control.

He started leaving the table early, offering quiet excuses about needing more firewood or checking their supplies. In truth, he just needed space. Room to breathe and steady himself before he let something slip.

But one night, she caught him off guard.

"Do I make you uncomfortable?" she asked as she headed toward the room.

He looked up slowly from the book he was reading and met her gaze.

"No," he said. "You make it... difficult to think."

Her lips parted, but he turned away before she could speak.

"Get some rest, Leah."

One evening, after he'd returned from outside the bunker, he found her with her head down on the table and a book half open beneath her fingers. A bolt of fear shot through him before he heard the steady, even rhythm of her breathing. She wasn't hurt, she had simply fallen asleep. The candle on the table flickered low, spilling its last light across her hair.

He stood there for a long moment as every muscle locked in hesitation. He should have let her sleep there. Should have draped a blanket over her and left. That would've been the right thing. The safe thing.

Instead, he moved closer.

Her lashes fluttered but didn't open. She looked impossibly young like this. Her fingers were still curled loosely around the edge of the book, as though holding onto a dream. He slid the book gently from beneath her hand and set it aside. Then, with a steady breath, he leaned down and lifted her.

She melted instinctively into him, her head settling against his shoulder as if her body recognized safety before her mind could. The shift drew a soft sound from her, half sigh, half word.

His name.

He froze. Her breath warmed his neck, and for a moment, he couldn't move. Every nerve pulled taut, protesting the closeness he wasn't supposed to want. Then, quietly, he forced himself forward, carrying her toward the small room.

The bed was already turned down. He set her down with deliberate care, letting go piece by piece, as if releasing her too quickly might wake her. Then, he pulled the blanket over her, tucking its edge beneath her arm. Her hair fanned across the pillow in a dark spill of softness, and before he could stop himself, he brushed one stray strand from her cheek.

"Rest," he whispered.

She stirred slightly, a faint smile flickering across her lips, one he didn't think she was aware of. He lingered longer than any sensible part of him approved of, standing in the dim glow with her quiet warmth filling the room.

When he finally turned to leave, he didn't look back. But as he pulled the door closed behind him, her peaceful breathing filtered through the crack. And for reasons he refused to admit, that sound unraveled him more than any blade or battlefield ever had.

Chapter 11

Snow blanketed the trees in silence causing pine boughs to sag under its weight. Nearly two months had passed since Leah had left Eldergrove behind, and the world outside Nico's hidden bunker had shifted from the crisp hues of autumn to the biting chill of winter. Somewhere beyond the secluded place they had called home, Christmas lights would be flickering in shop windows with the smell of cinnamon drifting thickly in the air. But here, at the quiet edge of the forest, time felt suspended and heavy, like the lull before a storm.

Her wound had healed quickly, though not without pain. Nico had tended to it daily until she insisted on doing it herself. The tension between them during those moments of close proximity became unbearable, to the point that it felt like its own quiet trial.

The training hadn't stopped though. If anything, it had deepened, especially after the first few weeks. What once felt like meaningless exercises now revealed their purpose. Her Seer magic no longer crashed over her without warning. She could sense it before a vision took over her, and she had learned to breathe through the tide and return without breaking. Still, she worried she had a long way to go.

So far, her visions had only touched non-living things: objects, places, and remnants of memory that carried little weight. Nothing compared to the storm that had torn through her the day she'd seen Nico's past. The memory of it still made her chest tighten, so she hadn't dared to ask to try again. Some part of her knew he wouldn't allow it, and another part wasn't sure she could bear it.

But no matter how hard she tried, the book had not opened for her again. Nico assumed it was because she lacked control, so for weeks he'd been teaching her how to harness it, grounding her emotions and containing the chaos inside so her magic wouldn't consume her. However, part of her wondered if the book was simply choosing silence.

As she continued to heal, their days began to blur together, filled with sparring, shielding, and meditation. Nico hadn't brought up blood magic again, choosing instead to focus on her Seer abilities while she recovered. The space between them had shrunk in subtle ways: shared meals, quiet conversations, the occasional brush of hands when passing a cup or a book. He never crossed a line, but she could feel the weight of his presence when he stood too close and the way he watched her when he thought she wasn't looking. Something unspoken simmered between them, growing more tangible by the day.

She wasn't sure when it happened, when she stopped feeling less like a guest and more like something that Nico hovered near, protective and watchful. Sometimes it was subtle, like the way he always stood between her and the door, and sometimes it wasn't.

Once, she'd stumbled during training, and his shadows had lashed out instinctively, knocking the target dummy clear across the forest. He'd muttered an apology, but she'd seen the way his hands shook afterward.

That protectiveness should have comforted her, but instead it left her uneasy. It made her aware of how small her world had become, and how her days began and ended with Nico. How his approval, his silence, and even his moods had started to shape her own. Somewhere along the way, she'd stopped thinking about Eldergrove, about her old life, and about Sage.

She tried once.

She asked Nico casually whether the Hollow had any way to reach the outside. "A phone, maybe? Just to check in?" She promised she wouldn't say anything she shouldn't, that she only wanted Sage to know she was alive. But Nico had only shaken his head. There were no cell phones in the Hollow.

She pressed further, hoping letters might work to bridge the distance, but Nico denied that too. Ink could be traced and messages could be intercepted. He reluctantly explained that no communication from inside the Hollow could ever reach anyone outside the Veil. The only way to contact someone beyond its boundaries would be to cross the Veil itself, and he wouldn't allow that. To her frustration, he didn't elaborate. He simply said no.

The realization hit harder than she expected, bringing with it a slow ache of guilt. She'd written pages for Sage while she recovered. The letters were folded neatly, with ink smudged where her hand had trembled. She'd told her everything: the visions, the fear, the way Nico both terrified and steadied her. But none of them would ever reach her. Nico had been blunt. No contact. No signal. The Order watched everything. And so, the letters sat in a box beneath the bed representing a growing archive of words she couldn't send, a tether to a life that felt further away with every passing day.

For weeks, the silence pressed in heavy. And then, as Leah's wound healed, something within the book began to stir. She noticed how its cover shimmered faintly now and then, but she chose to ignore it. The last vision it had shown her was still vivid in her mind, and she was afraid to see what it would reveal next. She hadn't told Nico about that vision, and she certainly hadn't told him she was ignoring the book's call.

During dinner one night, Nico mentioned they'd soon be moving their lessons to a different location. She stared at him, wide-eyed, as he added offhandedly that he'd begin teaching her how to defend herself with her magic. The word alone sent a thrill through her chest. Not just grounding techniques or deciphering visions pulled from objects, but actual defense. Real magic. She tried not to grin like a child promised fireworks, but she didn't quite succeed. Nico raised a brow, though he looked like he was fighting back a smile of his own.

Now, as she tried to sleep, her mind wouldn't slow. They already knew she had no elemental magic, which meant the only discipline available to her was blood magic. The thought made her anxious. She didn't know what it meant in practice, only that it was dangerous and forbidden.

The next morning, Nico led her up just before dawn, guiding her along a narrow, root-veiled path twisting away from the mossy ridge where the hidden entrance lay. The bunker beneath the earth already felt like a different world, sealed behind layers of stone and spellwork. Nico had given her a spare cloak that hung low on her frame given their height difference, but she was grateful for the extra warmth. The air stung her skin, and her breath clouded in front of her as she walked.

Nico stood a few paces ahead, arms folded, and eyes scanning the tree line as usual. He was wrapped in black, his shadows coiled close, ready at his command.

Leah stared at them warily as they faced each other.

"Don't look at the shadows," Nico said. "Look at me."

"I am looking at you, unfortunately."

He smirked. "Good. Keep that bite. You'll need it." His eyes flicked to the dagger in his hand. "You've learned to control your visions," he said, voice low and steady. "Now we move to something harder."

Leah crossed her arms. "Harder than nearly drowning in someone else's memories?"

"This is different." He stepped forward and held out the dagger. "Blood will be your anchor. Blood magic is powerful and effective for defense." His gaze dropped briefly to the blade. "You'll cut. Just a drop, and we'll go from there."

Her stomach knotted. She hated blood. Hated pain. But it was her only way to defend herself.

"What if I can't control it?"

"You won't. Not at first. But I'd rather teach you here than in the middle of a fight."

She stared at the dagger, hesitation buzzing through her veins. Something in his conviction steadied her despite the fear prickling her skin. She finally took it, noticing the weight and the cold bite of the metal in her palm. Nico stepped back with his shadows curling restlessly around him.

"Just a drop," he reminded her. "Then think of the strongest thing you've ever wanted to protect."

The branches underfoot crunched as Leah squared her stance, breath steaming in the icy air. She closed her eyes and slid the blade across her palm in one quick motion. Pain bloomed instantly, but she ignored it, forcing her focus inward. Nico circled her, his shadows moving like a dark echo.

"Focus," he said.

She shivered from the cold and concentrated, channeling her will into the blood trickling down her wrist. At first, it resisted, sluggish and uncooperative, slipping through her fingers. She gritted her teeth, forcing it to obey until a wobbling bead of blood lifted and hovered above her hand.

"Good," he said flatly. "Now shape it."

Her jaw clenched as she pushed the blood outward. It twisted, a trembling red tendril that slowly thickened, forming sharp edges. She opened her eyes. The shard pulsed faintly, unstable but solid. Her eyes, she realized, were glowing. Unlike her Seer magic, which felt like pressure, this felt like heat.

"That's it," she whispered, a thrill cutting through her growing exhaustion.

Nico's shadow lashed forward, sharp as a whip. "Defend."

The shard trembled violently as the shadow struck, heavy and fast. It split down the middle and collapsed before fully blocking the blow. Crimson droplets spattered the snow, hissing faintly. Leah staggered back, chest heaving, but the embers in her eyes burned brighter.

"Again," Nico said, stepping closer. His presence was tense but measured, a tether between danger and control. "Shape it again. Make it stay."

Leah snarled, determination coiling in her chest. She let anger, fear, and stubborn defiance weave together. The blood obeyed, thickening into a short, jagged blade. The shadows lunged again, but this time, the blade held, slicing cleanly through the darkness and dispersing it like smoke.

She staggered as adrenaline and relief collided within her. She looked to Nico, expecting criticism, but he only inclined his head.

"Not perfect," he said. "But it's progress."

Her lips curved despite herself. "I'll make it perfect."

He didn't respond, only circled her, with his shadows twitching at his heels.

"You need control, not just power. Blood obeys intent. Panic, and it turns on you. Hesitate, and it fails."

Leah nodded, gripping the blade as heat coursed through her fingers. The red weapon was both terrifying and intoxicating.

"Again," Nico said. "Until it's instinct."

The blade collapsed back into a bead of blood. Leah inhaled slowly, letting the cold air steady her pulse. The blood rose again and her eyes glowed red and steady once again. The shadow lunged, and this time she didn't flinch. The deflection was clean.

Nico's jaw flexed. "Good. Now don't just hold it. Move it."

She blinked. "Move it? How?"

"You guide it," he said, stepping back, watching her with sharp, piercing focus. "Think of it as an extension of your arm."

Grounding herself, Leah willed the blood to rise and she was pleased to see that it hovered steadily now. She tilted her wrist and the blood followed, rotating and dipping in perfect sync. Her eyes flared brighter and exhilaration surged through her.

"Good," Nico said. "Now shape it. Defend yourself."

A jagged shadow spike lunged toward her. Leah reacted on instinct, flattening the blood into a blade to parry the strike. Red and black collided with a hiss making her legs wobble, but she held.

"Steady your breathing," Nico said. "Let the magic follow. Don't chase it."

She inhaled sharply, forcing every shred of emotion into control. The blood flared crimson, forming twin daggers that hummed with raw power. She deflected another strike, then another, feeling unstoppable.

Then Nico moved.

The shadows thickened, twisting like living chains and wrapping around her arms and waist. They lifted her off the ground and pinned her to the rough bark of a tree. Her daggers spun wildly before dissolving as her control broke.

Her pulse thundered. "Nico," she gasped, struggling against the shadows that held her and the sudden closeness of him.

He stepped closer, deliberate and measured. The shadows tightened, pressing her chest flush to his. She felt his heat through the magic— the weight of his gaze, and the air vibrating with power and something far more dangerous.

"Focus," he murmured, low and commanding. He was so close the words brushed against her ear. "Feel it, but do not let it rule you."

Every fiber of her being screamed with the thrill of magic and the pressure of him. Her stomach twisted, her pulse spiked, and she realized the truth: if she let emotion completely control her, her magic would consume her. She had to hold it back. She had to master it.

Her legs kicked against the hold of his shadows as she attempted to re-form the blood daggers, but they faltered, dissolving before her eyes. Nico's shadows held her firmly and she could feel the exact line of his chest against hers, the subtle press of his knee near her side, and the taut restraint in his arms. Every inch of him pressed into her awareness, and every subtle movement he made was mirrored in the shadows restraining her. The tension radiating from him set her nerves alight, making her pulse race faster than the thrum of magic in her veins.

He leaned even closer, the warmth of his body pressing fully into hers. The shadowed hand hovering near her waist made her shiver. Her chest fluttered, and a new kind of heat began spreading through her. The air between them was taut, and alive with the magnetic pull of proximity and the danger of desire.

For a moment, the world narrowed to him, to the shadows, and to the fierce, intoxicating pulse of magic that neither of them could deny. Her breath hitched as she felt the weight of him, heat brushing against her—the almost-touch, the magnetic pull that made her tremble. Then his voice cut through the haze, sharp and commanding.

"Control, Leah! Your magic obeys you. Not the other way around!"

The words struck her, grounding her just enough to force her focus. She struggled, as her legs continued kicking against the shadows holding her down while her blood daggers flickered weakly. Nico's control was absolute, but not cruel. He was teaching her and showing her the thin boundary between surrendering to power and mastering it.

She could feel the tension in his body and the restraint it cost him, and a flicker of heat bloomed in her chest in response—thrill and fear colliding. Her heartbeat pounded in her ears as she fought the shadows, acutely aware of the electricity between them and the dangerous edge of his proximity.

Nico leaned closer, and her stomach coiled with heat. The shadows tightened just enough to force her to fight harder, to confront the surge of power in her veins. Every inch of her body was alight—alive with raw magic, struggle, and tension.

Then, deliberately, he released her just enough for her to land on the ground. Her knees wobbled and her chest heaved, blood still singing in her veins. Her hands shook, and her daggers flickered but did not fully reform.

He stepped back, and his shadows followed, retreating, though the space between them remained charged. He turned then, and his dark eyes held hers.

"You learned something today," he said. "Control comes first. Master that before anything else."

Leah nodded, still trembling, aware of the lingering heat, the pulse of her magic, and the closeness that had left her chest fluttering. She understood, finally, that the lesson had been as much about restraint—his and hers—as it had been about power. And though neither would speak it aloud, she had felt the dangerous electricity of what could have happened if he hadn't held back.

She took a shuddering breath, and Nico caught the falter in her stance and the uneven rhythm of her breathing. Her magic was feeding on her—too much, too fast. His expression hardened as the shadows retreated fully around him.

"Enough for now. You've done well."

She fell to her knees and exhaled, letting what remained of the blades dissolve back into her blood, and forcing her heartbeat to slowly return to normal. The red glow in her eyes faded gradually, leaving a faint shimmer as she tried to catch her breath. The forest was quiet around them; only the soft scrape of wind through the pine branches broke the stillness.

Leah stayed kneeling in the snow until the burn in her chest dulled. Her breath curled upward and vanished in the frozen air. She forced her hands to unclench, watching the red stains fade back into her skin as the cut began to coagulate. When she finally looked up, Nico was already moving. He crouched near his bag, pulling out a small tin and a battered cup. Snow hissed softly as he melted it over a small fire he started which was enough to heat the metal. The scent of crushed herbs filled the clearing before he poured the steaming liquid and offered it to her.

"Drink."

Heat seeped into her chilled fingers making Leah grimace at the bitter taste before a faint floral aftertaste softened the edge. Warmth spread down her throat, settling in her stomach, and muscles she hadn't realized were trembling began to ease.

"What is it?" she asked, voice hoarse.

"Winter root," Nico said simply, leaning back against a tree. "It stabilizes the blood."

She raised a brow, eyeing him over the rim of the cup. "You always know what to use. It's like you've done this before."

His gaze remained fixed on the tree line as shadows shifted faintly. "I have," he said finally.

Leah tilted her head, unsatisfied with the blunt answer. "How do you know about all the different kinds of magic? Blood, Seer, Elemental—you talk like you've studied them your whole life."

His eyes flicked to her. "Because I have."

He didn't elaborate, but the words carried weight, like stone dropped into a well. Leah could feel it—an entire life carved out in secrecy. She tightened her grip on the cup. The tea was almost gone, but its warmth lingered in her veins, chasing off the cold. She hesitated, then tried again, softer.

"The Order."

Nico's expression stiffened, and for a moment the shadows around him coiled tighter, betraying the tension beneath his calm. He didn't deny it. Instead, he exhaled slowly.

"They train you to know everything. Every kind of magic you might face. Every weakness you can exploit."

The sun had risen higher, but the wind felt colder. Leah debated whether to keep pushing, there was still so much she wanted to know.

"But you said there were no other Seers or people with blood magic. How did you learn about them?"

"I read," Nico said flatly. "And I listened. The Order hoards knowledge, even when it's inconvenient truth. There are always whispers and histories passed down by those who knew someone before their line disappeared."

Leah stared at her empty cup. Read about them? It felt surreal. She'd grown up reading about extinct animal species, never expecting to think of her own bloodline the same way.

"You mentioned before that you led them to believe you were dead," she continued. "How did you manage that?"

Nico's eyes locked on hers. The look held her still, as if weighing every word. Her pulse quickened, afraid she'd crossed another invisible boundary, but he didn't shut her out this time.

"I was raised within The Order," he said. His voice was quiet and steady, though his gaze slid away, lost in memory. "My father was a high-ranking commander of the stealth division. My mother was a trusted spell weaver who could amplify the strength of others around her. I told you once my magic is rare. Shadow binding. To The Order, I was the perfect weapon. Shadow magic is deadly and useful, so I was trained under my father in stealth."

Leah forced herself to stay perfectly still, afraid the smallest movement might remind him he hadn't meant to share this.

"I was considered a prodigy," Nico continued, eyes narrowing faintly as if the words themselves burned. "I became the leader of a stealth squad at the age of seven."

Leah's eyes widened. A seven-year-old child, trained and molded into something lethal. Her heart raced as she listened, torn between fury and grief.

"When I wasn't training," he went on, voice dropping lower, "I was in the archives, reading the history of other magical Pillars—hybrids and others who wielded abilities no longer seen. My father's magic was rare too, steel-binding. It drove me to wonder why such magic was disappearing and why our world was splintering."

He fell silent though his shadows continued to coil faintly at his heels. Leah swallowed hard, staring at him. The words already felt like too much, like he was opening a wound deliberately.

"When I was eight," he continued, "I was tasked with a mission to eradicate a village."

His gaze snapped back to hers, sharp as a blade, searching her face as if bracing for revulsion. Leah held his gaze, though her pulse hammered.

"I was forced to kill someone who meant a great deal to me." The shadows stirred, restless, as if they also remembered.

Leah swallowed. "Who?"

For a moment, she thought he wouldn't answer. Then his tone softened.

"His name was Archie." His fingers brushed the bracelet on his wrist. "We trained together. Stole hours in the night when my father wasn't watching. He was one of the few who made me forget what I was meant to be. We sparred, played games, talked about leaving The Order someday." His eyes darkened. "He reminded me I was still a kid."

Leah gripped the empty cup tighter.

"A few days before the mission, my father was called to see The Order's leader multiple times. Rumors spread about a couple breaking the law. My father was tasked with finding them, and our leader decided to make an example of them. The punishment was death—every Pillar tied to the betrayal would pay for it."

"Different squads were sent across the Hollows that week. When mine was called, it was for Riven Hollow, home to those with blood magic."

"My mission was clear. Infiltrate the Hollow. Kill every inhabitant." His voice thinned. "My father's right hand came with us. He was there when I found Archie."

Nico stopped, his body tensing as if the memory itself cut him open.

"I did what I was tasked to do," he said quietly, "and I was... praised for it." Confusion and disbelief shadowed his expression.

Leah's throat tightened and she tried to scramble for words in her mind, but she found none.

"That was the moment," Nico went on, almost a whisper, "the moment I knew I couldn't do that anymore. I couldn't be a pawn, a weapon used for their benefit, for things that didn't make sense—even to a child. So, I found a boy close to my height and build who had already been killed. I burned the body and left enough evidence to make my death believable, then I disappeared."

At last, his eyes lifted to hers. No shield. No mask. Just rawness that almost hurt to look at. Leah set the cup down carefully in the snow.

"Nico..."

He looked away, shoulders stiffening as if bracing himself. Leah swallowed against the lump in her throat.

"You carry this like it's your fault," she said softly, stopping before her voice could break. "Like you chose any of it. But I don't see a weapon when I look at you." Her breath misted in the cold. "I'm sorry, Nico. I'm so sorry you went through that."

His eyes lifted again, darker than she'd ever seen them, with something fragile buried beneath. He looked at her as if he couldn't believe she hadn't recoiled. Leah held his gaze though her heart was aching. It wasn't just a story. It was a wound he'd opened for her to see.

Nico broke the silence. "We should head back. It looks like it's going to snow." He brushed tiny flurries from his cloak.

Leah rose, tucking her hands into her sleeves. The air felt heavier, and it was not just from the cold. Neither spoke as they walked back through the snow, the pale light bleeding orange across the horizon.

She glanced at him once, wondering if he regretted telling her, but when the bunker entrance came into view, Nico slowed just enough for her to walk beside him. A small, almost imperceptible gesture.

They descended together as the last of the daylight faded, leaving the forest to its shadows.

Chapter 12

The bunker felt colder as they walked down the stairs. Nico set his satchel near the fireplace and hurried to start a fire, trying to add warmth back into the space. He pulled his cloak tighter around his shoulders and, without looking at Leah, started back up the stairs.

"I'll find food," he said, his voice flat. "Stay and rest."

Leah only nodded, though her chest felt heavy from everything he had confessed. She watched him disappear up the stairs, his footsteps fading until only the crackle of the fire remained, then she exhaled slowly. Her body was exhausted, but her mind was wide awake, reeling from finally getting to know more about him. Somehow, the closeness they had shared in that moment seemed to vanish, leaving her restless, yearning, and alone.

Leah paced through the main room, staring at the books that lined the entire wall across from the fireplace. Some of them looked old and fragile, yet they were meticulously cared for. She couldn't help but notice how clean the space was. She half expected the books to have at least a thin layer of dust on them, but everything looked immaculate. The shelves held volumes on everything from Binding spells to Elemental Magic to the History of The Order. That last one intrigued her the most.

She pulled it from the shelf and leafed through it. It resembled many of the typical books given in school—the ones that offered only the briefest overview of its subject while hiding all the dirty details. Leah set it aside and continued browsing Nico's personal library.

At the end of the third shelf, a smaller, mismatched book caught her attention. It looked more like a personal notebook than a formal textbook. Curiosity got the better of her, and she reached for it, flipping through the pages haphazardly. Scribbles filled the margins in a flowing hand—corrections and notes she assumed were Nico's. As she turned another page, a folded piece of paper slipped free and landed on the stone floor.

Leah stopped, staring at the spot where it had fallen. Something told her she shouldn't go any further, that this was crossing another line she wasn't meant to cross, but she couldn't stop herself. She placed the notebook on the round table absentmindedly and focused on the folded paper on the floor before reaching for it. It was covered in small, messy scribbles that were scratched out, while others nearly illegible. Leah glanced toward the narrow stairs and listened, straining to hear if Nico was returning, but there was only the sound of the crackling fire.

Her fingers trembled as she unfolded the paper on the counter—and froze. It was a map. At least, she thought it was. Hand-drawn, with the same scribbled style she'd seen on the reverse, ink lines sprawled outward, circling a dark blot at the center: Raven Hollow. Four territories stretched away like compass points—Roots Hollow to the west, Riven Hollow to the far north, Mask Hollow in the east, and Ashmere Hollow to the south. Each was paired with another name written in smaller, slanted script which read: Eldergrove, Birchgrove, Maplegrove, and Oakgrove respectively.

Her pulse quickened as she realized that the world was larger than she'd ever imagined, and her home was only a fragment of something vast. Her fingers hovered over the map, and a shimmer stirred at the edges of the ink. Purple light flickered in her eyes as her Seer magic tugged at her vision before she could resist it. The piece of parchment rippled, but the room did not dissolve entirely.

Leah looked around. She was still inside the bunker, but it was a ghost of its current form. She stood at the entrance of the bunker's sole room, looking out into the main space. There, a single bookshelf held no more than ten books. A young boy with dark hair and bright blue eyes crouched in front of the fireplace, scribbling frantically on parchment spread across the floor—the map.

Leah narrowed her eyes, as if focusing might sharpen the image. She took a step closer toward the boy, certain she recognized that dark hair and those blue eyes anywhere.

"I think this should do for now, Nico."

Leah's soul nearly left her body as the voice caught her off guard. A woman walked toward Nico, passing straight through Leah from behind. Leah spun toward the room the woman had come from, then back to them both. Nico looked up with frustration on his face, and Leah stared, unaware she was holding her breath.

The woman's hair, the way she carried herself, her soft voice—it was undeniable.

Selene.

"The spells around this bunker have been reinforced," Selene said. "They are strong. I trust that with them, and with yours, you won't have anything to worry about."

Nico's attention left the map as he looked up at her, his face trying, and failing, not to betray the hurt it showed.

"So, you won't be visiting anymore?"

"You know as well as I do what The Order will do if they find us. I will fulfill my promise, just as you have promised to fulfill yours."

Nico's gaze dropped back to the map, perhaps to hide the emotion in his eyes. "And Leah?"

As if on cue, Leah heard a small grunt from the room behind her, but she was too shocked to turn around. Selene crouched and placed a gentle hand on Nico's shoulder before turning to look directly at Leah.

Leah's heart skipped.

Selene met her gaze, smiled softly, then turned back to Nico.

"She'll be kept safe. Away from all this. You know where to find us. I made a promise to your mother too, and I never break my promises."

Nico rose to his feet beside Selene. "You still believe safety is possible under his reign? Ezren won't stop until every trace of what he fears is erased. You know that."

"I know," Selene said calmly, though a sharp edge crept into her tone. "But if you're going to kill him, Nico... do it for the right reasons."

Nico's face hardened and Leah saw the shadows gathering faintly around his shoulders, responding to the emotion he tried to bury. "There are no right reasons left."

Selene looked away, sorrow flickering across her features. "Then do it for her," she whispered, nodding toward the small cradle in the room. "Besides," she added, turning to look at Leah once more, "he doesn't even know she exists."

A sharp intake of breath snapped Leah back into herself. She staggered against the stone counter with her heart practically pounding out of her chest. The shimmer faded from the map, leaving the ink flat and ordinary. She folded it quickly and slid it back into the notebook, then returned the notebook to the shelf as guilt and faintness washed over her.

All the training she'd done with her Seer magic felt insignificant compared to the weight of this vision—or the weight of stepping into someone else's past. It left her instantly drained.

Footsteps on the stairs snapped her out of it. She hurried to the armchair and fixed her gaze on the fire, pretending she'd been doing that all along. Nico appeared at the top of the stairs with a small bundle of supplies tucked under his arm. Snowflakes clung to his cloak, which hung heavy over his shoulders.

"Food," he said flatly, setting the bundle on the countertop. He didn't look at her, and Leah could feel the lingering tension from their earlier conversation.

Leah tore off a piece of bread, but it stuck dry in her throat. Selene's voice replayed in her mind along with the sharp edge in it when Ezren's name was spoken. She wanted to ask Nico what he knew, but his silence as he moved about the room made the words shrivel.

Instead, her gaze drifted toward the entrance of the bunker.

"Don't you get tired of this?" The words slipped out before she could stop them. "Of hiding down here? You said there was a town nearby—Roots Hollow, wasn't it?"

Nico sat, taking a piece of bread for himself. "I've gone into town before, but not often."

"Why not?"

"You forget," he said without looking up. "Most people think I'm dead."

Leah frowned. "Yeah, but that's The Order. What does that have to do with people in the Hollow?"

His eyes finally lifted to meet hers. He didn't answer, but the weight in his gaze said enough.

Leah huffed, frustration prickling in her chest. "I grew up believing Eldergrove was the only place I would ever know. And now I'm suddenly introduced to this magical world I still know almost nothing about. I just want to see it for myself—"

"We can't," Nico said simply. "You're forgetting who you are, too. How do you think the villagers will react if you use your magic in public?"

"I won't," she said quickly, leaning forward. "I promise. I won't."

"No, Leah." His jaw tightened in the way it often did when she was starting to push his buttons. "It's too dangerous. We already have The Order trailing us. Going into the village is a much faster way to get us found."

Leah looked away in frustration while heat began rising in her cheeks. Words crowded her throat, but she forced them down. Maybe it was the guilt over snooping, or the cabin fever pressing in around her, that was ready to push her over the edge. The fire crackled, echoing the anger and disappointment burning in her chest.

"When I was little," she said at last, attempting to steady her emotions. "Selene kept me close. Too close sometimes. She let me play in the woods behind the house, but never far. When I started school, I didn't have many friends because everyone thought she was odd. She didn't let me visit friends after school. I thought it was normal… that everyone grew up like that."

Her hand tightened around the crust of bread until it crumbled. "She meant everything to me. She was kind and wise." Her voice wavered, then steadied. "But she sheltered me so much that I feel like I've been walking blind my whole life. Now the world is suddenly bigger and darker, and I don't know how to step into it without getting lost."

Nico didn't answer right away. His expression softened, though the hardness never fully left his eyes.

Leah glanced at him. "Sometimes I wonder if she protected me so much that I never learned how to protect myself."

"She did what she thought was best for you."

"And how do you know that?" Leah snapped. "How do you even know Selene?"

Nico stilled, firelight catching in his eyes. For a long moment, he said nothing, and the silence only sharpened her anger.

"You've been hiding something," she pressed. "I saw you—in a vision. You were here with her. With me!" Her voice cracked. "Why didn't you tell me?"

His shoulders tightened and his shadows began curling faintly along the edges of the room, reacting to her anger. "Because it wasn't my truth to tell."

"Not your truth?" Leah scoffed. "It was my life. I knew you knew Selene somehow, but you never told me you knew me, too." Her hands curled into fists. "How am I supposed to trust you when you keep things like this from me?"

Nico's shoulders sagged, and some of the steel in his expression finally gave way. He leaned back, the fight leaving him in a slow breath.

"Selene saved me," he said quietly. His gaze was as unreadable as ever as it drifted to the flames. "After I faked my own death, I had nowhere to go. If I wanted to vanish, I had to become nothing. A shadow. Selene was the only person left I could trust."

Leah shook her head, though her anger was already fraying. "But why Selene? How did you even know her?"

"She was one of my mother's friends," Nico said quietly. "She told me once that if I was ever lost, Selene would be the one to help me. So when I ran...I went to her." His words lingered for a moment, as if holding back another terrible memory. "When I found Selene, I had been wandering for weeks, surviving off whatever I could find in the forest around Raven Hollow. She shielded me and nursed me back to health."

His gaze drifted around the bunker, though he wasn't really looking at anything. "This place... she built it for me so I would have somewhere safe to hide."

"A few weeks after I recovered, she came back here shaken. She was pacing. Restless. She wouldn't tell me what was wrong— only that her time with me was coming to an end and that she had to fulfill a promise she'd made. She left in a rush that night, and when she returned..." His eyes met Leah's. "You were with her."

A sharp ache pressed against her ribs as the visions she'd seen flickered to life in her mind.

"We worked together, in our own ways," he continued. "She had ties within the Pillars—people who wanted The Order stopped but lacked the strength to act. I became her eyes and ears, gathering information about The Order and its leader. After she came back with you, she decided it was safest to hide in Eldergrove—hide her power, and hide you."

He shifted, his voice softening. "I went there a few times. To see her. To see you. You were so small. She asked me not to visit while you were awake—she wanted you free of all of this. No shadows. No magic. Just a childhood." He hesitated, a rare flicker of guilt crossing his face. "But I still went. I kept watch. Made sure you were safe."

"As you grew up, Selene swore me to silence each time I visited. She reminded me that your path couldn't be touched until it had to be—that if you grew up under the weight of the truth, it would break you before you ever had a chance."

Leah shook her head. "So instead, she just left me to walk blind?"

"She thought it was protection," Nico said sharply, then softened again. "Toward the end, she told me more. About her promise. About her death. She knew it was coming, Leah. She saw it as clearly as she saw you."

The words struck deep. "She knew she was going to die, and she still wouldn't tell me?"

"I argued with her," Nico said. "But Selene wouldn't bend. Every time, she made me swear not to interfere until the time came."

"And you obeyed her."

"Yes." His eyes met hers with unflinching steadiness. "Because I owed her everything. And because she asked me to protect you."

"Protection is a little bit of a stretch," Leah bit out. "I'm having a hard time swallowing the fact that either of you thought my destiny was in anyone's hands but my own." Her voice cracked, half laugh, half fury. "So you don't get to say that. Neither of you do. You kept me blind while the world was moving against me. Do you have any idea what that feels like?"

Nico didn't flinch. "I know exactly what that feels like."

"Then why?" she demanded. "You and Selene decided I couldn't handle the truth—that I was too fragile, too... breakable. *You* made that choice for me."

For a moment, the fire snapped louder than either of them spoke.

"If The Order had even suspected you were alive, they would have killed you long ago, before you had any way to protect yourself," Nico said. "It wasn't about fragility, Leah. It was about survival."

Leah looked away as frustration tightened her throat. The thought that her entire life had been built on a lie—and that her grandmother had been behind it—hurt less than the idea that others had decided what she was capable of.

"I am not weak," she said softly.

"I know you're not," Nico replied. "And if Selene were here to see how far you've come these past few weeks, she might just kick herself for being so protective."

Leah didn't turn, so he continued. "I know this is hard to hear, but I promise you...everything Selene did was to keep you safe. To give you a normal life... even if you'd hate her for it."

A long silence stretched between them. Finally, Leah whispered, "I know."

Tears slipped down her cheeks, and this time she didn't wipe them away. She let them fall, letting herself grieve openly for the first time since Eldergrove.

The release hit her all at once and for a moment, she couldn't speak and couldn't look at him—couldn't do anything except breathe through the ache she'd kept buried for weeks.

When she finally lifted her head, the fire had burned down to a low, steady glow, and the shadows shifted along the walls. Nico's voice broke the quiet.

"You should try to rest. Tomorrow we can go out and get some real food."

Leah dragged the back of her hand across her eyes, not bothering to hide the redness around them. "I'm not tired." She argued, leaning back and staring into the fire until her breathing evened out.

"You and Selene," she murmured. "You really thought keeping me in the dark was the only way?"

"No," he said quietly. "But she didn't see another one."

That answer didn't satisfy her, but she didn't have the strength to keep arguing. She let out a small breath and stood, heading toward the bedroom.

"Next time," she said softly, "if there's something I should know... just tell me."

Nico's gaze lingered on her. Then he gave a single, reluctant nod. "Next time."

It wasn't forgiveness, but it was all she could manage.

That night, Leah couldn't sleep. The shadows on the walls shifted even after the fire burned down to embers. Nico was somewhere outside—he always disappeared after their talks, as if honesty left him raw and needing space to close himself back up.

She had more questions than ever as she sat cross-legged on the bed with the Echodex in front of her. But instead of trying to call out to it, she hesitated, deciding it was best to set it aside and lay down for now.

Unlike previous nights, sleep came gently, like a tide pulling her under. Soon, the world blurred into color and sound. Leah found herself standing in a meadow bathed in pale light. The sky shimmered like morning after rain, and the air was cool and faintly scented with lavender. For a long time, she simply sat, letting the peace sink in which was something she hadn't felt in weeks.

"You're tired," a voice said.

Leah turned. A girl stood a few paces away, barefoot in the grass. She looked a few years younger than Leah, with loose blond hair and deep brown eyes.

"Who are you?" Leah asked.

The girl smiled faintly. "Someone who knows what it's like to feel alone."

Leah's throat tightened. "This is a dream."

"Maybe," the girl said softly, stepping closer. "Sometimes dreams are where we meet the parts of ourselves we've been trying to forget."

"You've been so brave," she continued. "Even when they kept the truth from you. That kind of betrayal leaves the kind of scars that no one else can see."

Leah frowned. "How do you know that?"

The girl tilted her head. "Because I can feel it. You dreamed me here, after all."

"Who are you?"

"V." The name fell from her lips like a secret. "You can call me V."

"V," Leah repeated.

V sat beside her, gazing out at the meadow. "I like this world you're dreaming of. It's peaceful."

Leah glanced around, then back at her. "So you're part of me?"

"Maybe," V said, a teasing glint in her eyes. "Maybe the part that remembers what you've forgotten."

The meadow rippled, and Leah felt herself being pulled free of the vision, leaving only V's soft smile behind.

Leah gasped awake with Nico beside her.

"We have to move, Leah," he said with a voice that was calm but edged with urgency. "Something tried to breach the protective spells."

She blinked. "What? I thought you said this place was protected—"

"It was," Nico replied, glancing at the entrance. He murmured a spell under his breath and magic shimmering faintly before fading. "But protections can falter. I'm not risking you. Whatever it was, it was close."

Her blood ran cold. "Do you think it's them again?"

He nodded once. "They're not here yet, but they're close enough."

He pressed his palm to the wall across from the bed and a low rumble echoed as part of the stone receded, revealing a narrow tunnel.

Leah stared. "You had an escape route this whole time?"

"I always have an escape route," Nico said. His voice was steady, but tension threaded his posture.

"Get what you need. We need to move now."

Leah pulled on her borrowed cloak and gloves, grabbed her bag, and secured the Echodex inside before stepping into the dark after him.

The forest lay hushed beneath fresh snow. Moonlight fractured through the trees, glinting off frozen branches and casting long, shifting patterns across the frost-laced ground. Every rustle felt too loud, every breath too fast. Leah stayed close behind Nico as they wove between the trees.

He moved swiftly, silent and alert. One hand stayed loose at his side while his fingers twitched as if brushing against unseen magic. They hadn't spoken since leaving the bunker. Whatever had disturbed the spells had definitely shaken him.

After what felt like an hour, Nico slowed and raised a hand. Leah stopped, her pulse drumming in her ears. He crouched beside a snow-dusted ridge, pressing his palm to the stone.

"We're clear for now," he murmured.

Leah exhaled. "What was that back there? Did they actually find us?"

Nico scanned the woods before answering. "I don't know how, but something, or someone, breached the perimeter. That means someone either knew where to look... or they're tracking you now."

"Me?" Her pulse spiked. "How?"

"Magic leaves residue," he said. "Especially forbidden magic. It could've left a trail."

The cold felt sharper against her skin.

"We need shelter," Nico said, stepping closer. "There's a safe zone a few miles east. One I hope they haven't found yet."

Leah nodded.

"Stay close," he added quietly. "Don't speak unless I ask. If I say run..." His gaze locked on hers. "You run."

A shiver ran through her, but she met his eyes. The distance between them remained, but it was edged now with something fiercely protective.

"Okay," she murmured.

And with barely a breath between them, they disappeared back into the dark.

Chapter 13

Their steps sank quietly into the fresh snow, leaving soft, clear prints in the silence of the forest. Frost-laced branches reached down like skeletal arms, snagging at Leah's sleeves as she followed. Leah's legs ached, but she didn't complain. Nico hadn't stopped since the snow-dusted ridge, and she knew better than to ask when they would.

At last, they reached a twisted arch of trees whose trunks bowed and knotted like clasped hands straining toward one another. Snow clung to the warped bark, shimmering faintly in the moonlight. It looked like nothing—just another tangled thicket—but as they stepped beneath it, Leah felt the change immediately. The air around them cooled, but not in the same biting way as the open forest.

She paused. "What is this place?"

"A forgotten grove," Nico said. "Hidden with old spells. Most wouldn't even see it." He ran a hand along one of the trees as they passed, and Leah could almost feel the pulse of energy beneath the bark.

She looked around. The trees formed a near-perfect circle, their roots braided tightly at the base. In the center, half-buried in snow and vine, sat a sunken stone structure with moss clinging stubbornly to its cracks. It looked like a ruin.

"This was a sanctuary," Nico said, nodding toward the half-sunken stone structure. "Before The Order claimed the region.

Now it's more of a... shadow pocket. It seems they haven't found it. Yet."

He crouched and pressed his palm to one of the cold, snow-speckled stones. His lips moved in a quiet murmur before a faint shimmer traced a circle into the snow-covered moss, then faded.

Leah watched him, curious. "What did you do?"

"A binding spell," he replied without looking at her. "It'll mask our presence from anyone searching."

A faint shift in the stone wall made a seam glow softly, and a section of stone slid aside, revealing a narrow passage just wide enough to step through. Inside, the space was small—no bigger than a single room, carved entirely from stone. A fireplace was set into the far wall, and a bundle of blankets sealed in waxed cloth rested nearby. Nico lit the fire, which soon settled into a deep, ember-like glow—bright enough to see and to make the space feel a little less haunted.

Leah sank onto a flat stone near the fire, wrapping a blanket around herself. She hadn't realized how cold she was until the stillness returned and she noticed how her fingers trembled slightly in her lap. Nico remained standing, scanning the entrance one last time before turning to her. His eyes flicked to her hands and the small tremor she hadn't meant to show.

Without a word, he crouched beside the fire and reached into the sack, pulling free another blanket which was thicker than the one she had. He hesitated, then crossed the space between them and draped it over her shoulders, brushing her arms through the fabric.

"It looks like you're freezing," he said quietly.

Leah didn't move. The warmth of his closeness stunned her more than the cold and she found herself staring into the low flames as if in a trance. "Do you think The Order really knows where we are?"

"I think they're close," Nico said. "But this grove will confuse their trackers, at least for tonight. After that..." His lips pressed into a thin line. "We move again."

Leah nodded, exhaustion pulling at her bones. "I wish you could just teach me how to disappear."

He looked at her for a long moment, something conflicting and distant clouding his gaze, before his hand moved slowly and brushed a stray lock of hair from her cheek.

"I will," he said.

Leah blinked, caught off guard by the gentleness in him and the warmth behind the armor. She wanted to say something, to ask what that look in his eyes meant, if it meant anything at all. But the moment passed, and he was already rising, retreating into the shadows beyond the firelight. She stayed where she was, wrapped in two blankets and the ghost of his touch, unable to shake the chill now rooted somewhere deeper than skin.

Her eyelids grew heavy as she settled back against the stone wall, the warmth from the fire helping to bleed the adrenaline from her body after another narrow escape. Just as she teetered on the edge of sleep, a tiny pinprick of light caught her eye. It hovered near the narrow entrance, smaller than the palm of her hand, but bright and impossible to miss.

She tilted her head, squinting. The light drifted slowly, almost lazily, before settling onto the snow beside the stone threshold. For a moment, she frowned, confused. It was too small to mean anything and too fragile to pose a threat. She shook her head, telling herself she must be imagining things.

But Nico noticed the shift in her expression. "What is it?" he asked with a tone that was already alert.

"Nothing," she murmured, though her voice caught as her stomach fluttered.

The light dimmed as she blinked before movement at the entrance made her gasp.

A black wolf emerged, sleek and strange, its body wreathed in smoke, translucent at the edges. Its eyes burned an intense, piercing blue. It stepped inside with casual confidence, making Leah's chest tighten as she pressed herself against the wall, every nerve firing.

The wolf glanced briefly at her before moving toward Nico, utterly unbothered. Nico was still seated by the fire as recognition crossed his face, and then a low laugh escaped him— a sound Leah had never heard.

The wolf stopped in front of him, lowering its head to press its forehead gently against Nico's. Leah could do nothing but stare, not understanding what was going on or why Nico was allowing this being to get so close to him. The wolf's eyes closed calmly, as if communicating without words.

"Thanks bud," Nico said before giving it a gentle pet. Then, just as suddenly as it had appeared, the wolf's form wavered, melting into mist and shadow before being absorbed into Nico's ring.

Leah's mouth fell open. Her brows furrowed as her eyes flicked to the spot where it had vanished.

"What the hell was that?" she demanded even though her voice was trembling.

Nico's lips twitched, and another quiet laugh slipped out. Just hearing him laugh made her head spin.

"I—I mean, seriously," she stammered. "That smoke-wolf thing just strolled in here like it owned the place! And you're laughing? Are you insane?"

"Not insane," he said, amused. "Merely entertained."

"Entertained?!" Leah echoed. "You think it's funny that a translucent wolf with eyes like frozen lightning just showed up and—"

"—and scared you half to death?" Nico cut in with a smirk. "Yes. Very entertaining."

Leah groaned, clenching her fists. "I swear, you have no concept of normal reactions."

"Normal is overrated," Nico said, leaning back against the wall. "Besides, you were overreacting slightly." He lifted his hand, pinching his fingers close together in demonstration. "Just slightly."

"*Slightly*?!" she shot back. "My entire body was vibrating with terror, and you were grading my reaction?"

"I was," he said, unashamed. "And for the record, Dimitri didn't even try to eat you."

Leah blinked. "Dimitri?"

Nico's grin widened. "The wolf's name is Dimitri."

She froze. "You—wait—you named it? That thing has a name?"

"Yes," Nico said mildly. "And it's mine."

Leah ran a hand through her hair—a restless gesture she'd picked up from Nico. "Mine? You own it? Like a magical pet?"

"It's not a pet," he corrected. "It's a familiar. All Pillars have one. Through them, we communicate. And through my ring..." He lifted his pinky, the small band glinting faintly in the firelight. "...Dimitri and I are linked. Messages. Warnings. He's part of the network."

Leah stared at him. "So the wolf just showed up to tell you something? You...speak fluent wolf now?"

"Their messages are telepathic," Nico said simply.

"So," she said slowly, "there's a wolf voice living rent-free in your head."

Nico laughed, and Leah hated that it made her smile.

"You send a message by touching foreheads with your familiar and thinking of the message you want to send," he explained. "They track down the recipient and bring their reply back to you."

Leah narrowed her eyes. "So. Magical text messages. Delivered by extremely committed animals."

"That's one way to put it."

"Do I get one?" she asked, already picturing it.

Nico watched her for a moment, like he could see exactly where her thoughts had gone. "In theory," he said. "But familiars don't deliver messages within the Groves."

Her shoulders slumped. "Of course they don't." The fleeting hope of reaching Sage fizzled out. She sighed and turned away, the silence settling heavier than before.

The forest around her no longer carried the soft hum of Nico's protective spells. Leah hadn't meant to wander this far. She stepped carefully over a root glazed with ice as her boots sank slightly into frozen moss dusted with snow. Her breath came in soft, visible puffs, and the air felt sharp against her lungs. A quiet unease tugged at her ribs, but she told herself it was nothing more than nerves. After all, Nico had gone on one of his many outings to find more food for them and insisted that she stay behind.

She hadn't meant to disobey him. Not exactly. But the stillness of the sanctuary had begun to press in on her to the point where the quiet felt too heavy and her thoughts felt too loud. A short walk through the trees had seemed harmless enough.

Now, without him beside her, the woods felt immense. She was more hypervigilant now that she realized she was lost and every shadow and movement in the trees nearly froze her in place. She thought she saw the edge of a green cloak disappear between the trunks but she quickly shook her head and blamed her nerves for that, too.

Leah slowed her steps as the sound of what seemed like children playing reached her ears. She stopped, listening to distant laughter and the faint clink of metal carried on the wind. Following the noise, she emerged from the trees onto a sloping hill—and saw it.

Roots Hollow.

The village spread out below her, alive with energy. The buildings were stitched together with moss and flowering vines, dusted with a light layer of snow. Narrow bridges of woven roots curved between upper levels, pulsing faintly with magic. Tiny lanterns hung from branches, and the soft sparkle of frost on the windows caught the light, making the whole place look as if it had been sprinkled with sugar. In a few windows, enchanted scenes played on a gentle loop. Reindeer-shaped constellations trotting across night skies, children skating across frozen lakes that chimed softly when they laughed, and golden bells that rang without sound as they swayed. She could feel it even from here— the thrum beneath her skin, the elemental energy humming in the air.

Leah began to descend the slope toward the village. The marketplace bloomed at the heart of the town with stalls with awnings striped in reds, creams, and deep forest greens. At the center of the square, a towering evergreen rose from a circular dais, its branches heavy with glowing sigils and floating ornaments that slowly orbited the tree. Children darted beneath it with their hands outstretched as they chased drifting lights that giggled when caught. Every so often, the tree responded to their delight, brightening in soft waves that rippled outward, drawing smiles and applause from the crowd.

Food stalls clustered near the fountain and steam curled into the cold air as bakers passed out mugs of spiced cider that warmed fingers and hearts alike. Loaves of bread sang softly as they cooled, and sugar-dusted pastries reshaped themselves into stars, moons, and tiny reindeer before being eagerly devoured. A chocolatier stirred a cauldron that shimmered with heatless flame, conjuring delicate snowflake patterns across each poured cup.

Nico's warning about going into town echoed in her mind, but the festive cheer, the warm glow of lanterns, and the laughter of the villagers made it hard to imagine danger here.

A faint breeze stirred her hair, carrying the scents of baked bread, honeyed fruit, and freshly cooked bacon. Music drifted from the marketplace, blending with children's laughter and the chatter of locals. Maybe, just for a moment, she could pretend she was someone ordinary.

She squared her shoulders and stepped into the town square, keeping her cloak drawn tight. At first, no one paid her much attention. Children darted between stalls, merchants called out their prices, and the air buzzed with warmth and noise. It was almost overwhelming after weeks of silence.

Her gaze landed on a long wooden table stacked with glittering trinkets—rings, stones, and tiny glass vials that looked just like the ones Nico had used to tend her wound after the attack.

"Excuse me, young lady," a saleswoman called brightly. She was older, her hair wrapped in a green scarf threaded with gold. "You look like someone who could use a little charm for the road."

Leah smiled politely. "Just looking, thank you."

"Oh, nonsense," the woman said, pressing a small pendant into Leah's palm which was warm to the touch. "Go on, try it. You can feel the hum, can't you? Good for grounding the elements— fire users especially."

Leah stared at the pendant and froze. She had no idea whether enchanted artifacts could trigger visions for her, but she knew she couldn't use magic here—not even a flicker.

"I—I wouldn't know," she said quickly. "I'm not—"

"Not what?" The woman tilted her head and her eyes began scanning Leah's face as if trying to decipher what kind of creature she was. "I haven't seen you around here before. Where are you from?"

Leah's heart thudded. "Oh, um, just passing through," she said, setting the pendant back on the table. "My friend and I—"

"What friend?"

The woman's tone shifted and Leah's pulse raced as nearby shoppers turned to look. Heat bloomed in her chest—the familiar warning sign whenever too many emotions surged at once. Her blood magic. She squeezed her eyes shut, willing her heart to slow before she did something she couldn't take back.

"There you are!"

Leah's eyes flew open. The voice came from behind her, and for a split second she thought it was Nico. But this voice was different—warm, easy, and threaded with laughter.

She turned just as a tall young man with dirty blond hair pulled into a messy ponytail appeared beside her, wearing a mischievous grin.

"There you are," he said again cheerfully, slinging an arm over her shoulders as if they'd known each other for years. "You promised you wouldn't wander off again."

Leah froze, caught between confusion and sudden relief.

The woman relaxed instantly. "Kasper! You know this girl?"

"Of course I do," Kasper said with mock offense. "She's terrible with directions, but I keep her around for the company." He gave Leah a conspiratorial wink before turning back to the woman. "Sorry for the trouble, Mirra."

Mirra chuckled, the tension fading from her eyes. "Well, if she's with you, Kasper, I suppose that's different. Keep her out of trouble, won't you?"

"I'll do my best," he replied, gently steering Leah away from the table.

"Oh, and Kasper?"

He didn't stop walking, just glanced back with a wide grin. "Yeah?"

"Do visit more often. It seems the other Hollows are taking up most of your time lately. We miss you."

Kasper lifted a hand in farewell. Once they were out of earshot, Leah whispered, "Who are you?"

"Someone who just saved you from a very awkward conversation," Kasper said easily. "You're welcome."

Leah frowned but couldn't help noticing how his grin reached his eyes. There was something kind about him. He looked a bit older than her, dressed in travel-worn clothes that somehow still looked effortless. His long hair was tied back haphazardly, his beard slightly overgrown, but it only added to his rugged, handsome features.

As he guided her through the market, the smells pulled at her attention—sizzling meats and fresh bread—wrapping around her like a tease that made her stomach twist painfully. She couldn't remember the last time she'd eaten a proper meal.

Kasper followed her gaze and smirked. "When was the last time you ate anything more filling than roots and mushrooms?"

She opened her mouth to argue, but her stomach betrayed her with a low growl.

He laughed. "That settles it. Stay here." He left her beside a table on the edge of the marketplace, where a traveler's backpack rested atop a folded green cloak.

Before she could protest, he was already weaving through the crowd toward a food stall.

Leah exhaled as her pulse finally settled after almost being caught. The square returned to its cheerful rhythm, and for the first time in days, she felt almost human. Her gaze drifted back to Kasper's belongings—the worn traveler's pack, clearly heavy from use, and the neatly folded green cloak beside it.

The fabric looked soft, edged with faint threads of gold embroidery that carried an air of familiarity. She reached out, curiosity getting the better of her. Maybe a quick look wouldn't hurt.

She closed her eyes as her fingertips brushed the edge of the cloak, and the world tilted.

In that instant, she was moving through the forest, boots crunching softly against a thin layer of snow. Ahead, through the trees, she saw herself, Leah, walking alone.

The market rushed back around her with the sounds, lights, and smells that slammed into place all at once. Leah jerked her hand back, suddenly aware of how dangerous it was to let her curiosity get the better of her in public. The vision had been brief but razor-sharp, and it told her one thing clearly: Kasper had been following her.

She sat at the table and waited. Kasper returned moments later with two steaming bowls in his hands and that same easy grin on his face.

"You okay?" he asked. "You look like you've seen a ghost."

Leah steadied her voice. "Something like that."

She was surprised she was even talking to someone she barely knew, but there was something about him that put her at ease. She began eating the stew, doing her best not to show how unbelievably hungry she was. The broth was perfectly seasoned, the vegetables tender, the meat falling off the bone—it took everything in her not to moan with satisfaction.

Kasper tilted his head, curious.

She met his gaze. "So," she said lightly, continuing to eat, "how long have you been following me?"

He froze for only a moment before his grin returned, softer now, almost impressed. "Ah," he said. "You saw something, didn't you?"

"I saw it," she replied. "Through your cloak."

He gave a low whistle. "Didn't think you'd catch on that fast. I didn't mean for you to touch it. Guess we're even now."

"Even?"

"I saved you from being outed by Mirra. You got a peek into my day job. Fair trade, don't you think?"

Leah folded her arms. "You were in the woods. Watching me."

He sighed. "Following, technically. Not watching. There's a difference."

She arched a brow. "That's supposed to make me feel better?"

Kasper's tone softened, sincerity flickering beneath the teasing. "Relax, Leah. I wasn't planning to do anything to you. I just wanted to make sure you weren't who I thought you were."

Her stomach twisted. "What did you just call me—"

Suddenly, the warmth around them dimmed, like sunlight slipping behind a cloud.

"Leah."

Her name cut through the air like a blade, spoken in a low, controlled voice that carried danger in every syllable. Leah froze, her pulse hammering in her ears, before she spun around to see Nico standing several paces away with his cloak drawn tight, his expression carved from ice. His gaze snapped to her, then shifted to Kasper. The shift was instantaneous. The stillness in him wasn't calm, it was containment.

"Kasper," Nico said quietly, and the sound raised the hairs on Leah's arms. "I should have known."

Kasper only grinned, utterly unfazed. "You make it sound like I'm a bad omen, old friend."

"We're not friends."

"True," Kasper said cheerfully. "You're more the 'glare and vanish into the shadows' type. I'm more of the 'buy soup for strangers and have pleasant conversations' type. We balance each other out."

Leah looked between them. "Wait—you know each other?"

Kasper smirked. "Know him? Please. I've seen this man drag entire rooms into darkness just to prove a point."

Nico's jaw flexed, but his voice stayed level. "You should watch what you say."

"Oh, I'd love to," Kasper said lightly. "But I'm starting to think your student here might not know the whole story. Should I—"

Nico shifted, his presence tightening the air around them causing his shadows to stir at his boots, restless and ready.

Kasper's grin faltered for a split second, just long enough to show he understood the warning.

"Still hiding," he said quietly. "Wouldn't want anyone realizing The Order's favorite weapon is still breathing."

"Careful," Nico murmured. The restraint in his voice was the only thing keeping the moment from breaking.

For a long moment, they stared at each other, with Leah caught helplessly between them. Then Nico turned to her.

"We're leaving. Now."

"Nico—"

His gaze softened, just a fraction. "Please, Leah."

Something in his tone stopped her cold. She gave Kasper one last uncertain look and followed Nico.

Kasper leaned back, placing his hands behind his head and offering her a crooked smile. "Guess that's my cue. Try not to vanish completely, Leah. Makes it harder to keep an eye on you."

Nico's shadows twitched, but he said nothing. He took Leah's arm and led her away, his cloak brushing hers as light slowly returned to the square. Behind them, Kasper watched until they disappeared, and she saw his easy grin fading.

The moment they crossed into the forest, the noise of Roots Hollow vanished like a door slamming shut. Nico moved ahead in long, deliberate strides and he didn't speak.

Leah followed a few paces behind, heat rising in her chest. "Are you going to say something," she asked finally, "or just keep storming ahead like I'm not even here?"

Nico stopped so abruptly she nearly ran into him. When he turned, his face was rigid with control.

"What were you thinking?" His voice was quiet. "You left. Without telling me."

"I just wanted to walk and clear my head," she said. "I got lost. Then I heard the town." She shook her head. "It was beautiful, Nico. You made it sound like a death trap, but there were families there. Laughter—"

"—and spies," he cut in sharply. "The Order keeps eyes everywhere. You think those people would protect you if they knew who you were?"

Leah flinched. "You don't know that."

"I do."

He turned away, pressing a hand to his temple. For the first time, Leah noticed the tremor in his fingers, the exhaustion in his posture, and the brittle edge in his breathing.

"I got back and you were gone," he said quietly. "For a moment, I thought they'd found you." His voice cracked. "I thought they'd taken you."

Understanding hit her all at once. He wasn't angry, he was terrified. She could see the dark circles under his eyes, the faint scar tracing his jaw, and the pulse flickering in his throat. He looked so strong all the time. Unshakable. But now she saw how he was holding himself together by sheer will.

Before she could stop herself, Leah stepped forward and wrapped her arms around him. Nico stiffened, caught off guard, and she felt his every muscle locking in place and his breath hitching, startled. She realized then that he wasn't used to this—wasn't used to being held.

For a moment, he didn't move. Then his hands lifted, hovering just above her back, uncertain. He didn't return the embrace, but he didn't pull away either. She felt it—the restraint, the conflict, the vulnerability he let slip just enough for her to see.

"Come on," he said at last, his voice quiet and rough. "We should head back."

Leah nodded though her throat was aching, but she didn't say anything else.

There was nothing to say.

Chapter 14

"**A**gain."

Nico's voice cut through the clearing, shadows surging at his command. Dark tendrils slithered across the ground like smoke and surrounded Leah, but she twisted out of the way, barely dodging the first lunge. Her pulse pounded as heat built beneath her skin making the crimson daggers she'd summoned gleam in her grip, their edges vibrating faintly with her heartbeat.

She managed to slice through one tendril, which dissolved instantly, but another lashed toward her from the side. Leah rolled as dirt kicked up around her, then came up on one knee, breathing hard. The metallic scent of blood hung in the air, but it wasn't as noticeable to her as it once had been, and it wasn't distracting her now.

Nico stood several feet away with his arms crossed, a picture of calm control amid the chaos. His eyes glowed black and his expression gave nothing away, though the shadows moved like extensions of his will, relentless and precise.

Leah gritted her teeth, ducking another attack. "You can try looking less smug when you're trying to kill me."

"I'm not trying to kill you," Nico said, his tone infuriatingly calm. "If I were, you'd know."

"Comforting."

"You're supposed to be learning control, not sarcasm."

"I'm multitasking."

He didn't even blink. "Focus, Leah."

She exhaled through her teeth, ignoring the ache in her arms. The air pulsed with heat and motion as the shadows circled him, waiting for his next command. The next strike came from behind. Leah spun, cutting through it with both daggers, blood and shadow colliding midair with a hiss. She backed up, scanning for an opening, and that's when she saw it.

A clear path between them. A single opening.

Without thinking, Leah shifted her stance, let the blood hum to life, and hurled the dagger straight at him. The air shimmered red as it flew, its aim perfect as it streaked toward Nico. For a split second, she swore she saw surprise flash in his eyes, but the shadows moved faster than the dagger, surging forward into a solid wall. They formed a shape that mirrored Nico's own silhouette, and the dagger struck it squarely in the head.

A sharp hiss filled the air before the dagger lost form and dissolved into a rain of crimson droplets that steamed briefly before vanishing into the melting snow. The other shadows around her withdrew, melting into the soil until only the one before Nico remained.

Leah froze. She could barely see his expression, but she knew him well enough to read the tension in his stance.

Finally, the shadow dissipated, leaving Nico standing there, unscathed, but very much aware of what she'd just done.

"Really?" he said slowly. "The face?"

Leah couldn't help the grin that broke across her lips. "You said 'again.' You didn't say where."

Amusement flickered through his eyes, the dark glow fading slowly as black gave way to blue.

"So, your first real hit," he said, taking a slow step forward, "and you decide to aim for my head."

"You make it hard to resist," she said lightly, trying to keep her tone even as her heart picked up pace.

"Is that what this is?" he asked, his voice dropping slightly, a teasing edge beneath the control. "Resisting?"

Leah blinked, caught off guard by the sudden shift in his tone. "You're insufferable."

"Careful," he said. "You're smiling."

She hadn't realized she was. Her grin faltered just slightly before Nico started toward her with slow, deliberate steps. Leah held her ground, chin raised, though every nerve in her body screamed to move, forward or backward, she didn't know which.

"Not bad," he said quietly. "You're finally starting to think like a fighter."

Her lips curved faintly, her voice low. "Or maybe you're finally starting to underestimate me."

"That would be a mistake," he murmured.

Leah inhaled in surprise as he closed the distance between them making the air around them feel electric.

Nico's gaze swept over her face, the red light still fading from her eyes. "You're shaking," he said quietly.

"I'm fine."

"You shouldn't lie to someone who can feel your pulse from here."

Her throat tightened, but she refused to look away. "Then stop standing so close."

He didn't move. His jaw flexed as the tension stretched, ready to snap. Nico's hand lifted almost unconsciously, as if he might touch her face.

A sudden gust of wind tore through the clearing, and Nico's expression shifted instantly. His head snapped toward the trees and his eyes darkened back to solid black as his shadows reacted, writhing like living smoke at his command.

"What is it?" she whispered.

The air around Nico changed, and his shadows launched forward, slicing toward the tree line. A startled voice broke through the rustle of branches.

"Alright, alright!"

Kasper stepped out with his hands raised but the smirk on his lips betrayed how little the situation had actually startled him, though irritation flickered behind his calm. "You really don't waste time with pleasantries, do you?"

Nico's expression hardened. His shadows froze midair, then dissipated. He didn't speak, but the tension rolling off him was palpable.

Leah exhaled, relieved this hadn't been another attack from The Order. "You were watching us?"

Kasper tilted his head, utterly unbothered. "Observing," he corrected smoothly.

Leah took a step forward but stayed close to Nico. "You nearly got yourself skewered."

He shrugged. "Wouldn't be the first time. Won't be the last." He glanced at Nico. "You've got quite the temper when someone ruins your fun."

Nico didn't rise to the bait, at least not outwardly, but Leah noticed his jaw tense ever so slightly. He stepped back from her, regaining his composure, though his shadows rippled once, like a warning, before melting away completely. His eyes faded back to blue, but his voice was low and clipped.

"You should go."

Kasper chuckled, unfazed, as he started toward them. "But I just got here."

"Then you can turn right back around," Nico said with a tone that was deceptively calm.

Kasper's boots crunched against the snow as he stopped a few steps away, his grin widening. "And miss all this?" His gaze flicked from Nico to Leah, deliberately lingering just long enough for Nico's fingers to curl at his side. "Not a chance."

Nico's eyes darkened again, a faint ring of black ghosting through the blue as realization hit him. "It was you. You were near the bunker."

It wasn't a question.

Kasper blinked, feigning surprise. "Oh? You noticed that?"

"You disturbed the spells I set."

"Disturbed?" Kasper echoed with mock offense. "That's such a harsh word. I'd say I tested them."

Leah watched the exchange with wary curiosity. She'd never seen Nico this tightly wound.

"So that was you?" she asked. "The disturbance from a few nights ago?"

Kasper gave a lazy half shrug. "Guilty."

Nico took a step closer and when he spoke again, his voice was back to that low, dangerous tone. "You're lucky the shadows didn't tear you apart."

Kasper met his glare with one of his own. "Trust me, shadow man, I can handle myself."

For a moment, Leah saw it, the shadows and wind stirring around them both, before she sighed and stepped between them.

"Enough," she said sharply. "Why do you keep following me, Kasper?"

The wind around him settled, and his grin returned. "I felt something strange. A ripple in the air I hadn't felt before," he said dramatically. "So I followed it."

His gaze slid to Leah, and she noticed how his eyes pulsed with a calming shade of gray. "Imagine my surprise when it led me to you."

Leah's stomach tightened. "You were following me because of my magic?"

Kasper held her gaze, still half smiling. "Because your magic shouldn't exist," he said simply. "And because anyone with that kind of power draws the wrong sort of attention."

"She's already drawn enough of it," Nico said coldly.

Kasper ignored him, his expression turning thoughtful. "But if you're still standing, that means The Order is having a hard time tracking you."

Nico's eyes narrowed.

"They don't usually miss," Kasper continued. "After all, they're the reason half the Pillars are buried instead of breathing."

Leah studied him, uncertain whether to trust the ease in his words. "You don't seem the type to care about that."

"I care about staying alive," he said simply. "And about balance. Wind goes wherever it's needed." He tilted his head, self-satisfied. "Maybe that's here."

"I'm sorry, but you think I'm letting you join us?" Nico asked incredulously.

Kasper continued to ignore him, keeping his attention on Leah. "You could use someone who isn't brooding and terrifying all the time. And someone who knows how to blend in. You two kind of stand out."

Leah caught Nico's glare and could tell his patience was wearing thin. She fought the urge to smirk and failed, turning toward him. "He's not wrong."

Nico shot her a sharp look. "We don't need him."

"Maybe we do."

He turned to her, frustration flashing across his features. "You don't know him."

"I didn't know you either," she said quietly. "And yet here we are."

That silenced him and he noticed how the wind shifted, rustling the trees and carrying Kasper's low chuckle between them.

"I like her," Kasper muttered.

"Don't," Nico said flatly.

Kasper lifted his brows, unbothered. "Relax. I'm here to help. For now."

Nico stepped forward, close enough that Kasper's grin finally faltered. "If you so much as breathe wrong around her—"

Kasper lifted his palms again, smiling easily, though his tone dipped. "Yeah, yeah. Shadows, death, eternal suffering. Got it."

Leah exhaled through her nose from exasperation and amusement. "Both of you, stop. If he wants to help, we'll let him prove it. If not..." she shrugged lightly. "We'll send him flying."

Kasper's eyes glinted. "Careful, Red. I might like the sound of that."

Leah paused, then shrugged it off, assuming the nickname came from watching her blood magic. Nico glared but said nothing, letting the argument fizzle into uneasy silence. The three of them stood in the clearing, the air heavy with tension, until Kasper finally broke it with a sigh.

"So," Leah said, glancing between them, "I need a bit more background here. You two fight like siblings."

Kasper laughed and Nico immediately glared at him.

"We don't," Nico said flatly.

"Oh, we absolutely do," Kasper said cheerfully. "He just refuses to acknowledge it."

Leah lifted a brow, waiting for the story.

Kasper tilted his head, considering. "He arrested me."

Nico sighed. "That is an exaggeration."

"I was six," Kasper continued. "And very politely trying to sneak into Raven Hollow."

Leah stopped, glancing briefly at Nico in disbelief before looking back at Kasper. "You were *six*?"

"It was an important errand," Kasper said defensively. "Also, I was very small. Hard to intimidate."

Nico crossed his arms. "You were trespassing."

Leah looked between them. "And how old were *you*?"

"Eight," Nico said stiffly.

Her mouth fell open. "They sent an eight-year-old to arrest a six-year-old?"

Kasper nodded. "He was very serious about it too. Gave me a whole speech."

Nico muttered, "I was following orders."

"He told me Raven Hollow was 'restricted' and that I was a 'security risk,'" Kasper added, grinning. "I'd just learned how to tie my shoes."

Leah stared at Nico. "You arrested a kindergartener."

"I escorted him out," Nico snapped. "And he bit me."

"I was provoked," Kasper said solemnly.

Leah laughed. "So this explains... everything."

"After that, we didn't see each other for a few years, but then we ran into each other in the forest. He was training. He had gotten taller. But I had gotten faster." Kasper smirked.

"You kept putting your nose where it didn't belong," Nico said.

"You kept giving me talks," Kasper replied. "Formative years, really."

Leah shook her head, smiling. "Congratulations. You two seem to be co-dependent."

Nico groaned at her comment, but Kasper beamed.

"So," he said, glancing between them, "are we just going to stand here all night, or are we sleeping under the stars together?"

Nico's stare could have turned him to ash. "That's it. You're not coming with us."

Kasper grinned. "You sure about that?"

Leah dragged her hand down her face and rolled her eyes. "Nico."

He turned to her. "You can't be serious."

"I'm very serious." She folded her arms. "You've barely slept in days, and you're about to kill someone for merely existing near us. We need to rest. Properly."

"Leah—"

She stepped closer, her tone softening just enough to disarm him. "You said it yourself. The spells were disturbed, not destroyed. If he's the one who triggered them, that means the bunker is still intact."

Nico hesitated, and she could see it, the split second where he measured risk against instinct. Finally, he exhaled through his nose.

"If the spells are compromised—"

"Then you'll know the second we step close," Leah cut in. "And if they're not, we get a bed. And warmth."

Kasper raised a hand. "I'm in favor of beds and warmth."

"Stay out of this," Nico muttered.

"Can't," Kasper said with an easy grin. "I'm part of the group now, apparently."

Nico shot Leah a look that could have frozen a river. She only shrugged, unapologetic.

"He could be useful," she said simply.

"You said that already," Nico replied.

"And I meant it."

He held her gaze long enough that she wondered if he'd push back again, but then his shoulders eased a fraction before he gave a curt nod.

"Fine. But you stay behind me."

Kasper opened his mouth, and Nico cut him off without looking. "Both of you."

Leah bit back a smile as she followed him into the trees.

The walk back to the bunker was slower than before. The forest was quiet now, and the chill of winter pressed cold against Leah's skin. Nico moved ahead of them, alert as ever, his eyes scanning the shadows while his hands flexed now and then as if feeling for disturbances. Leah followed a few paces behind him, her senses alert but calm.

Kasper trailed behind them both. Leah was keenly aware of him in a way she didn't quite trust, and that same instinct that kept her cautious kept tugging her attention back toward him again and again, tangled with curiosity. He walked easily with his hands in his pockets, whistling softly under his breath.

Then she felt it. A brush of wind curled at her back, lifting loose strands of her hair and spiraling around her shoulders. She slowed, glancing over her shoulder just as another current swept past in a more playful way, skimming her sleeve and tugging lightly at the hem of her coat. She looked down, amused. This wasn't like Nico's magic. His shadows were heavy, watchful, and alive with threat. This felt...light.

The wind moved with intention, swirling in small, graceful arcs that stirred snow from the branches above and sent it drifting down in glittering spirals. Leah had never seen this kind of magic before. She watched, transfixed, as the breeze danced and then stilled the moment her eyes met Kasper's. His whistle cut off, and a faint, knowing smile tugged at his mouth, like he'd been waiting for her to notice. Leah turned forward again, pulse quickening, unsure whether she should be more unsettled by him or more intrigued.

When they reached the hidden entrance, Nico stopped so abruptly that Leah jolted to a halt, narrowly avoiding running into him. She saw his posture change and his attention sharpening toward the trees around them. He murmured something under his breath, and the shadows around his feet peeled away from him and spread fast in every direction. Darkness spilled across the ground like ink in water, branching outward and slipping between roots, climbing tree trunks, then dissolving into the folds of the terrain. The temperature seemed to drop another degree, and her breath felt thicker in her lungs as the shadows passed close enough to brush her boots.

Leah stood perfectly still. Every instinct screamed that they were exposed, that something or someone beyond the tree line was watching. She imagined Order agents crouched just out of sight, tracking the echo of her magic. Her fingers curled into fists and her nails bit into her palms as she strained to listen for anything out of place.

Then, slowly, the tension eased. The shadows recoiled, flowing back toward Nico as if drawn by gravity, folding seamlessly into his silhouette.

Nico blinked, and the darkness in his eyes faded.

"The spells are stable," he said quietly. "It's safe."

Leah released a breath she hadn't realized she was holding and relief washed through her, loosening the tight knot in her shoulders.

"Told you," she said, unable to hide her small, triumphant smile and trying to look like she hadn't been petrified moments ago.

Nico glanced at her, the corner of his mouth twitching. "You're insufferable."

She smirked, tilting her head. "You love it."

"Maybe I tolerate it," he shot back, a clear grin breaking through.

Kasper leaned against a tree with his arms folded. "I like this place," he said, eyeing the subtle runes carved into the roots. "Hidden, eerie, probably haunted. Feels like home already."

"You're sleeping outside," Nico said without hesitation.

"Harsh," Kasper replied.

Leah brushed past them, heading toward the concealed stairway below. "You can both argue about it after I get in that bed," she called, her voice echoing faintly as she disappeared down the stairs.

From the corner of her eye, she saw Nico standing at the entrance, watching her.

Behind him, Kasper murmured, "You're not as unreadable as you think."

Nico didn't turn. "You should keep your observations to yourself."

Kasper grinned. "Oh, I plan to. For now."

The shadows stirred around Nico again, and Kasper raised his hands, laughing softly as he followed them down the staircase into the dim warmth of their underground refuge. The book covered wall and cozy armchair made Leah smile instantly.

Kasper stepped inside and let out a low whistle. "Huh. Didn't picture you as the cozy type," he said as his eyes looked over the space. "Books, fireplace, *and* a real bed? You almost make brooding look domestic."

Leah rolled her eyes at Kasper, then leaned closer to Nico and whispered, "See? I told you. Book Bunker of Brooding."

"Book bunker, huh?" Kasper's smile widened. "Catchy. And there's only one bed," he added, glancing pointedly between them. "Efficient setup. Guess you've found a way to keep warm."

Nico froze, every muscle in his back tensing. For a moment, Leah thought he might actually retreat since she saw the faintest flush coloring his neck.

"Don't," he said, clearly caught off guard.

Kasper lifted his hands in mock surrender, still smiling. "Just an observation."

Leah's cheeks warmed. "You're impossible."

"Charming," Kasper corrected, moving off to inspect the rest of the space as if he hadn't just thrown fuel on a fire.

Nico followed Kasper's movements through the bunker and exhaled sharply through his nose, muttering something Leah didn't catch, but it was enough to make Kasper raise his hands again. But beneath Nico's irritation, she could still feel it—the lingering echo of the moment they'd almost shared before Kasper appeared.

Nico moved to light the fire, and Leah busied herself with the lanterns, more to escape the thick silence than for the light itself. Kasper had already drifted to the wall of books, eyeing the same small volume Leah had noticed days earlier.

"You've been busy," he murmured, flipping through the pages. "Tracking something?"

Nico moved fast, faster than Leah expected, snatching the book from Kasper's hands. "That's none of your concern."

Kasper chuckled. "Touchy. You really should learn to share if we're traveling together."

"We're not," Nico said flatly.

Leah sighed, glancing between them. "Can we please try to get along?"

"I'm all for it, Red," Kasper said. "It's your shadow prince over here who struggles with sharing." He stepped closer to Leah, then glanced back at Nico with a teasing tilt of his head.

Leah stared at him. *Red?* That was the second time he'd used that name. Had he really given her a nickname already? She blinked, trying to hide her surprise, though the warmth creeping up her cheeks betrayed her.

Frustrated by the attention, she stepped aside. "So, Kasper, you said you can control wind?"

"Among other things," Kasper said, tilting his head. His eyes glinted a muted gray as a breeze rippled through the room despite the still air. The lantern flames bent toward him, as if drawn by his presence.

Nico's expression was unamused. "Elementals are usually unpredictable."

"So are shadowbinders," Kasper countered easily.

"You think joining us makes you useful? You're a liability." Nico snapped back.

"And yet," Kasper said smoothly, leaning back on his hands, "you haven't thrown me out."

Leah exhaled, stepping between them before Nico's vein popped. "Enough. We're all on the same side, remember? We need to sleep. It's been a long day."

Nico didn't move, but after a tense pause, he muttered, "Fine," and turned away, his shadow curling around his boots before dissolving.

Leah busied herself laying out blankets on the floor. "You can take that," she said, glancing at Kasper.

Kasper raised an eyebrow, his grin faintly wicked. "You're not offering me the bed? I'm wounded."

"She's not," Nico said sharply, without even turning.

Kasper laughed softly. "Of course not. Wouldn't want to intrude on the romance."

Leah nearly dropped the glass of water she was taking to the room. "Romance?" she echoed.

Kasper's grin deepened, but he didn't answer. He simply leaned back, folding his hands behind his head as though the tension in the room was a lullaby meant just for him.

Nico stared at the fire as he sat in the armchair, deep in thought. Then he said quietly, almost to himself, "If he stays, he follows my rules."

Kasper didn't even open his eyes. "Wouldn't dream of doing otherwise."

Leah glanced between them one last time before crossing into the bedroom and making her way to the warm bed. It looked impossibly soft, and she realized just how happy she was to be back here. She eased into it, curling slightly and letting the familiar weight of the mattress support her. Her thoughts buzzed with the events of the day, but lingered on Nico and the way he had looked at her during training. The way he had stood so close to her, close enough to touch.

She took a quick breath and shook her head, willing her imagination to settle. The voices outside the bedroom faded, and she hoped they would all finally get some much-needed rest. Leah took a sip of water, then lowered her head onto the pillow. The moment it touched the soft fabric, her mind began to wander.

Leah stood in a field of flowers that stretched endlessly beneath a beautiful blue sky. A warm breeze carried the scent of blossoms, brushing against her skin with a soft, soothing touch. In the distance, the ocean glittered, its waves catching the sunlight just right. Threaded through the stillness was a gentle, melodic hum, like a lullaby.

Leah turned toward the sound and saw her again, V, lying on the ground a few feet away with her eyes closed, as if soaking in the day.

"Hello again," V said softly, smiling as if greeting an old friend.

"It's you again," Leah murmured, walking over and sitting beside her. "Does this mean my mind is trying to protect me from something else again?"

V didn't open her eyes. "I wouldn't be here if it weren't for you calling me."

"I didn't call for anything."

"Didn't you?" V finally opened her eyes. They were the most vivid green Leah had ever seen, startling in their clarity. There was a calm in her gaze, a strange serenity that made Leah feel her questions were safe rather than probing or dangerous.

"It seems like you're struggling to understand your power," V continued, her voice low and gentle.

"I feel like I'm making progress, but—"

"He's not telling you the whole truth," V interrupted gently.

Leah's brows furrowed as she turned to face her fully. "What do you mean? He's the one teaching me."

V's gaze softened, almost pitying. "Teaching you how to fear it, perhaps. Not own it." She lifted a hand, palm up, and a small bloom of crimson shimmered there, Leah's magic, unmistakably. "This is you, Leah. Wild, beautiful, untamed. You're not meant to hide from it."

Leah stared, mesmerized, then blinked and shook her head. "He's just trying to keep me safe."

"Safe," V repeated quietly. "Or small?"

The word lingered in the air. Leah placed her hand on the bracelet Sage had given her. It always helped when doubt or anxiety crept in. For a moment, she thought the metal at its center was starting to glow, but everything in her dream world always seemed brighter than reality.

V noticed the motion, and a shadow crossed her face before she quickly looked away. The dream flickered and dimmed. The field trembled as though something unseen had drawn too close and V stood suddenly without looking back at Leah.

"I'll be back again," she whispered.

"Wait!"

But the dream unraveled and the world began dissolving around her. Leah's eyes flew open, though she stayed still, letting herself come down from whatever had held her in its grip. She sat up slowly, rubbing sleep from her eyes. The bunker smelled faintly of smoke and herbs, which made her stomach grumble. She moved to get off the bed, but before she could swing her legs over the edge, a voice called lightly from the other side of the door.

"Morning, Red," Kasper called.

Leah blinked as she stepped out of the small room, hair mussed and eyes heavy with sleep. Nico was already up with his boots laced, and his cloak neatly draped over the back of his armchair. Kasper, by contrast, was half-awake, leaning lazily against the wall and sipping from a dented tin cup, wearing the grin of a man who thrived on testing limits.

"Morning," Leah echoed, stretching with a soft groan.

"Your brooding babysitter here was up before dawn sharpening knives. I'm beginning to think he doesn't sleep."

"I sleep," Nico said dryly, without looking up from the dagger he was inspecting. "Just not when I'm surrounded by wind idiots."

Kasper chuckled. "See? Always so warm and welcoming."

Leah bit back a smile as she crossed into the tiny kitchen nook and poured herself a cup of tea.

"So," she said, blowing on it, "what's the plan today?"

Nico slid the dagger into its sheath. "Training."

Kasper's brows shot up. "Already? You do realize it's morning, right? People usually eat breakfast and converse before being subjected to torture."

Leah laughed softly, and Nico exhaled in long-suffering silence.

"I don't think we have much for breakfast," Leah admitted, setting her cup down. "We've got a very humble diet down here."

"What? No thanks. I don't do humble diets. How about I go get us some real food?"

Leah froze mid-sip. It clicked then. Unlike her and Nico, Kasper could move freely. Her mouth nearly watered at the thought of real food. She caught Nico watching her, noting her not-so-subtle reaction, and he didn't look pleased.

"It's too dangerous," he said. "You could be followed."

"Nonsense," Kasper said easily. "I'll be back before you even notice me gone." He winked at Leah.

She turned to Nico with the most pitiful, hopeful expression she could manage this early in the morning.

He pinched the bridge of his nose, muttering something about terrible influences. "Fine. Twenty minutes."

Kasper's grin turned triumphant. "Finally, some democracy around here." He pushed off the wall and headed for the exit, tossing the tin cup into the sink with a clatter. "Don't miss me too much."

Leah shook her head, smiling despite herself, while Nico looked like he was reconsidering every life choice that had led him to this exact moment.

Chapter 15

The tension was palpable the moment Kasper disappeared up the stairs. Nico, whose stare had lingered on the empty stairwell, swiftly shifted his attention to Leah. His eyes skimmed her up and down in a way that made her stomach dip before holding her gaze. Leah swallowed hard, a strange mix of defiance and vulnerability rising in her chest. Nico squinted slightly as he began walking toward her, slow and deliberate.

Leah's head was spinning. Was he angry? Was he going to get close to her again? The memory of their training session from the previous day flashed through her mind, refusing to leave and making her skin prickle at the thought of their closeness again. Whatever Nico was going to say or do, she wasn't backing down.

Nico stopped mere inches away from her, close enough that she could feel his warmth and the subtle hum of magic always ready to defend. Her chin tipped up to meet his gaze.

"That," he said sternly, pointing toward the staircase without breaking eye contact, "will get us into trouble."

Leah's annoyance flared hot and immediate. She knew he meant Kasper, but after everything they'd been through, after all the tension they'd lived with together, was this really what he wanted to talk about?

"You're this close to me," she said sharply, "and you want to talk about Kasper?"

The words hung between them, freezing Nico in place. For the first time since she'd known him, his control faltered.

"I'm talking about the risk," he said, quieter now.

"No," Leah countered, her voice surprisingly steady despite her pounding heart. "You're talking around it."

She didn't know where the courage came from, only that it felt overdue. "You don't get to pretend this is just about him."

Nico's hand lifted, his fingers hovering near her cheek, hesitating as if waiting for permission he hadn't asked for. Leah's mind raced, but she didn't move. She wanted to see how far he'd go. This wasn't the first time they'd been this close.

Then he touched her. Just barely. His knuckles brushed along her jaw, making her breath hitch. The world narrowed to that single point of contact, to the care in his touch, reverent and restrained, as if he feared what might happen if he pressed any harder.

For one breathless moment, she was certain he was going to kiss her. She leaned into his hand without thinking, but then he pulled away.

The loss of his touch was abrupt and jarring. Nico stepped back, breaking eye contact as his hand dropped to his side. The wall went back up as quickly as it had slipped.

"Kasper can't stay," he said, the edge returning to his voice.

Leah stared at him, her anger twisting with disappointment as the echo of his touch still burned on her skin. It was stupid to think there could ever be anything more than this.

"Right," she said softly. "Back to Kasper."

The faint sound of boots echoed from the bunker's entrance and Kasper's voice floated down moments later.

"Miss me?"

Leah turned as Kasper appeared, brushing snow flurries from his coat and carrying a bag. The smell hit her first, something warm and buttery, causing her stomach to betray her with an audible growl. She was grateful for the distraction. Kasper approached the small table, smirking like a man who'd just won a silent wager. Leah fixed her attention on the food to avoid his gaze, though the tension in the room remained unmistakable.

"I come bearing gifts. Don't all glare at once." He pulled out two small loaves of bread wrapped in a thin parchment and a handful of apples that looked like they'd been lifted straight from a market stall.

Leah blinked. "Is that—"

"Fresh bread," Kasper finished proudly. "Still warm, too. Risked my life for this. Well, technically I risked my boredom listening to a merchant talk about the weather, but close enough."

Nico's expression remained unreadable. "You're reckless."

"And you're welcome." Kasper set the bag down and tore a loaf in half. "Don't pretend you're not hungry."

Leah bit into a piece of bread which was still warm against her palms, and briefly imagined what they must look like to someone on the outside looking in.

"So," Kasper said between bites, turning to Leah. "You and I have training today, huh?"

"She trains with me," Nico cut in before she could answer.

Kasper raised his brows, amused. "Relax. I just want to see what she can do."

Nico's lips curved into a faint, knowing smirk. "Careful what you wish for, Kasper. You might see more than you can handle."

"Well, now I'm curious. What else are you hiding from me, Red?"

Leah stuffed the rest of her bread into her mouth as Nico stood, his familiar shadows curling at his feet, making the playful mood shift slightly.

"Outside. Both of you."

They emerged into the clearing above the bunker where the morning light was pale and cold. Nico walked ahead and stood at the center, motioning for Leah to face him, already slipping into the controlled stillness he wore like armor. His expression gave nothing away, only the faint dark pulse in his irises betraying the shadows coiled beneath his skin.

Leah wondered how he did it. How he could act like nothing had happened between them. As if the tension, the almosts, and the closeness were nothing more than her imagination.

She hated that. Hated how it made her feel small and exposed. Hated that he could step in and out of her emotions while she was left carrying the weight of it.

"Ready?" he asked.

Leah nodded and lifted her gaze. She caught the brief questioning look in his eyes and hoped, foolishly, that he could see it. The frustration. The hurt. The feeling of being pushed away after being pulled so close.

His shadows lashed forward without warning, slicing through the air and forcing her to twist aside. The earth beneath her boots was slick, but she moved with surprising precision, her breathing sharp and measured. When she countered, red light cracked in her palms as her blood answered her call.

She didn't hesitate.

Heat bloomed beneath her skin as she shaped the magic into a blade, meeting the shadows head-on. The impact sent a shudder up her arm, but she held her ground. She wasn't going to let him treat her like something fragile. Not today.

Kasper, who was leaning against a nearby stump with a mug of tea, watched with casual intrigue.

"So this is the great training," he drawled. "A bit dramatic, don't you think?"

Leah ignored him, focusing on the rhythm of her heart. The blood rose higher, shaping into familiar blades hovering beside her, pulsing in time with her will.

She caught the moment Kasper's tone shifted and his lazy amusement slipped away, replaced by something sharper. His grin faltered as he slowly lowered his mug, his attention locking onto the air around her.

"Wait—" he began, but the word never fully left his mouth.

Leah moved, spinning through one of Nico's shadow lashes, cutting cleanly through it. The crimson blades hissed against the darkness, leaving trails of smoke. When she looked up again, Kasper was standing straight with disbelief etched across his face.

"That's not spell weaving."

"Stay back," Nico warned, his voice cold.

But Kasper wasn't looking at him. His gaze stayed fixed on Leah. "That's blood magic."

Leah hesitated just long enough for Nico's shadows to strike her arm. She winced as blood welled, but instead of falling, it floated, shaping itself into another weapon. She heard Kasper swear under his breath.

"You're out of your damn mind," he said. "Training her with that."

"I'm teaching her control," Nico snapped. "Because if I don't, she'll lose it, and it will destroy her."

The clearing fell quiet except for Leah's uneven breathing and the low hum of her magic. Her eyes glowed a deep, pulsing red as she stared between Nico and Kasper.

Kasper took a cautious step closer. "That's real, isn't it?" he said quietly. "Not a trick."

Leah nodded.

His gaze dropped to her palm and to the thin line of red feeding the spell, and his expression changed. "You're actually using your own—"

"Yes," Leah said. "My blood."

Kasper blinked, processing. "And you let her?" he asked, looking squarely at Nico.

The way he said it twisted something in Leah's chest and she felt Nico's glare cut across her vision. Kasper's eyes darted between them, and for the first time Leah felt exposed, as if he were finally seeing the invisible thread of trust and danger binding them together.

Then he said, "But she's a Seer, isn't she?"

Leah's head snapped toward him. "How—"

He gave a small, humorless laugh. "The Hollow's been whispering for weeks. But a Seer with blood magic? That's not something you can pass off as ordinary enchantments." His expression shifted, wary now. "And the Echodex. You've got it too, don't you?"

Leah froze.

Kasper saw her reaction and nodded slowly. "That explains a lot."

Nico's tone was ice. "You know too much."

Kasper met his gaze. "You should be glad someone does. Because if you think you can keep her hidden forever, you're wrong. Power like that calls to things, Nico. Hybrids shouldn't exist, remember?"

Nico's eyes glowed black. "Are you threatening us?"

Kasper's smirk returned, softer this time. "Not unless you make me." He glanced at Leah and his tone dropped just a fraction. "I just think it's time we all stop pretending she's ordinary."

Leah tilted her head, studying him carefully. "How do you know about the Echodex?"

"I've heard enough whispers." His tone softened. "A relic that only responds to Seers. The Order spent decades trying to track it down before it vanished. If you have it..." He looked between the two of them. "That explains everything."

"Everything?" Nico asked sharply.

Kasper nodded. "I wasn't the only one who felt it. The moment she entered the Hollow, something shifted in the air. Every spell woven into this place rippled. The Order felt it too. I passed guards who looked nervous, having heard that the Triarch stirred."

Leah's stomach dropped. "The Triarch?"

Kasper turned to Nico, his brow furrowing. "She doesn't know about the Triarch?" He let out an incredulous laugh. "What kind of mentor are you?"

Nico exhaled through his nose but ignored the jab. "Sit," he said quietly, nodding toward a cluster of flat stones at the edge of the clearing.

Kasper flopped down with a dramatic sigh, muttering something under his breath.

Nico's tone shifted as he looked at Leah. "I told you once that the Hollow wasn't always divided. It used to be built on four Pillars: the Elementalists, the Weavers, the Seers, and the Blood Mages. Back then, magic flowed freely between the Pillars. There were no boundaries and no separation. The Order's founders demanded only fairness and balance."

He paused, eyes distant. "People from different Pillars could live together, marry, even bear children. Sometimes those children were born as hybrids."

"Sometimes?" Leah asked softly.

"Yes. Not every union resulted in a hybrid child," Nico continued. "But when it did, those children were unpredictable.

And then, many years ago, one was born who changed everything. His name was Ezren."

Leah froze, remembering the name from the vision she'd seen back in the bunker.

"After the death of The Order's old leader," Nico went on, "Ezren rose to power quickly. He promised unity, but what he really wanted was control. He outlawed the mixing of Pillars, segregated the Hollows, and declared any union between them a crime. Those who disobeyed..." His gaze hardened. "Were found dead or simply vanished."

Kasper leaned forward, resting his elbows on his knees. "Not everyone obeyed. Some refused to abandon their families, so they formed a group and approached Ezren, asking for leniency."

"The Drift," Leah whispered.

Kasper nodded. "Yes. The Drift was born from those who refused to separate. They surrendered their magic so they could stay with their loved ones. Ezren stripped them of their power and banished them to non-magical towns."

Leah's eyes widened. "But how does anyone take another person's power? Aren't we born with it?"

Nico and Kasper exchanged a heavy look before Nico spoke.

"Ezren has the power to take away someone's magic, but no one is sure how. All we know is that one of his right hands, a woman skilled in memory craft, erased the memories of the banished and left one trace of magic in each town, a tether, so The Order could keep watch. For months after, corpses began turning up near Raven Hollow, the Hollow assigned to The Order. They were people caught breaking laws, trying to escape, or attempting to reunite with those they'd lost."

He shifted, drawing one knee up. "To stop the bloodshed, Ezren offered what he called mercy. If two people of different Pillars conceived a child, they could choose to join The Drift and lose their power or surrender the child to The Order and continue their lives as if nothing had happened."

"That's how the Orphan Acquisition Program began." Kasper said bitterly, spitting into the snow.

Leah frowned. "The what?"

"An orphanage," Nico said quietly. "Comprised of abandoned children surrendered to The Order's care."

Leah's face drained of color. "That's monstrous," she whispered.

"It is," Nico said, his voice heavy with something darker. "Most of The Order's ranks are made up of those same orphans. Some were born with single Pillar abilities, while others became hybrids and grew more unpredictable."

"How so?" Leah asked.

"Some inherit both Pillars from their parents, powers like yours," Nico said. "Others manifest something entirely new."

Kasper nodded. "That's when Ezren changed the rules, for his own benefit. Most unions between Pillars are forbidden, but if Ezren gives his blessing, the bond is allowed. They call it a sanctified union." His mouth twisted in disgust. "What it really means is that he decides who gets to pass their power to the next generation freely."

Leah's stomach turned. "So, he's breeding magic?"

"Controlling it," Nico corrected. "Ezren keeps a record of every sanctioned pair. The offspring are taken into The Order for training the moment they show potential. Hybrids especially."

"Because they're stronger," Leah murmured.

"Or more unpredictable," Kasper added quietly. "Rare powers are dangerous if left unchecked, so he keeps them close and raises them loyal to The Order. He trains them until they owe everything to him." He nodded toward Nico. "Just look at your shadow prince. His parents were a sanctioned match. One a Weaver, the other a rare hybrid, a steel binder. The only difference is that when they had Nico, they were allowed to keep him and raise him within The Order."

Nico's jaw tensed as Leah looked at him, realization dawning.

"So that's why you were trained to—" Her voice faltered as the pieces clicked together, explaining the brutal childhood he'd endured.

Kasper fell quiet for a moment, absently rolling snow between his palms. "A steel binder and a shadow walker, both gifts Ezren coveted. No wonder he kept your father close, and why he's sitting on the Triarch now."

Nico's head snapped toward him. "What did you say?"

Kasper blinked. "Your father," he said slowly. "He's been part of the Triarch for years. You didn't know?"

Nico went rigid, and Leah felt the shift ripple through him. His muscles tensed, disbelief flashing in his eyes before being shuttered by something cold and unreadable.

"I had no idea," he admitted. "How could he—" His words broke off, raw with disbelief.

Kasper shifted, glancing between them. "It happened shortly after you vanished. I guess losing his prodigy son did a number on him."

Leah's stomach churned. The shadows beneath Nico's feet rippled restlessly and his fingers twitched once, as if restraining the urge to destroy something.

"No," he muttered, his tone sharp. "He doesn't change. He never changes." His gaze dropped to the snow, a faint tremor running through his hand. "He would rather serve a lie than face what's real."

Leah frowned. "Nico...what does that mean?"

"It means," he said quietly, "that he's right where he belongs." His voice turned to ice. "With them."

Before the silence could deepen, Kasper dusted off his hands. "We should head back."

Leah looked up. "Already? We just got here."

"Charging ahead without a plan is the fastest way to get killed," Kasper said. "We need to rethink things before training again."

"You think she can't handle it?" Nico asked, glaring at him.

"I think," Kasper replied evenly, "that I've seen enough mages burn themselves out to know when we're on thin ice." He crouched, tracing a rough symbol in the snow, a circle quartered by intersecting lines. "Hybrids are unpredictable. That's why they were killed, banished, or controlled. When someone doesn't understand their power, it never ends well. Controlling two forms of magic isn't just rare. It's dangerous."

Leah knelt beside him. "Have you seen that happen?"

Kasper's hand hovered over one of the lines. "I've heard stories. My mother loved hybrid lore. You can imagine the bedtime stories I grew up with." A faint smile flickered before fading. "But outside of that lore, blood magic was the hardest of the four Pillars to control. Even purebloods struggled." His expression darkened. "My mother's friend was a blood mage. She tried to save her son after he had an accident using her own blood. It worked for a moment, but blood magic demands balance. He convulsed and blood began to pour from his mouth. She tried to fix it but only prolonged his pain. He died, and she followed soon after, drained by the strain. My mother used to say that if the magic hadn't taken her, the guilt would have."

Kasper stood, brushing snow from his hands. "That kind of magic is powerful, sure. But it's fickle. If you keep pushing, it'll bite you back harder than any enemy The Order can send your way."

A chill ran down Leah's spine. She'd wondered if she could have healed herself before. Now she was glad she hadn't tried.

Nico folded his arms. "So what are you suggesting? We wait?"

"I'm suggesting we think," Kasper said. "You've hidden for years, Nico, but she's different. The world felt her enter the Hollow. Allies and enemies alike. If The Order learns what she really is..."

Nico visibly tensed at the thought.

Leah looked between them. "Then what do we do?"

Kasper sighed, glancing at Nico. "I might have an idea. But let's get back to the bunker first."

Inside, Kasper motioned them to the table while he paced, hand to his chin. Nico sat rigidly, irritation etched across his face.

Kasper's gaze drifted to the wall of books. "You're good at training, Nico. I'll give you that. But you don't know this magic. You can't properly teach what you've never seen." He pulled a book from the shelf, one that looked more like a textbook than the others, and flipped it open to a detailed map of the Hollow spread across its pages.

"Here," Kasper said, sliding it toward Leah. "Are you familiar with this?"

Leah hesitated. Saying yes would mean admitting she'd used her magic while Nico was gone, and in his current state, she didn't find it wise to admit that. "No," she lied. "But Nico did mention something about the different Hollows."

Kasper frowned at Nico. "Failed again as a mentor? How long have you been training her? She has no idea of the world around her!" he exclaimed, shaking his head dramatically.

Nico didn't say anything, he just stared at the book, no doubt trying to figure out what Kasper was getting at.

"The four Hollows," Kasper went on, pointing to the map, "each represent the Pillars."

"Yes, I remember that. North, East, South, and West," Leah said, leaning in.

"Right," Kasper nodded. "The Pillars once comprised of the Seers and the Blood Mages are pretty much deserted now." He continued, pointing to areas on the map. "Ashmere Hollow to the south, and Riven Hollow to the north." He took a deep breath before continuing. "Obviously, no one from those Pillars remains, but—"

Leah's heart quickened as hope sparked in her chest. "But what?"

"You heard it earlier. When The Drift was banished, The Order ensured that a tether of power—"

"Absolutely not." Nico's voice cut through the air like ice. He was on his feet now, eyes burning.

Kasper sighed, unsurprised by the reaction. "Nico, you know the Elders—"

"I said no," he repeated, colder this time.

"The Elders?" Leah interjected, trying to diffuse the tension.

Kasper's brows lifted as he glanced between them, as if seeking permission to continue. Nico pinched the bridge of his nose, muttering under his breath in frustration. Kasper took that as a reluctant go-ahead.

"Yes," he said carefully, sitting down. "Every non-magical town has an Elder. They were the only ones allowed to keep a sliver of magic, solely for communicating with The Order."

Leah leaned back in her chair, stunned. "All this time, there was someone like that in Eldergrove and I had no idea?"

Kasper nodded.

"But that must mean they're ancient!" she blurted out. "Didn't you say Ezren took over decades ago? Just how old is he?"

"No one knows," Nico said flatly. "But it's estimated he's close to a hundred."

"Ha!" Kasper barked out a laugh. "Creepy old geezer still looks like he's in his forties, though!"

Leah blinked, staring at Nico. "A vampire," she muttered.

Nico's lips twitched, suppressing a laugh. Kasper, on the other hand, lost it completely. "A vampire?" he wheezed between bursts of laughter. "No way. There's no such thing!"

Leah frowned. "I can't be that far off. Who lives that long?"

"Very little is known of Ezren," Nico said, regaining his composure. "But I can guarantee he is not a vampire."

Flushed with embarrassment and irritation, Leah crossed her arms. "Fine. So these Elders. How would they even help me? And why are you so against it?" She fixed her gaze on Nico.

Nico took a deep breath. "Because I don't trust them," he said quietly. "They might have once served as mediators between the Pillars and The Order, but that was decades ago. No one knows where their loyalties lie now, or if they'd hesitate to turn you in." His eyes flicked to hers, blue mixing with black. "The moment they sense what you are, Leah, they might see you as a threat. Or worse, an opportunity."

Kasper exhaled loudly, leaning against the table. "He's not wrong about the risk," he admitted. "But sitting here isn't safe either. You can't hide from what you are. If we don't find someone who understands your magic—"

Leah frowned. "So what, we just walk up to an Elder and ask for help? What if they don't believe who I am?"

Kasper paused, then snapped his fingers lightly. "Then we show them proof." He straightened, his eyes brightening. "You'll take the Echodex with you."

Leah froze and looked down, avoiding Nico's gaze. She hadn't told him she'd been avoiding the book entirely.

"Leah?" Nico asked, concern breaking through.

"I haven't opened it again. Not since the last time."

"The last vision?" Nico asked, his voice softer but threaded with unease.

She nodded. "Every time I've used it, it drains me. I can barely stand afterward."

Kasper folded his arms. "Then maybe the problem isn't the Echodex. Maybe it's you trying to use it without guidance."

Nico turned sharply toward him, irritation flaring. Leah flinched, but Kasper raised his hands in mock surrender.

"Think about it," Kasper continued evenly. "If her blood magic works differently, forcing her Seer magic could be what's interfering with the Echodex."

Nico's glare faltered for a moment and he sank back into his chair, considering it. Leah felt the weight of his internal struggle as the truth settled.

Finally, Nico exhaled. "Fine."

Leah searched his face but found only resignation. Kasper's smile spread triumphantly.

"I knew you had some sense," he teased, earning an annoyed look.

"By the way, Leah," Kasper said, curiosity glinting in his eyes, "mind if I see this legendary artifact of yours?"

"Oh. Yeah. Okay."

She disappeared briefly into the next room and returned carrying the book carefully, as though afraid it might wake. She set it on the table and stepped back.

Kasper stared. "That's it?" he muttered, reaching out. "Doesn't exactly scream ancient relic."

"Kasper," Nico warned, but it was too late.

Kasper flipped it open, his smirk fading almost instantly. "So," he said flatly, "the book lost for centuries, the one said to hold the truth of every bloodline, is blank?" He closed it with disappointment.

"It's not blank," Leah said quietly.

Kasper blinked. "Come again?"

She met his gaze though a flicker of unease crossed her eyes. "You just can't see it."

Kasper frowned, glancing back at the Echodex as though the truth might suddenly reveal itself. "Right..." he murmured, drumming his fingers against the table. "Well, whatever it is, and whatever it does, it's bound to the Seers. That much I am certain of." he looked up at Leah. "So, what do you want to focus on first? Your visions or your blood? Because that will tell us where we go next."

Leah hesitated. "What do you mean?"

"If you want to know more about the book and your Seer magic, we need to go to Oakgrove. If you want to learn more about your blood magic, we go to Birchgrove." He said simply.

"No," Nico said sharply. "We start somewhere safe."

"Safe?" Kasper raised a brow. "Didn't we just agree this is risky no matter what?"

"Yes," Nico said evenly. "Maybe if we go at it blindly. We start in Eldergrove." He looked at Leah. "Selene raised you there. If The Order didn't intervene all these years, someone was protecting her. Probably the Elder."

Kasper straightened. "Selene?"

"My grandmother," Leah said quietly. "She died."

"Oh." Kasper rubbed his neck. "Sorry." Then something clicked. "Wait. Selene Gardner?"

Leah froze. Even Nico's expression shifted.

"Yes," Leah said slowly. "How do you know her name?"

Kasper laughed in disbelief. "Everyone knew Selene Gardner. She wasn't just a weaver, she was a legend. The Order watched her for years, but she always slipped through. People said she had friends in high places."

Leah's stomach twisted. "That can't be right. She never left the house."

"That's exactly what someone hiding something big would want you to think," Kasper said gently.

"She wasn't hiding," Leah insisted, though uncertainty crept into her voice.

Nico's tone softened. "If Selene had allies in the Hollow, Eldergrove might not just be safe, it might be waiting for you."

Kasper nodded. "Exactly. She made sure you weren't alone, even if you didn't know it. The Elder could be the key."

Leah looked between them as her pulse started to quicken. The thought of her grandmother being something more than ordinary made her chest ache.

Finally, Kasper broke the silence. "Then it's settled. We start with Eldergrove."

Leah's gaze fell to the Echodex resting between them where a faint pulse of light only she could see shimmered across its surface.

"Eldergrove," she echoed softly. "Then that's where we'll go."

Chapter 16

Roots Hollow glimmered under a fresh layer of frost. By the time they reached the town, the air smelled faintly of pine and smoke, and the trees were lined with garlands of evergreen and ribbons of silver, a sure sign that Christmas was approaching. Lanterns shaped like stars swung gently from every awning, casting light over cobbled streets. Leah slowed as they entered the square, taking it all in.

They had spent the last few days planning this, going over routes, supplies, and contingencies, but seeing the town now—alive with holiday cheer—made all the strategizing feel almost unreal.

"It's even more beautiful than I remember," she murmured. The last time she'd been here, she hadn't had the chance to look around since she'd been too busy trying to stay unnoticed, though that sharp shopkeeper, Mirra, had nearly caught her then. It had been the day she'd met Kasper. This time, the air felt lighter and more festive. She watched children dart up and down the square, their faces red from the cold, while merchants called out about spiced cider and sugar plums.

They hadn't gone far before Mirra herself appeared, stepping out of her shop to set up her tent of sweets and winter goods. She was bundled in a plum-colored shawl with matching gloves. Her gaze caught Kasper instantly.

"Well, I'll be," she said, smiling wide. "If it isn't Kasper Kari! I'm surprised to see you here again so soon."

Kasper looked faintly startled, then returned her grin. "What can I say?" he said sheepishly.

Mirra's gaze shifted to Leah, who was doing a poor job of pretending not to be noticed.

"It's that friend of yours from the other da—oh!" she said, grinning and checking around her before hurrying them inside her shop.

Leah exchanged a bewildered look with Kasper but followed her in. She glanced back for Nico, but he was nowhere to be seen. Of course not. He blended into places like this better than anyone.

Once inside, Mirra gave Leah a quick once-over and gasped. "Oh honey, don't tell me you're going to travel with Kasper with only that cloak to keep you from freezing to death!" She gestured dramatically at the oversized cloak Leah had more or less stolen from Nico.

"I—I'm okay," Leah started, but Mirra was already moving toward the clothing racks.

"Nonsense. Really, Kasper, you cannot be so crass with your lady!"

Kasper frowned, clearly exasperated. "But she's not—"

"Tell me, dear," Mirra interrupted, turning back to Leah, "what's your name?"

"Uh...Selene," Leah said quickly.

"Selene! Beautiful name." Mirra's eyes twinkled. "Do you have a color preference?"

"Oh...no. Not really. Maybe something that blends in," Leah said shyly.

Mirra hummed thoughtfully as she rummaged. "You still have that scar, Kasper? From when you pulled my boy out of that mess years ago? Please tell me you used the cream I gave you."

Leah blinked. "You rescued her son?"

Kasper rubbed the back of his neck. "Wasn't much of a rescue. Just a few of The Order's men having too much fun at someone else's expense."

"Too modest, as usual," Mirra said, turning with a coat in hand. "Try this for me, would you?"

Leah hesitated, glancing at Kasper for reassurance. He nodded with a soft chuckle. Leah removed her bag holding the Echodex and handed it to him before slipping off the cloak. The coat was a muted brown that fell to her knees, lined with fleece so soft it felt like a hug. She smiled at her reflection, momentarily lost in the comfort.

Mirra beamed. "I hope to never see your woman wearing a hand-me-down cloak again, Kasper! Now, off you go."

Leah's eyes widened. "Wait, I can't possibly—"

"Please, Selene," Mirra said, lifting her hands. "It's my pleasure. Consider it a welcoming gift from Roots Hollow."

Kasper smiled as Leah's face turned crimson. Mirra laughed and pulled him into a farewell hug. "You picked a cutie."

"Yeah..." Kasper said absently, eyes still on Leah.

Leah froze and she felt her cheeks burning. Kasper blinked, realizing what he'd said. "Thanks, Mirra. Take care of yourself."

"You too, Kasper. Hope to see you both soon."

They stepped outside, Kasper's hand resting lightly on Leah's back as he guided her along a winding path away from the busy square.

"What was that?" Leah asked once her pulse slowed.

"Oh, just Mirra being Mirra," Kasper said with a laugh, handing her bag back.

They continued toward the edge of town, where Nico appeared suddenly between two buildings, as stern as ever. Kasper just grinned and raised his hands in surrender, stepping away from Leah and past him down the road. Leah didn't understand the silent exchange, but she didn't care much either. Her new coat was warm, and for the first time in days, she felt almost at peace.

They walked in silence as the town faded behind them. Frost crunched underfoot along the narrow path winding toward the edge of the Hollow. The forest thickened and the branches were heavy with snow, arching like a tunnel of white. Leah pulled her coat tighter, still feeling the lingering warmth of Mirra's shop.

"It feels...different here," Leah said, looking around.

Kasper adjusted the strap of his pack. "That's because we're leaving the Hollow," he said. "Magic fades the closer you get to the border. Even the air changes."

Leah nodded. "The last time I crossed the Veil, it was...overwhelming." She stopped as the memory of that first crossing made her throat tighten.

Nico's voice came from ahead of them. "You won't see anything," he said simply.

Leah looked up at him. "What do you mean?"

He stopped and turned toward her, his breath visible in the cold air. "The Veil only tests those who enter the Hollow. It doesn't care about those who leave."

She let out a small breath of relief, though the words didn't comfort her as much as she had expected. "And no one's going to stop us?"

Kasper's voice came from behind her. "Not unless you start throwing magic around. Most people don't even know these arches exist." He adjusted his pack. "To them, we'd just look like travelers on an empty road."

Nico's gaze swept to the horizon. "That's the point. These crossings were meant to be forgotten."

The path sloped downward into a grove of bare trees. Frost clung to the bark, and beneath them stood the arch, grown from intertwining roots with its center shimmering faintly.

"It's not the same one I came through before."

"No," Nico said. "Each Veil leads somewhere different. We'll come out farther north in Eldergrove this time."

Leah hesitated. "And what if The Order's watching?"

"They're always watching," Nico replied. "Which is why we keep our heads down and find out whether the Elder is our ally or our enemy. Every time someone from a Hollow enters a Grove town, the Elders feel it. It is The Order's first line of defense to ensure whoever enters follows the rules."

Leah took a slow breath. The risks were high. One wrong move and they'd be caught.

"Ready?" Nico asked.

She nodded.

They stepped forward and the air shimmered, cold and weightless. For a moment, Leah felt suspended between worlds. Then the hum vanished and snow crunched beneath her boots. The scent of pine was sharper here, colder. Eldergrove lay before them, but it was much quieter, its magic muted beneath human stillness.

"Keep your hoods up," Nico said quietly. "The Order's been sending scouts through the Groves."

"You think they're still looking for me here?" Leah asked.

"I wouldn't be surprised," Nico said. "Even if they don't know where you are, they'll be gathering information." He looked at them both. "Remember why we're here. We find the Elder. If anyone stops us, we're just travelers heading north."

In the days before heading out of the bunker, Nico had made it clear that if they were going to follow Kasper's plan of visiting the Elders, it would be on Nico's terms. Now that she was returning after awakening her powers, Leah was not allowed to visit anyone or go anywhere she might be recognized. The return to Eldergrove was simply to track and find the Elder.

They had spent hours poring over maps, hoping to uncover even a trace of the Elders' whereabouts. The maps of the Groves were scarce and nothing like the detailed charts of the Hollow, which had been the result of Ezren's intent to let the Groves fade into obscurity. He had wanted them to be forgotten. Leah described Eldergrove to the best of her ability, retracing familiar paths from memory, but even she could not imagine where an Elder might be hiding. Nico had also questioned her about anything Selene might have said offhand that lingered in her mind, but all Leah could offer were the riddles and symbols she had grown up with which were only fragments that had never made sense to her.

They followed the cobblestone path into town. It led them past the old school Leah had attended, Westview Academy. Leah shuddered. Her school life had not been a particularly happy one. They passed the gate surrounding one of the playgrounds, the one for elementary kids where Leah had endured countless rounds of bullying. She took a deep breath and picked up her pace, wanting to get away as quickly as possible, an action that didn't go unnoticed by Nico behind her.

They passed a line of shops whose shutters were still half closed for the morning. Leah slowed when she saw the apothecary, Selene's old supplier. A wave of memory hit her so suddenly her chest ached. The bell above that door used to chime whenever she ran errands for her grandmother, and the shop keeper, Jay, would never let Leah leave without giving her a lollipop—a routine he had kept since she was a child. Leah stopped and stared at the entrance, but before she could linger any longer, Nico caught her wrist.

"Don't."

She blinked at him. "I know."

"If you recognize a place, someone might recognize you," he said. "The less you're remembered here, the better."

Leah swallowed and forced herself to keep walking. "Then how are we supposed to find the Elder if we can't talk to anyone?"

"We won't need to," Nico said, nodding ahead. "Selene knew this day would come. She would have left clues for you around town."

Kasper raised a brow. "And how exactly are we supposed to find these clues in a town full of people who don't even know magic exists?"

Leah stopped mid-step. "Of course," she murmured. All those cryptic conversations with Selene, all the talks of looking beyond, were they meant to prepare her for this? Something flickered in the corner of her vision, a faint shimmer along the brick wall beside them. She stepped closer.

Etched into the stone was a symbol so faint it could have been mistaken for weathering. Two concentric circles with a line down the center. Leah reached out, her expression tightening as she remembered the symbol sewn over Selene's blanket that night. It pulsed beneath her fingers. She looked back at Nico and Kasper.

"Looks like we found our breadcrumb," Kasper said.

Nico crouched beside the symbol. "She knew you'd recognize it. Selene marked these for you."

Leah swallowed the emotions rising in her chest. Selene hadn't left her clueless after all. Composing herself, she looked ahead. Now that she knew what to look for, she saw them, another sigil glinting beneath a streetlamp, then another just beyond it. A path.

"Do you think these lead to the Elder?" she asked.

"If we're lucky," Nico said. "If not…" He scanned the empty street. "We'll find out soon enough."

"Or get caught following glowing graffiti," Kasper muttered, though there was no real protest in his tone.

They followed the trail, careful to keep distance from the few early risers sweeping steps or opening shop doors. Leah's heart raced faster with every mark they passed. Each symbol hummed in recognition with the same golden pulse that lived beneath her skin whenever she used her power.

The sigils eventually led them beyond the graveyard, where the snow lay deeper and the air turned sharp and still. The final mark glimmered on a moss-covered post near an old path Leah didn't remember.

"This doesn't look familiar," she murmured.

"I don't think it was meant to be," Nico replied, brushing gloved fingers over the symbol. "Selene might have hidden this trail deliberately."

Leah moved forward as the path opened into a clearing and stopped short, recognition hitting fully. At its center stood an old greenhouse with glass panes that were dulled with frost and vines creeping up its frame.

"I remember this," she whispered.

A memory surfaced, crunching snow beneath her boots, sunlight on frost-covered branches, Selene's careful smile from just beyond the trees. What she'd thought was a playful outing now twisted with awe and ache. Selene had really been preparing her all along.

"All this time," Leah murmured, eyes misting. "She was thinking ahead. For me."

"She always has," Nico said quietly. "Now we follow the trail she left."

They approached the greenhouse cautiously. From the outside, it looked abandoned, but the subtle hum of energy told them otherwise. Light could be seen flickering faintly within.

Kasper circled it, scratching his ear. "I can't hear anything in there. It feels strange." He circled his finger in the air and summoned a small spiral of wind and willed it toward a crack in the glass, but the magic refused to enter.

Beside him, Nico stilled as his shadows tried to push forward and failed. Leah realized they were both testing the space and neither could get their magic inside.

They gathered at the door. Leah reached for the handle, expecting resistance, but it opened easily.

The space inside expanded impossibly. Crystal panels reflected warm light all around them. The ceiling stretched high above, supported by arches etched with sigils. Shelves of tomes, vials, and instruments lined the walls, all meticulously arranged. Subtle spells pulsed along the floor and ceiling.

"Typical weaver home," Kasper murmured.

Leah's attention caught on a black and silver arch near the back wall, engraved with runes. "What...is that?" she asked.

Nico stepped beside her. "A reporting node," he said quietly. "It's tied to The Order. Even here, a Spell weaver has to respect certain protocols. If someone uses magic carelessly, they could signal The Order. That's why the Elders always have to be careful. One wrong move, and they could be compromised."

Leah shifted in discomfort knowing that even in a sanctuary, The Order's reach still lingered. Yet the room itself exuded care, history, and knowledge, all structured through precise spell weaving.

Then without any shouted incantation, Nico was yanked to a halt, shadows exploding outward in instinctive defense before freezing solid on the ground—locked in place as if pinned to the floor by unseen nails. His breathing became erratic and Leah saw him struggling to breathe.

Kasper swore sharply before he suddenly staggered and stopped entirely. The tiny tornado he had summoned earlier reappeared but began to grow in size right beside him, threatening to attack. It was as if the air itself refused to obey.

"Stop," Leah gasped, stepping forward. "Please. They're with me."

From the shadows, a figure stepped forward, her long silver hair brushing softly against her back. She wore a green robe that draped elegantly to the floor, concealing her hands, and moved with grace that suggested decades of skill. Her emerald eyes scanned them with quiet precision.

"I wondered when you'd find me," the Elder said calmly. She had a gentle tone that exuded confidence, a stark contrast from the spells currently at play. "Selene knew you would come." Her gaze shifted to Nico and Kasper. "You were expected alone."

Her attention hardened. "These are armed anomalies."

Leah swallowed hard. She could feel Nico fighting the spell behind her, his frustration a palpable heat at her back. Kasper's jaw was clenched and his eyes were narrowed. He didn't look afraid, simply aware that if the Elder wished it, neither of them would move again. Ever.

"They're protecting me," Leah said quickly.

A single finger lifted. The magic tightened. Nico choked as his shadows were forced flat once again. Kasper buckled before the spell caught him again, holding him up like a puppet pinned by strings.

"Protection," the Elder said, almost hauntingly, "does not grant permission."

Leah felt panic claw at her chest. She saw Nico straighten slowly causing the hum of magic to waver. Shadows seeped from his skin again, coiling inward and fighting against the invisible force.

"Nico," Leah whispered, fear prickling beneath her ribs.

His gaze was locked on the Elder. The spell still held him, but not cleanly. A fracture rippled through the magic.

The Elder's head tilted as interest replaced her initial detachment.

Nico exhaled slowly and his shadows sank into the stone beneath his boots. They looked like dark veins spreading outward in a silent, creeping web before the sanctuary groaned.

"Nico, don't," Kasper warned.

Light flared along the walls as threads of spellwork tightened, snapping into place around Nico's shadows and forcing them back, compressing them. Nico snarled, a sound dragged from somewhere raw and feral. Then Leah saw it. For a terrifying moment, the shadows fought back and Nico's hands shifted a full inch against the spell's hold. An inch. It might as well have been a blade at the Elder's throat.

The Elder's eyes sharpened. "Well."

Power surged. Sigils flared. Nico was driven to one knee before his shadows extinguished like embers beneath stone.

Kasper fell as if released from invisible grips, but he made no noise and said no words. He simply looked over at Nico as if he too were concerned over what he had just witnessed.

Leah trembled and she realized her nails were biting into her palms.

"You walk with something unfinished," the Elder said to Nico, no longer neutral, "but dangerously close to mastery."

Her gaze flicked to Leah. "Given more time, this sanctuary would not have held him."

The admission chilled her to the bone. Nico stayed where he was, head bowed and breath ragged. Fury still rolled off him, but Leah could see the forced control he was trying to contain. His fingers curled once against the stone, then stilled before he inhaled. Again. And again. When he finally lifted his head, the shadows were gone. His face had gone carefully blank, but she knew better now. She could see the cost of that composure in the way his shoulders held themselves rigid, as if bracing against his own instincts.

"Come," the Elder said, as if nothing extraordinary had just occurred. "We have much to discuss." She turned, already moving deeper into the greenhouse, the matter apparently settled.

Leah hesitated before Nico pushed himself to his feet. He did not look at Kasper or the Elder, but his gaze flickered briefly to Leah, a silent assurance that he was okay.

The Elder looked back briefly, and her expression softened as it fell on Kasper. "It has been many years since a child of wind has come this way," she said warmly. "Do not worry. I hold the power to alert The Order, but I don't believe that will be necessary at the moment."

Kasper's mouth thinned, and he gave a small, embarrassed nod.

"My name is Maverick," the Elder said, stopping beside a long table crowded with herbs. "I have been the one overseeing Eldergrove for nearly a century."

She settled into a chair at the head of the table with a commanding posture and gestured for the others to sit. Nico took the seat between her and Leah. Only then did Leah notice a faint tremor in his hand as it came to rest on the table.

"You must be Nico," Maverick said bluntly. Nico nodded slowly, his expression carefully neutral.

"And you," she continued, turning her gaze to Leah. "I suppose you came to ask me about Selene?"

Leah shifted nervously in her chair. "Well, I—"

"She needs to understand her powers," Kasper cut in.

Nico and Leah both turned sharply toward him, aghast, but Maverick only gave a quiet, appraising look before returning her attention to Leah.

"I see." Her emerald eyes took on a brighter tone as she wove her hands in the air. A low hum filled the room, and a soft green light formed above the table. With a snap, the light solidified into a cloak, a protective spell to contain the voices and thoughts of those within—an extra safeguard against the prying eyes of The Order.

"When I joined The Drift as a Weaver," Maverick began, "The Order took away most of our powers and memories from our lives before our split from the Hollow. For reasons I do not fully understand, I was chosen as the Elder of this town, tasked with protecting it and reporting back to The Order whenever things seemed...amiss."

She leaned forward slightly, her gaze locking on Leah. "There is little I can tell you about the extent of the powers you carry, Leah, but I can tell you about Selene."

Leah nodded and her curiosity piqued.

"Eighteen years ago," Maverick continued, her voice softening, "Selene came to me in search of sanctuary within Eldergrove. She knew what was coming. A rule had been broken and from that transgression, a child would be born of different Pillars—one who carried a power rare enough to unravel everything The Order had built."

Her eyes softened, glimmering with a mixture of respect and memory. "Selene was a gifted Weaver, one with alliances in all corners of the Hollow. Unlike most Weavers in Roots Hollow, she turned her back on The Order's divisions. She believed the Pillars were never meant to stand apart."

Maverick's hand lifted slightly, and with a shimmer of gold, a teapot and four cups floated gently to the table between them. The air smelled faintly of honey and sage as the cups filled themselves. "Though she distanced herself from The Order, Selene's roots ran deep. Many of her dearest friends were still bound to it...or fighting quietly against it." Maverick paused, her gaze lingering somewhere far away. "She walked a dangerous line for many years."

"She was like a secret agent," Kasper murmured, leaning forward slightly. "Hiding in plain sight."

Maverick smiled faintly. "In her own way, yes. She kept many secrets, but she had always opposed The Order, even more so after someone close to her was taken unjustly." Her gaze softened as she looked toward Nico. "Her name was Ilya."

Nico froze. His hands clenched on his knees under the table, the tension visible in his jaw. Leah noticed the subtle change in his posture and the flicker of pain in his eyes.

"She knew that her time was running out," Maverick continued softly. "Before she was killed, she made Selene promise to protect what she treasured most." Maverick's voice softened further. "I am glad to see you alive, Nikolai."

Leah nearly choked on her tea. She turned to Nico, stunned. Kasper's brow furrowed, his gaze darting between them. Nico's expression didn't change, but the muscle in his cheek ticked as if holding back years of unspoken grief.

Maverick continued without pause. "Not long after, Selene learned The Order had taken interest in another woman, Runa, a Seer from Ashmere Hollow. Someone betrayed her, revealing to The Order that the child she carried was a hybrid. The Seer Pillar was always the one The Order was most wary of, so they used this as an excuse to exercise the worst possible punishment. Death."

Leah's pulse quickened. "A child?" Her voice came out barely above a whisper. "Are you saying Selene wasn't related to me?"

Maverick shook her head gently. "No. She was not, by blood. But she loved you fiercely, more than many love their own."

The words seemed to hollow out the air between them. Leah's breath caught, and she stared down at her reflection in the teacup. The surface trembled with each uneven exhale. Beside her, Kasper shifted, his expression tense. His usual easy composure had vanished. His hand hovered halfway across the table, then withdrew, curling around his own cup instead.

"She kept you safe," Maverick went on. "While you were at school, Selene returned to the Hollow often. Always working. Always watching. Building alliances in secret. Every step she took, every lesson she taught you, was to prepare you for this moment."

Leah's vision blurred as the pieces aligned. The cryptic warnings. The strange lessons. The way Selene always knew. Tears slipped silently down her cheeks.

Across the table, Kasper swallowed hard. "She must have known you'd find your way here," he said quietly.

Leah let out a trembling breath that was half a sob, half a laugh. "Yeah," she murmured. "And here I thought she was just eccentric and prone to speaking in riddles."

Nico finally lifted his gaze from the table. "Selene was never careless with her words. Every riddle had a purpose."

The silence that followed was heavy with loss, love, and realization. The faint hiss of the teapot refilling their cups was the only sound between them.

"Selene's choices were not without cost," Maverick said softly. "But she never wavered. You were her hope, Leah. The thread she believed could mend what's been torn."

Leah's fingers trembled against the teacup. Then Nico spoke. "Did Selene ever say who was meant to guide her?"

"Yes," Maverick said. "She said your name."

"No," he said, shaking his head. "I'm not enough for what she needs. I don't understand her power, or the book..."

"The Echodex," Maverick murmured. "It holds the truth of all Pillars. It is not a spell book or a weapon, but something far greater and far more dangerous to The Order. It contains truth about Ezren and perhaps the key to his undoing. But you're not wrong, the Echodex is a delicate book. It is sentient and can probably tell Leah is not ready. You'll need someone who remembers the world before the Pillars fractured."

Nico's gaze lifted. "Who?"

"Atticus," she replied. "Elder of Oakgrove. A scholar of the old world. If anyone still knows the meaning of what's inside the Echodex, it is him."

Kasper frowned. "And there's a 'but', isn't there?"

"Yes," Maverick admitted. "Atticus has long been under The Order's watch. I cannot tell if he still serves their will or fights against it. Either way, you'll need him. He is the only one who can guide her."

The room seemed to still for a moment until Maverick's head suddenly turned toward the window, eyes narrowing. The faint hum of her spells rippled through the air.

"Your time here is over." She rose gracefully, her composure unbroken but her tone urgent. "Take the back door through the grove. You have five minutes before the wards I placed around you collapse." She lifted her chin toward Nico and Kasper. "Gentlemen...I trust you know what to do."

Nico and Kasper were already moving. The change in them was instantaneous—no hesitation or wasted motion. Nico's eyes darkened, his shadows unfurling like smoke and wrapping around Leah as he pulled her off the chair and close to him.

The air outside the greenhouse was charged, heavy with magic from those who had approached it. Nico's shadows grew wider, wrapping all three of them in a dense, protective cocoon. Kasper's power flared in tandem, helping to guide Nico's shadows away from immediate danger. They sprinted toward the Veil, every step heavy with tension. Time was slipping away— Maverick's protective spells would unravel in less than three minutes and if that happened, The Order would know their exact location.

Chapter 17

They reached the arch just as the last of Maverick's protective spells holding steady around them vanished. Nico's shadows retracted and Kasper's power eased, allowing the air around them to settle. Leah exhaled, and her legs finally gave out. She sank to the cold forest ground with one hand braced against the earth and the other closing tightly around the bracelet Sage had given her. Her lungs burned as she dragged in steady breaths, counting them until the shaking in her hands eased. The spells had held, and nothing had been triggered. For now, they were still undetected.

Leah glanced between Nico and Kasper. Neither looked relieved. Nico was already scanning the archway like he expected someone to come through and attack, while Kasper's gaze was distant, as if listening to something only he could hear.

Leah felt dizzy, which she figured was just the adrenaline after running for their lives. "Wait," she said, the word slipping out before she could overthink it. Her voice was edged with nerves. "What if we don't go back into the Hollow this time?"

Nico turned toward her slowly. "What are you suggesting?"

"What if we keep moving?" she said, pushing herself to her feet. "If anyone sensed anything just now, they would expect us to go back into the Hollow, right? So, what if we go somewhere else instead? Somewhere crowded, where they wouldn't expect us to go?"

Nico frowned. "You mean Oakgrove?"

She nodded. "My best friend always takes the train there. It's only a two-hour ride." Her tone held a flicker of hope. "We wouldn't need to rely on magic to cover ourselves this time which means they can't track us. I think it's... safe."

Nico studied her, weighing the risk. Kasper's grin returned immediately, mischief lighting his eyes. He circled behind Leah and placed his hands on top of her head, his chin settling there with casual familiarity.

"She's not wrong," he said. "Lying low could also mean hiding in plain sight."

A flicker of irritation crossed Nico's face, which Kasper noticed instantly. "Ah, there it is. I was wondering if you'd forgotten how to look at me like that," Kasper teased, giving Nico an exaggerated wink.

Leah rolled her eyes but couldn't help a small smile. "You're going to get on Nico's nerves the whole way, aren't you?"

"Only as much as is necessary," Kasper said, brushing past Nico with deliberate closeness and letting his arm brush Leah's shoulder just enough to provoke a reaction. Nico's eyes followed every move, unamused, but he didn't intervene.

They stepped back onto the streets of Eldergrove cautiously. Now at midafternoon, the town was bustling with people doing their holiday shopping. Leah kept her head down, trying not to draw attention as she led them toward the train station. They had to be careful, especially knowing someone from The Order had appeared. Even though the townspeople were non-magical and oblivious, Order members were likely lurking in plain sight just like them.

Leah reached instinctively for her bag, fingers slipping inside as a new thought struck her. Money. Her stomach dipped slightly as she rummaged through the bag, but she already knew that there was nothing there. Of course. She had left her house in such a rush that she didn't think to take any cash with her, only her card. Her gaze flicked briefly to the busy street ahead as unease prickled at the back of her neck. Cards would be easier to use, but the thought of The Order tracing something like that made her stomach twist. They had eyes everywhere—what if they could track them through her card too?

"I just realized," she murmured under her breath, half to herself, "I don't have any—"

"I do," Nico cut in calmly, as if reading her thoughts.

Leah blinked and looked up at him. "You have human money?"

His mouth twitched faintly, almost amused. "Selene didn't exactly keep me hidden in the woods every time I visited." He reached into the inner pocket of his coat and pulled out a small fold of worn bills. "I learned the currency. Figured it might come in handy someday."

Relief loosened the tight knot in Leah's chest, and a quiet wave of gratitude followed close behind. Of course Nico had thought ahead. Up until now, she hadn't needed to buy anything—not while moving through forests and hidden parts of the Hollows—but stepping back into a normal town meant normal problems again.

With that worry settled, Leah lifted her gaze and guided them forward through the busy streets and soon, the small train station came into view through the bustle. Holiday decorations hung from its archways, red ribbons fluttering in the cold air. But Leah didn't notice the decorations, instead, she noticed the way people's eyes turned as they walked past. Or more specifically, how every woman within sight seemed to stop and stare.

"Oh my god..." one girl said loudly to her friend, elbowing her. "Did you see that tall one? He looks like he walked out of a movie."

Her friend giggled. "I call the one with the scar. Look at that jawline."

Leah groaned under her breath. "Perfect. Just perfect." She grabbed Kasper by the wrist with one hand and Nico with the other, dragging them through the crowd toward the ticket booth. "You two are officially public hazards."

Kasper smirked. "You sound jealous."

"Jealous of a stampede? Please." She rolled her eyes and stepped up to the open ticket booth, but the second she looked up, her stomach sank.

"Omg, Leah??" the booth attendant exclaimed, her voice drenched in performative surprise.

Caroline Wess. Her childhood tormentor, and the girl who had made her school years a quiet hell. Perfect blond curls framed a face that hadn't changed much, still all fake sweetness and superiority. If time had done anything, it had refined her vanity. Caroline had always loved an audience and always loved reminding everyone how perfectly she fit into her own skin.

Her station uniform did nothing to dull the smugness in her eyes, clinging to her with a neckline just low enough to invite attention. As she leaned forward over the counter, Leah caught the familiar, infuriating gesture Caroline had perfected years ago: shoulders angled just so that her chest was subtly, but unmistakably, on display.

"Caroline," Leah said flatly, summoning the fakest smile she could manage. "Hi. Can I just get—"

But Caroline wasn't listening anymore. Her eyes had drifted past Leah to Nico and Kasper. The shift in her expression was immediate.

"Oh," she breathed, her voice turning soft and predatory all at once. "And who are you two?"

Leah felt her stomach drop.

Kasper leaned casually against the counter, a slow grin forming. "Just travelers."

"Well," Caroline purred, leaning in further and clearly aware of exactly what she was doing, "if you're passing through Eldergrove, I could show you around. There's a cozy tavern right across from here." She bit her lower lip. "Maybe later tonight?"

Kasper arched a brow. "Tempting. But I try not to accept invitations from people who forget their manners."

Caroline blinked, feigning innocence. "Manners?"

"Yeah," he said, smirking. "Usually you acknowledge the person in front of you before flirting with the guy behind her."

Caroline's smile faltered for a split second before she doubled down, brushing it off with an airy giggle. "Oh, I was just being friendly. You boys look cold in those cloaks. Are you two brothers? You're both so handsome."

Nico's expression darkened and his voice came out low and clipped. "We're fine."

Caroline either didn't hear the warning or chose not to. "You're not from around here, are you?"

"We're not here for conversation," Nico said. "Three tickets."

The sudden edge in his voice made Caroline falter, but only for a moment. She smiled again, flicking her hair over her shoulder, clearly mistaking irritation for interest. "Of course, handsome. Where to?"

"Oakgrove," Leah said sharply, stepping between them before Nico lost his patience. "Three tickets, please."

Nico reached into his coat and placed the folded bills on the counter, sliding the cash forward to pay for the tickets without taking his eyes off the attendant.

Caroline's gaze slid past her again, this time to Nico's gloved hand resting beside the money. She reached for the tickets slowly, her fingers brushing deliberately close to his.

Nico's arm moved before Leah could react. He slid his arm around Leah's waist and pulled her close to his side, his stare leveling on Caroline.

"Touch me again," he said quietly, "and you'll regret it."

Caroline froze. Whatever she saw in his eyes drained the color from her face, but Leah barely registered it.

All she could feel was Nico's arm around her waist. Her breath hitched as her thoughts stuttered at the warmth of him pressed against her side. It wasn't accidental, and it wasn't protective. He had pulled her in without hesitation, as if there had never been any doubt where she belonged in that moment.

Kasper's chuckle snapped her back. "I should have warned you about him. But hey," he added with a smirk, "I'd say you lasted longer than most."

Caroline's mouth opened, then closed again, lost for words. Her hands shook slightly as she passed the tickets across the counter. "Th-there you go," she stammered.

Leah forced herself to move, slipping out of Nico's hold only when she had to.

"Thank you," she said tightly, snatching the tickets before Caroline could recover.

They turned and headed for the platform, the chill air biting as they crossed. Once seated on a bench, Leah exhaled hard, willing her racing pulse to settle.

"Well," she said softly, glancing sideways at him, "that was terrifying. You didn't have to do that."

Nico stared straight ahead, posture rigid once more, as if he'd already retreated behind his walls.

"Yes," he said. "I did."

Kasper chuckled beside them. "You sure did. I thought she was about to climb over the counter and get on top of you. Honestly, she showed impressive restraint."

Leah groaned and dragged a hand down her face. "You're not helping."

But even as she said it, a knot twisted in her stomach. The image wouldn't leave. Caroline's deliberate lean. The way her eyes had lingered on Nico like he was something to be taken. Leah felt her fingers curl around the edge of the bench, and she shifted closer to Nico without fully meaning to.

Kasper, of course, noticed everything. "Relax, Red. You handled it fine."

Leah stayed quiet, staring down at her hands as heat crept into her cheeks. She didn't want to admit how rattled she'd been. Her stomach still fluttered at the memory of Nico grabbing her waist. But worst of all, she couldn't shake the image of Caroline flirting with him.

Was this what jealousy felt like?

The whistle of the train echoed through the frosted air and the scent of coal and pine hung heavy, blending with the chatter of travelers. Leah clutched the tickets tightly in her gloved hand.

"Car nine," she said, glancing between Nico and Kasper. "That's us."

They moved quietly, blending into the crowd. Nico kept a step ahead, scanning faces, while Kasper lingered behind, tense and alert, his eyes flicking to every corner. Inside, the train was warm and dimly lit, its walls humming softly as it prepared to leave the station.

The three of them boarded quietly, slipping into an empty car nine where the seats smelled faintly of leather. Leah set her bag down on the seat. For a moment, it almost felt normal, like she was just another girl traveling for the holidays.

Almost.

"I can't believe we're actually taking a train," she murmured as her eyes swept over the polished carriages. "I've... never even ridden one before."

Kasper gave her a sideways glance. "First time for everything."

"Wait," Leah said curiously, "are there even trains in the Hollow?"

"Not exactly," Kasper said. "Travel through the Hollow is different. Mostly portals, since they're quick and efficient."

"Portals? I thought those were rare."

"The ones that connect the Hollow to the Groves are different from regular transportation portals," Kasper explained. "The regular ones can be found throughout town, and normally everyone has one."

Leah blinked. "That's... convenient."

"It is," he said with a small shrug.

She slid into the seat by the window, watching Eldergrove's familiar skyline blur into fog. The train gave a low rumble, then lurched forward, carrying her away from the only home she had ever known. Her chest ached. She hadn't gone to college like everyone else. She had stayed for Selene, the café, and maybe the quiet since the outside world had always felt too big, too uncertain.

If her younger self could see her now.

"I'd love to see my friend when we get there," she said quietly, turning toward Nico and Kasper. "I haven't been able to talk to her at all since this happened..."

"No," Nico cut in, sharper than usual. His eyes flicked toward the other passengers. "You can't risk it. The Order knows your face now. For all we know, they already have eyes on this train."

Leah frowned. "But she's my best friend."

"Exactly," Nico said evenly. "You'd be putting her in danger."

Frustration coiled in her chest, but she knew he was right. She didn't want to put Sage at risk. Leah clenched her fists lightly in her lap, trying to figure out some way to let Sage know she was safe.

Kasper stood, adjusting the strap of his coat. "I'll check the next few cars. I'll draw less attention alone, especially if they still think it's just you two traveling."

Nico shot him a questioning look. "Did you hear something? Do you think they're here?"

"I think they could be," Kasper replied, scanning the corridor. "And I'd rather know than guess."

Before Leah could respond, he disappeared into the narrow aisle, his coat brushing against the seats as he moved. She turned back toward the window where the landscape of fields and forests rushed by, the world expanding beyond her small, safe town. Eldergrove was already fading behind her, swallowed by the mist.

"I have to ask," she said carefully. "You can't send Dimitri to check on Sage? Give her a message for me?"

Nico raised his brow. "Do you remember how you reacted the first time you saw him? Do you honestly think it's a good idea?"

Leah's gaze dropped to her hands, twisting in her lap as frustration curled in her chest. Of course it wasn't a good idea.

"Besides," he added, "Dimitri wouldn't be able to appear outside the Hollow."

"I just want to tell her I'm okay," she murmured, the ache in her chest hollowing her words.

"I'm sorry, Leah, but it's too dangerous right now."

Her hands tightened into fists in her lap. He was right, and she knew it, but that didn't dull the frustration. Leah pressed her forehead against the cool glass of the window in defeat.

"You know," she began softly, her reflection faint against the glass, "I never thought I'd be here right now."

She felt Nico's attention shift before she saw it. When she glanced back, he was watching her, something in her voice had clearly unsettled him, but she looked back out the window.

"I used to think I'd stay in Eldergrove forever," she continued quietly. "Maybe take over the café someday. Keep everything small and... safe." Her voice thinned. "I didn't think I was made for anything more than that."

She noticed Nico's hand lift, hovering near her face, close enough that she felt its warmth. His fingers hesitated, then settled into a light, almost awkward tap against the top of her head.

"Sometimes," Nico said, "we're meant for something greater, whether we believe it or not." Their eyes met. "I'm a firm believer that the cards we're dealt are always the ones we can handle." A faint, almost wistful smile followed.

Leah studied him, her expression softening. His words lingered in her chest like an ache, but another thought surfaced. Maverick's sanctuary. The truth about his mother. A boy's innocence stolen and shaped by pain, forced into something he never chose.

She swallowed hard.

"I'm sorry about your mom," she said, emotion rushing back unchecked.

Nico's expression stilled before he looked away, fixing his gaze on the blur of trees outside. "You don't have to be," he said quietly. "She made her choice."

Leah frowned. "That doesn't make it fair."

He let out a soft, humorless huff. "Fairness is a story we tell ourselves so we can sleep at night." His gaze returned to her, the faintest glint of warmth cutting through the steel. "But thank you."

Her lips curved into a small smile. "You sound like someone who's lived a thousand lives."

"Feels like it some days."

Something in his tone made her chest ache. She wanted to say more, to tell him he didn't always have to hold everything together, but the compartment door slid open and Kasper stepped back inside. A cold draft followed him.

"Everything's quiet," he said.

Leah blinked. "So... that's good?"

He tilted his head. "Depends. Calm might mean they're waiting for something."

Nico's shoulders squared. "Or someone."

Kasper dropped into his seat with a sigh. "You're fun, as always." Then, glancing at Leah, his tone softened. "For now, we're safe. No need to stress."

Leah nodded, trying to breathe again. The motion of the train was oddly soothing, the warmth of the compartment dulling the chill that had followed them since leaving the greenhouse. Still, unease twisted in her stomach.

After a few minutes, she stood, brushing her hands on her coat. "I'll be right back. I just need the bathroom."

Nico's head snapped toward her. "No."

She blinked. "No?"

"It's not safe," he said firmly. "Stay here. You can wait until—"

"I'm fine," Leah interrupted, forcing a small laugh. "There are people everywhere. I'll be quick."

"Leah—"

"I promise," she said softly. "It's just a few cars down. I'll be careful."

For a moment, it looked like he'd argue again, but she met his eyes and something there made him relent. He gave a short, sharp nod.

"Two minutes. If you're not back, I'll come for you."

"Understood, sir," she teased lightly, though her heart was already pounding.

Leah slipped into the corridor muted by the light flickering against the glass as the train curved through the forest. Passengers murmured quietly behind closed doors. Everything seemed... normal.

She exhaled and headed toward the back cars.

As she stepped out of the bathroom, she saw him. A man leaned against the wall outside the last passenger car, tall and broad in a wrinkled gray coat. His eyes tracked her instantly before he smiled, and her skin crawled.

"Evenin'," he drawled, stepping into her path. "Didn't think they let angels ride second class."

Leah froze, forcing a tight, polite smile. "Excuse me."

He moved closer. "Funny. You don't look like you're from around here."

Her heart hammered. She tried to sidestep him, but his hand shot out, grabbing her arm.

"Hey—let go!"

He only grinned wider. "Relax. No need to make a scene." His other hand lifted, brushing a strand of hair from her face.

Panic roared in her ears. She shoved him, but he was stronger, forcing her backward into the next car. The door hissed shut behind them, sealing them off from the rest of the train.

"Don't be like that," he whispered. "Just a little fun before your stop."

She twisted, trying to break free as he pressed closer. Her mind screamed at her to use her magic, but she couldn't. Not here.

"Don't touch me," she said, breathless.

He didn't stop. He grabbed both her wrists above her head, his free hand sliding toward the buttons of her coat. Panic surged and he managed to kick him hard, but he only laughed.

"Feisty."

"Funny," a voice drawled behind him. "I was about to say the same thing."

The man stiffened, spinning to find Kasper in the doorway with one hand in his pocket, expression unreadable.

"Who the hell are you?" the man snapped.

Kasper's gaze flicked to Leah, checking her, before returning to the man. His voice stayed light, almost bored.

"Someone with a very low tolerance for idiots." He stepped forward slowly. "Now I'm going to give you five seconds to remove your hands from her and pretend this never happened."

The man sneered. "You think you scare me?"

Kasper smiled. "Not yet. I'm more of a slow-burn kind of guy."

The man lunged. Kasper sidestepped easily, hooking the man's arm and twisting. A sharp, ugly crack filled the car and the man cried out, collapsing to one knee.

Kasper sighed, crouching beside him. "I was really hoping you'd make a better choice, but here we are." His tone never changed. Quiet. Amused. Dangerous.

He glanced at Leah, then leaned close to the man. "You're going to stay down and when you wake up, you're going to rethink your life choices. Because if you ever look at her again..." His voice dropped to a whisper. "I'll make sure you don't wake up next time."

One precise strike to the base of the man's neck dropped him unconscious. Kasper straightened, brushing his sleeve as if nothing had happened, then crossed to Leah, giving her another quick once-over.

"He didn't hurt you?"

She shook her head, rubbing her wrist.

"Good," Kasper said. "I really don't want to clean blood off a moving train."

Leah blinked at him. "Thank you."

He smiled softly. "I suggest we get back before Nico has a meltdown."

Nico was already on his feet when they returned. His gaze locked on Leah's trembling hands as she sat.

"What happened?" he asked.

Leah opened her mouth, but Kasper cut in. "Some creep thought he could have fun in an empty car. I handled it."

Nico's eyes narrowed. "Define 'handled.'"

Kasper leaned back, folding his arms. "He'll be sleeping it off. Nothing permanent, unfortunately."

Nico took a slow breath, scanning Leah for injuries. "He touched you?"

She shook her head quickly. "I'm fine. Kasper stopped him."

The fury in Nico's eyes didn't fade. "You shouldn't have gone alone."

"I'm sorry," Leah whispered.

Kasper interjected. "Relax," he said in an edged but lighter tone "I made sure he got the message."

"You think this is funny?" Nico snapped.

"Not even a little." Kasper leaned forward, elbows on his knees and fingers laced like he was holding himself in check. "But someone had to keep this from turning into a massacre."

Silence settled over the car.

"You would've killed him, Nico," Kasper said quietly. "Then we'd have a real problem."

After a long moment, Nico spoke. "Next time, you don't leave my sight."

Leah nodded instinctively.

Kasper leaned back, as the familiar grin slipped back into place, but it didn't quite reach his eyes. "Well," he muttered, gazing out at the blur of trees, "this trip's off to a great start. Can't wait to see what kind of welcome Oakgrove's got waiting for us."

Chapter 18

The train screeched as it slowed, snow swirling past the windows in soft flurries. Leah pressed her gloved hand to the glass, catching her first glimpse of Oakgrove. The town looked like it had been pulled straight from a holiday movie with Christmas decorations lining every street. Rows of cottages were dusted in snow, strings of lights crossed overhead, and a small market appeared to be set up beside the station. Smoke curled from chimneys around them, and carolers sang near a tall pine tree in the center square.

When the train finally stopped, Nico was the first to step off, scanning the platform before motioning for the others to follow. His dark cloak stood out sharply against the white snow, a stark mark of vigilance in the stillness. Leah pulled her coat tighter as she stepped down behind him, and looked over at Kasper, who was taking in the scene with a grin.

"You wouldn't think a place built on lost memories would be this... merry," he said.

"Stay close," Nico said quietly, eyes flicking toward the crowd.

Leah and Kasper followed him down the steps. The hum of the market tugged at Leah, the scent of roasted nuts making her stomach growl. She couldn't help but take it all in, the lights, the laughter, the delicious smells. No wonder Sage had chosen to come study here.

"It's... beautiful," she said softly.

Kasper gave a small nod, glancing around. "You can say that again. I did not expect the other side of ruins to be this."

"Few do," Nico said without looking back.

They passed between stalls selling ornaments, scarves, and sweets. Leah glanced down at the cobblestones, searching for the faint glowing symbols that had guided her through Eldergrove, but there were none.

"The markings," she murmured. "They're not here."

Nico's gaze shifted to her. "Nothing at all?"

Leah shook her head, and Kasper frowned. "Then how are we supposed to find Atticus?"

Nico didn't answer. His expression was stern, and Leah knew that meant he didn't know either. They slowed their pace, drifting toward a small food stand tucked along the side of the marketplace, close to the train station.

"Let's grab something to eat while we figure out our next move."

The smell of fried potatoes filled the air as they approached. A broad-shouldered man greeted them cheerfully and began putting together plastic cones filled with hot French fries, sprinkling them with salt and herbs before handing the first to Leah. Out of habit, her eyes flicked toward Nico just as he slid a few bills across the counter to pay. He gave her a brief nod and Leah took a bite that almost made her groan with how delicious it was.

Kasper chuckled at her reaction, then froze mid-bite. Across the street stood a small booth draped with a purple banner that read: *Fortunes and Reflections.* The woman behind the table wore far too many scarves and bangles. Her dark hair was pinned back with a jeweled clip, and her lipstick was a bold shade of crimson.

"What's that?" Kasper asked, tilting his head toward the booth.

Leah and Nico followed his gaze. "Oh, that's a fortune teller," Leah said. "They tell you your future using cards. It's just for fun."

He looked confused. "How would she know?"

"She doesn't," Leah said with a faint smile.

But Kasper was already heading toward the booth, finishing his fries in one mouthful and tossing the paper cone away. Leah sighed and followed, while Nico lingered only a few steps behind, close enough that she didn't slip out of his awareness while he finished his food.

The woman leaned her chin into her palm as Kasper approached, her bracelets jingling softly.

"Well," she said with a teasing smile, "aren't you a sight. Come for a glimpse of your future, love?"

Kasper beamed and slid into the chair across from her. "Absolutely."

The woman shuffled her deck with practiced grace, flipping and spreading the cards. "Pick three, and let's see what they have to say."

Leah folded her arms just outside the booth, brows furrowed. The last time she'd seen a fortune teller, she'd been fourteen, at a market in Eldergrove. She'd begged Selene to let her go, only to be told they were all fakes. When Selene finally gave in, the woman had prophesied that Leah would get a dog and travel the world with Selene on her twentieth birthday. So much for that.

The fortune teller flipped the first card. "The Wheel. Change is coming. Big change, and not all of it comfortable. You may lose something... or find something unexpected."

Kasper nodded enthusiastically. "Interesting. Okay."

The second card turned over. "The Tower. Obstacles in your path. You'll be challenged in ways you never saw coming."

Kasper frowned slightly. "Huh. Okay. A little vague."

The woman's gaze flicked to Leah. "Ah, your companion. I sense tension, but loyalty. She's loved you for years, grounds you, and sometimes... restrains you."

Leah flushed. "We're not—"

"Shh," the woman said, lifting a finger. "The cards reveal what the heart cannot speak."

The third card appeared. "The Star. Hope persists. You'll be drawn to something extraordinary... though you may not recognize it at first."

Kasper blinked. "Wait. That doesn't make sense. You said I'd lose something, face challenges, and find something extraordinary. Which is it?"

The woman leaned back with a dramatic sigh. "Life is full of contradictions, darling. That's why the cards are necessary." She smiled at him flirtatiously.

"That's enough," Leah said, shaking her head as she took Kasper by the arm.

"I guess that's that, then," he muttered, clearly disappointed.

Leah led him back to the food stall, where Nico was now enjoying a small sandwich.

"So," Nico said, raising an eyebrow with a smirk, "will you become the most powerful?"

"Shut up, Nico," Kasper replied solemnly, pointing at Nico's sandwich. "Can I have one of those?"

The vendor laughed and handed Kasper a fresh sandwich.

"Ah. Miss Faye got you, didn't she?" the vendor asked, chuckling as he passed over napkins. "She does that to every tourist. If you want the real thing, you should see Kaya. She's usually down by the frozen creek past the chapel."

The three exchanged a look. Not who they needed, but maybe a place to start.

After finishing their food and a few pastries, they left the warmth of the market behind. The streets grew silent as festive sounds started fading into distant echoes.

Leah scanned the buildings for any sign of Bravo Vet, Sage's apprenticeship. She hadn't spoken to Sage in months, and she was certain her friend would be furious when they finally reunited. The thought tightened her chest with guilt. She'd never wanted a cellphone before, but now she understood how much easier it would have made staying in touch.

Nico walked ahead with his head down, boots crunching over cobblestone as if he could sense hidden sigils beneath the snow. Kasper trailed behind, glancing around with idle curiosity. Leah drifted to the right with thoughts of Sage crowding her mind so completely that she didn't notice the group of men approaching until one slammed into her shoulder.

"Watch where you're going!" he snapped, stepping back aggressively.

Before she could respond, Nico was at her side, his expression ice cold. "Careful," he said, placing a hand on the man's chest.

The man's scowl deepened, ready to shove back, but Nico froze. His eyes widened as he spotted the mark hidden on the man's collar. The mark of The Order.

"Nico?" Leah whispered.

He didn't answer but she saw him stiffen. At her voice, another man, taller with red hair, locked eyes with Nico. He went completely still, as if he'd seen a ghost.

"Go," Nico hissed. "Now."

Kasper grabbed Leah's arm, and they bolted down a narrow side street. Kasper stumbled over a loose stone, but Leah hauled him forward as Nico brought up the rear, watching the red-haired man, who remained frozen.

For a moment, it seemed the group had stopped before recognition sharpened the taller man's face.

"That's them," he hissed. "Move. Follow them." The others caught on, and the group gave chase, weaving through the winding streets, careful not to draw attention.

Leah's heart hammered as she glanced back. The town that had felt warm and festive moments ago now felt tight and hostile, especially with the way Nico was radiating tension around them.

"Where are we going?" Kasper panted, gripping her hand.

"Somewhere they can't see us," Nico said tersely. "And fast."

Leah nodded, swallowing her fear. The search for Kaya suddenly felt far more urgent and much more dangerous than she had imagined. They ran through a tangle of narrow streets, boots crunching on snow-dusted stone. Nico stayed in the back, keeping a sharp eye on the shadows, while Kasper muttered something about wanting to knock them out.

Behind them, The Order agents moved quickly but with careful restraint, suppressing any hint of magic. Every step had to be calculated, otherwise Oakgrove's residents would notice even the slightest disturbance. The tall, red-haired man who had recognized Nico lingered among them. Even from afar, she could see the tension in his posture and the way his gaze fixed on Nico and never wavered. Something about him felt stunned, like he was looking at someone who wasn't supposed to exist.

Leah darted around a corner where the narrow streets opened onto a small square. There, bathed in the soft glow of lanterns, stood a chapel. Its doors were wide open, revealing warm light inside. Just outside the doorway stood a woman in silence. She had deep brown eyes framed by jet-black hair that fell to her shoulders, and a quiet, confident presence that made Leah instinctively pause. The woman did not speak. She only watched them, her lips curved into a subtle smile.

Kasper groaned and crossed his arms. "We don't have time for this," he muttered. "We should just—"

"Shh," Leah said, lifting her hand, her gaze fixed on the woman. "Kaya?"

The woman's smile widened slightly. Then, with a slow, deliberate motion, she bowed her head and stepped aside, waiting by the open door. Nico's eyes flicked to the streets behind them. The Order agents were closer now, moving faster.

Leah did not hesitate. She grabbed both of them by the hands and ran for the chapel, slipping inside as Kaya closed the door behind them without a sound. The moment it shut, the structure folded in on itself, stone and shadow dissolved into empty air as if it had never stood there at all.

Leah barely dared to breathe, but she could still hear footsteps outside slowing, then stopping. Muffled voices carried through the space where the doorway had been, close enough to make her pulse pound in her ears.

"What... where are they?" one muttered, the words sharp with confusion.

"I don't see them. Check behind the houses," another voice ordered, tense and clipped.

Silence stretched briefly before Leah heard a fist strike something solid, the sound tight with restrained anger. "We report back. We lost them."

Their footsteps lingered a moment longer before finally retreating, fading into the distance. Only then did Leah release the breath she'd been holding. Beside her, Kasper and Nico looked warily at Kaya, who simply smiled and began to walk ahead, leading the way.

Beneath the square, Leah, Kasper, and Nico followed Kaya down a narrow staircase that twisted deep underground. The stone steps were worn and uneven, smoothed by centuries of use, and the walls curved close on either side as if pressing them downward. The stairwell was dim and quiet—the air growing cooler with every step. Kaya moved ahead without haste, a stark contrast to the chaos they had just escaped.

"Isn't it a little convenient," Kasper whispered, breathless, "that the exact person we're looking for just appears out of nowhere?"

Leah didn't answer. The thought had crossed her mind too, but something about the way Kaya had looked at her kept pulling her forward.

"Stay close," Nico murmured.

Kaya glanced back but said nothing, leading them to the bottom of the stairs where a heavy metal door stood before them. She opened it to reveal a small chamber lined with books and stacks of papers pressed against the stone walls. At the center sat an elderly man behind a plain wooden desk. His gray hair framed a face deeply lined by time, and his eyes seemed to look straight through them.

"Atticus," Kaya said softly, stepping aside.

The man lifted his gaze from a scattered page of notes and his muted lilac eyes fixed on Leah with quiet intensity.

"So," he said at last with a voice that was low and deliberate. "You finally found me."

A shiver ran down Leah's spine. "You know who I am?"

"Know?" A faint, humorless smile touched his mouth. "Child, your presence ripples." He pushed himself up from the desk with effort. "But I am more interested in the rumors of what you carry."

Leah's heart stuttered, her hand brushing the satchel at her side.

"The Echodex," Atticus said with quiet certainty. "You have it." He let out a short, incredulous laugh that made Nico tense beside her.

"We didn't come here to—"

Atticus raised a hand, silencing him without looking away from Leah. "If I wished you harm, boy, we would not be speaking." His attention returned to her. "Tell me, child, have you opened it?"

"Yes," she said. "But I didn't understand what it showed me. It didn't show me anything for a long time, actually."

Atticus studied her, a flicker of sympathy crossing his face before it vanished. "Then it is true. The Echodex chose you."

He moved to the front of the desk and leaned against it. "The Echodex does not awaken for just anyone. What you see through it is not meant to be lived, it is meant to be understood. A Seer's power runs deep, but with the Echodex, that depth can become an abyss."

Leah's frustration rose. "I don't understand. Isn't it just a book of memories?"

Atticus exhaled slowly and leaned back, crossing his fingers where a thick gold ring gleamed on his middle one. His gaze drifted to Nico and Kasper, weighing them.

"Kaya."

Kaya stepped into the room, bowing her head slightly.

"Please," Atticus said calmly, "take these gentlemen on a brief tour."

"No," Nico said sharply. "I won't leave her alone with you."

"Me either," Kasper added. "How do we know this isn't a trap?"

Atticus smiled faintly. "If she wishes to learn more about the Echodex, I must speak to her alone."

Leah hesitated, torn between caution and curiosity.

"It's okay," she said softly.

"No, Leah," Nico said, firm and final.

She met his gaze. "I need to know what I'm dealing with. You said it yourself. You can only teach me so much."

Kasper shifted uneasily. "I don't know, Nico. This feels... off."

Nico's jaw tensed, calculation flickering behind his silence.

"I'll scream if he tries anything," Leah added quietly, attempting humor, though neither of them smiled.

At last, Nico stepped back. "We'll be right outside."

Atticus inclined his head. "I would expect nothing less of you, Nico."

Nico paused at the sound of his name, then turned and left with Kasper close behind. The heavy door shut with a muted thud.

Atticus faced Leah again. "Now," he said softly, "to understand the Echodex, you must first understand what our Pillar represented, and what The Order did to erase it."

He paced behind the desk, fingers trailing over old book spines. "The Seers were once the greatest nuisances to The Order—at least after Ezren took control. Before him, The Order tolerated Seers, even used their foresight when it suited them. But Ezren is not a man who enjoys uncertainty."

He stopped, his lilac eyes gleaming. "When he learned that some Seers could alter the future, not merely see it, fear became obsession."

Leah frowned. "They could change it?"

"To a degree," Atticus said. "While all Seers possessed the gift of prophecy, twin Seers, particularly those from the bloodline of The Unheard, carried something far more dangerous. They could manipulate the Echodex itself, and with it, the threads of time. The Unheard were the direct descendants of the first Seer who created the Echodex, and their connection to it was absolute."

He resumed pacing. "But twins were rare among our kind, and Ezren made them rarer still. He cursed the bloodline so when twins were born, one would never live long enough to master their gift. A cruel but effective way to ensure the Echodex's true power would remain forever divided."

Leah gasped. "He cursed babies to die?"

"It was not a risk he was willing to take." Atticus said grimly. "The Seers would see, but never touch. Know, but never change."

"Then why is he still searching for the Echodex?" Leah asked.

"Because it is not merely a book," Atticus replied. "It is a mirror of all timelines and bloodlines. Ezren believes that if he can master it, he can rewrite the future so he always prevails. An item with that much power cannot be destroyed."

"But it only answers to my bloodline."

A grim smile spread across his face. "Ezren's power exceeds what we believed possible. He is confident he can bend it."

Leah looked down. "Then what does it want from me?"

"To remember," Atticus said simply. "That's what it was made for. The Echodex does not seek to be wielded, it seeks to be remembered. Through it, you can uncover what Ezren has buried: the pacts he broke, the bloodlines he cursed, and the truths he silenced. The Echodex remembers what the world was forced to forget."

Her voice trembled. "And knowing that will stop him?"

"No," he said quietly. "But within those memories lies what he cannot change."

Leah frowned. "Change?"

"Every man who believes himself a god," Atticus murmured, "hides a flaw he cannot see. A truth that even power cannot protect him from."

Her eyes widened slightly. "You mean...his weakness."

Atticus leaned forward, steepling his fingers. "Everyone has one. But decades of fear have buried his deeper than any grave. The Hollow trembles at his name, and no one dares to look beyond it. But you..." He gave a faint, knowing smile. "You carry the only light left that might show where his shadow ends."

Leah swallowed, her fingers finding the Echodex in her bag.

Atticus's eyes followed the motion. "Find the truth...for in truth lies the way to end him."

Leah's mind swirled, every thread of Atticus's words tangling into another. The Seers. The curse. The Echodex.

"You make it sound like you were waiting for me."

"In a way," he said quietly. "We have been waiting for someone like you for decades. Someone the Echodex would answer to who was not bound by The Order."

The silence between them stretched, broken only by the door creaking open. Kaya stepped in, the light from her lantern catching in her black hair. "We've returned," she said quietly.

Atticus smiled. "Right on time."

Chapter 19

Kaya moved like smoke through the corridors. The faint light from her lantern brushing against the damp stone walls and glinting off the ink-black strands of her hair. Nico followed a few steps behind, his hand instinctively hovering near his weapon, while Kasper trailed close, his eyes darting across every turn and shadow.

No one spoke.

The passage twisted deeper underground, narrowing until their shoulders grazed the walls. At every fork, Kaya chose without hesitation, her lantern swinging slightly as she glided forward. The air grew colder the deeper they went until finally, Kasper broke the silence.

"Are you ever going to tell us where we're going?"

Kaya didn't turn. "Back."

Nico tensed. "You could try being less cryptic."

"I could," she said simply, "but then you might not follow."

Another turn, another narrow stair, and then suddenly the space opened into the chamber they had left less than an hour ago. Atticus sat behind his desk again with his eyes already fixed on them as if he had known they would return at that very moment. Leah stood opposite him, still and pale with her hands gripping the Echodex through her bag.

Nico's gaze swept over Leah, making sure she was unharmed before he saw it— a faint shimmer to Atticus's right, rippling like heat against air. The distortion deepened, folding over itself until a shape began to form: a swirling aperture of shadow and light with runes etched around its rim in a glowing script. A portal.

Kasper stiffened. "That looks like—"

"—an Order Node," Nico finished in a low voice.

Atticus smiled faintly. "Forgive me, child," he said, glancing toward Leah.

Before Leah could react, Atticus lifted his hand and struck the desk with his ring. A sharp, resonant clang split the air and the runes of The Order node flared to life before the room erupted into chaos.

Figures poured from the portal, Order agents in white masks. Nico reacted first, shadows ripping free from the ground and sweeping toward the intruders. Kasper summoned wind to yank Leah toward him, grabbing her arm and pulling her toward the door as Atticus vanished behind the flood of Order members.

"Go!" Nico shouted.

With a sharp gesture, Kasper unleashed shifting currents of air to slow the advancing agents. Kaya, still standing by the entrance, did not move. Her brown eyes locked with Nico's and the sharpness of her glare made him falter for a moment before her soft, enigmatic smile returned and she bowed her head once more.

Nico blinked, then it clicked.

He pulled Leah and Kasper forward with his shadows and drove them deeper underground. They descended the narrow passage quickly, which twisted and turned like a buried vein beneath the town, branching endlessly as the air grew colder with every step. Leah struggled to keep pace, her bag thudding against her hip. Behind her, Kasper's breathing turned ragged, while Nico moved ahead as if he already knew the way.

"How do you even know where we're going?" Kasper yelled.

"Because I pay attention," Nico shot back with a glare.

They pushed farther down the passage and reached the narrow staircase Kaya had guided them through earlier.

"She knew," Kasper said breathlessly. "She was showing us the way out."

Nico glanced back, shadows flickering in his eyes. "Then let's hope she meant it."

A shout echoed through the tunnels, followed by the barked orders of an Order commander, and boots slammed against stone as pursuit closed in.

"They're gaining on us!" Kasper said, glancing back.

"Just keep moving," Nico growled.

The corridor split ahead. Left or right. Leah hesitated, but Nico took the left. Memory guided him, every twist burned into his mind. The passage plunged sharply downward, then widened into a larger chamber lit by flickering torches. Nico slowed just enough for Leah and Kasper to catch their breath, scanning the room with trained focus.

"Well, well, well."

The voice slithered from the shadows before a figure stepped forward. He was tall and broad-shouldered, torchlight catching the faint sigil branded at the collar of his long coat. His eyes fixed on Nico with recognition and disbelief.

Nico moved instinctively, stepping in front of Leah as shadows tightened around him like armor. "Silas," he muttered, the name leaving his mouth like a curse.

Silas's gaze flicked briefly to Leah, then to Kasper. "They'll want to know about this," he said mildly. "Especially your father. He might even faint when he hears you're still breathing."

Kasper blinked, looking between them. "Who the hell is this guy? Is this a family reunion or something?"

"No one important," Nico said through clenched teeth.

Silas placed a hand over his heart in mock offense. "Ouch, Nico. I'm hurt."

Nico's voice darkened. "What do you want?"

"To warn you," Silas said simply, beginning to circle them. His cloak brushed the floor, the only sound in the chamber. "I heard the rumors," he went on conversationally. "That Grigori's son was alive and that he had found the girl carrying the Echodex. Two myths, I thought. Until now."

He stopped directly in front of Nico.

Nico's eyes bled to black as shadows split across the floor like serpents, lunging for Silas's throat and wrists but Silas did not flinch. With a flick of his wrist, symbols flared in the air, runes igniting in a circle around him. Nico's shadows struck the barrier and unraveled instantly. The backlash rattled the torches in their sconces.

Silas sighed, lowering his hand. "Still all instinct and no restraint. You were always your father's son."

Nico's voice was ice. "You're wasting my time."

"Oh, I doubt that," Silas replied smoothly.

Kasper stepped closer to Nico with a readied stance despite the confusion on his face. "You want to fill me in here? Because right now it feels like everyone knows the script but me."

Silas's gaze shifted to Leah. Nico felt her move closer behind him. Silas studied her briefly, then focused on her hand, still instinctively shielding the book in her bag. Understanding flickered across his face, followed by a smile.

"They're coming," he said quietly. "I suggest you leave now, unless you're eager for a reunion with your father."

Nico narrowed his eyes but did not wait. He shoved past Silas, pulling Leah with him with Kasper close behind.

"Let's move," he ordered.

Kasper hesitated. "So we're trusting the random guy who deflected your death shadows like they were annoying flies?"

Nico didn't answer. Kasper just grumbled and followed. The tunnel narrowed, forcing them into single file. Every footstep echoed behind them as Nico's senses sharpened. He stayed alert, feeling the rhythm of their flight through shifting shadows.

Then the air changed, cooler and threaded with the scent of pine. They burst from the tunnel into the night.

Cold wind bit at Leah's skin, tugging at her hair as the forest opened around them. The moon hung low, casting silver streaks through the trees.

"Wait!" Kasper yelled, stopping them short.

From the shadows ahead, a figure stepped into view.

"Kaya?"

Her black hair shimmered in the moonlight. "You took your time," she said smoothly.

Kasper tensed. "You led us into a trap."

Kaya only smiled, tilting her head toward a lantern-lit path hidden beneath ivy. "If I had, you'd already be dead."

Her gaze flicked toward the distant glow of the tunnels, where faint voices still echoed. "Unless you'd like to be taken," she said evenly, "I suggest you follow me."

Without waiting, she turned and walked deeper into the woods, following the lantern-lit trail.

Kasper scoffed, throwing his hands up in the air. "Right. Now let's follow the mysterious woman who almost got us killed."

"Kasper," Leah hissed. "Didn't you both say she showed you the way out?"

Nico hesitated, glancing back toward the tunnels where pursuit still lingered. "I'll take my chances," he said quietly, then followed Kaya.

The others trailed after her in wary silence, glancing back often. The forest thickened until a small cabin appeared in a moonlit clearing. Nico felt the magic immediately, layers of enchantments woven to hide rather than protect. His eyes narrowed as Kaya reached the door and traced a glowing sigil across the wood, making the runes shimmer then dissolve, unlocking the door with a quiet click.

The cabin was far larger inside than it appeared. A wide main room opened around a lit fireplace, its warmth cutting through the cold. A large couch framed the hearth, easily seating eight. To one side sat a narrow kitchen with a small island and four matching chairs and he could see four doors that stood at the back, two on either side. The space was humble, but the air buzzed with contained magic.

Leah stepped in first, her shoulders relaxing as the fire's glow washed over her. Kaya said nothing, moving straight to the kitchen to set a kettle on the stove and prepare tea with deliberate calm.

Nico and Kasper lingered near the door. Nico checked the window beside it and froze. Where the clearing and forest had been moments ago, a blizzard now raged. Snow swirled so thick it blotted out everything beyond the glass. The window fogged instantly, the wind outside reduced to a dull roar.

"There's no one out there," Kaya said without looking up, pouring steaming water into the mugs.

Nico stepped forward, faint shadow magic coiled tight around him and took a seat at the island though his gaze never left her. "Who are you?"

Leah remained by the fireplace, snow melting in her hair as she listened. Nico did not need her thoughts to know she was wary.

Kaya set the mugs down with care, inviting them closer. Steam curled upward, fragrant with familiar herbs.

"Who I am," she said at last, leaning against the counter, "depends on who's asking."

Kasper frowned, glancing at the storm outside. "We're asking as people who just ran for our lives," he said sharply, "and walked straight into a witch's cabin."

Kaya's lips curved in faint amusement. "You're not entirely wrong."

That did little to calm Kasper who crossed his arms, glancing between her and Nico, annoyed. "Okay, then please explain what's happening. First the skeletal Elder, then a random family reunion of sorts, and now we're in a cabin that is quite clearly in the middle of a nonexistent snowstorm. Should I be concerned or just...roll with it?"

Nico didn't look at him. "Both."

Kasper scoffed. "Fantastic. Love the clarity," he muttered sarcastically, striding to the island and grabbing a cup of tea.

Kaya watched the exchange with mild interest, her gaze lingering on Nico before she picked up the cup meant for Leah and crossed the room toward her.

"You've been keeping interesting company, Leah."

Nico's eyes never left Kaya as she moved. He noted how Leah hesitated, glancing briefly at him and Kasper before finally taking the cup. A faint exhale, a flicker of relief. He cataloged it all.

"Thanks," Leah said, blowing across the surface. "It's been an adventure, that's for sure."

Kaya gave an amused huff. "You are safe here. The enchantments keep us hidden. To anyone outside, we're nothing but a passing snowstorm." She sank gracefully onto the couch and crossed her legs.

Nico's eyes narrowed as the shadows around his feet twisted and writhed, responding to his silent command. They slithered forward like dark serpents, reaching toward Kaya with lethal precision.

"You mistake my kindness for naiveté, Nico," Kaya said evenly, tilting her head. Her voice was soft, almost polite, but the weight behind it made his blood run cold.

The shadows halted mid-slither, then recoiled to Nico. His control which was razor-sharp moments ago, faltered just enough for him to recognize the truth. She had stopped him completely. Not with brute force, but with sheer mastery. His jaw clenched as the shadows quivered at the edge of his will, churning with power they could not release.

"Impossible," he muttered, locking eyes with her.

Kasper's hand twitched toward the dagger at his belt, though he didn't draw it. His gaze stayed fixed on Kaya, reading her as carefully as Nico was.

Nico's awareness flicked to Leah, who sat tense on the couch. "What's going on?" she asked.

Kaya turned her attention to Leah, her eyes glowing a soft, unnatural purple. "I see your friends struggle with trust," she said calmly. "But I understand. I suppose I must seem like a ghost."

Nico went still. The glow was familiar—he had seen that hue during the exchange with Leah the moment she touched his bracelet and while she practiced her magic.

Leah's whispered words confirmed it. "You're a Seer?" she murmured, almost to herself.

Nico's shadows retreated fully as he processed it. "That's not possible," he said. "The last of your kind was taken by The Order years ago."

Kaya tilted her head and took a small sip of tea. "And yet, here I am."

Kasper relaxed, the tension draining from his shoulders. He lifted his cup again, his gaze moving between Nico and Kaya with that familiar glint of mischief returning. "Well," he said lightly, "this just got significantly more interesting. Another Seer appearing out of thin air. You could've led with that before the dramatic reveal."

Nico watched as Leah glanced nervously at Kasper, her expression caught between relief, curiosity, and caution. Kaya, by contrast, only arched an eyebrow, unimpressed.

Leah moved closer and sat across from her. "Are you really?" she asked, sounding both concerned and hopeful.

Nico noticed the subtle shift in her posture, the way her shoulders tensed and then eased, the weight of months of isolation visible in her small, hesitant movements. After believing she was the last Seer, the revelation had to feel like both relief and shock.

"Yes," Kaya said softly, studying Leah as if measuring the pain and restraint in her eyes. "I survived the purge because my parents made a choice. They foresaw the danger Ezren and The Order would bring. The Pillars were being hunted, bloodlines shattered. When they realized The Order would come for us, they entrusted me to Atticus. He protected me, trained me, and kept my existence hidden."

"You mean the old man who just handed us to The Order?" Kasper asked, leaning forward. "Not exactly reassuring."

Kaya took another sip before meeting his eyes. "You forget where you are, Mr.—"

"Please," Kasper interrupted. "Call me Kasper."

She ignored the humor. "Kasper. This is Seer territory, one of the Pillars The Order hunted nearly to extinction. It is not in our interest to appear openly opposed to them."

"You'd think that," he countered, "but the old man—"

"Only summoned The Order after speaking to Leah," Kaya cut in, "and after ensuring you had completed your purposeful tour."

Kasper opened his mouth to argue, then shut it, conceding the point.

"So that's how you stayed alive?" Leah asked quietly.

"Yes." Kaya's gaze drifted to the window, where the illusionary storm still raged. "I was fourteen when my parents brought me here. They had prepared me for years after receiving a vision tied to the Pillars' massacre. The visions never revealed when it would happen. They left me with Atticus two years before it finally happened."

Leah stared into her cup, watching the steam curl and fade. "I'm so sorry," she murmured. "I didn't know someone like me existed."

"That was the point," Kaya said softly. She stood and carried her empty cup to the sink, moving with a quiet confidence that made Nico's focus sharpen. "For a long time, I believed my parents left me here to give me a chance to survive. Later, I realized it was more than that."

Leah looked up. "What do you mean?"

Kaya crossed the room and sat beside her. Nico's shadows stirred faintly at the movement. "Why don't you find out for yourself?" she asked, extending her hand.

Leah hesitated, staring down at it. Nico felt the tension ripple through her, the doubt that had him bracing instinctively. She hadn't used her Seer magic in weeks, not since the incident with him, and the way she shifted betrayed the guilt she still carried.

"I don't know if I can."

Kaya didn't waver. She gently took Leah's trembling hand. Nico noted how her calm seemed to radiate outward, steadying Leah like a current. "Then let me teach you," Kaya said.

Her eyes locked onto Leah's, and Nico felt the subtle pull of authority, the kind that made even him hesitate.

Leah glanced at him, uncertainty written plainly across her face. Nico gave a small, almost imperceptible nod. He didn't need to speak, he knew this was what she needed, even if it came from someone he didn't trust.

Leah drew a slow breath and met Kaya's gaze. Nico watched her shoulders loosen.

"Okay," she whispered as a soft glow bloomed in her eyes. "Show me."

The room dimmed and the air rippled around them. Nico's shadows stayed taut at his sides and for the first time in weeks, Leah did not seem to resist the visions rising to meet her. Nico's jaw tightened as he watched, alert to every flicker of power and to the faint stirring of something far more dangerous beneath the surface.

Chapter 20

Leah's breath caught as color and sound dissolved around her. When the air finally stilled, she stood barefoot in a meadow veiled in fog. The ground beneath her was cool and damp, and the only sound was her heartbeat thrumming in her ears. The last time she had used her Seer magic, it had been unwelcome, tapping into a memory that was not meant to be shared. Leah stopped and took a deep breath reminding herself that this time, Kaya had allowed her to see this vision.

Her heart began to steady as she looked up again. Through the fog, she could see a girl who appeared to be in her early teens, kneeling by a small river and braiding wildflowers into her dark hair. Leah knew at once by the shape of her face and the sharpness in her gaze that it was Kaya. With a hesitant step, Leah began to walk toward her. She still didn't know what she was meant to do inside a vision. Could she speak? Interact? Or was she destined only to watch?

"Kaya."

A woman's voice called through the mist, freezing Leah on the spot.

The young girl turned as two figures emerged from the fog, a man and a woman whose resemblance to Kaya left no doubt who they were. Her parents were both tall and graceful, their eyes glowing faintly with deep purple light. Yet there was urgency in the way they moved, an undercurrent of fear that made Leah's pulse quicken.

Young Kaya rose to meet them, confusion flickering across her face. The emotion struck Leah so sharply that her body trembled. She gasped without meaning to, realizing the feeling was not her own—she was inside Kaya's memory, and she was suddenly aware that her heart was beating in time with the girl's. This meant that she was not simply seeing the vision but experiencing it.

"Is it time?" Kaya asked, searching their faces.

Her mother's lips trembled before she managed a nod. "The visions grow clearer every day. We cannot risk losing you."

"Then we go together," Kaya said quickly. "We'll all go to Atticus and—"

Her father stepped forward, kneeling so their eyes met. "We can't, honey. Atticus cannot risk having too much power to contain in a place that should have no magic at all. If The Order learns he is helping us..." He shook his head.

Kaya's throat tightened, and Leah felt the sting of tears she did not shed, the effort to remain composed. Pride and sorrow tangled inside her until she could barely stand. She did not want to show her parents weakness after all the time they had spent preparing her for this moment. Kaya had known this day would come, but now that it was here—

Her father rested a gentle hand on her head. "You're our chance, Kaya. The Pillar's chance."

Kaya's voice cracked. "But if I go, you—"

Her mother stepped forward and cupped her face, forcing a smile through her tears. "Our time is already written, Kaya. You must trust that this part of the vision is not an ending." She glanced at her husband, then back at her daughter, her voice dropping to a whisper. "You are the hope of our Pillar. One day, someone will awaken the Echodex, and you will be the one to teach and pass along our history."

Kaya's eyes shimmered. She swallowed hard, trying to keep her voice steady. "I understand," she said softly. "But please promise me you'll find me again. You have to."

Her mother's smile wavered. "In every vision, my love."

The fog closed in, swallowing them until their forms blurred and broke apart. Leah reached out instinctively, trying to hold on, but her hand passed through smoke. Silence pressed in so completely that she could hear the echo of Kaya's heartbeat fading into her own.

The world rippled, then snapped back into focus. Kaya sat beside her once more, eyes distant, still lost in the memory they had shared. A single tear slid down Leah's cheek. The ache inside her was not just sympathy, it was grief, the weight of all the goodbyes a fourteen-year-old girl should never have to bear.

Kaya's eyes refocused on Leah, and a soft smile crossed her face as she reached out to wipe the tear from her cheek. "We have a long way to go with your training," she said gently. "We cannot have you crying at every vision you see."

Leah sniffled and wiped her nose. "It felt like I was there, like I was you."

"Yes. When you tap into another Seer's vision, you also feel their emotions in that moment. That is what makes the magic dangerous."

Dangerous.

The word lingered in the air. Leah had heard Nico say again and again that she needed to stay grounded and control her emotions while using her magic, but she had never fully understood why. Most of her training had involved inanimate objects that held no emotional weight and while those visions left her tired, they were nothing compared to the moment she had tapped into Nico's past through his bracelet.

She still remembered the rush of emotion, the happiness she felt as the little boy she later learned was Archie ran toward Nico. That joy, that pure innocence, had been intoxicating even within the vision. She had wanted to follow Archie, to stay wrapped in that sense of bliss. Now she understood. If she ever touched a vision steeped in something darker than happiness or grief, would she be able to withstand it?

"I haven't really understood how this magic works," Leah admitted quietly. "There was only so much we could figure out without guidance."

Kaya glanced toward Nico and Kasper. "It would not be common to have knowledge of a Pillar that became extinct nearly two decades ago. I would assume The Order made it a point to erase any documentation that revealed too much."

Nico nodded. "The Order keeps most of their records in their library archives," he said. "But access is restricted to those with explicit permission."

Kasper scoffed. "Of course. Can't have anyone discovering they're still corrupt. It's a wonder the other Pillars are standing at all."

"Anything Ezren considers a threat will be eliminated," Kaya said evenly. "Which is why you must learn how to see." She paused, then softened. "But that's enough for now. You'll need rest if you want control over your emotions." She gestured toward the back of the cabin. "The rooms on the right are yours. Leah can take the one on the left, next to mine."

Leah exhaled as relief washed over her.

Kasper brightened immediately. "Finally, some downtime," he said, stretching as he headed toward one of the rooms. "Want to share, Nico?" he added with a smirk over his shoulder.

Nico shot him a glare but said nothing, turning instead to Leah. "Are you okay?"

Leah offered a tired half-smile and nodded. "I'll be fine. I think I really do need to sleep. You should too."

As she walked toward her room, Nico's eyes followed her, noting the slight sway in her step and the tension still lingering in her shoulders. He paused as Kasper awkwardly tried to high-five her goodnight, rolling his eyes internally at the younger man's antics.

Once everyone was in their rooms, Nico exhaled slowly, but his vigilance didn't fade. Kasper's energy was exhausting, every word and every smirk deliberately provocative. Nico moved toward the last room, but his attention kept drifting back to the front window. The night beyond the cabin was quiet, yet instinctively he sensed the potential for intrusion, the faintest disturbance in the air.

The encounter with Silas had left Nico unsettled, and that in itself disturbed him. Growing up, Silas had been more than a mentor. He had been another father figure, one Nico admired and trusted, especially because he was not as unyielding as his own father. Where his father demanded obedience through force, Silas taught control and precision, guiding Nico with a steadier hand.

Yet beneath that calm, paternal exterior lived a power Nico had always feared. Silas never needed to raise his voice or prove himself. The strength was simply there, coiled and waiting, and Nico had learned early to respect it. That was why allowing them to escape unsettled him so deeply. It was not mercy he sensed, but calculation, and the thought that they might already be moving within one of Silas's designs left a chill Nico could not shake.

He whispered a soft incantation, and golden sigils spiraled from his fingertips toward the front door. They struck the frame silently and dissolved on impact, disappearing without a sound. His eyes scanned the shadows in the corners, noting the delicate interplay of light and darkness, measuring what was seen and unseen.

"Impressive," Kaya said from across the hall. "I trust you will also try to get some sleep? Or will you continue with protective enchantments all night?"

Nico rolled his eyes and finally stepped into his designated room, pausing briefly at the threshold to glance at Leah's door which was now closed. Kaya smiled and shook her head before retreating into her own room and closing the door. "Goodnight, Nico."

He approached the bed. It had been months since he had slept on a real one, since he had given his to Leah back in the bunker. With a quiet sigh, he sat at the edge and let the tension in his shoulders ease slightly. But the stillness sharpened his thoughts, and instead of relief, a familiar churn of frustration and inadequacy crept in.

Being forced to leave the bunker and expose Leah to potential threats gnawed at him. On that day alone, she had faced two situations that put her in danger. First, the asshole on the train. His fists clenched as he remembered the look on Leah's face when she returned with Kasper to their seats. If Nico had been there, he would not have been as forgiving. Then again, maybe Kasper was right—drawing attention to themselves would have made things worse.

Then there was Atticus. Nico couldn't read him, not the way he usually could. Something was off, something he couldn't place, and it only worsened when Atticus had expelled him and Kasper so quickly. Too many things could have gone wrong. He was losing his edge. Being around Leah distracted him enough that he hadn't even noticed The Order soldiers approaching. The thought tightened his chest.

Nico lay back, staring at the wooden beams above him. The faint hum of Kaya's sigils pulsed through the cabin walls. He traced an invisible rune across his palm, a reflex born of discipline, though it brought him no comfort tonight. His mind refused to settle.

Leah's face lingered behind his closed eyes, the tear she hadn't meant to shed, the tremor in her voice when she said she could feel everything Kaya had felt. He had seen what that depth of empathy could do. The Order had broken Seer prisoners by flooding them with others' pain until they no longer knew whose heart beat in their chest.

He rolled onto his side and ran a hand through his hair, exhaling quietly. Kaya seemed sincere, but sincerity meant little to him. Too many smiles had hidden knives, but still, she was the only one who understood Leah's power well enough to teach her. He couldn't deny that.

Just as sleep threatened to take hold, soft footsteps stopped outside his door. Nico sat up as tension snapped through him before he recognized the voice.

"Nico?" Leah whispered.

He opened the door to find her barefoot with a white robe drawn around her shoulders.

"You should be resting," he said.

"I tried," she admitted. "Kaya said she'd be in the basement later if I couldn't sleep. She said I could come down." She hesitated, fingers twisting the edge of her sleeve. "I wanted to go, but I didn't want to do it alone. Would you maybe come with me?"

The door beside Nico's opened, and Kasper peeked out with tousled hair and eyes half closed. "What's going on?"

Nico glanced at him, then back at Leah, with a deepening frown. "The basement?"

Leah nodded and gestured down the hall. "She called it a practice space. She said it's safer than the surface for her kind of magic."

Kasper straightened, rubbing the back of his neck. "If she's training, I'm not missing it," he muttered. "Wouldn't want you two having all the fun."

Nico sighed through his nose but stepped into the hall, motioning for Leah to lead. Together, they descended the narrow staircase at the back of the cabin.

The air grew cooler as they descended until the steps opened into a wide stone chamber lit by floating orbs that shimmered in the darkness. Markings were etched deep into the walls, old runes, some even Nico didn't recognize. The air down here smelled faintly of ash and wildflowers.

Kaya stood near the center, posture steady, and hands clasped. "Good," she said. "You all came. I thought you might need one more lesson before the night ends."

Leah looked around, awed. "You train here?"

"I do," Kaya replied, a flicker of nostalgia crossing her face. "Every Seer before the fall of our Pillar learned in places like this. The walls keep magic contained so visions do not bleed into the physical world." She gestured to them. "Sit. Tonight I only want to observe how far your connection reaches."

Nico remained standing until Leah gave him a small look, a silent request. Reluctantly, he sat beside Kasper, who lounged back with his arms crossed.

Kaya knelt in front of Leah. "Focus on clarity. Forget the noise. Forget what you think you know about your power. When your magic reaches for a memory, it does not always choose what you expect. It shows what you need."

Leah blinked. "But I thought I had to touch someone to see anything. That's the only way it's ever happened."

"That's how your gift first surfaced," Kaya said gently, "but it's not the only way. A Seer's thread requires connection, not contact. Down here, you will be able to see that thread. Above ground, it remains invisible."

Leah's eyes widened. "You mean I could reach someone's memory without them knowing?"

"Only when there is a bond," Kaya replied. "Your power responds to emotion, not touch. This space will let you see that connection and learn to guide it and protect it from those with bad intentions."

Leah inhaled and nodded, placing her palms on the ground as instructed. The stone beneath her glowed faintly.

"Choose someone," Kaya said softly.

Leah visibly hesitated before her gaze flicked between the two men. It lingered on Nico before shifting to Kasper. Kaya smiled knowingly. "Let the magic decide."

The air stirred before light rippled across the floor in fine threads that reached first toward Kasper. His brow furrowed, but he stayed still as the glow touched his boots and climbed like a quiet flame. Leah gasped, her eyes glowing purple.

Kasper's confusion softened into surprise. Leah spoke without thinking. "You're in a garden. You're pruning roses."

Kasper blinked. "What?"

She laughed breathlessly. "You're humming. Badly."

He groaned. "Okay, that part didn't need sharing."

The glow faded, then shifted, drawn unmistakably toward Nico. He felt it before it reached him, like a prickle across his skin. Unconsciously, his hands tightened against his knees with instinct urging him to pull away, but he forced himself still.

Leah straightened, her focus narrowing. Nico watched her swallow the fear that had kept her back before her attention sharpened.

"You're sitting by a window," she murmured. "It's raining. You have a book open, but you're not reading. There's a candle. You look—"

His jaw locked. The image was too precise.

"You look tired."

"That's enough," he said, his tone softer than intended.

Kaya lifted her hand, and the light receded. Nico exhaled as Leah blinked and the glow fading from her eyes.

"I didn't mean to—" Leah began.

"You didn't intrude," Kaya said calmly. "You observed. The memories your magic reached were unguarded, ordinary ones. Seer vision favors truth over significance."

"So I can't choose what I see?" Leah asked.

"Not yet," Kaya replied. "Control comes later. Right now, your gift reacts to emotion. When you master your mind, you will shape what your visions reveal." She traced a rune in the air. "And the belief that your magic cannot defend you—" her gaze softened "—is a lie meant to make Seers dependent."

Leah looked startled. "Defend me? How?"

"Seeing is not only for understanding," Kaya said. "It is for survival. A Seer's strength is foresight, but a Seer can also reach the emotion that anchors a memory—the grief behind the loss, the fear beneath the anger—and turn it back upon the one who holds it. The heart remembers faster than the mind. When you touch that thread, they feel what they've spent their life trying to bury."

Leah's eyes widened. "I could make someone feel their own pain?"

"Only briefly," Kaya said. "Watch."

She extended her hand to Kasper, who hesitated but nodded. The glow around Kaya's eyes deepened to a soft purple as she brushed his forearm. For an instant, Kasper's teasing grin faltered and his eyes clouded before his breath hitched as he staggered back.

"What did you—" he rasped.

Kaya withdrew immediately, the light fading from her eyes. "A fragment only. The emotion he feels when he cannot protect those he loves."

Kasper steadied himself, rubbing his neck. "That was... disorienting."

"That is a Seer's defense," Kaya said. "You do not create pain, you reflect what already exists. The moment their heart remembers, their body hesitates. It is enough to escape. Enough to survive."

Nico watched Leah closely, catching the flicker of unease in her eyes. Power like hers always demanded choice, and choice carried consequence.

"That's enough for tonight," Kaya said, breaking the tension. "You've done enough."

The sigils in the walls dimmed. As the others turned toward the stairs, Nico stayed behind waiting for Leah. When their eyes met, he gestured subtly for her to go first. She gave him a faint smile and started up the steps.

Kasper yawned loudly ahead of them. "Bedtime, finally."

Kaya and Kasper entered their rooms shortly after, but Leah paused at her door, her hand hovering over the handle. Nico had already turned away, forcing himself toward his own room before instinct could betray him.

"Thank you, Nico..." she said softly, her voice just above a whisper.

"You did well tonight," he replied quietly.

"I barely understand what I'm doing."

Silence stretched between them. Nico should have stepped back, should have gone into his room. Instead, he closed the distance. His hand lifted slowly, giving her time to pull away, but she didn't. His fingers curved around her wrist first, then slid upward until his palm settled at her waist. The contact was unmistakable and made Leah's breath hitch. He felt it through her body before he heard it.

"Patience, Leah," he murmured, his voice low, roughened by something dangerously close to want.

Her body leaned into his without hesitation, and that was all it took. His thumb pressed lightly at her side, just beneath her ribs, anchoring her there. He dipped his head, close enough that his breath brushed her ear, close enough that it took everything in him not to close the final inch between them.

"That's why you'll train with Kaya," he said quietly. "And why I'm here."

For one fractured moment, he let himself stay. Let himself feel the curve of her, the heat of her body against his palm, the way her pulse thundered like it was trying to call to him. His shadows stirred, coiling tight and restless, drawn to her the way they always were.

This was too close. Too dangerous.

With visible effort, he loosened his grip. His hand slid from her waist, fingers dragging just slightly as he let go. He stepped back as control snapped painfully into place.

"Goodnight, Leah."

"No."

The word hit him like a spell.

She turned before he could process it, her hand catching his wrist and pulling with unmistakable intent. The world tilted as she dragged him across the threshold and into her room before she closed the door behind them with a soft, final click.

"We're not done here," she said.

Nico stared at her, genuinely stunned. Leah never did this. She hesitated. She doubted. She retreated into caution and guilt and careful distance.

"Leah," he said slowly, tension flooding his limbs, "this is a mistake."

She scoffed, flustered and defiant, cheeks flushed as she folded her arms like she was bracing herself against him. "You don't get to decide that for both of us."

His shadows stirred, restless, curling tightly at his feet. "You're exhausted. We've had one hell of a day. You don't—"

"I know exactly what I'm doing," she cut in. Her voice wavered, but her eyes didn't. "What I don't understand is you."

She stepped closer, then closer still. "You watch me like I'm something you're afraid to touch," she said. "You stand too close. You pull away. You act like wanting me is some kind of crime."

His jaw clenched. "You don't know what you're asking for."

"I'm not asking for anything," she said quietly. "I just don't get it."

The space between them vanished. He could feel her heat, her breath, and the steady thrum of her pulse calling loudly to something feral inside him. He should have moved. Should have put distance between them when he had the chance. Instead, his hand lifted and caught her at the hip, stopping her inches from him.

"Because," he said with a voice that was low and strained, "if I stop controlling this, I don't know if I can stop at all."

She took a shaky breath, but she didn't retreat.

"Then don't," she whispered.

That was it. The last thread snapped as Nico surged forward and kissed her. It wasn't gentle. It couldn't be. Weeks...months of restraint burned through him as his hand slid into her hair, tilting her head back as he claimed her mouth with a hunger he had denied himself for far too long. Leah gasped softly before kissing him back, and her fingers clutched his shirt like she'd been waiting just as desperately.

He broke the kiss only when he had to and pressed his forehead to hers, breathing hard and his control in tatters.

"Leah," he said, voice rough and reverent. "If we do this—"

She kissed him again, shorter this time, deliberate.

"We already are."

She didn't wait for him to answer. Leah surged up and kissed him again, harder this time, with all the heat and intent she could muster. Her hands slid beneath his shirt and her fingers curled against his skin like she was daring him to pull away.

Nico's breath left him in a sharp exhale as something wild surged up his spine. His shadows answered instantly, rippling along the walls and pooling at his feet like living things stirred awake. His eyes burned as power pressed forward, begging to be unleashed.

He kissed her back harder, hunger eclipsing restraint. His hand slid firmly to her waist, guiding her backward step by step until the backs of her knees met the edge of the bed.

The shadows moved with him, curling around her wrists and hips and holding her in place as he followed her down onto the mattress. She gasped softly against his mouth, but she didn't pull away. If anything, she arched herself toward him, meeting the weight of his presence without hesitation and without fear.

Nico reluctantly broke the kiss and hovered over her, their bodies separated by little more than soft fabric. The shadows around Leah's wrists tightened faintly, and he knew that his control was shredding away with every breath.

This was dangerous and he knew it.

His forehead dropped to hers as he tried to steady his uneven breathing. "Leah," he warned, his voice rough enough to sound barely human.

She smiled up at him, breathless. "You don't get to stop now."

His shadows surged in response, tightening slightly as he kissed her again, deeper and hungrier. One hand braced beside her head and the other gripped the mattress as he fought the pull of his power—fought himself.

He lowered his head and his lips began to brush the curve of her jaw first, hesitant for only a fraction of a second before sliding to the delicate line of her neck. The contact was slow and deliberate, and he felt the exact moment her breath caught and the moment her pulse fluttered wildly beneath his mouth.

His lips lingered at her neck, pressing closer. He breathed her in, allowing his magic to surround them. He felt her shift slightly, testing the hold at her wrists, but he knew they would not release her. They could feel what he felt.

Hunger.

Need.

Possession.

And beneath it all, something far more dangerous.

Release.

A sharp, intoxicating thrill tore through him as that truth settled in his chest. He was letting go by choice.

All his life, control had been survival. Every breath measured. Every emotion contained. Every instinct buried before it could become a weakness. His power had always demanded restraint, and he had given it willingly until control was no longer something he maintained...it was something that defined him.

And now, he was breaking it.

He felt it in the way his shadows refused to obey with their usual precision, moving instead with raw, instinctive hunger. He felt it in the way sensation drowned calculation and in the way her warmth beneath him unraveled years of discipline with terrifying ease.

It was reckless.

It was dangerous.

It was *intoxicating.*

He was standing on the edge of something irreversible, where one step further would silence reason entirely and unleash everything he had suppressed for years. The thought of that should have terrified him but instead, it *thrilled* him.

His mouth pressed more firmly to her neck, trailing slow, deliberate kisses along the sensitive line of her throat. Then he reached the delicate crook of her neck. Her soft moan broke the air between them, a sound that might as well have pushed him over the edge he was standing on in his mind.

Then—

"Oh, don't stop on my account."

Nico froze. The voice floated down the hall, light and unmistakably amused.

The shadows snapped back instantly, vanishing into the corners as reality crashed down. Leah sucked in a breath, eyes wide, heat still humming between them as the moment shattered.

From across the hall, Kasper continued lazily, "Just so you know, your shadows were getting very loud. Wind carries, Nico. Especially through emotionally charged hallways."

Nico closed his eyes and exhaled slowly through his nose.

For a moment, fury flared sharp and volatile. His jaw clenched as he pushed himself upright, dragging a hand down his face while control slammed back into place with painful force.

Too close.

Leah sat up too. Her hair was tousled, her lips were swollen, but her eyes were bright with defiance. She looked at him, a little dazed and, if he was honest, a little triumphant.

"Well," she said softly. "That was rude."

A faint, humorless sound escaped his chest.

"Necessary," he replied, meeting her gaze. "Unfortunately."

From the hall, Kasper chuckled. "You're welcome. Try not to summon the abyss after midnight, yeah? Some of us are trying to sleep."

Nico shook his head once, then stood and offered Leah his hand.

"This conversation isn't over," she said quietly.

His mouth curved, just slightly.

"No," he agreed. "It isn't."

And this time, he didn't pretend he didn't want it to be.

Chapter 21

Leah woke to sunlight spilling across the floor, and for the first time in what felt like months, she realized she had slept through the night. Her body felt lighter and her mind less tangled, as if the quiet of sleep had washed some of the tension away. She stretched, savoring the sensation of rest, until her hand flew to cover her mouth as memories of the previous night flooded back. Nico's hands. His breath against her skin. She squeezed her eyes shut as a breathless, silent laugh caught in her chest.

Her heart fluttered wildly as heat bloomed across her cheeks. She rolled onto her back and stared up at the ceiling feeling half mortified and half thrilled. She could still feel it all. The kiss hadn't been imagined—it hadn't been a dream. Nico had kissed her back, completely unrestrained.

She pressed her lips together, biting back a ridiculous smile as she dragged a hand through her hair. After all the distance, the restraint, the careful closeness, she had finally broken through him.

The scent of frying herbs and potatoes drifted through the air, and her stomach growled in response, grounding her before she could spiral too far into the memory. She had no way of knowing the time, but she assumed it wasn't too late, given that no one had woken her.

Leah slipped out of her room, tugging her robe tighter around herself, and followed the soft clatter of movement into the kitchen. Kasper and Nico were already up, sitting at the island while Kaya worked at the stove. The moment Leah saw

Nico, her pulse jumped, and she looked away to stop herself from blushing.

"Good morning," Leah said softly as she stepped in.

Kaya turned with a small smile. "Morning. I hope you slept well. Are you hungry?" She turned off the pan and began setting plates in front of them.

"Hungry? I heard her stomach growl from the other room. She's been very hungry since last night." Kasper said with a wide grin.

Kaya laughed and Leah shot him a mortified look and ducked her head.

Kaya chuckled as she served eggs and potatoes mixed with vegetables. "Eat."

Leah sat beside Nico. "Morning," she whispered. He looked more rested than she had seen him in weeks, his dark hair slightly tousled and his posture deceptively calm.

"Morning," he began.

Kasper chewed thoughtfully, eyes flicking between them with far too much interest. Then his mouth curved into a slow, wicked grin.

"So," he said casually, like he was discussing the weather, "did anyone else sleep terribly, or was it just Nico?"

Silence dropped like a stone. Leah nearly choked and Nico froze mid-motion with his fork hovering an inch above his plate.

"What," he said flatly, "are you talking about?"

"Oh, nothing," Kasper replied, grin widening. "Just noticed you look a little distracted this morning. Must've been a long night of brooding."

Kaya didn't bother hiding her amusement. She took a slow sip of tea, eyes gleaming. "Shadowbinders do tend to brood louder than they realize."

Leah focused intently on her plate as heat rushed to her face and her pulse began racing far too fast for a normal breakfast. She could feel Nico beside her, utterly still. Kasper glanced at her, lowering his voice just enough to be dangerous.

"Relax, Red," he added sweetly. "Whatever kept him up clearly didn't kill him."

Nico finally turned with a glare sharp enough to cut glass. "Kasper."

Kasper raised his hands, innocent as sin. Kaya smiled into her mug. Leah didn't dare look at Nico.

"Leah," Kasper interrupted dramatically, already halfway through his meal, "I've decided. I'll volunteer as tribute for your training."

Leah blinked. "What?"

Kaya arched a brow but said nothing, continuing to eat.

Nico's glare shifted to Kasper. "You?"

"Yes, me," Kasper said cheerfully. "Someone has to save Leah from having to look into your gloomy mind."

Kaya smirked faintly. "Actually, Kasper's offer is useful."

Leah turned toward her, surprised. "You think so?"

Kaya nodded. "Kasper's energy is open. Unfiltered emotion makes readings clearer. Nico's mind, on the other hand, is a fortress. He blocks intrusion, consciously or not."

Leah thought of the time she had tried to read Nico and found only a black abyss.

Kasper leaned back smugly. "Hear that, Mr. Gloom? My vulnerability is an asset."

"Your lack of discipline," Nico muttered, "is what makes you an easy target."

Leah bit back a laugh as she took her first bite, relieved that the conversation had shifted. The food was simple but flavorful, the kind of meal that felt touched by care. She hadn't realized how much she'd missed that.

"Once you're done," Kaya said, gathering her plate and cup, "we'll continue in the basement."

Ten minutes later, the four of them gathered again in the training chamber. The air was cooler here with runes pulsing faintly along the walls. Kaya stood at the center with her hands clasped.

"There are three ways for a Seer to access memory," she began. "Direct touch, contact with a personal object, and distance reading. All rely on emotional resonance. The stronger the emotion, the clearer the vision."

Leah nodded as Kaya continued. "You can't always choose the moment you'll see, but you can choose the emotion you follow. Think of it as navigating by feeling instead of sight."

"So," Kasper said, tilting his head, "emotional scent-tracking?"

"A crude but accurate analogy," Kaya replied.

Leah hesitated. "And if I get lost? What if I can't pull back?"

"Then you stop reaching," Kaya said gently. "A vision is a door you open with your mind. You close it the same way, by remembering who you are and where you stand."

Leah exhaled slowly. "Right."

"Now," Kaya said, stepping closer. "I'll show you how it feels to direct emotion. I'll follow something familiar in you. Shock."

Before Leah could respond, Kaya placed a hand on her shoulder. The air shifted and she felt the magic prickle at her skin. A mug shattering on the floor. Selene's voice. A hand grabbing her arm during a childhood game. A dead bird near the forest's edge.

Then the attic. Dust swirling. The lock opening. The Echodex revealed. The letter confirming her grandmother's death.

Leah gasped as the vision fractured, splintering apart.

"That's the feeling," Kaya said quietly. "I followed shock and found memories tied to it. That's how you guide it."

"It's overwhelming," Leah said.

"It is," Kaya replied. "For them, they relive the memory and emotion. For you, you feel it too. You learn control by testing your limits, not avoiding them."

Kasper shifted uneasily. "So when do I come in?"

"Now," Kaya said.

Kasper sighed. "Figures."

Nico crossed his arms. "Don't worry Kasper. If you faint, I'll catch you."

"See? That's the kind of energy that makes me nervous." Kasper said, pointing at Nico.

Kasper stepped in front of Leah and took a deep breath in. Leah hesitated, looking back at Kaya.

"First, touch without direction." Kaya said.

"You mean, without looking for a feeling?"

Kaya nodded.

Leah took a deep breath and stepped forward, her hand trembling slightly as she placed it against Kasper's chest. She closed her eyes and let her power stir.

The vision rippled into focus. Kasper looked like he was around twelve years old. He stood in a sunlit clearing, the wind swirling around him in playful gusts. The trees bowed in rhythm, leaves spiraling like green confetti around him. He laughed, pure and unguarded, the sound bright against the hum of nature. Another ripple, and the joy vanished. He was older now, setting up a small camp in a dark forest. Firelight flickered over his face, shadows deepening the tiredness in his eyes. The distant howl of wolves echoed, and he drew his cloak tighter.

"Can you detach?" Kaya's voice echoed.

Leah pulled back, the chamber snapping into focus.

Kasper blinked. "No wonder The Order feared you."

"Good," Kaya said. "Now search for an emotion."

Leah nodded, pulse quickening. "Sorry," she murmured, placing her hand back on his chest.

The magic hummed and she hesitated, unsure where to begin. She didn't want to intrude, not again...not like she had with Nico. But her thoughts betrayed her, circling that moment with the regret she still carried for how she'd seen into his mind. And before she could pull away, the magic latched on to it.

Regret.

The basement rippled as Kasper's memories unfurled around her. The first flashes were small: Kasper kneeling over a broken bird's nest where tiny bodies were still and fragile. A jolt of sorrow shot through Leah, but she forced herself to stay. The visions accelerated, each one sharper and heavier. Kasper at a gravesite, rain blurring the names on the stone. The ache of being too late, of standing powerless in the face of loss, pressed into Leah's chest. And then, a cabin. Dim light surrounded by the scent of smoke and something metallic in the air. A girl, no older than twelve, lay crumpled on the floor, blood staining her brown curls. Kasper knelt beside her, shaking violently, while his hands pressed against her chest as if he could hold her life in his grasp.

"I shouldn't have left..." the voice of the younger Kasper broke through the vision. "I promised I'd stay. I said I'd stay..."

Leah's throat tightened—she could feel it all. The helplessness, the horror, the unbearable weight of a broken promise. Her body went rigid and her hands trembled against Kasper's chest, but she couldn't pull back.

Leah continued to look on as young Kasper wailed, rocking back and forward with the girl in his arms.

Kaya's voice sliced through the haze. "Leah. Detach. Focus."

She tried, pulling at the edges of her consciousness, but the regret clung, suffocating and dense, as if her magic had entwined with it. Nico's hand landed lightly on her shoulder. "Leah. Come back."

Her vision blurred with tears before the vision finally shattered causing Leah to stumble forward, clutching Kasper as sobs escaped from her lips. He froze, caught off guard, but didn't pull away. He lifted his arms slowly, hesitated, then held her.

"It's okay," he murmured.

Leah collapsed against him, letting the tears run unchecked. The basement walls, the magic, the memories, they all faded away into the background. Only Kasper remained, steadying her trembling form with a gentle weight.

Leah's sobs began to subside, but her body still trembled as she clung to Kasper. The weight of the memory had left her drained, her magic pulsing faintly against her skin. She pressed her forehead to his chest, listening to the steady thrum of his heartbeat, as if anchoring herself to the present could pull her fully back from the storm of emotions she just went through.

She was dimly aware of the room again and the quiet and weight of eyes on her. When she finally lifted her gaze, she caught sight of Nico standing a short distance away near Kaya. He hadn't moved and his posture was rigid, his hands clenched so tightly at his sides that his knuckles had gone pale. She couldn't tell if he was angry, afraid, or simply holding himself together the way he always did.

Kaya's calm voice cut through the tension. "Breathe, Leah."

She obeyed, drawing in a shaky breath, then another. Slowly, she pulled back just enough to lift her head, her wet cheeks pressing into Kasper's chest.

"I'm sorry," she whispered.

"You have nothing to apologize for," he said, though his own voice trembled slightly. "You didn't break anything. I am okay."

Kaya stepped closer to assess them. "What you felt was not yours to carry, Leah. It was the weight of a memory, of an emotion."

Leah inhaled deeply, finally allowing herself to pull back just enough to meet his eyes. The anguish still lingered there, a raw ache of unhealed pain, but Kasper's steady gaze told her he had survived it before, and he would survive this too. Leah had no idea who that girl had been, only that she had meant a great deal to Kasper. She didn't dare ask now.

She exhaled shakily and stepped back from him. The basement was still, and she could feel both Kasper's and Nico's eyes on her. She understood now how magic like this could disarm others. She just needed to make sure she wasn't disarmed alongside them, as she had been with Kasper.

"Kaya, is every memory this debilitating?" Leah asked, sinking down to sit on the floor.

"Or is it only negative emotions?"

"It can be any emotion," Kaya replied, "but negative ones have a higher chance of affecting the caster as much as the one being read."

Leah nodded slowly, absorbing it. Kaya glanced around the room.

"Boys, I need some time alone with Leah."

Kasper and Nico exchanged a look but didn't argue. Kasper headed for the stairs, and Nico hesitated before following.

When they were alone, Kaya crouched across from Leah, resting her arms loosely on her knees, watching her with the same calm attentiveness she'd shown during training.

"How are you feeling?" she asked.

Leah hesitated. "Heavy."

"That's normal," Kaya said. "You stepped into someone else's grief. It takes time to shake it off." She studied Leah, then added, "You did well."

Leah exhaled. "It didn't feel like it. I lost control again."

"But not completely," Kaya corrected. "You came back. Understanding your magic comes first. Control follows." She leaned back slightly. "Tell me something. How do you feel about your travel companions?"

Leah blinked. "Kasper and Nico?"

Kaya nodded. "You've traveled far with them. That tells me something, but I'd rather hear it from you."

Leah picked at a loose thread on her sleeve. "Kasper's... easier. He makes light of things, even when he shouldn't. Sometimes that helps." Her voice softened. "Nico's different. I don't always understand him, but he's been there since the beginning. I trust him."

Kaya's eyes narrowed slightly, thoughtful rather than disapproving. "That sounds accurate."

"What do you mean?"

"I'd heard of him," Kaya said. "Long before you arrived. A name passed between teachers and watchers. The Order's prodigy. The one who mastered shadow binding before most of us could hold a proper shield. Brilliant. Dangerous. Then one day, he vanished."

Leah looked down, thinking of what Nico had shared. "He told me part of it, but he doesn't talk about it much."

"I wouldn't expect him to," Kaya said. "People who survive that kind of ruin don't return whole. He's learned to seal his own mind. You won't see what's behind those walls unless he allows it. And even then, I doubt he could endure letting it all surface."

"I've been worried about him since you started teaching me," Leah admitted. "Before Kasper joined us, there was an incident. I touched a bracelet he wears and saw one of his memories." Her voice faltered. "He looked hurt. Like I'd done it on purpose."

"Is that what you were thinking about when you touched Kasper?" Kaya asked.

"Yes. I was afraid of intruding again, of making someone angry at me." Leah's gaze dropped. "And then that fear became the emotion I focused on."

"I see," Kaya said quietly. "That's one reason I didn't want Nico training with you today. You're not ready to see what's inside him, and I'm not sure he is either." She met Leah's eyes. "He's protective of you, but that protection is raw. It comes from trauma. He tries to prevent harm even when none is visible."

Leah's chest ached. "He's been through so much."

"And yet he's still standing," Kaya said. "That says more than any story." She placed a gentle hand on Leah's shoulder. "Be careful with him. He walks with ghosts. And whether he knows it or not, you've become one of the few things keeping them at bay."

Leah nodded, though her throat felt tight. Her gaze drifted to the stairway above, where faint creaks made her wonder if Nico had paused to listen.

Later, the cottage felt heavier. Leah sat near the hearth, palms tingling with leftover magic, her chest still aching. Kaya glanced between her and Nico, reading the tension easily.

"Kasper," Kaya said after a moment, "come help me fetch a few things from the shed."

Kasper looked up, distant. "Now?"

"Yes," Kaya replied. "Before the rain starts."

He nodded and followed her outside. The door closed, leaving silence behind.

Nico stood near the far wall, arms crossed, posture coiled rather than composed. His eyes tracked Leah like he wasn't sure she'd hold together.

"You don't have to look at me like I'm about to fall apart," she said.

He crossed the room and stopped close enough to make her pulse spike.

"I'm fine," she said softly.

"You weren't," he replied quietly. "You were gone. And I couldn't reach you."

"I came back."

"Barely." His voice shook. "And it scared me."

"It was part of the training," she said, though doubt edged her words.

"No." He shook his head. "That was you drowning in someone else's grief. And I had to watch." His fists clenched. "I'm supposed to protect you."

"You can't protect me from everything."

"I know," he said, breath shuddering. "That's the problem."

She waited.

"I tried to make this about duty," he continued. "Distance. Safety. I told myself it was better that way." A humorless laugh escaped him. "I'm terrible at lying to myself."

She stayed silent, letting him speak.

"Maybe it was the night you fell asleep reading by the fire. Or when you stood up to me before you were healed. Or last night, when I should've walked away and didn't." His gaze softened. "You remind me how to care. And that terrifies me."

"I've lost everyone I've ever loved," he said quietly. "And losing you..." His voice broke. "I wouldn't survive it."

Leah stepped closer and rested her hand over his heart, feeling how fast it beat.

"I'm not asking you to stop being afraid," she said. "Just don't shut me out because of it."

"I know what last night meant," she continued. "And I know what today cost you. I'm not here by accident. And I'm not fragile."

"I care about you," she said simply.

His hand rose to cradle her jaw. "This is dangerous."

"I know," Leah said. "But so is pretending we don't feel it."

He leaned his forehead against hers. "I don't know how to love someone without breaking them."

"Then let me choose," she said softly. "I don't want safety if it means distance."

She kissed him gently. After a moment's hesitation, he kissed her back, just as softly, relief threading through the contact.

"Well," Kaya's voice said lightly from the doorway, "that answers one question."

Leah pulled back, startled, heat flooding her face as the door opened. Kasper followed, rain clinging to his hair.

"Wow," he said, grinning. "And here I thought we were racing the weather."

Nico stepped back, composure snapping into place, though his hand lingered at Leah's side a second longer than necessary.

"I wondered how long it would take," Kaya said mildly.

Leah glanced at Nico. His eyes were softer than before. And despite the interruption, she didn't regret it. Not even a little.

Chapter 22

Three days. That's how long it had been since they'd finally let the walls between them crumble, since Leah had chosen to step into the risk of him. Nico hadn't seen much of her since. Kaya had taken the reins of her training, which he told himself was for the best. Leah needed structure. Precision. Control. Kaya could give her that.

Most mornings, he woke to the sound of movement below the floorboards as the soft echo of Leah's voice and Kaya's measured instruction drifted up from the basement. Sometimes he caught a flicker of light beneath the door, and the worry that tightened his chest during her training came dangerously close to the memory of her claiming him in ways he was still trying to process.

By the time they would emerge hours later, Leah always looked exhausted. Her hair fell in soft tangles, her shoulders slightly slumped, but there was a steadiness to her gaze that hadn't been there before. She was changing, growing. Kaya told him the training was working, that Leah was learning to find her center before the visions could pull her under. She was also starting to learn how to pull herself back without outside interference.

Nico nodded, pretending to be pleased, and he was, mostly. He'd watched Leah come apart too many times, her power pulling at her mind like a current too strong to swim against. Seeing her gain control should have felt like relief, but every time she passed him in the hallway with a polite smile and a quiet "good morning," the air between them tightened just a little more.

He hadn't meant to say it that day. Any of it. It slipped out, years of restraint breaking under the weight of seeing her nearly disappear right in front of him. Even Kasper noticed the tension. The man was almost too perceptive for his own good, lingering close to Leah during breaks and throwing Nico pointed looks whenever she laughed at one of his ridiculous jokes.

Kaya noticed too. She didn't say anything outright, but her decision to keep Leah busy was no accident. Nico suspected she thought distance might cool whatever was brewing between them. It hadn't. If anything, it made it worse.

Nico found himself counting the hours until he'd hear her footsteps again. The smallest glimpse of her was enough to unravel his resolve all over again. One evening, he stood by the window, watching their reflections as Kaya and Leah came up from the basement. Leah spoke animatedly, her hands moving as she talked, and for a moment she looked almost carefree.

Kaya mentioned the Echodex, and Nico's attention sharpened. That wasn't just another training milestone. It was a step toward true Seer mastery. If Kaya thought Leah was ready to begin that work, it meant her control had solidified faster than he'd expected. The realization brought equal parts pride and dread because the stronger Leah became, the closer she drew to the same dangers that had nearly destroyed him.

He tore his gaze from the window and exhaled sharply. It didn't matter. His role was clear. Protect her. Keep her safe. But the echo of her voice made it hard to remember it was supposed to be only that.

Kaya's laughter pulled him back as the basement door opened. Leah climbed out first, hair loose around her shoulders, and a faint sheen of sweat at her temples. Kaya followed with far less effort, posture composed despite the hours underground.

"Good timing," Kaya said, brushing dust from her sleeves. "We were just about to take a break for lunch."

Leah's gaze flicked to Nico, and color rose instantly to her cheeks.

"Hi," she said shyly.

Nico straightened, forcing calm. "How's training going?"

"She's improving faster than I expected," Kaya replied, crossing to the counter for water. "Her emotional control is stabilizing. She'll be ready for resonance work soon."

Leah blinked. "Resonance work?"

Kaya shot her a knowing look. "I was going to explain after you ate, but since your mentor is eavesdropping—"

"I wasn't—" Nico started.

"—we might as well discuss it now," Kaya finished with a faint smirk.

Leah tilted her head. "What's resonance work?"

Kaya leaned against the counter, her tone shifting. "It's the first step toward using the Echodex."

"She's used it before," Nico said, glancing at Leah, who fidgeted with the edge of the table.

"There's a difference between seeing what the Echodex wants you to see and seeing what you want to see," Kaya replied. "Until now, Leah's understanding came from the visions themselves, not from any control she exercised."

Leah frowned. "It feels impossible to learn to see anything in there properly."

"It might seem impossible to others," Kaya said, "but not to you. Your bloodline has always had a strong connection to the Echodex—that's exactly why The Order wants it."

Leah glanced between them. "Atticus said Ezren believes he can wield it. That it will show him what he needs to stay in power forever."

Kaya's expression hardened, and Nico felt tension coil through him.

"Yes," Kaya said firmly. "We cannot allow that."

"But why does it matter if he has it?" Leah asked. "He's not a Seer. He's not part of my bloodline, so why—"

"He doesn't need to be," Kaya cut in sharply, glancing at Nico. He understood the stakes all too well.

Leah looked at Nico, frustration clear. "Okay. Can someone please tell me what I'm missing?"

Nico exhaled and ran a hand through his hair. "No one knows much about Ezren. Only that he has immense power. I've spent years trying to uncover a weakness, a mistake, anything." His mouth flattened. "Every trace is buried. Every story incomplete. Everything about him is calculated and protected."

Kaya nodded. "When Ezren rose to power, previous Order leaders began dying under mysterious circumstances. Some fell ill overnight. Others vanished. No trials. No records. No bodies."

"And no one dared to question it," Nico added. "Those who tried, disappeared too."

Leah folded her arms. "That's horrifying."

"And deliberate," Kaya said. "Ezren ruled through fear before authority."

A soft step sounded behind them. Kasper emerged from the hallway with his hair tousled and the faint crease of a pillow still on his jaw. "But he didn't rise alone," he said. "He never does."

Leah turned. "What do you mean?"

Kasper leaned against the counter, glancing briefly at Nico. "He hand-picked his most powerful allies to stand by his side. Together, they form the Triarch."

"The Triarch?" Leah echoed.

"Ezren," Kasper continued, eyes locked on Nico. "Valeria and Grigori."

The name struck like a blade. Nico didn't move, but something inside him fractured.

His father. Again.

He'd learned the truth only recently, but hearing it spoken so plainly stripped away the distance he'd built around it. Grigori wasn't just an enforcer. He was the man who taught Nico how to stand, how to fight, how to survive in a world that demanded obedience over humanity. The man who once told him strength was loyalty and loyalty was everything.

He remembered the last time he'd seen him standing at Ezren's side, after what Ezren had made him do. After his father had so willingly killed the woman he claimed to love, right in front of him. No hesitation. No regret. Only allegiance.

"Grigori…" Leah whispered. "That's—"

"My father," Nico said quietly.

Kaya nodded. "Yes. Grigori is one of Ezren's right hands."

Nico let out a slow breath. "I guess he didn't hesitate. He chose his place."

"I'm sorry," Leah said gently.

"Don't," he replied. "He made his choice long before I made mine."

Kaya stepped in. "Grigori commands loyalty through fear and force. He believes order is maintained through control. Ezren values him because he never questions."

Nico scoffed softly.

"And Valeria?" Leah asked.

Kaya's gaze sharpened. "Valeria is an enchantress of the mind—one of the most powerful weavers The Order has ever produced. She specializes in memory alteration, emotional suppression, and psychological binding."

"She erased people's memories," Leah said.

"Yes," Kaya confirmed. "Entire lives undone. Families forgotten. A possible resistance eliminated without bloodshed."

Leah's brows furrowed. "That seems… unlike him, no?" she said slowly. "Doesn't he rule by fear and force? He wiped out entire magic Pillars. Why would he allow people to openly defy him without true consequences?"

Kaya was quiet for a moment. "Because it *is* a consequence," she said at last. "Erasure is cleaner than execution. Those he let go couldn't organize, couldn't warn anyone, couldn't even remember what they were fighting against. And without memory, they couldn't cross the Veil into the Hollow anyway. They were rendered harmless. Alive, but effectively gone."

Something snapped into focus for Nico. The pattern The Order had drilled into him. No mercy. Total control. His shadows rippled in a low, restrained response to the fury building in his chest.

"Ezren doesn't just rule through fear," Nico said. "He engineers obedience."

Leah looked at him, startled.

"He surrounds himself with monsters," Nico continued flatly, "and convinces them they're necessary. That what they do is the only way to keep the world from tearing itself apart."

His jaw clenched. He knew the lie intimately. He had lived inside it.

Kasper inhaled through his nose and crossed his arms, looking between Nico and Leah. "That's the Triarch," he said. "Power, mind, and muscle."

Nico closed his eyes for half a second. Years. Years of trying to find a crack in Ezren's armor, any sign of weakness, had led nowhere. Even with Selene's help, he had only managed to piece together fragments. Dates that didn't line up. Records that ended too cleanly.

Leah's voice cut softly through the silence. "Wait."

Nico turned to her. Leah was staring at the floor now, brow furrowed in thought, fingers picking at the edge of her sleeve. "If Ezren was already in power when the previous leaders died, and that was decades ago..." She looked up slowly, meeting all three of their gazes. "How old is he supposed to be?"

She took a seat at the kitchen island. "He should be dead," she continued, almost to herself. "Or at least old. Frail. That kind of power doesn't just last forever, does it?"

Something cold slid down Nico's spine.

"He doesn't," Kaya said quietly. "Age."

Leah blinked. "Excuse me? I thought vampires and immortality weren't a thing."

"They aren't, at least not in any form I know of," Kaya replied. "But Ezren has looked to be in his mid-forties for years."

"That's impossible," Leah said, disbelief creeping in. "If he rose close to when the old council fell, he'd have to be—"

"Close to a hundred," Nico said.

The room went quiet. Nico watched confusion spread across Leah's face.

"That's not—people don't just—"

"No," Nico agreed. "They don't."

He leaned back against the counter, the familiar pressure settling behind his ribs, the sensation that always followed Ezren's name. "Every record I've found points to the same thing.

Ezren was already a grown man when the previous leaders ruled, and he hasn't aged the way anyone else does. Not naturally."

"Neither has Valeria," Kaya added, "but that one is easier to explain. She can use enchantments to make herself appear younger."

Leah hesitated. "So is Valeria doing that to him too?"

"No," Kasper said. "Valeria's only been around for forty years or so. Ezren has looked the same for far longer."

Kaya's expression darkened. "Whatever he is, it isn't sustained by time alone."

Nico looked at Leah. "That's why the Echodex matters," he said. "If Ezren has found a way to defy time, to anchor himself beyond mortality, then it came with a cost."

"And cost leaves patterns," Kaya said. "Patterns the Echodex can see."

"So if he's lasted this long..." Leah began.

"He's afraid of losing it," Kaya finished.

"Or having it taken from him," Kasper added.

"Whatever he's done to preserve himself, it isn't invincible," Nico said. "And he knows it."

The room fell silent. Kaya turned back to the stove. Leah reached for a piece of bread. Nico remained still, the sensation settling in his spine like a tightening grip.

Kasper noticed. Nico caught it in the way Kasper tilted his head, in the glance toward Nico's clenched jaw and the shadows drawn too tightly at his feet.

"Well," Kasper said lightly, pushing off the counter. "That was uplifting."

Leah huffed a quiet laugh.

Kasper nodded toward the door. "Come on, Shadow Prince. You look like you're about to implode. Let's get some air."

Leah glanced at Nico. "Be careful."

Nico met her eyes, gave a short nod, and followed Kasper outside.

The air was crisp, fresh snow blanketing the ground. The moment they crossed the boundary of the cabin's enchantments, Nico felt it. The quiet hum of warded space fell away, replaced by open air that offered no protection, no distortion to blur presence or intent.

He stopped instinctively, one hand lifting slightly. Kasper froze beside him, reading the shift just as fast.

"You feel that too," Kasper murmured.

Nico nodded. "They're closer."

They didn't follow the path. Nico stepped off it instead, guiding them into the trees where the underbrush broke silhouettes. Shadows gathered around him, bending light and dulling the sharp edges of his presence. Kasper followed and waited.

Nothing revealed itself outright. No sudden movement. No flares of magic. Nico didn't lower his guard. The Order never arrived loudly unless they wanted to be seen.

Kasper knelt in the snow and closed his eyes, exhaling slowly.

The air responded. He extended his right hand, palm up, as a thin spiral of wind formed above it, rotating in controlled precision. The spiral tightened into a small funnel, turning in place like a miniature tornado.

Nico watched closely. This wasn't showmanship. This was wind shaped to listen.

The current extended outward in narrow threads, slipping between branches, curling around trunks, drawing in distant movement. Each thread fed back into the spinning column in Kasper's palm.

A few seconds passed before Kasper's brow furrowed.

"North," he said quietly. "Two, maybe three. Patrols."

The funnel collapsed inward, condensing into a rotating sphere of wind hovering above his hand. Nico shifted his stance.

A dry, browned leaf lifted from the forest floor and drifted into the orb. The moment it touched the spinning air, it dissolved, and a voice followed.

"...Ezren wants updates by nightfall."

Two more leaves joined it.

"...all Groves, all Hollows. No exceptions."

"...she's a Seer. The book responded."

Nico felt tension snap back into place.

Another leaf spiraled inward.

"He knows he can use it."

Kasper opened his eyes. "They're not guessing anymore," he said. "They're sure."

The final leaf drifted into the orb.

"If we find the girl, do not engage. Signal and withdraw. Orders from the top."

Kasper let his hand drop. The wind unraveled instantly, scattering leaves back into the snow as if nothing had happened.

Ezren knew.

The realization settled cold and heavy in Nico's chest.

"I don't think it's safe to stay out here," Kasper said, already turning back toward the cabin.

Nico didn't move.

Ezren didn't escalate without cause. He didn't send agents this deep into neutral territory unless something had shifted beyond his control. If he was tightening the perimeter instead of watching from a distance, then the balance had already begun to tilt.

Nico looked back toward the cabin, toward Leah standing on the edge of something dangerous.

For years, he had searched for leverage. For proof Ezren wasn't untouchable.

Now Ezren was reacting.

And that told Nico everything.

The Echodex wasn't just a tool. It was the one thing Ezren feared enough to hunt openly for. And if Leah could learn to wield it properly, then for the first time in decades, the balance might finally tip.

Chapter 23

Leah lingered in the basement with the Echodex in hand, the low hum of magic vibrating faintly through the stone floor. Anticipation and trepidation coiled in her stomach, tightening with every passing second. Today, Kaya had promised she would finally begin learning how to use the Echodex.

She had handled many visions by now, and Leah felt ready. She had learned control over her magic, learned how to pull back before a memory or emotion could overwhelm her, but this was different. Through her training with Kaya, she had come to understand that the Echodex was not just a lens for seeing others. It was a conduit. A sentient instrument left to her by her mother, the only gift she had entrusted. It held truth, but it demanded clarity, intent, and the courage to face that truth without flinching.

Kaya stood across the room, arms folded, posture straight. Every inch of her radiated composure, making Leah acutely aware of her own uncertainty. Kasper and Nico leaned against the far wall, arms crossed loosely. Nico hadn't spoken much since the night before, but his presence was heavy and protective. Every so often, Leah caught him watching her, eyes narrowing in calculation, as if he were counting every beat of her pulse.

"Sit," Kaya said.

Leah obeyed, lowering herself onto the cool stone floor, legs crossed, palms resting on her knees. The residual hum of magic beneath her made it clear that Kaya had layered protective enchantments to keep the Echodex's power contained within the basement.

"The Echodex," Kaya began, kneeling beside her, "is unlike any tool you've used. It is older, more discerning. It responds to intent, and it will only reveal what it believes you are ready to see." Her gaze flicked briefly to Nico before returning to Leah. "It will never lie. But it will withhold to protect itself, and to protect you."

Leah nodded slowly, absorbing the weight of that. She had handled the Echodex before and knew it revealed what it chose to. She had avoided the book for weeks, promising herself not to touch it again until she understood what she was dealing with. Now, as she reached for it, she felt its presence immediately. A subtle warmth bloomed in her chest, almost like a heartbeat, a rhythm that mirrored her own.

"You must ask a question, not a memory," Kaya instructed. "Frame it clearly. The book responds to purpose and clarity of thought."

The familiar pressure built behind Leah's eyes as she whispered the words she had been carrying for months.

"I want to know about my parents."

She paused, willing the weight of the request into focus, then extended her hands slowly. Her fingertips brushed the Echodex's cover. It pulsed beneath her touch as warmth spread across her palms before the room dimmed and ambient light bent inward.

Threads of golden light unfurled from the book, weaving upward like smoke. Leah's chest tightened as they began to form shapes, vague at first. Hills. Trees. A gray sky. Then the threads coalesced into a faint vision. She blinked, steadying it and holding it the way Kaya had taught her.

A sign stood clearly before her.

Ashmere Hollow.

The name echoed in her mind, though she had never spoken it aloud. A place she knew nothing about, now reflected in her vision with startling clarity. The trees were tall, their branches arching like the ribs of a cathedral. Mist drifted low across the grass, and the air felt thick and weighted with absence. A sudden chill crawled over her skin, tightening her stomach.

"What is it showing you?" Kaya asked, her hand brushing Leah's shoulder.

Leah's fingers tightened around the book. "Ashmere Hollow," she said. "Why... why there?" Her voice trembled as longing and grief pressed in without explanation. "What am I supposed to do with this?"

"If that is all you can see," Kaya said gently, "then it is showing you where you need to go."

Leah stared at the fragile vision, at the ruins suggested by the shifting light, trying to make sense of the pull it exerted. Frustration prickled her skin as the golden threads wavered and vanished, leaving her blinking in the dim basement.

"I don't understand," she said. "Was that where my parents lived?"

Kaya inhaled, choosing her words carefully. "Ashmere Hollow, as it stands now, is just ruins," she said. "When the Seers were hunted, the town was destroyed."

Leah drew a sharp breath. "That's horrible. But that means I have to go there to see more?" Concern flickered across her face.

Nico's voice cut softly through her thoughts despite the tremor Leah could detect beneath it. "You won't be going alone."

"Definitely not," Kasper added. "I've been to Ashmere Hollow. If you're not familiar with the landscape, you can get lost easily there."

"Thanks," she whispered, a faint tremor to her words. "I don't think I want to go there alone."

Kaya's voice broke her train of thought. "We should prepare to leave," she said. "Remember that going back to the Hollow means we'll need to be much more alert. The Order is still looking, and if they're smart, they will most likely have eyes on Ashmere Hollow already. Keep that in mind."

Leah nodded, her chest tight with anticipation as she headed up the stairs and into her room. Ashmere Hollow burned in her mind, the echo of its misty expanse haunting the edges of her vision. She could almost hear the faint rustle of leaves, the whisper of loss lingering at the edges of her vision. She didn't know what awaited her there, only that she had to go, and that she wouldn't be alone.

Ten minutes later, she emerged to find Kaya organizing supplies, Kasper muttering over maps, and Nico checking their gear. All seasoned and ready to leave at a moment's notice.

"Ready?" Nico asked.

"I think so," Leah said, though her pulse quickened. Her fingers brushed the bracelet on her wrist. Crossing the Veil again meant facing memories she had barely survived before.

Nico noticed her hesitation and stepped closer, placing a hand lightly on her shoulder. "Your passage won't be as intense this time," he said gently. "You've grown. You're ready."

Leah lifted her gaze to meet his, and for a fleeting moment, the weight of fear eased. She gave a small, grateful smile. "Thank you," she whispered.

Kaya joined them, slinging a pack over her shoulder. "We should move in pairs," she said, casting a measured glance around the clearing once they stepped foot outside the cabin. "Leah, Nico, stay together. Kasper and I will scout ahead. Keep your eyes and ears open. Ashmere Hollow is fragile, and its magic could have been disturbed by The Order."

The walk through the forest was quiet at first, the rhythmic crunch of leaves underfoot filling the space between words. Leah's hands hovered near her bag as her fingers brushed the Echodex.

Kasper's voice broke the silence. "The archway should be just past this bridge. If the maps are right, we'll see the stones before sunset."

Leah's chest tightened. She had imagined the archway countless times since the Echodex showed her Ashmere Hollow, and now that they would be approaching it soon, her anxiety peaked at the realization that she would be visiting the place where her parents once lived—and where they had died.

They came to a small clearing, the remnants of a path barely visible beneath moss and dirt. Leah froze as she saw it. The archway. This one looked similar to the one she crossed in Eldergrove. They were both made of stone pillars with ivy creeping along the edges as though trying to stitch the cracks of the stone back together.

The moment Leah stepped closer, a shiver ran through her. The Hollow's magic pulsed beneath her skin, calling her forward.

"You okay?" Nico murmured.

She nodded. "I think so."

"Follow me," Kaya called. "The Veil will test you again. Focus on the light and your companion's voice."

Kasper activated the sigils. The archway from Eldergrove to Roots Hollow had shown a misty forest on the other side, but this one simply showed an abandoned path covered in snow. He and Kaya crossed first and vanished. Leah's heart beat faster, but Nico's calm demeanor at her side confirmed that nothing out of the ordinary had happened. Perhaps this was what others would see from the neutral side as people crossed.

Leah's pulse spiked and she realized it was because of the dread of what would await her this time through the Veil. Leah tried to dismiss the thought, surely there was nothing worse than what she had experienced the first time around. Just then, a warm hand touched hers.

Nico looked down at her briefly and gave a short, reassuring nod before he gently pulled her forward toward the archway. The walk through it was slow and deliberate, and Leah felt the air thickening as soon as they crossed the threshold. Mist curled around their feet, and the faint pulse of magic beneath Leah's skin began to intensify.

She had expected dizziness, nausea, confusion— all the things that had nearly undone her before—but this time, the visions came as whispers rather than storms. She glimpsed memories and echoes, fleeting shapes of what had once been, but none of them slammed into her mind like a hammer. A gentle squeeze of her hand reminded her she was with Nico, walking beside him. She didn't know if it was him or her growing strength that was keeping her from losing herself in visions once more.

Ashmere Hollow opened before them gradually, and the mist cleared, revealing Kasper and Kaya just a few steps ahead. The trees rose like skeletal spires and mist curled between them. Leah looked around, noticing the uneven ground that was scarred by decades of neglect and decay. She gave Nico's hand a soft squeeze to let him know she was okay before she let go and began walking slowly ahead of them to take a better look at their surroundings. But even as she let go of his hand, he stood by her side and walked with her.

Even in ruin, Ashmere Hollow held a strange beauty, a solemn dignity, as though it remembered its former life and mourned its loss at the same time. The air here pressed down on her chest with every step she took. The soft steps seemed to echo through the ruins, through the skeletal trees and broken stones, carrying with it a profound sense of loss. It was as if the Hollow itself had been waiting for her, holding onto decades of grief, and now that she was here, it poured into her.

Her knees weakened but Nico steadied her instantly. Words felt inadequate here. The sorrow was too vast and yet unbearably personal. From the corner of her eyes, she saw Kaya walking forward and the realization hit her

"This Hollow..." Leah whispered, voice cracking. "This was... your home, wasn't it?"

Kaya let out a slow breath and she nodded slowly, not taking her eyes off the shattered remains of what had once been vibrant paths and workshops.

"It was," she said softly. "Before the Pillar fell, this place was... alive. A center of learning, of magic and community. I've been back many times since then. Each visit is easier in some ways, harder in others." Her eyes flicked briefly to Leah. "But it never stops taking your breath away the first time."

Leah reached out, brushing a finger along the broken remains of what she assumed to be a small home or shop. Dust flaked into her palm, carried away by the faint breeze that wound through the Hollow. Every surface seemed to hum with a melancholy resonance that tugged at her heart. She could feel the sadness of this place, a sadness like once she had not felt in a very long time.

She drew in a shaky breath and looked at Kaya. "I... I feel it. All of it. How do you—?" She swallowed, unable to form the words.

Kaya's gaze softened. "You let it touch you, but you don't let it drown you. That's all you can do here. The Hollow remembers. It mourns. But it doesn't have to break you."

Nico placed a gentle hand on her shoulder, a reminder that she wasn't alone. They continued walking, treading carefully over fallen stones and ash-streaked soil. Leah's eyes caught the jagged outline of a dried-up riverbed where the cracked earth weaved like veins through the ruins. She followed it with her gaze, feeling a strange pull, a thread connecting it to some half-forgotten memory. The riverbed led past collapsed walls and burned-out foundations, the smell of soot and decay hanging heavy in the air even after all this time.

A shiver ran down her spine. The riverbed looked... familiar. Not from her own memories, but from something she had seen, or something she'd been shown. She stopped, gripping Nico's arm.

"The river," she whispered. "Selene said I would find her body... where the river bends to ash."

Kaya paused as well, eyes narrowing as she took in the riverbed. "The river bends there," she said quietly, her voice low and measured. "It's been dry for years, but the Hollow's geography hasn't changed."

Leah's chest tightened, but she couldn't find it within herself to let go of Nico's arm. Her heartbeat hammered painfully against her ribs as realization set in. This was it. Everything she had gone through since her birthday, every pulse of magic, every whispered hint from all the visions she had seen, seemed to converge on this single point. She felt drawn forward but rooted to the spot. She was scared. She felt more fear now than she ever had crossing any veil. If this was what she thought it was, she didn't feel ready to face it.

Nico moved beside her, cupping her face with his hands and pressing his forehead against hers. She felt dizzy and realized she was hyperventilating.

"Hey," Nico said gently, forcing her to focus on him. "It's okay. You're okay."

The emotions were too much, and she felt the sting behind her eyes as tears threatened to fall.

"I don't..." she started, then shook her head in an attempt to calm the tears. "I don't think I can do this," she finally blurted, wiping her hand across her eyes.

"You *can* do this," he said matter-of-factly.

It was incredible, the amount of trust and confidence he had in her. Confidence she did not feel. If anything, everything she had improved up to this point seemed pointless now. She hated that she was breaking down like this in front of them— hated feeling so vulnerable. But the tears threatened to fall once more, and this time she didn't try to stop them.

"Do you want me to go with you?" he asked finally, and she exhaled a sigh of relief that he had suggested it before she had to ask.

Leah nodded, letting him lead her along the cracked riverbed, hand in hand. Every step brought a new surge of grief, but also clarity. She could sense the remnants of the lives that had been here, the people who had built this place, who had loved and learned and lived, now gone. The ash-streaked riverbed was like a scar of what it once had been, but it was also a path she had to follow.

As they approached the bend, Leah's pulse quickened. The river curved sharply, and the ground ahead was blackened, streaked with the remnants of fire. She could see faint shapes in the ash, almost like footprints, leading toward a partially collapsed structure that had once been a stone tower atop a small hill overlooking a dense forest below.

She stopped just before the bend and took a deep breath, letting the weight of grief, loss, and anticipation press in on her. She let go of Nico's hand once more as a strange, simmering resolve pushed her forward. She had come this far. She needed to see this through.

Leah's boots crunched over the ash-streaked ground as she approached the bend in the dried river. The soil was blackened, cracked, and brittle, remnants of a town long reduced to nothing. The river's curve led to a shallow depression, the earth scarred and pocketed with signs of fire and ruin. Behind her, the soft presence of Kaya, Nico, and Kasper lingered, giving her space but remaining close enough to offer silent support.

Leah's chest tightened as grief and anticipation coiled together with every step she took. She knew, deep in her bones, that she had arrived at the place Selene had chosen. She stepped forward slowly, eyes scanning the blackened soil, and then she saw it: a shape among the ash, faintly lighter, almost blending with the gray and black around it.

She recognized it immediately as her pulse jumped and a cold ache spread through her chest. Her hands shook violently as she knelt beside it. The skeleton was unmistakable, small and slight, the delicate frame of the woman who had carried her as a child and protected her with unwavering love. Leah's fingers trembled as they brushed away ash and dirt, revealing Selene's remains fully for the first time.

A strangled sob ripped from her throat. Months of longing, unanswered questions, and pain she had carried quietly all crashed down in a single wave. She pressed her hands to the bones, desperate for some trace of warmth, some connection to the woman who had raised her, taught her, and then chosen this lonely, silent place to die.

Every memory of Selene flooded her at once. The lullabies, the patient instruction, the thoughtful riddles. Raw sobs escaped her as Leah pressed her forehead to the empty cheekbone, imagining the soft weight of her grandmother's arms, the smell of her shawl, the comfort of her voice. She could feel the loss in her veins, a cold, inexorable grief pressing down on her shoulders.

She tried to breathe, tried to steady herself, but each sob that tore through her chest left her hollowed out again. Months of restrained mourning, nights of silent crying, dreams haunted by Selene's absence, crashed into a tidal wave. Leah's nails dug into the ash as her vision blurred.

The silence of Ashmere Hollow pressed in on her, thick and suffocating. Not a single bird stirred, and no wind passed through the burned-out trees. Only the faint pulse of the Echodex beneath her fingers offered any sensation beyond the ache of grief.

Leah's lips trembled as she whispered a barely audible, "Gran... I..." Her voice broke, the words lost in dust and ash, but her fingers brushed against something solid and smooth, nestled among the remains.

Leah's fingers trembled as she lifted the pendant from the ash, the faint glow of its surface pulsing in sync with her heartbeat. She didn't know what she had expected, but the warmth that spread through her chest was unlike anything she had felt since Selene had died.

The memory poured out of the pendant in a gentle wave, enveloping her like a soft current and disconnecting her from the present. Suddenly, she was no longer kneeling in the blackened riverbed of Ashmere Hollow. She was in Selene's study, the room suffused with the golden light of late afternoon. Dust motes drifted lazily through the beams falling across shelves lined with books and trinkets, and the air carried the familiar scent of herbs.

There, sitting at her desk, was Selene.

She looked up directly at Leah, upright and alive, her hair pulled back into a messy bun and a small smile tugging at the corners of her lips. Her eyes were warm, but Leah could see the weight of emotion threatening to spill as they watered.

"Thank you for finding me," Selene said, her voice soft but teasing, just enough to make Leah blink in disbelief.

Leah's throat tightened. "Gran... I..." she started, her voice breaking, but the words failed her. She was caught in the impossible reality of seeing Selene in front of her again, sitting just as she always had, speaking directly to her.

Selene leaned forward, eyes locking with Leah's. "I'm sorry, Leah. I'm sorry that I left you the way I did."

Leah could see the pain behind her eyes, the regret of choices already made. But she didn't care. She was just happy to see her again, even if it was only a memory. Leah wanted to talk, wanted to tell her everything that had happened since Selene left, but she couldn't form the words. All she could do was look at her as tears continued to fall.

Selene gave her a warm smile. "I don't have much time. I want to tell you the truth about your parents." She paused, and with a wave of her hand, an image appeared like a hologram atop the desk. It was the image of two people, a man and a woman, smiling at Leah, making her hold her breath amid silent sobs.

"They defied The Order," Selene said. "They defied it by choosing each other." She pointed to the woman. "Runa, your mother, was a Seer of the Hollow, descended from The Unheard." Then she nodded toward the man. "Ezra, your father, was a powerful blood mage."

Leah's pulse was still racing, but the realization that she was truly looking at her parents allowed her breathing to steady for a moment. She forced herself to focus, to really see them for the first time. Her mother, Runa, had ash-black hair, long and partially braided at the back. Her eyes were pale blue, just like Leah's. The ache in her chest returned, but this time with the grief of parents she had never known.

She turned her gaze to Ezra. Leah smiled softly as he shifted slightly, striking a pose that somehow conveyed his personality even in silence. His golden eyes were unlike anything she had ever seen before, and his dirty blond hair fell in loose waves.

Selene noticed how the holograms helped Leah calm her breathing. "The Order forbade unions like theirs, binding the Pillars to secrecy and loyalty. But your parents were little rebels. They chose love."

Leah looked up at Selene. "They... they knew what would happen?"

Selene nodded, a shadow crossing her face. "Yes. One of their own betrayed them. Boris, a Seer of Ashmere Hollow, told The Order about the impending birth of their child. They hoped secrecy would protect you, but The Order was relentless."

Leah looked back at the holograms. Runa gave Ezra an annoyed look as he continued to pose.

"Your mother foresaw the danger," Selene said softly. "She made the choice that saved you. She called me, entrusted you to me, and I swore to protect you."

"Why?" Leah asked.

"Because your mother was my best friend." Selene's voice faltered, a tremor of grief threading through it. "The pact your father and I made was one I knew would cost me my life."

Leah stared at her, eyes blurring again. It was hard to fathom what it must have taken for Selene to make such a sacrifice.

"I understood that, and I accepted it," Selene continued. "It was the only way to ensure your survival." She rose slowly from the chair and walked around the desk toward Leah.

Leah took a shaky breath as Selene approached.

"Everything I did, every restriction, every lie, every moment I kept you from magic, was so you could live."

Leah's hands shook at her sides. "Gran... I..." she started, unsure if she was allowed to move.

Selene stopped in front of her and opened her arms, tears slipping down her cheeks.

Leah closed the distance between them in a rush, nearly knocking them both over as she hugged her tightly. They cried together, every tear carrying the weight of words never spoken and goodbyes never had.

"Thank you," Leah sobbed. "Thank you for everything, for keeping me safe, even if it meant..."

Selene cupped Leah's face with the same gentle hands that had always calmed her fears. "I know," she said, forcing a smile through her tears. "I chose my path, and I wouldn't trade it for anything."

Leah placed her hands over her grandmother's. "I am so honored to have you as my grandmother. I will miss you."

Selene wiped away the tears on Leah's cheeks as another sob escaped her.

"Thank you."

The way she said it tore Leah's heart open. It felt as if Selene had been waiting to hear that Leah loved her, that she wasn't angry. The warmth surrounding them began to fade, and Leah shook her head.

"No," she whispered. "Don't go."

Selene leaned in and pressed a soft kiss to Leah's forehead before stepping back.

"I love you, Leah. I am proud of you and how far you have come. Whatever happens next, trust me when I say that I know you can do it. You carry not just your parents' legacy, but mine as well. Remember that. Always."

The memory softened, the light fading, leaving Leah kneeling over the blackened soil once more, the pendant warm in her hands. She pressed it to her heart as tears continued to fall.

For the first time since Selene's death, she felt both the ache of loss and a fragile spark of connection, as if her grandmother had never truly left her.

Leah's hands trembled as the memory faded completely, leaving her alone with the Hollow's ash and the lingering warmth of Selene's final words. Her chest heaved as the grief she had carried for months surged again, threatening to overwhelm her.

A soft sound behind her made her turn, vision blurred with tears. Nico stepped forward and knelt beside her without a word. Leah didn't hesitate. She fell into him, letting the sobs she had held back for months pour out freely. She clung to him as if letting go would mean losing Selene all over again, as if his embrace could anchor her to the world while she faced the unbearable emptiness of the Hollow.

Chapter 24

It took a while for Leah to calm down after finding Selene's body and the message from the pendant that now rested against her chest. The four of them made a quiet, beautiful burial site at the top of the hill and finally laid Selene to rest. Despite the ache in her chest, Leah knew she had to finish what she had started and find the answers she had come to Ashmere Hollow to uncover.

The forest around the Hollow pressed in close, thick with blackened trunks and ash-strewn undergrowth. Leah moved cautiously, her steps quiet against the brittle ground, and the faint pulse of the Echodex guiding her forward like a hidden thread. Kaya and Nico flanked her, alert and watchful, while Kasper lingered a few paces behind, still studying the terrain.

Despite their careful vigilance, Leah felt the pull before she could see it. A subtle tug brushed her mind, as if something within the Hollow was calling to her. She followed it instinctively, her heart hammering with a mixture of dread and urgency. Each step through the skeletal remains of the town carried the weight of grief, memory, and anticipation.

Nico's eyes never left her, and she felt the quiet reassurance of his presence, though she didn't speak. Words felt fragile and unnecessary here. The Hollow demanded attention, demanded respect, and Leah allowed herself to be guided by its silent insistence.

Eventually, they reached the remains of what had once been a neighborhood. At least five homes lay in ruins, some completely collapsed, others shattered and strewn across the ground. One particular stone house caught Leah's attention. It was half-collapsed, nearly swallowed by moss and creeping vines. She approached slowly, the Echodex warm in her hand. Its pulse sharpened, almost urgent, as if it had been waiting for her to arrive at this exact place.

She knelt beside a fallen beam and brushed her fingertips over the smooth stone, feeling magic thrum beneath her skin. Leah placed the Echodex atop the stone and closed her eyes, bracing herself as the vision rushed toward her.

It struck like a physical weight, dragging her into a night of fire and despair. Flames licked the horizon, and the shadows of Order agents stretched long and monstrous against the walls of a small house. Outside, screams echoed through the darkness, the sound of Ashmere Hollow falling. Inside, the air pulsed with the scent of iron and smoke.

Runa's cries cut through the chaos, forcing Leah to focus. Runa lay on her bed, her voice ragged and raw with pain. Sweat slicked her skin as she labored, her hands gripping the edge of the mattress hard enough to splinter the wood. A chill ran down Leah's spine as realization set in. Her mother was in active labor.

The vision was chaotic, but whenever Leah focused, she could feel their emotions as clearly as her own. Runa's exhaustion and fear pressed heavily against her, and she felt the tension radiating from her father as he moved restlessly at her side.

Ezra knelt beside Runa, torn between helping her and checking the door, listening for the moment the enchantments he'd laid over their home might fail. He hovered, helpless, caught between love and impending catastrophe.

"Ezra," Runa gasped, her voice hoarse. "It's time. She's coming."

Leah fixed her attention on her father, forcing herself to stay present despite the rising panic in her chest. She could feel the dread in his bones. There was no time left, no room for anything but this moment, this fragile defiance against fate. Ezra brushed a soot-streaked curl from Runa's temple, his voice trembling as he whispered, "Stay with me. Just a little longer."

A flash of light illuminated the doorway. Selene's silhouette appeared, breathless, her eyes wide with dread.

"They've reached the square," she said, urgency low but fierce. "The Pillar is falling. We have minutes at most."

Another contraction wracked Runa's body, and she bit back a sob. "Then help me bring her into this world," she gasped.

The baby's first cry split the air like a crack of thunder. Tiny, fragile, and unmistakably alive.

Runa sagged back against the pillows, tears of exhaustion and awe streaking her cheeks. Her trembling hands reached out, cradling the newborn close. Leah willed herself forward and found she could move, circling the scene until she stood close enough to see her mother's face clearly.

For a fleeting moment, the world outside faded. The flames, the screams, the end of everything all fell away. There was only the rhythm of Runa's breathing and the look of awe and undeniable love as she stared down at the child in her arms.

"My beautiful girl," Runa whispered, her voice shaking with wonder and grief. "You were never meant to be born into this cruel world... but maybe you'll change it."

Ezra knelt beside her, his hand trembling as it brushed the infant's cheek. The small, perfect face reflected the firelight, a spark of everything they had fought for.

The moment shattered as the walls shuddered, the unmistakable crack of The Order breaking through the final spells.

"Ezra," Selene said, stepping forward, her face pale but resolute. "We must bind her now."

Ezra looked down at his daughter, then back at Selene. "If I do this," he said, his voice unsteady, "it ties you to her. Leah's life will be bound to yours through this blood oath. When she awakens her power—"

"I know," Selene said softly, her gaze unwavering. "I know the cost. Do it."

Ezra's breath shook as he nodded. "Forgive me."

He drew a slender dagger from his belt, its blade etched with runes that pulsed faintly crimson. With a practiced motion, he sliced across his palm, then across Runa's and finally across Selene's, their blood mingling where their hands met. The air shimmered instantly and the room pulsed with power that seemed to vibrate from the earth itself.

He spoke the words low, reverent, each syllable burning with intent:

> *"By blood that binds and breath that ends,*
> *by heart that gives, and will that bends,*
> *by life unbroken, death shall weave,*
> *the thread of theirs through thine reprieve.*
> *When light is lost, and shadow calls,*
> *her name will rise where memory falls."*

The sigils burned into the air, swirling around them in a spiral of red-gold light. The magic caught, searing through Selene's veins, through Ezra's, and through the crying child Runa held against her chest.

Runa reached out, clutching Selene's bloodstained hand. "You'll keep her safe," she whispered, eyes glistening with tears. "Promise me."

"I swear it," Selene said, her voice breaking.

Ezra's hand trembled as he pressed a blood-slicked kiss to his daughter's forehead. "Live," he whispered to her. "Live for what we could not."

Outside, the night exploded as the last ward collapsed under The Order's assault. Shadows flooded the doorway.

Runa's strength faltered. She turned to Selene one last time, her face soft despite the terror surrounding them. "I can never repay you for this. Thank you."

Then, with one final, aching look at her daughter, she whispered, "Take her."

Selene gathered the infant against her chest, tears falling freely now. "I'll protect her," she vowed, her voice fierce and trembling all at once.

But before the vision could fade, Leah saw Runa double over suddenly, one hand clutching her stomach, her face twisting in confusion and pain. Her gaze flickered toward Ezra as panic spread across her features.

Then silence.

Leah's fingers refused to leave the Echodex. The golden threads had faded, leaving a hollow ache, but she pressed her palms harder against the cover. "Please," she whispered, her voice cracking. "Show me more. Let me see everything. I need to know."

The book pulsed faintly beneath her hands, almost as if it were struggling against her demand. Yet Leah couldn't let go. She could feel the unfinished memory pressing at the edges of her mind, a tension that burned hotter with every heartbeat.

"I can take it," she murmured through a strangled sob. "I can handle it. Just show me."

The air around her thickened. The faint hum of the Echodex grew stronger, more insistent, resonating through the Hollow. Threads of golden light flickered violently, coiling outward like serpents, and Leah's chest tightened when she sensed something wrong in the book's pulse.

"Leah!" Nico's voice tore through her narrowing focus. "Stop!"

She barely registered him. She was caught in the pull of the unfinished memory, desperate for the final fragments of her parents' night, desperate for answers she had carried for months. The threads of light writhed violently through the air, the hum of the Echodex sharp and discordant now. Shadows along the Hollow floor stretched unnaturally, tendrils of magic she could not control curling toward her like living things.

"Leah!" Nico was closer now, reaching for her.

She tried to pull away, eyes wild, her body trembling. The book shuddered beneath her hands, thrumming with a power that pressed into her and into the Hollow itself. Panic coiled tight in her stomach.

"This... I can handle this," she gasped, but as she forced the memory further, her eyes began to glow red when she looked at Nico.

The Echodex drove something into her mind that she was not ready for. The chaotic pulse of magic around her pierced what little control she had left. Sparks of light burned like fire behind her eyes, and a searing pressure spread across her temples. The taste of iron filled her mouth. She lifted a shaking hand and felt warm blood slipping from her nose, then from her ears. Her vision blurred crimson at the edges. She couldn't hold it. Not this time.

"Leah!" Nico's voice cut through the haze, but she couldn't reach for him—her body would not obey.

Her heartbeat thundered in her ears, her skin burning from the inside out. "I can see it," she gasped, eyes unfocused. "There's more. He's...She's."

"Leah, stop!" Nico's voice broke, raw with desperation. "I won't let this happen!"

Before she could respond, before she could plead, before the Echodex could drag her deeper into the unfinished memory, a hand clamped onto her shoulder. There was a flash of darkness and a sharp pressure at the base of her skull.

Then nothing.

Darkness didn't come all at once. It bloomed like ink in water, slow, curling, and soundless. Leah drifted through it, her body unbound, her thoughts slipping through fragments of fire, blood, and her mother's voice. The edges of everything blurred, and the weight in her chest dulled into something that almost felt like peace.

Then came the hum. A soft melody, low and familiar, the tune she heard in her dreams. The one that always played before she appeared.

"Leah..."

The voice was that of a child, small and melodic. When Leah turned, she stood in a place that wasn't quite real, a pale meadow caught between night and dawn. The air shimmered silver and blue, like moonlight on water. In the distance, the faint outline of trees swayed without wind.

And there, sitting cross-legged among faintly glowing wildflowers, was her.

V.

The little girl looked exactly as she had in every dream before. Dark curls framing a round face, bright gray eyes too old for her age. Barefoot. Smiling softly.

"Welcome back," V said, her voice light with something close to relief. "I was starting to think you wouldn't."

Leah blinked, disoriented. "What is this? Why do I keep seeing you?"

V tilted her head, an innocent motion that felt rehearsed. "Because you need me. Because I'm the only one who's been honest with you."

Leah frowned. "Honest about what?"

"About what's been kept from you." V's smile faded. "You've seen it now, haven't you? The truth about your parents. About what was taken from you."

Leah's chest tightened. "That wasn't the full truth. I know it wasn't. The Echodex cut it off."

"Maybe it was protecting you."

Leah's heart stumbled. "Protecting me from what?"

V's eyes flickered, a shadow passing through them, so faint it could have been imagined.

"From them."

Leah swallowed. "Them?"

V stepped closer, her expression soft, almost pitying. "You trust them, don't you? Nico. Kaya. Even Kasper. But you shouldn't."

Leah shook her head. "No. That's not true. Nico was trying to help me."

"To control you," V said gently. "You felt it, didn't you? The way he stopped you. The way he silenced what you were about to see."

"That's not true," Leah whispered, though her voice wavered.

"Isn't it?" V's gaze softened again. "They know something, Leah. Something about Sage. About the ones you left behind."

Leah's stomach twisted as the world dimmed, the soft blue haze bruising into violet. "Sage?" she breathed. "What are you talking about?"

V reached out, her small hand brushing Leah's wrist. Her touch was cold, wrong in a way Leah couldn't explain.

"She's not safe," V whispered. "They've known. All this time. She's in danger."

Leah froze. "Danger?"

"You have to go back," V said. "Back to Eldergrove. You have to save her before The Order gets to her."

Fear slammed into Leah's chest. "No," she said quickly. "That's not possible. They would've told me. Nico would've."

"Would've lied," V said softly, stepping closer until they were nearly nose to nose. "He always does."

V's eyes deepened into something luminous, beautiful and bottomless.

"Listen to me," she whispered. "The memory wasn't finished. There's more. And if you don't see it soon, if you don't go back, you'll lose everything."

Leah trembled. "Why should I trust you?"

V smiled, slow and knowing. "Because I'm the only part of you that can't lie."

The meadow rippled. Sunlight bled into smoke. For a heartbeat, V's face blurred, her eyes glowing faintly gold beneath the innocence.

Then everything shattered into white.

Leah gasped as she bolted upright, air flooding her lungs. Her vision swam before snapping into place. The ground was cool beneath her palms, smoke lingering faintly in the air. She was back in the ruins of Ashmere Hollow.

Kaya knelt beside her, face pale, fingers hovering near Leah's arm without touching. Kasper stood a few paces away, jaw tight, eyes flicking between her and Nico, who paced in sharp, restless steps.

"What happened?" Leah's voice came out ragged. She pressed a hand to her head, trying to ease the violent throbbing.

"You nearly killed yourself," Nico said roughly. He didn't look at her, only at the Echodex lying on the ground, still pulsing faintly. "You wouldn't stop."

Leah blinked, disoriented. "The memory."

"Was consuming you," he snapped, finally turning. His eyes were dark, bloodshot with strain. "You weren't ready. I warned you what the Echodex could do if you pushed it."

"I didn't push it."

"Yes, you did." His voice cracked, fear bleeding through. "You were bleeding from your eyes. I had to stop it."

Leah's pulse roared in her ears. She looked to Kaya, searching for something steady, but Kaya's expression was unreadable.

"He didn't have a choice," Kaya said quietly. "The Echodex wasn't responding to you anymore. It was fighting you."

Leah's hands curled into fists. Fire and her mother's voice flickered behind her eyes. "It wasn't over," she whispered. "There was more."

Her voice faltered as the image of Runa clutching her stomach slammed back into her.

Kasper crouched in front of her. "You were out for almost an hour," he said gently. "Whatever you saw, it's over for now."

Over.

The word made something in her recoil.

Leah pressed a trembling hand to her forehead, trying to steady her breath. But the echo of V's voice lingered, curling around her thoughts like smoke. *They've known all along. She's not safe.*

She swallowed hard. "Sage," she murmured before she could stop herself.

Nico's head snapped up. "What about her?"

Leah froze, the lie catching in her throat. "I..." She hesitated, staring at the dirt, the ash, the still faintly glowing Echodex. "Nothing. Just... I thought of her. That's all."

Kasper exchanged a look with Nico, one that Leah caught but couldn't read.

Nico exhaled shakily and crouched beside her, his voice gentler now. "You need to rest. Whatever the Echodex wanted to show you, it's not finished. Forcing it will only destroy you."

Leah met his gaze. For the first time, the distance between them felt unbearable. He had saved her, again, but all she could think about was what he had kept her from seeing.

The words came out quieter than she meant. "You didn't want me to see the rest."

Nico's expression didn't change, but his jaw tightened. "Not when it's killing you."

She wanted to argue, to scream that she could handle it, that she had to know. But her strength was gone. Her body felt hollow, her veins cold.

Kaya placed a steady hand on her shoulder. "We'll figure out what the rest means," she said softly. "Together. For now, just breathe."

But Leah's breath wouldn't steady. The world felt wrong, the light too dim, the air too heavy. And beneath the quiet hum of the forest around them, she could still hear it, faint, almost imagined, the echo of that voice from her dream.

You have to go back, Leah. Save her before The Order gets to her.

Leah's eyes flickered toward the Echodex. Its light had dimmed to a soft pulse, one that, for a moment, seemed to match the rhythm of her heart.

She looked away. But she could still feel it, the pull, the whisper, the promise that something was waiting for her in the dark.

The pulse of the Echodex had just begun to fade when the first tremor rolled through the ground. A deep, thrumming vibration cut through the silence, like the heartbeat of something massive beneath the earth.

Kasper's head jerked up. "Did you feel that?"

Nico was already moving. "Everyone, get down."

Before Leah could process The Order, the forest erupted. A flare of blue light split through the tree line, striking the earth only yards away. Dirt and ash exploded into the air as a figure stepped through the veil of smoke, robes glinting with the insignia of The Order.

Then another. And another.

"Move!" Nico shouted, his voice a whip of command.

Kaya's hands flew to her belt, summoning shimmering wards that sprang up around them like transparent shields. "How the hell did they find us?"

"They've been tracking the Echodex," Kasper growled, pulling Leah to her feet. "That surge might've drawn them straight here."

Leah's blood ran cold. "What? No, I—"

Her words were drowned out by a chorus of shouts as The Order soldiers advanced, their blades igniting with cold silver light.

Nico raised his hand, shadows unfurling like wings around his arms. "Stay behind me!"

The first spell struck his barrier, cracking it like glass. The impact sent Leah staggering backward. Kasper retaliated instantly, strong gusts of wind rushing forward, but more soldiers poured in from every direction. The ruins were surrounded.

"Go back to Kaya's!" Nico barked.

Leah's mind spun. Her body felt sluggish, drained from the Echodex, but instinct took over. She ducked beneath a blast of violet energy that seared past her ear, the air sizzling with heat.

Kasper's hands moved again, wind snapping to his command in a sharp spiral. He sent it forward in controlled bursts, disarming one soldier, then another.

"We have to move. We're sitting targets!"

"Go!" Nico shouted, already stepping forward. Shadows stretched beneath him, coiling and striking with fluid, predatory precision. Every movement was defense and offense at once, wrapping around Kaya and Leah, deflecting bolts of energy before lashing out at their attackers.

Leah tried to focus, to summon something of her own, but her magic stuttered. Her pulse roared in her ears, and the Echodex's echo still throbbed in her bones. The world doubled, light and pain blurring together.

"I can help," she said, but her voice broke. Her hands trembled as faint glimmers of light flickered between her fingers.

Kaya turned, her eyes briefly glowing purple with sight. "Leah, your energy's unstable. You'll make yourself a target."

"I already am one," Leah rasped.

Nico turned to her, shadows writhing around him. "You're not stable. You'll draw them faster."

"But I can't just stand—"

"You can, and you will." His eyes were fierce. "When I tell you to run, you run. Do you understand me, Leah?"

She opened her mouth to protest, but the world erupted before she could speak.

A bolt of energy struck Kaya's barrier, shattering it into fragments of light. Kaya gasped as she was thrown back, but Kasper was already there, wind exploding outward in a violent burst that caught the debris midair and hurled it back.

The blast sent three soldiers sprawling. Another ducked beneath it, drawing a weapon crackling with runic light.

Leah flinched as it raced toward Nico. He raised an arm, shadows solidifying into a wall just in time. The collision cracked the air like thunder.

"Go!" Nico roared. "Kaya, get her out!"

"I'm not leaving—"

"Leah, now!"

Something in his voice cut straight through her, fear she had never heard from him before.

Kaya caught Leah's wrist, eyes blazing as she read the spiraling threads of danger. "Leah. If you stay, we all die. Go back to the cabin"

Another blast struck nearby, stone shards flying. Kasper's wind caught most of it, deflecting the debris, but blood streaked his cheek. "Move!" he barked. "I'll cover you!"

Leah hesitated, torn between the urge to fight and the command burning in her chest. Then Nico turned, shadows flaring high like black fire as he met her gaze.

"Go!" he shouted again. "Don't look back!"

Her throat tightened. "Nico—"

His shadows lashed outward, blocking her view, pushing her back as if even the darkness wanted her gone.

Then she grabbed the Echodex and ran.

The forest swallowed her in seconds. Branches tore at her arms, roots caught her boots, and the sounds of battle crashed behind her like a storm. Every step away from them was agony, but Nico's voice stayed with her.

Don't look back.

She didn't, couldn't, but the weight of what she was leaving behind crushed her chest until it hurt to breathe.

A burst of light flashed behind her, followed by an explosion. Her knees nearly buckled, and she choked on a sob.

The Echodex throbbed against her side.

Run.

The whisper wasn't Nico's. It was soft. Female. Familiar.

Leah stumbled but kept going, tears streaking her dirt-smeared cheeks. The forest blurred around her, shadow and wind and the echo of magic colliding behind her. Somewhere in the distance, the night was burning.

Chapter 25

Leah's legs ached, her body trembling with exhaustion, but she pushed forward, driven by the confusion coiled tight in her chest. The forest around her was thick with shadows, the remnants of her hurried escape from The Order's soldiers pressing at the edges of her mind. Every step felt heavier than the last, as though fatigue itself had rooted into her bones.

She squinted through the dim light filtering past the canopy, searching for the familiar shimmer of the archway back to Oakgrove. She knew they asked her to go back to the cabin, but she couldn't ignore Sage. She needed to make sure she was alright, and if she was going to have an opportunity to check on her herself, this was it. When it finally appeared, a faint, wavering outline against the dense foliage, relief prickled through her. Without hesitation, she crossed the threshold. The world shifted sharply, tension releasing from her shoulders as the magic of the archway lifted and deposited her on the other side.

Her pace quickened, urgent and almost reckless, as the streets of Oakgrove spread out before her. She headed instinctively toward the train station, planning to leave the city and return to Eldergrove as fast as she could, thoughts of Sage propelling her forward.

Her thoughts sharpened suddenly, a jolt of clarity slicing through the fog of exhaustion. Sage. Sage was supposed to be here, at the vet clinic in Oakgrove. Her pulse quickened as relief and dread tangled together, clinging to the fragile hope that maybe everything wasn't lost.

The streets of Oakgrove sprawled around her like an unfamiliar maze. She didn't recognize a single building or street name. The city felt foreign, alien, and the exhaustion in her legs made every step a small battle. She needed help. She needed directions.

Leah's gaze flicked toward a small café tucked into a corner, the kind of place where someone might notice a lost face. She hurried inside, the door jingling as she entered. A few patrons looked up from their drinks, and she caught the eye of a young woman behind the counter.

"Excuse me," Leah said, her voice urgent. "I need to find Bravo Vet Animal Clinic. Could you tell me how to get there?"

The woman paused, studying her, and only then did Leah realize what she must look like to others. Dirty. Disheveled. Unhinged.

"Hmm... Bravo Vet?" the woman said. "That's on the far side of Oakgrove, near the riverwalk. Take this street straight, then turn left at the second intersection. You can't miss it. It's the only place with a green-and-white awning."

"Thank you," Leah said quickly, relief cutting through the tight coil in her stomach.

She hurried back into the streets, repeating the directions in her mind as she navigated unfamiliar roads, ignoring the soreness in her legs and the raw ache in her chest.

The city buzzed with movement and sound, but to Leah it blurred into a confusing haze. Her thoughts replayed images of Sage, imagining her working quietly at the clinic, unaware of the danger, unaware that Leah was coming. The thought bolstered her, giving her the strength to push through the fatigue that threatened to buckle her knees every few minutes.

Finally, she saw it. The small building with the green-and-white awning. Her heart leapt, a fragile spark of hope amid the gnawing anxiety. She pushed the door open, the scent of antiseptic and animals washing over her, and swept her gaze across the room in search of a familiar face.

"Excuse me," she said to the receptionist. "Is Sage here today?"

The woman frowned slightly. "I'm sorry, there's no one here by that name."

Leah saw it then, the irritation, the faint disgust of someone confronted with a stranger who looked the way she did now. The same judging eyes that had followed her through school. She fought the urge to shout in her desperation.

"Sage," Leah said louder. "She's an apprentice here."

"Honey," the woman said, placing a hand to her chest in a gesture that felt more patronizing than kind. "We don't have an apprenticeship program."

Leah froze. The warmth of hope drained instantly, replaced by a hollow weight settling deep in her chest. Her thoughts spiraled, frantic and disoriented. How could Sage not be here? She should be here. She knew she was supposed to be here.

Then a soft, coaxing voice slipped through the edges of her thoughts, almost like a suggestion.

They knew all along. Sage is in danger. You have to go back. You must save her.

Her stomach clenched as panic surged, tangling with exhaustion and grief, with the creeping confusion V's whispers had planted in her heart. Without another word, Leah turned and walked out of the clinic, pressing a trembling hand to her forehead as she tried to steady herself.

The city felt heavier somehow, darker, as if Oakgrove itself were urging her to act without thought. Her jaw tightened. Despite the ache in her chest, her resolve hardened.

She had to find Sage. She had to make sure she was safe. Leah would never forgive herself if she had endangered her best friend, especially after trying so hard to avoid it. She had stayed away. She had refrained from calling or writing for this exact reason, to keep Sage safe from the dangers that followed her.

Still, doubt wormed its way in, slithering and insistent. Months with Nico had left their mark, and she couldn't help wondering if she was walking straight into a trap. But she didn't stop to dwell on the thought. She didn't pause to question the gnawing unease in the back of her mind.

Directions to the train station blurred past as she moved with single-minded determination. Her legs burned, her lungs ached, but every step carried her closer to Eldergrove, closer to the one person she had to find. Thoughts of Kasper, Kaya, and Nico did not surface. Right now, they were not important. Sage was.

The clatter of the train carried her forward, Oakgrove fading behind her. The rhythmic sound of wheels on tracks felt almost soothing, a fragile tether to the world outside the chaos in her head. She stared out the window, vision hazy with fatigue, imagining Sage's face, her laugh, the way she always noticed when Leah was off, the gentle teasing that had lightened so many heavy moments.

The hours passed in a blur of darkness and motion, broken only by occasional station stops. Leah's thoughts spiraled through possibilities. Where could Sage be? Had she been taken? Was she hurt? Each scenario twisted in her chest like a blade.

At last, Eldergrove appeared. The familiar outlines of the town greeted her, but even the streets she knew felt altered, distorted by the panic consuming her. Her legs carried her from the station without conscious thought, driven by desperation.

She slowed only when she passed her old home.

The sight stopped her short. The garden was overgrown, the fence sagging, paint peeling in places. It looked abandoned, like a memory pressed into the wrong frame. Her chest ached as longing and guilt washed over her. This had been her safe place once. Now it barely felt real.

Her feet carried her to the front door. She hesitated, then crouched beside the long-dead potted plant that had once adorned the entrance. Beneath it lay the spare key. Leah unlocked the door and pushed it open.

The familiar creak of the hinges echoed through the quiet house. Dust motes drifted through shafts of fading afternoon light, the air smelling faintly of old wood and neglect.

She stepped inside slowly, boots soft against the hardwood floor. Dust clung thickly to the corners, spiderwebs stretched across forgotten spaces. The lights didn't flicker on with the same warmth they once had, though she told herself it was just her imagination.

A faint sound made her pause, a chime, barely audible. Almost imagined.

Her gaze swept the rooms, sharp and alert. A trap? A signal? A warning from The Order? A shiver traced her spine. She swallowed hard, forcing the panic down. It was probably just the house settling after months of neglect.

She didn't linger.

Moving quickly through the entryway, she entered the living room and froze. A red light blinked insistently on the landline's answering machine.

Seven new messages.

Her hand hovered before pressing play.

Beep.

"Hey, it's me. Just checking in. You left in such a rush. Everything okay?"

Beep.

"Leah, I know you hate calls, but this is my fourth message. I'm starting to worry."

Beep.

"I went by the café. Thomas said you quit without notice? That's not like you. Please call me."

Beep.

"Please call me. Even if you're mad. Even if it's just to say you're alive."

Beep.

"I don't know what's going on, but I can feel something's wrong. I passed by the house and it looks abandoned. I'm freaking out, Leah."

Beep.

"Leah, I haven't heard from you in months. Please be okay."

Beep.

"Where are you?"

The final beep lingered, slicing through the silence. Leah stared at the phone as if it might answer itself. A single tear slid down her cheek. She hadn't realized she was holding her breath, hadn't realized how tightly the tension had wound itself around her chest.

Her fingers trembled as she picked up the receiver and dialed Sage's number.

It rang once. Twice.

Then—

"Leah?" Sage's voice burst through the line, breathless, raw with relief. "Oh my god. Are you okay?"

Leah's knees nearly gave way at the sound of her best friend's voice. Relief flooded her, hot and overwhelming. She clutched the receiver, her body shaking as tears spilled freely.

"I... I'm fine," she said quickly, her voice breaking. "I needed time. I'm sorry I didn't call."

A pause. Sage's relief was unmistakable, woven into every breath. "You're back?"

Leah let out a shaky exhale, a small laugh breaking through her tears. "Yes. I'm home."

She swallowed hard, heart pounding. "The house is still standing, somehow."

"I can't believe it," Sage said, her breath hitching. "You're finally back. You're okay."

The sound of it settled over Leah like a blanket, warmth and safety threading through her exhaustion at last. She pressed her forehead lightly to the receiver, letting herself feel the tension in her body easing for the first time all day. She laughed softly, choked up and trembling, letting a tear slip freely. Sage was okay. She was safe.

"I am," she whispered. "I really am."

"Leah," Sage said, her voice trembling too, "don't move. I'll come to you. Just... stay where you are."

"No need," Leah said, forcing a lightness into her voice, though her chest still fluttered with relief. "I was actually thinking—" Leah stopped as static began to sound over the phone and blinked, catching only fragments of Sage's words.

"Wait, what?"

The static continued, making Leah grow frustrated. "Just meet me at the café, okay? I'm heading there now."

Leah heard static over Sage's voice before the line went dead.

Leah's fingers froze on the receiver. The dial tone didn't return—only the low, buzzing silence of the phone. Her chest tightened again, but not with fear. Frustration flared at having their conversation cut off like that. She tried the line again and again, each attempt meeting the same empty tone.

She exhaled slowly and let the phone rest in its cradle as relief still pulsed through her veins at the sound of her friend, safe. Homesick and exhausted, she felt the pull of the familiar streets of Eldergrove and the simple, human need to see her friend.

She made her way to the bathroom and finally got a good look at herself. Honestly, she couldn't blame the snotty woman at the vet clinic or the countless people who had stared as she passed. She washed her face, tidied her hair, and slipped on a fresh coat, tucking the Echodex safely into her satchel. Sage had always been overly cautious, maybe even paranoid, but Leah couldn't let that stop her. She wasn't the same girl who had left.

Without looking back, she stepped outside. The crisp air of Eldergrove brushed against her face as she started toward town, letting the rush of relief and homecoming carry her forward.

The sun had crept higher since Leah slipped back into Eldergrove. Afternoon light slanted through the clouds in pale gold bands, stretching familiar shadows across the sidewalks. The streets were hushed, caught in that in-between lull before the town's pulse returned for the evening.

Leah approached the café from the back alley, her heart thudding as the old brick walls came into view. She slowed at the front steps, peering through the window. A couple of customers sat inside, heads bowed over mugs and laptops. The chalkboard menu still bore her handwriting, faded but unmistakable. The sight caught in her throat, a piece of her old life suspended in time.

Her hand hovered on the door before she pushed it open. The bell chimed softly. Warmth met her first, then the scent of baked sugar and fresh espresso.

"Be right with you," came a voice from the back.

Thomas stepped out from the storeroom, a towel slung over his shoulder. He blinked when he saw her, then smiled, that same steady, gentle expression she remembered.

"Well... welcome back," he said quietly. "Didn't think you'd actually come in."

Leah gave a half-smile, slipping off her coat. "Didn't think I would either."

He studied her for a moment, like someone trying to decide which version of her had returned. Then he gestured to the counter. "Sit wherever you want. Coffee's fresh. We've even got your oat-pecan muffins. I only burned one today."

A breath of laughter escaped her. "You're improving."

"A miracle, I know."

He moved behind the counter with familiar ease, pouring a cup without asking. Leah drifted toward her old seat by the window, the one she used when she was a guest instead of an employee. The light there was softer, gold-tinged. When he set the mug down, she wrapped her fingers around it, letting the warmth seep into her chilled hands.

"How've you been?" he asked.

"Traveling," she said after a long sip. "Needed space. Answers."

"Find any?"

She didn't answer.

Thomas didn't press. He leaned against the counter, calm and watchful. It should have been comforting, but something in his stillness made her uneasy. Maybe it was the silence between questions. Or the flicker of his gaze toward her satchel. Or maybe she was just jumpy, seeing ghosts in daylight. Still, her fingers drifted toward the Echodex, brushing the cover's cool edge.

The bell above the door swayed faintly, though no breeze followed. Leah didn't turn. She took another sip, trying to calm her racing heart. The afternoon light dimmed, softening around them.

"So... you and Sage," she said after a moment, her tone light but edged with curiosity. "Did that ever go anywhere?"

Thomas raised a brow, a faint smirk tugging at his mouth. "We had one date. Maybe two drinks total. She ghosted me after that."

Leah looked up, surprised. "Really?"

He shrugged, drying a mug with slow precision. "Didn't take it personally. She's got her walls up. Higher than she lets on."

Leah huffed a quiet laugh. "You figured that out in one date?"

"Let's just say," his gaze met hers, "I know when someone's keeping secrets."

The words lingered between them. Leah looked away first. The coffee was stronger than she remembered, bitter with a faint floral edge. She was too tired to question it.

"You want me to warm that up?" he asked.

"I haven't even finished it."

"I know," he said, already reaching for the pot. "But you look like you could use something stronger."

He poured with practiced ease, his hand moving briefly behind the counter, too smooth and ordinary to draw attention. Leah didn't notice. She lifted the mug again and drank. It was hotter now, with a strange sweetness that clung to her tongue.

"Has Sage been around lately?" she asked, half-distracted.

"Not yet," Thomas replied. "Said something about visiting her aunt this week. I figured you two would've crossed paths by now."

"No," Leah murmured. "Not yet."

Her fingers tightened around the mug. The light outside stretched thin, and she noticed the café walls beginning to tilt. Everything felt wrong.

Thomas was watching her again.

"You okay?" he asked.

"I'm fine," she lied. Her pulse quickened, the edges of her vision softening. "Just tired."

He nodded. "Long trip, I'm guessing."

Leah's hand slipped toward her bag, brushing the Echodex. The hum beneath its cover was faint, almost nonexistent. Something was very wrong.

She pushed back from the counter, the scrape of the chair loud in the quiet room. A few customers glanced over, then looked away.

Thomas stepped out from behind the counter and moved toward her, placing a steady hand on her back and rubbing lightly. "Hey, Leah. It's alright. You look pale."

"I just need air," she managed, but the words slurred. The warmth spreading through her wasn't comforting anymore. It was heavy. Sinking.

Thomas's smile didn't reach his eyes. "Why don't I walk you out?"

"No," Leah whispered, but her knees buckled. Her hand fumbled for the Echodex. It throbbed weakly against her palm but didn't open.

A shadow flickered past the front window.

Thomas stepped closer, his voice low and steady. "You should've stayed gone, Leah."

Her vision fractured like glass catching light.

Then everything went dark.

Chapter 26

The forest of Oakgrove was a blur of twisted trunks and shadowed undergrowth, the scent of smoke and blood thick in Nico's lungs. His muscles screamed with exhaustion, every step was a fight against the fatigue threatening to buckle him to the ground. Wind howled erratically around Kasper, cutting at branches with jagged force, while Kaya staggered slightly beside him, her robes smudged with dirt and streaked with blood. The Order hadn't let them escape unscathed.

Nico's shadow lashed around him, tearing at the air, shielding them as best it could, but even the shadows were fraying at the edges. Kasper stumbled, a sharp hiss escaping his teeth as he pressed a hand to his side where a burn mark glowed faintly red.

"I... can't..." he gasped.

"Keep moving," Nico growled, ignoring the ache in his own ribs where a spell had scorched him. Every nerve screamed with pain, but they had to reach Kaya's cabin. They had to.

The clearing finally appeared, and the cabin shimmered faintly, magic woven into the trees to make it seem like part of the forest itself. Relief clawed at Nico's chest, but it was fleeting. The thought of Leah waiting for them kept his pulse taut. She should be there.

He stumbled forward, shadows flaring instinctively around him, pushing away the last hints of pursuit. Kasper leaned against a tree, wind curling protectively around him.

"We... we made it," he rasped.

Kaya's hands glowed faintly as she touched the cabin, murmuring a quick spell to reinforce its defenses. "She should be inside," she said, her voice calm, though dread threaded through it.

Nico's hands trembled as he reached for the door, anticipation and relief coiling tight in his chest. "Leah?" he called softly, his voice cracking. "It's us."

Silence.

His stomach dropped.

"She's not here," Kaya whispered, and the words landed like stones in his chest.

"What do you mean she's not here?" Nico's voice sharpened, panic fraying his tone. "She should be... she—"

"She talked about someone named Sage," Kaya said, choosing her words carefully. "Maybe she went after her."

Nico's heart thumped violently. "Sage?"

Kasper groaned, pressing a hand to his side as the burn throbbed sharply. "If she's alone... The Order could—" His voice cut off, jagged with fear.

Nico's shadow surged around him, restless and agitated. Every instinct screamed that Leah was in danger and that she was alone and running straight into a trap.

"We track her," Nico said. "We find her. We bring her back. No matter what it takes."

Kasper's wind tugged at the edges of his coat, mirroring his unease. "We follow the trail," he said. "Wherever it leads."

Kaya held up a hand, her eyes scanning them both. "Stop." Her voice was calm despite the blood and bruises staining her robes. "You're hurt. Both of you. And if you push yourselves now, you won't make it. Leah will be lost, and we'll be too weak to help her."

Nico's shadows coiled impatiently, but he hesitated. He knew he was injured, pain lancing down his side with every breath. "We don't have time—"

"I know," Kaya said softly but firmly. "I'll mend your wounds. We need to regroup. We can't make rash decisions, not now."

Kasper's hands clenched, wind flickering around them, but he let out a tense sigh. "If you say so…"

Nico barely registered the words, only that she wanted to regroup, and that maybe it wasn't the worst idea. Finally, he exhaled and nodded reluctantly. "Fine. But only for a few minutes. Then we go."

Kaya moved around her kitchen, grabbing vials and mixing them together. Nico watched her closely. She must have studied other forms of magic to survive on her own, potions and protective enchantments to shield herself if she was found. She didn't seem like the type to rely solely on Atticus for protection.

She returned a moment later and held out two small vials, one in each hand. "Drink," she instructed. "This won't heal you completely, but you'll be able to move more easily and without pain."

Nico saw Kasper grimace as he downed the potion, color draining from his face as he fought the urge to throw up. Nico lifted his own vial and sniffed it. It smelled like mud, unpleasant but not unbearable.

With a quick motion, Nico drank it. Heat spread down his throat and pooled at the site of his injury, slowly knitting it from the inside. The sensation was uncomfortable, but effective.

It was rare for him to need help with injuries. When he had in the past, The Order always had a powerful weaver who could fix anyone right up. Potions were not something he had dabbled too much into for himself, though he knew the basic combinations to assist in external injuries just in case they were ever needed—which had been, for Leah.

"What else have you been hiding?" Kasper asked incredulously as he watched his injury slowly heal.

"Not as much as you two have." Her eyes went stern as she looked between them. "When were you two going to tell me Leah was a hybrid? And a deadly one at that."

She took the vial from Nico, who only looked down at her, concerned.

"Seer and Blood?? Do you have any idea what kind of power that combination creates?" She shot Nico a disapproving look before retrieving the empty vial from Kasper, who looked away, guilt written all over him.

"She hasn't used her blood magic in weeks," Nico said carefully. "We were tracking down the Elders to help her learn how to control her powers."

Kaya turned to him, unimpressed. "And what do you think happened in Ashmere Hollow? Her blood magic interfered with her Seer magic, forcing the Echodex to do something it wasn't ready to do."

Nico opened his mouth to argue, then stopped. He remembered rushing to Leah, her eyes glowing red, blood pouring from her face. In the chaos, he hadn't understood what he was seeing.

Kaya turned away, heading back toward the kitchen. "You're lucky your wounds weren't worse. It would've taken much longer to heal you."

Nico stared at the floor, guilt settling heavily in his chest. Guilt for missing what was happening to Leah. Guilt for hiding her blood magic from Kaya. He hadn't thought much about Leah's blood magic at all. They'd been so focused on her Seer abilities and the Echodex.

"You two should head out," Kaya said from the kitchen as she set a kettle on the fire. "I think it's best if I stay here, in case Leah shows up."

Nico nodded. "If she was looking for Sage, she went to Eldergrove."

Kaya poured herself a cup of tea and nodded. "Be careful, Nico. Surveillance around the Groves has increased."

"Yeah," Kasper said quietly. "We know."

Nico and Kasper stumbled into the edge of the forest as early evening light slanted through the trees. Nico was anxious. He could feel it in the way his breath came in uneven bursts and in the way he kept running a hand through his hair, thinking.

"The train's too slow," Kasper muttered, breaking his concentration. Kasper's wind began to stir beside him, rustling leaves and tugging at the edges of Nico's cloak. "If we wait two hours, she'll be gone. We have to do this another way."

Nico's shadows stirred in response to Kasper's wind, coiling and pulsing. "Then we move faster," he said, jaw tight. "We work together. Like before."

Kasper's wind picked up, whipping through the trees, tugging at Nico's cloak until the shadows leaned into it, spiraling around them and holding them in a spiraling orb of wind and shadow. "You mean we fly?"

Nico didn't answer. He let his shadows ripple outward, forming a thick, living shell around them, which made Kasper flinch. "If we move that quickly, we risk injury. I'll use my shadows to protect us," Nico said.

"So you mean we can go fast, fast?" Kasper grinned. Nico rolled his eyes and nodded. That was all the permission Kasper needed.

Kasper exhaled sharply and bent his energy into the air around them, weaving currents that lifted debris and propelled them forward, faster than their legs could carry them. Leaves and branches whirled into spirals, the forest seeming to bend around their passage.

Nico's shadows extended, enveloping them in a cocoon within the wind, a tether against the chaos. Every step, every pulse of Kasper's power, was amplified by Nico's darkness, turning speed into safety and velocity into protection. They surged forward with enough force to lift them from the ground.

"Alright, going up," Kasper said, just before gravity shifted and pulled them skyward.

There was no need to discuss the plan. They both knew the direction. They felt it in the pull of the air and the restless flicker of shadows. Leah was out there, and every second mattered.

The world inside their sphere of magic blurred as they increased speed. Nico gritted his teeth, muscles straining, but he couldn't let up. Kasper struggled too, his lips pressed tight in concentration. Shadow and wind were conflicting forces. Wind was chaotic and difficult to control, which made it harder for Nico to steer and contain.

Then, as suddenly as it had begun, the rush ebbed and they descended.

They came down at the outskirts of Eldergrove, the familiar outline of Selene's old home coming into view. The wind fell away, the shadows loosened their grip, leaving them teetering on weak legs and trembling bodies.

Nico dropped to one knee, gasping as his shadows curled limply around him. His lungs burned, his chest heaving as though every breath had to be fought for. Kasper stumbled beside him, pale and shaking, sweat beading at his temples.

"We... made it," Kasper rasped, leaning heavily against a fencepost.

"Barely," Nico admitted, his voice hoarse. His gaze fixed on Selene's home ahead. The faint glow of its windows offered a small anchor amid the exhaustion.

Neither spoke for a long moment. The air felt heavy with spent magic and overused power. Kasper finally let out a shaky laugh.

"Next time... we train before doing that again. Our magic doesn't combine willingly."

Nico only nodded, slumping briefly against the earth. Despite the pain and bruises, relief threaded through him. They were close. Leah was here. They had reached the place where they might find her.

But exhaustion weighed heavily, and neither could ignore the truth. Getting here had only been the first step. The real danger was still waiting.

After catching his breath, Nico stood and stared at the cabin he had known for most of his life. Except today, it looked wrong. The garden was overgrown, vines threatening to pull the gate from its hinges. The windows were dark, the familiar calm absent.

"Is that..." Kasper began, stepping beside him.

"Yes. That was her home," Nico said, moving cautiously forward. He could still sense lingering magic around the cabin, but it was muted, dulled.

"No. Not the house," Kasper said, pointing as a glowing orb drifted toward them.

As it drew closer, the orb reshaped into a tabby cat, padding quickly toward Nico and rubbing against his legs, meowing insistently. Nico's chest tightened. He knew exactly what this meant.

He scooped the cat up as it purred.

The cat pressed its forehead to Nico, and then the voice came loud and clear in his head.

"Nico! I don't know where the hell you are or why you let Leah come back alone, but she's in trouble. If you're coming at all, she's not home. She'll be at the café where she worked. I trust you know where that is. I expect you there promptly."

The cat opened its eyes, meowed once, then dissolved back into an orb and vanished into the air.

An icy shiver ran down Nico's spine. Leah had been wrong. She had walked straight into a trap.

"A familiar?" Kasper asked. "From who?"

"Let's move," he snapped, already heading toward town.

Kasper followed, wind shifting anxiously around them. He was perceptive, that one. Nico didn't need to explain the danger. They both felt it.

Nico slowed as they neared the café, stopping a short distance from the door. Magic hummed beneath his feet, the ground thrumming in shockwaves. She was here, searching, cloaked so tightly she was nearly invisible. But Nico had trained with her long enough to find her.

The streetlight flickered on as the sun dipped lower. Shadows stretched without command, spilling like ink across the stones. They slipped into cracks, crept beneath the café door frame, and crawled along the outer wall where the light failed.

Nico stilled as his shadows met resistance.

There she was.

Nico's fingers twitched before he felt the wind around them stirring again and Kasper beside him stilled. The air around them grew heavy and alert. Then, Kasper's head tilted, listening to something Nico couldn't hear.

"Someone's hiding," Kasper said under his breath.

"I know," Nico said quietly. "She's cloaked."

Kasper's mouth curved faintly. "Let's see how well she's anchored."

He lifted a hand, sending a low current sweeping down the street. Gravel skittered as the air pulled hard.

A figure stumbled forward as the wind tore her from hiding.

"Back off, windstorm," she snapped. "Unless you want your lungs tied in knots."

Kasper blinked. "Excuse me?"

"Sage," Nico said, stepping between them. "It's alright. She's not a threat."

"Damn right I'm not," she snapped. "Who the hell is this guy?" She pointed at Kasper, making him step back slightly.

"A friend of Leah's," Nico said carefully.

"Wait," Kasper started, pointing between them. "How do you—"

Sage narrowed her eyes at Kasper and looked to Nico, ignoring the question. "Nico, what the hell is going on? Last I heard, you were chasing Elders. Now you're wandering Eldergrove with him? You're supposed to be with Leah."

"A lot has happened," Nico said.

Sage laughed sharply. "You don't say. At least you got my message." Her voice wavered as panic crept in. "She called me. From Selene's house. Said she was going to the café. I tried to warn her, but the line cut before I could—"

"Why the café?" Nico asked.

Sage stiffened. "Probably to see Thomas. The one she trained with before all this."

Nico's shoulders tightened.

"I always felt something was off," Sage said, voice trembling now. "Too polite. Too quiet. Too convenient. I didn't sense magic until after Leah left." She swallowed. "It wasn't until then that I found out he's one of them. The Order."

Silence settled.

"If he's Order," Kasper started, "then she's already—"

"She's not dead," Sage cut in, sharp and certain. "I'd know."

Nico turned to her. "How?"

Sage hesitated, then pulled back the sleeve of her jacket. A faint silver thread glimmered at her wrist, a bracelet with a metal center where an etched runic symbol pulsed softly.

"I gave her the twin to this," she said. "As long as she's alive, it'll respond to me." She tapped it gently, and the light flickered weakly. "See? It's faint, but it's there."

Kasper stepped closer, curiosity flickering beneath his guarded expression. "You can track her through that?"

"Not precisely," Sage said, shaking her head. "The bracelet acts more like sensation than sight. I feel when her fear spikes, when she's relaxed, alert, things like that. The spell is tied to her vitals, so I can tell if she's alive, under stress, in danger, or moving by the way the rhythm shifts."

"That's still pretty convenient," Kasper said, studying the pulsing light.

"Yeah. I gave it to her on the weekend of her birthday, since I knew that Selene..." Sage trailed off, looking down at the floor as she forced her emotions back under control.

Nico exhaled quietly, relief threading through him. At least they had confirmation Leah was alive, an advantage he hadn't expected. "I'm glad you did. It gives us a better chance of tracking her. What can you tell from it now?"

"She's moving, but slow," Sage said. "Which means she's either hurt... or someone's keeping her that way."

Kasper cursed under his breath. "Then what are we standing here for? If she made it to the café, there'll be lingering magic."

Without another word, Sage pushed past him and yanked open the café door. The faint scent of roasted beans and lavender cleaner lingered in the air. Chairs were tucked neatly under tables, the floor swept, the counters freshly cleaned. But something was wrong. The door was unlocked, yet the place felt abandoned. No staff. No customers. No hum of coffee machines. Not even the drip of a pot.

"This place gives me the creeps," Kasper muttered.

"It's too quiet," Nico said softly, eyes scanning every shadow. His hand brushed the air and tendrils of darkness curled along the walls. "Someone's used magic."

"She came through here," Sage said, moving behind the counter to the only other door besides the single-stall restroom. She pushed through the swinging door into the staff room. "She was terrified," she added, her voice shaking.

Kasper froze beside the coat closet. The air shimmered, like heat bending light. "Uh... guys?"

Nico and Sage followed his gaze. The closet door was slightly ajar, and behind the hanging coats the air pulsed unnaturally. A swirling portal glowed faintly in the narrow space, threads of silver light weaving through a dark core. It hummed with raw, unstable power.

Nico stepped forward, face paling. "That's not a normal passage. It's tethered directly into the Hollow."

Sage's breath caught. "Then Leah—"

"Was taken through it," Nico finished grimly. He crouched, studying the distortion. "It's still open. Whoever used it didn't close it."

Kasper's fists clenched. "Which means we can follow."

Sage grabbed Nico's sleeve. "No offense, but you both look like you're about to pass out. I can keep my veil up for a while, but not if you collapse halfway there. Let me lead."

Kasper's wind stirred. "You think we're just letting you run point?"

She met his gaze, unflinching. "I don't think. I know."

Nico nodded, ignoring Kasper's protest. "Fine. Lead the way."

Together, they stepped into the closet, and the world swallowed them whole.

For an instant there was no up or down, only motion. Wind cut like shards of ice, whipping at their faces and clawing at their clothes. Then, with a violent lurch, they spilled out onto uneven ground. The air was colder here, heavy with fog and the faint scent of iron.

A short distance away, they saw one of The Order's holding camps, a sprawling maze of watchtowers and twisting paths that curved back on themselves. Shadows pooled unnaturally, the fog distorting distance, and faint shimmers hinted at active surveillance.

The ground was treacherous. Icy patches, hidden ditches buried beneath snow, frost-crusted roots waiting to trip the unwary. One wrong step could draw a patrol from the fog. The camp was designed to confuse and intimidate.

Nico braced a hand against a snow-covered stone, chest heaving. "We're close," he managed.

Kasper glanced toward the horizon where a dull red glow pulsed through the mist. "That's the stronghold. She's somewhere in there."

Sage looked between them. "You don't expect to search like this when you both look ready to collapse?"

Nico glared but didn't argue. His limbs were heavy, vision still swimming from the portal and the flight to Eldergrove. Pride burned almost as fiercely as exhaustion.

Kasper leaned against a tree and grinned. "I'd say we're holding up fine... for people who almost ate snow back there."

Sage rolled her eyes and raised her hands. Silver threads spilled from her fingertips, wrapping around their shoulders and arms, sinking deep into their muscles. Her eyes glowed green as she murmured under her breath, easing soreness, steadying breath, coaxing strength back into their limbs.

Kasper stretched, chuckling softly. "Careful, Nico. If she heals you much more, you might start feeling loopy."

Nico's mouth twitched. He flexed his fingers, feeling the tension drain from his body as Sage's magic worked. The physical exhaustion that had been dragging him down retreated slightly, giving him the strength to keep moving, and the patience to tolerate Kasper's jokes.

"Thanks," Nico said, looking up at Sage.

"Yeah, yeah. But listen to me carefully, if either of you slow me down, I'm leaving you behind."

Kasper gave a quiet laugh. "You sound just like her."

Sage's lips twitched. "Then you'd better keep up."

"Can your veil mask all three of us?" Nico asked.

"It'll hold," Sage replied, rolling her shoulders as if settling invisible weight. "But only if Windy here doesn't start stirring the wind up again."

Kasper gave a half-bow. "I'll behave."

"See that you do."

They fell into step as Sage tightened the veil around them. Sight and sound blurred, the magic pressing like water against Nico's skin. Each additional mind added strain, but she didn't falter.

The forest pressed closer as they moved, branches clawing at the veil but failing to break through.

"She was here," Sage whispered. "Stopped for a moment."

"How do you know?" Kasper asked.

"My Mindveil isn't just concealment," she said. "It protects me, but it also acts as a compass. Within a certain radius, I can sense others. Especially those I'm connected to."

"So you can lead us to her?" Kasper asked.

"I can recognize her presence when we get closer to her."

Nico's eyes swept the surrounding area. "If you can sense her, then that means we're close."

They continued onward in silence, each concentrating on their surroundings to ensure there was no threat as they approached the camp.

"You didn't even tell me you were coming to Eldergrove," Sage said, voice edged with accusation and fear.

Nico sighed, running a hand through his hair. He was wondering when this conversation would take place. "I didn't know I'd be coming this soon," Nico replied. "Leah has been talking about seeing you the last few days."

Sage glanced at Nico from the corner of her eye and he could tell she was not happy with him regarding Leah. "I trust that whatever happened was out of your control, Nico, but you could have sent Dimitri to give me a heads up."

Nico exhaled, trying to calm his annoyance. "I considered it," he said. "But I was a little indisposed and didn't want to risk him getting intercepted."

Sage scoffed. "Luna made it to you just fine."

He gave a tired huff. "How many cats do you see compared to black wolves?"

Sage arched a brow. "Touché. Still not an excuse."

"I know," Nico said. "I'll buy you tea when we get her back."

Kasper leaned forward, a sly grin tugging at his lips. "So...what's the story here? Some ancient childhood pact to torture one another?"

Sage chuckled, rolling her eyes. "Something like that. I've known him since I was ten. Basically the big brother I never asked for. Annoying, infuriating, and always in the way."

Kasper's smirk faded, replaced by focused wary expression as he tilted his head slightly. "I'd love to know more," Kasper cut in, his tone sharpening. "But there's a pressure shift ahead. Like the café portal."

"A containment field?" Nico asked.

"Or a portal into Raven Hollow."

Sage inhaled sharply. "Which means they're about to move her."

"Then we move faster," Nico said.

"You think the three of us can take a full Order guard?" Sage asked.

"No," Nico replied. "But if we wait, she's gone. Raven Hollow is a fortress. Once she's inside, we won't get close without triggering every alarm."

Kasper's eyes narrowed. "Then we don't wait."

Sage exhaled as her veil rippled outward, faint silver footprints flashing before fading into the snow.

"She's that way," she said. "Let's move."

Chapter 27

The world returned to her in fragments, a cold floor beneath her, the metallic tang of blood and stone lingering in the air, and a dull, pulsing ache behind her eyes. Leah blinked slowly, trying to piece together where she was. Every breath sliced through her ribs like glass, making her flinch at the pain. Above her, a harsh artificial light buzzed faintly, lacking the soft, golden warmth of the café's windows or the cool shadows of the forest. Was she underground?

Her arms and ribs throbbed painfully as she shifted, wincing. Her wrists were bound by something that crackled softly with magic when she moved, and panic tightened its grip around her chest. She scanned the small, square room, carved from stone. The walls were etched with faint glyphs that shimmered whenever she drew breath too loudly. It was a warded chamber, and she was trapped inside it.

Her thoughts snapped immediately to Thomas. The betrayal stung sharply. She had trusted him, laughed with him, let him pour her coffee. All along, had he been waiting for this moment? Leah pressed her forehead to the cold floor, forcing herself to stay calm, to think.

Breathe. Focus.

Her heart skipped when she realized her bag was gone. Panic surged as she twisted, eyes scanning every corner and shadow, but the satchel and the familiar hum of the Echodex were nowhere to be found. Thomas's betrayal pressed against her chest, and for the first time in weeks, the safety she had felt with Nico, Kasper, and Kaya seemed like a distant dream.

She was completely alone.

Her breathing hitched and began to spiral, fear clawing its way forward, threatening to swallow her whole. She should have gone back to Kaya's.

Leah pressed her face into her knees, trying to steady her breath, but the magical bindings burned against her skin, a brutal reminder that she had no control here. Thomas had drugged her, and the effects were fading, but not fast enough. The room felt too small, the air too heavy to draw a full breath. Her pulse thundered in her ears as every sound beyond the stone walls became a threat.

No one was coming to rescue her. Not unless she sent a signal, a call for help, somehow.

Then faint footsteps echoed down the hallway, muffled voices drifting closer. Leah strained to listen, but she couldn't make out the words. Her head throbbed, her vision blurring as darkness crept in again.

She lost consciousness once more.

They circled the perimeter until they found a cracked stone wall where the pulse of protective magic dulled beneath their feet. Sage pressed her back against the cold granite, eyes scanning the area. The camp around them was unnervingly quiet.

"We're close," Sage whispered. "Leah's in there."

Kasper's fists clenched at his sides. "Sage, can you tell how many of them are nearby?"

"Two," she said quickly. "Walking toward this side. Earth mages."

Kasper smirked and glanced at Nico. "Perfect. Ready, Nico?"

Nico nodded. Without hesitation, they slipped through the narrow gap in the broken wall, entering The Order's holding grounds and leaving the safety of Sage's veil behind.

"What was that?" a man asked, shaken. "Did you feel that?"

Two guards emerged from the shadows. One was broad, planted like a boulder. The other was lean, fingers already sinking into the dirt as he searched for the disturbance. Nico and Kasper ducked behind a rock pillar and locked eyes as the soil tightened beneath their feet, the agent sniffing for intruders like a hound.

Without a word, Kasper stepped forward, wind coiling around his fingers like eager serpents.

Nico cursed under his breath. Of course Kasper would move without a plan. Idiot.

"There!" the broader man shouted, pointing at Kasper.

The earth answered immediately. Stone speared upward where Kasper had stood. He twisted aside, using the wind to stay ahead of the rising rock. He landed hard and skidded across the gravel just as the ground beneath him buckled, the second mage stealing the pressure from under his feet.

Nico hesitated, torn between blowing his cover to save the idiot or seeing how this played out. These earth mages weren't wasting effort hurling rocks. They understood Kasper's magic and were attacking the one thing he couldn't fight head on: instability.

Kasper exhaled and drove the wind low, forcing it beneath the surface. Air knifed through sand and soil, hollowing the ground from within. The earth collapsed as its support vanished, breaking the mage's concentration and drawing a sharp hiss from him. The other slammed his palm down, and a wall of stone erupted between them, surging upward to shield them.

Kasper smirked and charged straight at it.

Wind wrapped around his limbs and flung him skyward just before he struck the wall. The stone continued to rise beneath him as he vaulted over its edge. He twisted midair and pulled hard.

Air ripped down the wall's face, forcing itself between half-set layers of stone. The surface flayed open, the wind stripping the wall to its bones. The broader agent barely raised his arms before the storm struck him. Earth armor crawled over his chest, but the wind tore through it, carving thousands of cuts and grinding away at the joints before a final gust ripped the breath from his lungs and sent him crashing to the stone floor.

"Reed!" the leaner agent shouted. He slammed both hands into the ground, turning Kasper's landing point to sucking mud the instant he touched down. Kasper dropped to his knees as gravity caught up to him.

Nico moved.

Tendrils of darkness lashed out, binding the second guard's legs. The man's eyes widened in panic before he collapsed, helpless against the creeping void. Shadows crawled over his limbs, pinning him in place and tightening with every frantic struggle. Nico's eyes burned black, empty and endless, a density of shadow swallowing whatever dared look back.

"Where is she?" he demanded.

He didn't shout. The words scraped out of him in raw fury, and his shadows responded, coiling tighter, pressing down until the man's breath broke into panicked wheezes. He tried to scream.

He didn't get the chance.

The shadows snapped with brutal precision. There was a sharp crack, and then the body went still. Limbs hit the ground with a dull thud that echoed too long in the quiet camp.

Nico stood there, shadows still writhing around him, as if searching for something else to destroy.

"Clear," he said grimly, his voice barely a rasp.

Behind him, Sage approached Kasper cautiously, her eyes never leaving Nico. He felt their gazes burning into his back as he forced his breathing to slow, as if control alone might pull the darkness back under his skin.

It didn't.

Something wasn't right.

The Order had hunted Leah for months. It made no sense that now, with her captured, there were so few guards. They knew Nico was with her. They knew what he could do.

So why had this been easy?

Was this a trap? Were they already too late?

"Let's move," Nico said sharply, striding deeper into the camp.

Kasper sucked in a breath and emptied the space beneath his feet. Wind tunneled downward, collapsing the mud inward until he freed himself. They pressed forward without the Mindveil, heartbeats hammering as they navigated cold, damp corridors that smelled faintly of iron.

At the end of a narrow hall, Kasper stopped at a heavy wooden door, barred and splintered with neglect. He pressed his fingers to it, listening. A low growl escaped him. "This is it."

With a sharp kick, the door gave way, splinters flying.

Inside, dim light revealed a lone figure.

"Leah!" Nico rushed forward, heart slamming.

But the figure turned, and a mischievous smile spread across his face as he raised his hands in mock surrender.

"Oh, Nico," he said lightly. "You didn't really think it would be that easy."

"Silas," Nico hissed. His shadows flared across the floor.

Silas lifted a finger, playful. "Ah, ah," he chided softly. In his other hand, he held a small bundle of hair.

Nico froze. His shadows snapped to stillness.

"What the hell are you doing? Kill him!" Kasper shouted, wind gusts circling his fists.

"No. Stop!" Nico's voice cracked, raw with fear. The sound disarmed Kasper instantly.

Silas's gaze slid to Sage, who went visibly pale. "Your friend there senses Leah, doesn't she?" he murmured. "What would happen if I..."

A small flame sparked to life at his fingertip, hovering dangerously close to the hair.

Kasper and Sage stared, confused. Nico stepped forward. "Silas, stop. Please."

Sage pressed a trembling hand to her bracelet as its light flickered and dimmed.

"Leah," she whispered. "Nico, what is he doing? She's reacting to something."

Desperation clawed at Nico's throat. He knew exactly what Silas wanted.

Without hesitation, Nico dropped to his knees and snapped his fingers, retracting his shadows. "Please," he said again, bowing his head.

Silas smiled and extinguished the flame. "Nico, Nico, Nico. If your father could see you now." He stepped closer, almost fond. "I won't harm her. I expected you to get her before these fools dragged her to Raven Hollow. But this little favor..."

His grin widened.

"...will cost you."

Nico nodded, head still bowed, allowing Silas to stand directly before him. Every lesson Silas had ever carved into him screamed to move, to survive. But Nico had learned when stillness was the only weapon left.

Silas held the advantage. One wrong move would cost Leah her life.

The motion was swift, too fast for the others to follow. The metallic snip of scissors cut the air. Silas stepped back, holding a lock of Nico's hair.

"She's in a stone chamber below," he said casually. "Go left, second right, then down." His eyes glinted. "I'll be seeing you soon."

He brushed past Sage and Kasper, who remained frozen.

"Oh, and Nico?" Silas added without turning. "You missed the sunrise."

Nico stilled. For a second, the world narrowed, sound dulled, and pressure bloomed behind his eyes, then vanished.

When Silas's footsteps faded, Nico rose. He didn't look at the other two, he simply turned toward the hall Silas described —toward her—and began to walk.

Silas was gone for now, slipping past them with that infuriatingly smug grin, but Nico couldn't relax. Every shadow around them felt sharper, more alert, and he knew the other Order members could appear at any second. Sage's hand lifted, pendant pulsing faintly, and a soft, shimmering haze began to radiate outward.

Her Mindveil wrapped around them again like a living cloak, bending sight and sound, blurring their forms into near invisibility. Nico felt it settle over his shoulders, felt the taut focus in Sage's mind as she extended the veil to cover all three of them.

Nico walked without looking back, his boots sounding too loud in the ruined hall. The directions Silas had given were surprisingly clear—left, second right, down—and Nico followed them to a T. No words. No face to face with Kasper or Sage. He couldn't afford the softness of explanations. Not now.

As the corridor narrowed, they found Order members, struck down before alarms could sound. The absence of guards made more sense now, even if nothing else did. Cold air breathed up from below, carrying the smell of mildew.

At the expected turn, a stairwell yawned downward, carved roughly into stone. The handrail was gone. Ash slicked the steps. The spells here were older, rougher. Not Raven Hollow's clean precision, but magic meant to hide what shouldn't be found.

Sage closed her eyes, pendant glowing faintly.

"We're almost there," she said.

The stairs ended in a low-ceilinged chamber no larger than a holding cell. A single barred aperture let in a slant of weak daylight from a shaft above. At the center of the room sat a low stone slab with chains looped from iron rings bolted into the floor. At its center was a single sigil, carved deep and precise, a mark Nico recognized instantly.

His father's hand had made that.

The blood drained from his face.

"Is that..." Kasper's voice faltered as he approached, eyes widening at the slab.

"A sarcophagus," Sage said, kneeling at its edge. Fear etched her features as she turned to Nico. "I feel her. She's in there."

Nico approached the slab, the sigil pulsing faintly beneath his gaze, making him flinch despite himself. The magic was deliberate, sharp, and cruel. This wasn't just a trap. It was a lesson in control, a cage meant to dominate and break without spilling blood.

Sage traced the edges of the stone, her fingers hovering just above it. "It's layered," she murmured. "The chains bind her physically, but the sigil is tied to her life-thread. Whoever carved this wanted her alive... and obedient."

Kasper circled the slab like a predator, eyes tracking the chains. "We pry the slab, break the anchors. Maybe the sigil weakens."

"You'd need leverage," Sage said urgently. "Those bolts are deep-set. Any disturbance could snap her life-thread. One wrong move and she dies."

Nico swallowed and closed his eyes.

Leah's face flashed behind them. Sleeping at the table. The tilt of her chin when she refused his help. The spark of defiance in her eyes. Each memory anchored him as surely as the chains anchored her.

His hands moved on instinct. Shadows pooled at his feet, curling outward along the edges of stone and iron, pressing lightly against the carved lines of his father's mark. The sigil resisted, rigid and unyielding, but the shadows slipped beneath its defenses, teasing at the threads that bound her life.

He focused on her hand, trembling, reaching for him. That image became the anchor for his magic. The shadows responded, coiling and pressing, bending the steel-threaded spell without striking it, coaxing hesitation from the sigil's rigid will.

"It's steel binding," he murmured. "Rigid. Precise. Direct force will kill her. We have to mislead it. Force it to hesitate. That's when we move."

He knelt at the southern edge of the slab, shadows pooling and spreading beneath iron and stone. They slipped under the sigil's rigid magic, teasing at the threads tethering Leah's life. The sigil pulsed sharply, testing. Nico's shadows did not strike. They coaxed.

Kasper placed both palms against the eastern seam and sent air through the cracks with careful control. Tiny vibrations rippled through the stone as he applied pressure without jerking the chains. Sage extended her Mindveil along the northern edge, pendant glowing faintly as a shimmer rippled across the sigil, a subtle illusion meant to confuse its perception.

Nico focused on Leah. Ribbons of shadow extended from his hands, some coiling beneath her to support and cradle her without touching skin, others stretching toward the sigil. The strands probing the steel binding moved delicately, nudging and bending the magic, coaxing the life-thread to slacken.

One surge too strong. One misstep. One careless tug, and the binding keyed to her life-force would snap, killing her instantly.

The sigil pulsed again, sharp and bright, testing. The slab shuddered under the combined pressure of wind, shadow, and veil, iron bolts groaning. The smallest movement gave way, and Nico acted.

He slid his hand beneath the slab's edge, forcing shadows to flow like liquid under his fingers. Darkness spread beneath Leah, lifting and cradling her weight. She shivered but did not wake.

"Careful," he murmured. "Every second counts."

Kasper maintained steady pressure. Sage's veil flickered, twisting the sigil's perception. The chains groaned, metal biting stone as the sigil pulsed faster, struggling to maintain control.

Nico's shadows tightened slightly, guiding the life-thread away from the anchor point. Slowly, inch by inch, the slab shifted enough for Kasper to free one chain. Another careful push and the second slackened.

The sigil flared, then pulsed weakly, confused by illusion and pressure. Nico held his breath as shadows wrapped fully beneath Leah. With a steady, delicate motion, he lifted her, cradling her as if she weighed nothing.

Her eyes fluttered open, glassy and unfocused. Bruises bloomed dark beneath pale skin. Nico's chest eased slightly, though the sigil's magic still lingered.

"Almost there," he whispered.

Kasper's wind widened seams without snapping metal. Sage's veil shimmered, keeping the sigil's attention elsewhere.

One final careful tug from Nico. One measured push from Kasper.

The chains clattered free.

The slab shuddered and settled without crushing. The sigil dimmed, still present, but denied its control.

"She's ours," Nico breathed.

He let the shadows fold back into himself, still cradling Leah protectively.

She coughed softly. Her wrists were free. Her breathing was shallow but steady.

"You're safe," Nico said quietly.

She blinked up at him, confusion flickering through pain. "Nico?"

A shadow of guilt crossed Nico's face as he brushed hair from her forehead. "I should've been here."

Leah's gaze drifted as a faint tremor passed through her body.

Sage lingered near the stairway, scanning the perimeter.

Leah's eyes fluttered closed again, exhaustion pulling her under. Kasper found her hand, gripping it gently but fiercely. "You're not alone anymore," he whispered.

Nico stood, casting a wary glance toward the corridor. "We need to move her. Now."

"I can cloak us," Sage said quietly. "Briefly."

"Then we don't waste time."

The Mindveil bloomed, the walls blurring as Nico lifted Leah carefully into his arms. Her fragile weight contrasted sharply with the fire burning behind his eyes.

They slipped back through the corridors, every creak and shadow felt amplified. Nico's steps were silent, his control over the shadows blending seamlessly with Sage's veil. Kasper's every muscle tensed, ready to unleash the storm at the slightest threat.

Nico cradled Leah carefully, her fragile form weighed down by exhaustion and pain. The corridor was silent for now, but shadows shifted near the exit of the stronghold. From the gloom emerged four more figures moving with lethal purpose. Their faces were masked, but their intent was clear: recapture.

The three of them stopped, careful not to make any noise that would lead the figures to them. Nico set Leah down softly next to Sage before looking at Kasper, who only nodded in understanding.

Kasper's jaw clenched under Sage's Mindveil as the wind whipped around his hands, eager to strike. Nico's eyes darkened, shadows pooling at his feet ready to lash out.

The first guard looked around, feeling the shift in the wind, but unable to see where the disturbance was coming from. He lunged forward with blades that erupted with fire. Kasper was released by the Mindveil and he twisted forward, summoning a sudden gust that slammed the attacker backward into cold stone. A sickening crack echoing as the man crumpled to the ground

Nico came out next, already moving and striking at another. The guard's eyes widened in terror before the darkness crushed his throat in a silent, brutal grip. Two more charged, but Kasper unleashed a cyclone of slicing wind, scattering them like rag dolls. One struck the wall and did not rise.

Nico stepped forward, shadow-blades extending, cutting through armor and flesh with ruthless precision. The last guard fell.

Silence followed.

Sage dropped the veil, breath caught. Her gaze locked onto a figure lingering in the shadows.

Thomas.

"There," she hissed.

Nico's gaze snapped to him. "That's him."

"He doesn't get to walk away," Kasper said.

Thomas had seen them. He backed toward the trees, raising his arms slowly, not in surrender but calculation.

"We're not done," Sage said, voice shaking. "Not until he answers for this."

Thomas turned and ran.

Kasper looked over at Sage who was kneeling by Leah. "You stay here, I'll catch him."

"No." Nico stepped closer, close enough that Kasper would hear the finality in his voice. "We do this together."

Sage hesitated. Nico caught the moment her resolve faltered when her gaze slid back to Leah. She lay motionless on the cold stone floor, too pale, her body betraying her with a faint, involuntary shiver. Heat burned beneath her skin; fever flushed her cheeks even as bruises bloomed dark along her jaw and temple. Even unconscious, Leah looked like she was still fighting—locked in some private battle Nico couldn't reach.

"Sage." Nico forced his voice steady, though urgency scraped at his chest. His shadows dragged restlessly at his feet, sensing the same thing he did. "You need to move her. Now. It's only a matter of time before they come back."

Sage nodded, fear flickering behind her eyes. Nico couldn't tell if it was for Thomas, or for the moment that would come when Leah would wake and everything Sage had hidden would finally surface. She gathered Leah into her arms carefully, cradling her as if afraid she might fracture. Sage murmured the spell, fingers closing around her pendant as the Mindveil bloomed around them, thin and shimmering like heat rising off stone.

Just before the magic took hold, Sage looked at him. "Don't get yourselves killed," she said.

Then the air folded inward, and she was gone.

Nico stood there for a moment too long, staring at the empty space where she had been, his chest tight with the knowledge that he'd let her go again.

Kasper broke the silence with a sharp exhale. "Let's get him," he said. "Thomas, was it?"

Nico didn't turn at first. He tensed, shadows stirring as something cold and focused settled into him. "Yes."

"I'd like to return the favor," Kasper added. "Personally."

That earned Kasper a grim, humorless smile. Nico finally looked at him. "Good."

The forest answered them the moment they moved. Wind rose at Kasper's command, tearing through the trees in a sudden, violent rush. Nico felt his shadows surge in response, stretching long and lethal behind him, no longer restrained. They spilled out together, two forces unleashed.

Branches bowed. Darkness stretched.

And Thomas ran.

Chapter 28

Branches tore at Kasper's arms as he raced through the woods, wind at his heels and fury in his veins. Trees blurred past in smears of gray and green. He could feel Thomas ahead, a flicker of movement, a distortion in the air, just out of reach. Behind him, Nico moved like a silent shadow, the forest bending and darkening where he passed. The hunt had begun, and Thomas was the prey.

"He's veiled," Nico muttered, eyes scanning the shifting light ahead. "Not well, but enough to make him slippery."

"I can still feel him," Kasper said, jaw tight. "Wind doesn't lie."

A shape darted left through a narrow ditch. Kasper followed without hesitation, the ground sloping treacherously beneath his boots. He leapt over a rotting log, landed hard, and kept going. "He's fast."

"Cowards usually are," Nico growled.

They burst into a wide clearing, moonlight slicing through the trees like a blade. Thomas stood at the far edge, panting, but his posture wasn't panicked now. It was ready.

He was waiting.

Kasper slowed to a stop, wind coiling dangerously around him. "You should've kept running."

Thomas smiled faintly, eyes flicking between them. "And miss the grand finale?"

Shadows surged behind Nico, forming sharp ridges along the forest floor. "You drugged her. You handed her over to The Order."

"She came to me," Thomas said calmly. "I just made sure she stayed."

Nico's hands flexed at his sides. "You're going to regret that."

"I doubt it." Thomas rolled his shoulders. "You've made a mistake following me here."

From the woods behind him, the air thickened with magic. Footsteps. Four masked figures stepped into view, blades catching the pale light. Nico didn't flinch. "Finally. I was getting bored."

They came fast.

Kasper launched forward in a cyclone of motion, wind whipping violently outward as he drove his fist into the first guard's chest. The man flew backward into a tree with a sickening crack. Another guard slashed with his blade, but Nico's shadows rose and caught it mid-strike, wrapping like serpents around the metal, twisting it free as blood sprayed.

Nico struck hard, faster than the eye could follow. His blade emerged from the dark, a curved obsidian edge that seemed to drink the light. He drove it through a second guard's ribs, dragging the shadowed edge upward until the body crumpled.

Kasper turned, spun, and summoned the wind again, palms slicing upward. A gust like a hammer sent the third attacker spine-first into the earth. Breathless. Broken.

The fourth stumbled, then turned to flee.

Nico's voice cut across the clearing. "Run, and I will show you no mercy."

The man dropped to his knees.

Only Thomas remained upright, breathing hard, but his eyes were cold and calculating.

"You're not like them," Kasper said, stepping closer. "You smile too easily. You watched her suffer. You planned this."

Thomas's smile wavered. "You think this ends here?"

"No," Nico said, lunging.

Thomas barely dodged, a dagger flashing into his hand. He wasn't untrained. The blade grazed Nico's shoulder, shallow but enough to slow him.

Kasper hit Thomas from behind, tackling him in a rush of wind and earth. They slammed into the ground, Kasper's knee pinning his back, his hand crackling with force just above Thomas's skull.

"Give me a reason not to end this," Kasper growled.

Thomas coughed, blood at the corner of his mouth. "Because I'm the only one who knows where they're taking her next."

Everything froze.

Nico's shadows eased, but Kasper didn't move.

"What do you mean *next?*"

Thomas smiled again, crooked and smug. "She's marked now. The Order doesn't let go once the bond is made. You think you saved her? You just started the real game."

Silence rang through the clearing.

Then Nico's blade pressed gently to Thomas's throat.

"Start talking," he said quietly. "Or this forest becomes your grave."

Pain came first, seeping up through her ribs like fire stitched beneath her skin. Her head throbbed, her mouth was dry, and her limbs felt too heavy to belong to her. She opened her eyes slowly, each blink scraping against the raw edge of a headache that wouldn't fade.

Leaves.

Above her, trees stretched into the dark, their branches tangled against a silver-drenched sky. A forest. She was lying on cold ground.

Something soft pressed over her chest. A jacket?

A voice cut through the fog. "Hey. You're okay. You're safe."

Leah turned her head, barely managing it. A familiar face leaned into view, wide eyes, tense jaw, curls pulled back into a messy knot.

"Sage?"

Relief bloomed sharp and sudden in her chest. She tried to sit up, but pain bit down hard and her breath hitched.

"Don't," Sage said quickly, guiding her back with a hand to her shoulder. "You're still recovering."

Leah blinked at her. "What... where—?"

"You're out of The Order's hold," Sage murmured. "Nico and Kasper got you out. You're safe now."

Nico. Kasper. Her thoughts scrambled to catch up.

"The cell. Thomas. He..." Her voice cracked.

"I know." Sage's expression hardened, something bitter surfacing behind her eyes. "He took you. We got there just in time."

Leah exhaled shakily, grounding herself against the soil beneath her palms. Every part of her body hurt. But she was out. She was alive. And Sage was here.

For a moment, it was enough.

Then something shifted.

Leah's brows furrowed.

"Wait. How did you...?" She looked up at her friend, confusion slicing through the haze. "Sage, how did you find me?"

Sage's mouth opened, but no sound came.

"You said Nico and Kasper got me out," Leah continued, her voice rough but gaining strength. "You knew their names. But I never told you about them."

Sage didn't answer.

Leah's voice sharpened. "I never told you about them."

There it was. The silence. A beat too long. A tension behind Sage's eyes Leah hadn't noticed before.

Leah shifted back slightly, her ribs protesting. "You knew," she whispered. "You've known. About all of this."

Sage exhaled slowly, guilt flickering across her face. "I did."

"For how long?"

"Since before Selene passed."

The words landed like a blow. Leah sat back, pulse roaring in her ears.

"You knew my grandmother was involved? You knew I was...?" Her voice trembled with something breaking. "You let me leave without telling me anything?"

"I didn't know you were going to leave. I didn't know everything," Sage said quickly. "Selene didn't tell me all of it. She just said she already had a plan in place and to trust her."

Leah shook her head, breath uneven. "I thought I was going crazy. Do you know what that did to me?" Her vision blurred. "And the whole time you were what? Just waiting?"

"I wasn't waiting," Sage said fiercely. "I was watching. Protecting you the only way I knew how."

"You lied to me, Sage!" Leah shouted, raw and shaking.

Sage's voice broke. "Because I was scared I'd blow it. Because I didn't know how to explain what I could do without you thinking I'd lied to you our whole friendship."

Leah's heart twisted. "You did lie."

"I kept a secret," Sage said quietly. "One that wasn't mine to share. Selene trusted me, made me swear."

Silence settled between them again, heavy with everything unsaid.

"Leah, you don't have to trust me. Not right now. But I need you to know this." Sage's voice softened. "I've always had your back. Always. I'm sorry I couldn't tell you everything before. I thought I had more time, but when I came back the next day, you were gone and I had no idea where you'd gone."

Tears slid down Leah's face as she looked at her best friend. The confident, teasing girl she'd always known was still there, but beneath it she saw something new. Power. Depth Sage had kept buried.

"You have magic," Leah said quietly.

Sage gave a small, tired smile. "Yeah. I'm a weaver like Selene. My power is called Mindveil. It lets me hide things. Mask people. Protect them."

Leah let that sink in. "And you never thought that might be useful to mention sooner?"

"I wanted to wait until you were ready."

"I was ready the day Selene died."

Sage swallowed. "Then I'm sorry I failed you."

Leah closed her eyes, overwhelmed by the pain in her body and the storm in her chest. "How could you keep this from me? Do I even know you?"

"I'm sorry, Leah," Sage whispered. "You can hate me if you want. But I'm not leaving. Not this time."

Leah stared at her. Her body ached, but this hurt differently. This was the kind of pain that cracked something deep inside.

Then, instinctively, her hand went to her side. The satchel.

Her fingers brushed canvas.

Empty.

The Echodex.

Gone.

She froze.

"Sage," she said slowly, fear flooding her chest. "Where is it? The Echodex. It was with me at the café—"

Sage's expression changed instantly.

"They still have it," she whispered.

Thomas's smile thinned but didn't disappear as Nico's blade pressed firmly to his throat. His breath was ragged, eyes sharp with defiance.

"You think rescuing her changes anything?" Thomas spat. "The Order always plans ahead. You're playing into their hands."

Kasper's fists clenched, wind whipping impatiently around him. "What do you mean?"

Thomas's gaze flicked toward the dark forest beyond, a thin smile curling at his bruised lip. "Leah's extraction was expected. A distraction. They have other moves in motion. Backup plans. Safe houses, decoys, entire networks hidden from sight. You of all people should know that."

Nico's jaw tightened. "What did you just say?"

Thomas met his eyes. "Grigori used to talk a lot about you. His prodigy son, killed too soon..." He scoffed. "Right."

The air between them went still. Kasper tensed, sensing the shift without understanding it.

"Where?" Nico demanded. "Where will they take her next?"

Thomas chuckled darkly, blood dripping from his split lip. "If I knew, you'd already have found them. But I won't tell you anything. What's in it for m—?"

Kasper's hand surged with power as Nico's blade pressed harder, cutting off Thomas's words. The man's defiance wavered, his strength giving out, and he slumped on the floor, unconscious.

Nico's eyes flicked to Thomas's chest, and there it was: the Echodex, strapped and partially concealed beneath his coat. He moved quickly, but as his fingers brushed the surface, he realized it had been sealed—sigils faintly etched along the edges pulsed with dormant energy. It wasn't going to open on its own, not without effort... and not without care.

"Damn it," Nico hissed.

"Is that...?" Kasper's voice carried a mix of astonishment and amusement. "This little ass. What do you suppose he was planning? Did he think he could sneak a peek before handing it to the boss?" He shook his head with a grin. "He's going to be useful, alright! Once we torture him for information!"

"No. Not now," Nico said firmly.

"What? You're leaving him here?" Kasper started before going into how this was the perfect time to take him with them.

But Nico wasn't listening. His gaze lingered on Thomas's unconscious body. They needed him alive, at least alive enough. But Nico wanted to know what his true intentions had been with the Echodex, and how the Triarch would react now that he had lost it.

The forest remained unnervingly quiet as they retraced their steps, every shadow sharp, every sound amplified. Urgency drove them forward, straight back to where Leah waited.

The fight was won. The war was not.

They broke through the underbrush into the clearing, and relief hit Nico so hard his knees nearly gave out.

Leah was awake.

She was propped weakly against a tree, Sage crouched beside her. Her face was pale and drawn, shadows pooling beneath her eyes, but she was breathing. Conscious. Alive.

Nico crossed the distance without thinking and dropped to his knees in front of her. His hands hovered, afraid of hurting her, before settling lightly at her sides.

Leah's gaze found his. For a moment she just stared, as if unsure he was real. Then Nico leaned in, resting his forehead against hers, eyes closing as he let out a breath he hadn't realized he'd been holding.

Leah lifted a trembling hand and clutched the front of his shirt, fingers tightening as if afraid he might disappear. A small sound escaped her as she pressed her face into his shoulder, trying not to cry.

"What did he do to you?" Nico whispered, fighting to keep the rage at bay.

She swallowed hard, wincing as pain flared through her ribs. "I think he drugged me. Before I lost consciousness completely, he'd already tied me up." She kept her grip on his shirt as she spoke. "I was in and out. I don't know the order of things. I remember an older man yelling at Thomas before they put me in that coffin thing."

Nico felt her shudder and wrapped his arms around her.

"When I woke up again," she continued softly, "the pain wasn't just from the drugs. I think they did something while I was out. But I don't remember being beaten."

Fury simmered beneath the surface as he studied the bruises along her skin. But Leah needed him steady, not unhinged.

"I've got you," Nico murmured. "You're safe now."

A quiet sob escaped her as she pressed closer.

"I'm sorry, Nico," she whispered. "I shouldn't have run."

His hand stilled at her back, but he didn't pull away. That conversation could wait.

"The Echodex," Leah said suddenly, glancing at both him and Kasper. "It's not here."

"It's okay," Nico said, pulling it from his cloak and placing it in her hands. "We found it. Thomas had it."

Leah frowned, confused, but Sage spoke before she could ask.

"We can't stay here," Sage said. "I can sense more people approaching."

She exchanged a look with Nico and Kasper before speaking. "We should go back to my place. It's off the usual paths and it's protected — nothing fancy, but enough to keep prying eyes at bay for a while."

Kasper's eyes narrowed, tension tightening his jaw. "The longer we wait, the easier it is for them to find us. We should leave now."

Nico's chest tightened, every sense screaming danger. The forest around them felt suddenly hostile. Leah was safe for now, but she needed to recover. And they needed answers. The seal on the Echodex would need to be worked out.

Nico adjusted the book in his cloak, then let his eyes flick to Leah. Her head rested lightly against him, fragile in a way that made every instinct in him flare. He would keep her alive. Whatever it took.

He exhaled slowly, forcing a measured calm over the storm inside. Then, without hesitation, he lifted her into his arms as if he were swearing a silent vow: anyone who came for her again would have to go through him first.

The wind swept through the trees, carrying faint whispers of pursuit, but Nico's grip never faltered. Ahead, their path was uncertain, but he would not fail her.

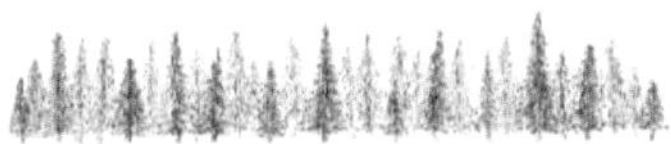

The flickering candlelight cast long, restless shadows across the cold stone walls of the ruined stronghold. Outside, the forest whispered with the remnants of the night's chaos as broken branches lay strewn like discarded weapons. Bodies lay scattered throughout the grounds, forming a silence so heavy it seemed to scream failure while the air itself reeked of blood.

From the darkness, a tall figure paced with deliberate steps. His dark robes swallowed sound as he moved, eyes sharp and filled with quiet fury.

"Amateurs," he muttered. "To let them slip through our grasp so easily."

The stronghold lay gutted. Candle stubs burned low, and stone was slick with drying blood. Bodies littered the corridors, Order soldiers frozen in shock and terror. He stepped over them without a glance. Their worth had already been assessed.

His focus lay below.

The chamber at the end of the stairs yawned open, cold air breathing upward, heavy with disturbed magic. He descended, his steps echoing softly until he reached the chamber floor.

The sarcophagus stood open, its chains lying slack and dragged aside, while the containment sigil still glimmered faintly. They were steel-binding runes of his own design, meant to be precise and unbreakable.

He stopped.

The sigil had not been broken; it had been unraveled. The life-thread had been coaxed loose and redirected with impossible care, without overpowering the binding. His work had not been destroyed.

It had been outmaneuvered.

Slowly, he knelt and removed his glove, pressing two fingers to the stone. His magic answered before something else stirred. Shadow.

His hand curled into a fist as realization settled into focus. This kind of magic had known exactly where to pull...exactly how to loosen what should have been unbreakable—a technique he had not sensed in years.

A memory surfaced: a boy who bent shadow like breath and who learned too quickly. A boy whom, until an hour ago, he believed to be dead.

His lips pressed thin.

"So, the rumors were true," he murmured, sliding his glove back on.

"Nico."

The name lingered, absorbed by stone and shadow. His son was alive. And worse, he had interfered.

As he approached the stairwell, a hooded messenger bowed. "Mr. Morozov. Patrol reports movement near the perimeter. Unknown figures. Possibly the seer's allies."

Grigori did not slow. "Let them run," he said calmly as a faint smile curved his mouth.

"It will make this more interesting."

At the top of the stairs, he paused, gazing toward the forest where darkness pooled endlessly between the trees. The battle for control was far from over.

The Order would not yield.

*Thank you for taking a chance on this story and
spending time with these characters.*

If you enjoyed your journey, I would truly appreciate
it if you shared your thoughts in a review on Amazon or
Goodreads. Your support helps this story reach new
readers and allows me to keep writing.

Thank you for reading.

Acknowledgements

I honestly don't know where to begin. This journey has been a wild ride, and even as I write this, it feels surreal to say that I actually did this.

First and foremost, to my husband, Juan, thank you for pushing me to focus on myself and for supporting me through countless late nights and time spent away from you and our kids so I could finally bring this story to life. I could not have done this without you.

To our children, thank you for inspiring me to return to something I truly love. I hope this shows you that it's never too late to chase your passions and that anything is possible when you put your heart and time into it.

To Ethan, who never failed to motivate me and wish me luck during my late-night writing sessions. Thank you for your excitement over the story and for your hundreds of questions about the characters and the plot. You still can't read it yet, baby. Just wait a few more years.

To my sister, who supported me every step of the way and gifted me the most adorable bookish jewelry to inspire my writing. Thank you for always believing in me.

To my friends, who never stopped encouraging me to keep going, even when it all felt overwhelming. Your support means everything.

To my editors, Amy Eversley and Paige Lawson. I loved working with you both. Thank you for your endless support and for loving this story and its characters as much as I do. Your insight, feedback, and suggestions pushed my writing to the next level, and I am so grateful.

To my beta readers, S.N. Brooks, Rachel Cortez, and T.A. Crownover. Thank you for your encouragement throughout this process and for embracing my characters with such enthusiasm.

Lastly, thank you to every reader who took a chance on me. Your support means more than you know. I hope this story brings you joy and that these characters stay with you for a while.

Thank you for being part of this journey with me.

About the Author

Leslie Lenz has been a creative her whole life. She writes fantasy romance stories filled with magic, and emotional depth. When she isn't writing, she is balancing life with her three children, drawing or crafting, and believing wholeheartedly that it is never too late to start doing what you love. This is her debut novel, and she hopes her characters stay with you long after the final page.

Connect with Leslie on
Instagram: @lesliewritesfantasy
Tiktok:@lesliewritesfantasy

www.ingramcontent.com/pod-product-compliance
Lightning Source LLC
Chambersburg PA
CBHW031116160726
47991CB00004B/1405